Deep
Focus

Gloria Repp

Gloria Repp

THE DUMONT CHRONICLES
BOOK 2

Deep Focus

Cover design by Tugboat Design
Interior photos courtesy of Jon Repp and Bill Beck
Scripture quotations are from the English Standard Version.

Copyright © 2013 by Gloria Repp
http://www.gloriarepp.com

Published by MTL Resources LLC, South Carolina
Printed in the United States of America

ISBN-13: 978-1493683765
ISBN-10: 1493683764

Men were deceivers ever,
One foot in sea and one on shore,
To one thing constant never.
~Shakespeare

caption:

Discard

The blond woman at the front desk wore a smile, but her voice grew brisk at Lindsey's worried questions.

"I'm sure he'll get here just fine," she said. "Perhaps he had to take a later flight. Here's Karl to carry up your luggage."

Lindsey wanted to say, "He would have phoned me!" but she picked up her camera case and followed young Karl through the elegant lobby to the elevator.

Well . . . maybe Vance would have phoned. But it wasn't like him to miss a flight.

Karl was saying something upbeat about the traffic and the weather and the local market, but the elevator ride soon ended, and he stopped talking to escort her down a long yellow hall.

The room was as luxurious as Vance had promised, with a downy coverlet on the bed, potted plants in a corner, and Native American carvings on the wall.

Good thing she had decided to pay for it herself. She would have felt guilty charging the company for such magnificence.

Karl put down her bags, grinned, and surveyed the

room with a proprietary air. "Welcome to Seattle!"

He pulled the draperies fully open with a flourish. "Well, whaddya know," he said. "Looks like a bit of blue sky out there."

He gestured across the rippled gray-blue water that Vance had called Elliott Bay. "You can laugh, ma'am, but when we see blue sky, it's like *wow!*"

Lindsey didn't feel like laughing. "That's what I hear." Had he seen the dismay on her face, or was he always so cheerful?

He moved back towards the door and paused at her camera case. "Nikon, huh? Digital! I bet it's one of those hot new models."

"Fairly new."

Please, let him not be another one of those photo fanatics.

Karl nodded, his grin widening. "Something told me you're not just my average tourist. Had you pegged right away for a professional. What's your company?"

"A small magazine."

And for these three days she wasn't going to even think about work. That was the plan, anyway. What had happened to Vance?

"Magazine? What's it called?"

They always asked this. Maybe someday she could get the name changed, and she could answer without a faint sense of embarrassment: *"DogTales Magazine."*

Karl's gaze didn't falter. "Dogs, huh? Stories?"

"More like in-depth articles about dogs, with lots of photos."

He leaned back against the open door. "Sounds great!"

She'd already given him his tip. Why didn't he go away?

"Bet you can take great photos with that Nikon," he said. "Color, though. I'm a black-and-white man myself.

2

What d'you think about digital?"

Better to ask her partner—Edric—that question. Karl and the old guy could talk all day about digital versus film.

She shrugged. "It's okay."

He straightened up, as if remembering his duties, and stepped into the hall. "Have a great time in Seattle, ma'am," he said. "It's the Emerald City, ya know." He closed the door and was gone at last.

She moved to the window, staring at the streak of blue sky, hoping it would widen. If Vance got here soon, they could still go out to eat. A special place, he'd said, like Maximilien's.

Yes, Elliott Bay was beautiful, even under a fretted gray sky. And look at that backdrop of shining white-veined peaks—the Olympic Mountains. Vance would tell her more about them.

If he ever got here.

The first doubts crept into her mind, like the wisps of cloud that were edging up from the horizon. Had he decided not to come? She should phone and find out.

But after she opened her cell phone, she paused. Did she really want to do this? He didn't like her phoning him, and anyway, her rule was, "Don't pursue." At least, "Don't look like you're pursuing."

Yes, phone him. This was important. She pressed his speed-dial number and tried not to hold her breath.

"Hey, this is Vance! Leave me a message, and I'll get right back to you."

She snapped the phone shut. No message. Maybe he was on the plane. He would notice that she had phoned and call back.

Meanwhile, she could make sure she was ready. She unzipped a suitcase and began to unpack, quickly and efficiently. After so many trips, it was almost automatic.

Put the small items in this drawer. Take the cosmetic

3

bag to the bathroom. Hang up the things she'd need for the weekend. Here was the moss-green sweater she'd bought for the trip. A good color with her dark hair, Vance would say. He always commented on what she wore.

She yawned. Only three hours difference from the East coast, and she was used to jet lag, but somehow . . .

She emptied her carry-on suitcase and put the Nikon into it, along with her favorite film camera, the Mamiya. Better keep them out of sight. From the small suitcase—her portable office—she took a folder of notes about the South Carolina dogs and zipped everything else shut.

How about that shower she'd been promising herself? Then she'd check out the rooftop garden they had read about on the Inn's website. Half the fun of this trip had been planning it together.

She had known Vance was going to Seattle for a conference, and she'd scheduled her research trip for the same time. Vance had taken it from there, suggesting that they both come a few days early. "The Inn is the best place downtown," he'd assured her.

He had made reservations for adjoining rooms, which made her think twice, but she'd hurried to assure herself that she could trust him.

In the huge bathroom mirror she caught sight of her frown and rubbed her forehead smooth. They'd never done much besides talk and eat lunch together. He'd kissed her a few times, and he was good at it.

Her face grew warm. She pushed the memory away, picked up one of the oversize fluffy towels, and unzipped her cosmetic bag.

Vance was such a private person, she never quite knew what to expect from him, but she would manage. She had her boundaries, and she could take care of herself.

By morning light, everything looked worse instead of better, the way it was supposed to.

She didn't feel like eating, so she took her coffee out to the Inn's little rooftop garden and lowered herself into a deck chair.

The mountains had disappeared, and Elliott Bay had become an expanse of choppy gray. A cruise ship slid past, its lighted decks speaking of warmth and laughter.

She tried another sip of her coffee. It tasted fine but did nothing to dispel the effects of a wakeful night.

Often, when she couldn't sleep, she would amuse herself by attaching captions to the day's events, as if they were a series of photographic images, and last night she couldn't picture anything except his face.

Caption: *Vance grinning.*

Caption: *Vance talking.*

Caption: *Vance teasing.*

But she'd heard nothing from him—not by text or phone or email.

To her left stood a tub of bronze chrysanthemums, and beside it, a pair of equally round women leaned over the rail. They exclaimed at the sights below, reading to each other from a tour book. That incandescent orange sign? It was the Pike Place Market. World famous. Seven acres of Northwest arts, flower stalls, fresh produce, antique shops, and cafés.

Their voices shrilled through her gloom. Vance had told her that the Market was a great place. They could explore it and have breakfast there.

Her neck twinged of its own accord, and she stood to her feet with a jerk. She wasn't going to sit here all day and wait for him. Besides, it was too late for breakfast.

On the map that came with her Seattle Sights brochure, she'd noticed a camera shop. It was just up the street and would be a diverting place to browse. Might as well get some exercise.

She gathered up her purse, decided against taking a

camera, and left through the Inn's courtyard, a place that had delighted her at first sight. It was like an enclosed garden, complete with flowering plants and a tiny pool.

She looked away from the Market's neon sign, turned left and strolled up the hill, watching the people who hurried past. While she stood waiting for the light to change at First and Pine, she realized that she'd forgotten the map.

First Street? Wasn't she supposed to turn here?

She joined the office workers and tourists who were crossing the street and continued on past the colorful window displays.

In front of a coffee shop called the First Hill Bakery, she paused. The windows were hung with antique baking implements and old-fashioned coffee pots. Trays of enticing breads and cookies invited her to come in.

More coffee? She had to figure out what to do about Vance. Maybe another cup would help.

She hesitated, annoyed by her own indecision, and, carried in the wake of a chattering family, let herself be swept in through the open door.

The fragrance of cinnamon greeted her, lifting her spirits. At her elbow was a glass case filled with pastries and scones, and along the side and back walls, small round tables jostled each other for space.

The family ahead of her laid claim to three tables, and rather than push past them, she chose a seat near the door.

The coffee was good, but after a few minutes her blueberry scone began to taste like dust, and she found herself crumpling one paper napkin after another.

She scolded herself. This is Seattle. You've always wanted to come here. Look around.

Two men at a back table caught her eye. They were discussing something, but their voices weren't particularly loud. Perhaps it was their intensity that made her watch.

6

One was just a boy—no more than twenty—hunched stiffly over the table, as if to protect himself.

His profile was a study in black: black hair falling into his eyes, oversized black nylon jacket, black jeans.

What a shot he'd make! She should have brought her Mamiya, after all.

The sharp angle of the boy's chin was belligerent as he listened to the dark-haired man across from him. The man said something emphatic and paused.

The boy snapped out a reply. The man, with a quiet smile, spoke again. From the way they held their heads, the two of them seemed to be sparring, locked in mental combat.

She pushed her napkins into a pile at the edge of the table. Should she go back to the Inn? Stay here and drink more coffee? Check around for that camera shop?

The boy leaped to his feet with a cry, overturning his chair. He clattered a knife onto the table, whirled, and ran down the aisle. The edge of his jacket brushed her napkins to the floor, but he ducked through the entrance without a backward glance.

The dark-haired man, looking much like a troubled father, swiftly pocketed the knife, set right the chair, and started after the boy.

He paused by her table to snatch up the napkins and murmur an apology, his attention on the street beyond. She glimpsed shadowed blue eyes and a taut face, and then he disappeared.

The family next to her continued to eat and talk and laugh, as if such scenes were not worth more than a glance, and before long, Vance's face reappeared in her mind, superimposing itself over that of the dark-haired man. Once again she began the weary round of questions. What had happened? Where was he?

At the very least, he could have phoned.

An unwelcome memory came to mind. Two or three times during the past few months, Vance had "forgotten" one of their private lunches. He was always apologetic, charmingly so, but his explanations never quite rang true.

Someone must know where he was. His conference trip had been duly scheduled through Darlene, their receptionist-secretary.

The cool, reasonable part of her spoke up: why not call the office and nonchalantly ask a few questions? If he'd been run over by a truck or something, Darlene would know.

What day was this? Friday. Early afternoon in New York. Yes, Darlene would be there, and she'd know. Darlene made it her business to know everything.

Lindsey took out her phone and pressed the speed-dial number.

"Good afternoon!" Darlene said. "*DogTales Magazine.* How may I assist you today?"

"This is Lindsey," she said. "Just checking in."

"Hi, Lin! I thought you'd be calling us one of these days. How was the sunny south?"

"Hot and humid. Not so great for tramping the Savannah River with a bunch of dogs."

Darlene made sympathetic noises, and finally Lindsey asked, "Everything going okay? Is Edric still his sweet old self?"

"Until yesterday," Darlene said. "He's been a bear ever since."

Darlene liked to give out information in tidbits.

Lindsey smoothed a wrinkled napkin onto the table. "What's got into him now?"

"It's our golden boy, Vance. He didn't come in to wrap up things like he was supposed to."

She paused.

Lindsey snatched up a handful of napkins. What was

8

this about Vance?

"After a while we found out," Darlene said.

Lindsey waited.

"His wife had emergency surgery. A perforated ulcer."

Something inside her turned to ice. She couldn't move. She couldn't breathe.

Darlene was still talking, but she couldn't seem to hear. Was it the rushing in her ears, or the noisy family standing up to leave?

She looked down at the napkins, still clutched in her hand.

Should get rid of those. Should say something.

"Okay, Darlene, got to run." Her voice rasped, and she smoothed it with an effort. "Tell Edric I'll call him."

She closed her phone.

His wife? Vance had a wife?

She stood up from the table, moving carefully because her bones seemed brittle enough to break. She edged out onto the sidewalk and turned back the way she had come.

In front of the toy shop she had to pause for breath, had to choke back the great gasping sobs that sucked up all her air. She stared at the cheery red cars on display, waiting for her brain to shift into gear.

What was she going to do?

It seemed a long way back to the Inn, and by the time she reached the little courtyard, she had made up her mind. She was going to hit DELETE and move on.

Lindsey marched across the lobby to the desk. "I'll be checking out in half an hour," she said. "Please have the valet bring my car around."

caption:

Fog

Don't think about him, Lindsey told herself.

She should get to the ferry. Weekend traffic would be heavy, and she'd probably have to wait.

Follow the plan she'd already mapped out for Monday morning when Vance would have left for his conference: drive up Interstate 5 and take the Edmonds-Kingston ferry, the simplest way to get to the Olympic Peninsula.

Be sure to phone the hotel in Cameron Bay; tell them she was coming two days early.

A drizzle had started to fall by the time she drove onto the ferry, and part of her wanted to hide in the car, but the tough part of her—the adventurer—insisted that she do something.

The passenger deck was crowded with tourists wearing colorful Gore-Tex and tired-looking commuters in black, gray, or brown, but she found a seat next to one of the wide windows.

If she were doing a travel feature, what photos would she take? Maybe those white-trimmed wavelets or those swooping gulls? Yes, and that distant island, hung with thin gray streamers of cloud. She'd shoot it in black-and-white.

What a contrast to the South Carolina low country,

with its longleaf pines and cypress swamps, and the marvelous Carolina dogs! But she was on her way to see their Northwest cousins, dingo dogs, as she called them, and rainy skies didn't matter.

The ferry slid into the dock with notable grinding sounds. Time to look at the map again. Cross the Hood Canal and turn north along 112 to Cameron Bay. Those misted blue mountains on her left must be the Olympics.

She didn't need to worry about arriving after dark because the woman at the hotel, Cameron's Roost, had given her directions in considerable detail, along with strange little asides.

When she was planning this trip and had asked Remi for advice, he'd suggested that she stay at Cameron's Roost.

She smiled to herself, remembering. Remi Lavelle— that young man with a mysterious past—lived here, and she'd met him after he had somehow ended up in New Jersey.

He'd turned out to be a good friend, the brightest, most engaging youngster she'd ever worked with. It was his intriguing description of the dingo dogs that jump-started her thoughts about this magazine feature.

An official sign directed her toward the towns of Port Townsend, Sequim, and Port Angeles, and a broad valley gave way to trees interspersed with the occasional house or farm. Rain began to fall in earnest, bringing on a dreary dusk.

By now she would have been dressing for supper with Vance. He'd never before taken her out to an expensive restaurant, but he said he wanted to make up for that.

Her throat tightened until her neck began to ache. Don't think about him.

She concentrated on the rhythmic motion of the windshield wipers until she began to yawn. Had she forgotten to eat lunch? She dug into her shoulder bag for

11

her emergency rations of water and granola bars.

Not hungry, although coffee might help. But maybe there wasn't a coffee shop out here since the trees seemed to outnumber the people.

Living in New Jersey's Pine Barrens, she'd seen plenty of trees and wilderness. The trees she knew were mostly pines, some tall, some fire-blackened, some gaunt, struggling to stay alive in the sandy soil.

But this was a world apart, a wild profusion of lush green accented with fall tints, thousands and thousands of trees covering the hillsides.

She turned onto Route 112 and passed through the little town of Joyce with its general store. She saw glimpses of water through the trees, and a mobile home advertising fresh-smoked salmon, and a tiny blue hut with a large sign: THANKS-A-LATTE. It looked closed.

Just as well. Even a latte didn't sound good anymore. She'd better pay attention to this rain-slick road with its hills and dips and hairpin curves.

Trees crowded close, darkening the twilight. No lights here, not a single one for miles, but Vance had told her that Seattle was beautiful at night. He said he'd take her over to West Seattle to see the lights of the city across the water. He'd been full of plans.

How many women had he taken to West Seattle?

A twinge of pain needled one temple. Her rental Jeep careened off onto the shoulder, and she wrenched it back to the road.

Don't think about him.

Here was somebody's Marine Service. And more trees. A few were already leafless, others hung with moss. Tiny fir trees, perfectly shaped, grew by the side of the road. Look here: an entire hillside was covered with gray stumps.

Thank goodness she'd found out about Vance before this weekend.

No, thank God. Had he protected her, kept her from doing something she'd regret?

She didn't deserve it. She speeded up, rounding a curve too fast.

Her front tires hit mud and the Jeep slewed sideways. She steered into the skid, and the Jeep powered through, missing a mud-spattered log and bumping over rocks as it left the mudslide behind.

The rain increased to a downpour that sent water sluicing across the windshield, defeating the wipers. Every once in a while a gust of wind swept the rain aside, and she caught sight of the road, glimmering in her headlights.

A rain-streaked sign beside the road advised her: *Slides and washouts next 3 miles.*

Uh-huh. We noticed.

She drove more and more slowly, straining to see ahead, to follow the muddy torrent that flowed down the middle of the road. The Jeep churned on through it all, and she felt as if she were navigating an endless tunnel of water with unseen dangers on either side.

Her eyes burned from staring through the windshield, her back had stiffened, and her temple still pulsed with pain. Should she pull off the road? No—this storm might go on for hours. Wasn't she almost there?

A wooden sign, the size of a billboard and lit with small white spotlights, loomed out of the mist: CAMERON BAY WELCOMES YOU.

Thank you, Cameron Bay.

She turned off onto a road that slanted downhill, curving along the edge of a small bay. Lights shone from rows of houses banked above the road.

At the far end of the bay, she found the driveway for Cameron's Roost and followed it through rain-swept trees to a large house.

At last.

She parked beside a green Subaru, and sat listening to the trees drip, trying to gather enough energy to get out of the car.

The house was sturdy and square-built, probably old. Someone had added a few window boxes and Victorian gingerbread-work, and the effect was somewhat discordant, like a mastiff wearing a lacy hat, but at the moment, she didn't care.

A welcoming light blinked on over the door and a woman hurried out. She was as solidly built as the house, and she was smiling. "Welcome to Cameron's Roost," she cried in a high voice. "I am Belinda Cameron."

She helped Lindsey unload the car, chattering about the terribly long trip from Seattle and how she hoped the ferry crossing hadn't been too rough and how heavy the rain had been, and certainly it was a blessing the roads hadn't washed out.

She paused for breath, "And driving in the dark too! I'm sure you must be exhausted."

Lindsey didn't answer. Her headache was swelling into her brain, and fortunately, the woman's spate of words left her no opportunity.

Belinda pushed open an impressive wooden door, and they stepped inside. A fireplace glowed in the room to her left, and a steep flight of stairs rose in front of her.

Belinda gestured toward the fireplace. "Won't you sit down and have a nice cup of tea?" Her eyes glistened with curiosity behind her glasses.

"Thank you, but not now," Lindsey said.

Just get up those stairs, she told herself.

She picked up her camera case and the carry-on bag, leaving the other two for Belinda, who looked strong enough to manage them.

At the top of the stairs, Belinda turned to the right and unlocked a door. "This is the master suite," she said. "My grandfather, Samuel Cameron, had it built especially for himself. I think you'll find it comfortable."

Lindsey had the impression of a long room, massive furniture, and many windows.

She sat down on the bed, closing her eyes. "Thank you for letting me come early," she said, and mumbled something about jet lag.

Belinda, sounding sympathetic, took a long while to describe the terrible jet lag she'd experienced during her trip to Paris.

Lindsey made an effort to open her eyes. "I seem to be coming down with a migraine. Don't worry if I sleep all day tomorrow."

After that, the woman must have left because there was silence.

Lindsey stood up, slowly, and fumbled through her shoulder bag for the pills. They would knock her out, but that was better than nothing. Her lips had already gone numb, and her vision was blurring.

Cold.

Moving cautiously, she put on her pajamas and robe, wishing they were flannel instead of satin, added a thick sweater, and slipped into the bed. Pain throbbed and pulsed through her head, keeping time with her heart-beats, but finally everything faded into a thick gray fog.

Dreams. Vance's face, wearing a sly smile . . . One of the Carolina dogs leading her through a swamp until she fell into mud . . . Tall trees, like the ones in Tolkien's Old Forest, swaying above a stream of muddy water.

Later . . . soft light filtering into the room and someone's high voice. Belinda. The woman held out a steaming cup, and Lindsey managed to choke down the dark, pungent tea.

She sank back into sleep and more fog-blurred dreams. A smooth, silky voice—Vance at his best. Then a harsh

15

voice from the past, warning her of sin.

When she opened her eyes, it was dark again.

More tea from Belinda and some crackers that she couldn't eat. But she welcomed the bitter-tasting tea.

No more nightmares. Better dreams. Remi's face with his cocky grin. And oddly enough, something about a gray cat.

She awoke to find it watching her from the top of a chair. Its green eyes were alight with curiosity.

Belinda came in, carrying a tray. "Oh, good, you're awake." She wore gray too, a tailored wool skirt with a silk blouse and chunky silver jewelry. "Shula said you'd be better by Sunday, but the way you looked, I couldn't believe it."

A distant phone rang as she put down the tray. "I'll go answer that. Why people have to disturb a Sunday afternoon is beyond me, but here's some more of Shula's tea and my special soup. Skookum, get down from there."

Belinda left, taking the cat with her.

Sunday afternoon? She must have slept right through Saturday. Not unusual for a bad one.

Lindsey sat up to drink the tea. The bed had a flotilla of pillows, and she piled three of them behind herself. She drank the soup, which was thick and beefy, and ate all the little pieces of buttered toast.

My thanks to you, Shula, whoever you are.

She tried standing up. The headache was really gone. Now for the big test.

She stepped to the plum-colored draperies and pulled them aside. Light poured through tall windows and a sliding glass door, but she could face it without flinching.

She peered out at a weathered balcony. Beyond were fir trees, a yellow-tinted maple, and gray water.

She turned back to survey the room. Old Samuel Cameron must have been a big man who liked his comfort.

The dark leather club chair was sumptuously soft, as was the brown corduroy overstuffed chair and the king-sized bed. It would make a fine honeymoon suite.

An absurd thought.

With an effort, she swallowed her sadness.

Vance was gone. Face it.

She stumbled toward the kitchenette and paused at the bathroom door. Just what she needed. That long counter, that wide old tub—she could set up a workable darkroom in there.

She'd have to tell Remi how much she liked his choice of lodging.

What next? Unpack. The pigeonhole desk had room for her laptop and folders. The black trunk would be a good place to stack her suitcases. The cherry wood bureau by the bed had plenty of drawers.

Today she would get herself pulled together, and tomorrow morning she'd phone Remi to confirm the arrangements for interviewing the owner of Cedar Run Kennels. For months, she'd been looking forward to meeting this remarkable man.

Remi liked to talk about his adopted father, Ben Fletcher, a Makah Indian who was—as Remi put it—a wizard with dogs. Besides boarding and training dogs, Ben Fletcher raised a rare Makah breed that seemed to have the same traits as the dogs she'd researched in South Carolina.

Those dogs would be the focus of the best photo essay she'd ever produced, and equally important would be firsthand information from the owner: his background, experience, and observations.

She had finished unpacking and was thinking about going out onto the balcony when Belinda knocked at the door and came in, carrying a teapot.

"Brought you one more dose of tea," she said, her eyes

darting across the room. "It looks as if you've already been up and about, I'm sure."

She put four yellow packets on the kitchenette counter. "I'll leave these so you have some extra in case the headache comes back."

"Thank you very much," Lindsey said. "That tea certainly did the trick. Who is Shula?"

Belinda settled her hips into the leather chair, looking complacent. "She's a very wise and talented woman who just happens to be my best friend. Shula does marvelous things with herbs and makes all kinds of teas. She calls this one PainFree."

Lindsey sat down and filled her cup. "What's in it?"

"Feverfew and meadowsweet and chamomile, she says, plus a few of her secret ingredients."

"You'll have to tell her it worked wonders."

"Oh, you'll meet her. I told her all about you. It's not every day we have a famous photographer come to our little town, I'm sure."

Lindsey groaned inside. She had to think of something graceful to say when people made extravagant statements like that.

Belinda nodded, making her tight gray curls bounce. "When Remi told me about you, I expected an older lady. I never thought you'd be so young."

Better to just smile and drink the tea. She didn't feel very young today. But to Belinda, who was probably in her sixties, a person in her forties might seem young.

Lindsey blinked, trying to focus. The light seemed to be growing hazy. Did Shula's wonder tea have sedative properties as well?

Belinda kept on, telling her how the house was built in 1895 by her great-grandfather, Ezekiel Cameron, and saying something about the beach, just outside, that was nice for walking, and that Lindsey would want to take her camera.

People always said that. They didn't realize that a camera—at least one of them—went wherever she did.

She tried to smile and nod at intervals while Belinda talked about other sights, but she must have sat without answering for a while because Belinda stood up, saying, "You're looking sleepy again, so I'll let you get some rest. An early bedtime wouldn't hurt you, I'm sure. Come down for breakfast tomorrow, if you wish."

It took an effort to get to her feet and see Belinda to the door, but at last she was alone. She locked the door, closed the draperies, and crawled back into bed with a sigh. Oblivion was not necessarily a bad thing.

The tea, or whatever it was, must have eventually worn off because she slept for only a few hours before the dreams began. They were all of Vance, and they made her long for him, whether she should or not.

By five o'clock in the morning, she was awake. She took a shower, humming, "Gonna wash that man right out of my hair," a song she'd heard her grandma sing. Certainly appropriate now. Too bad it wasn't that easy.

By six o'clock she'd put fresh polish on her toenails, dressed, and turned on her laptop. It took a while to figure out how to connect to the local network, but finally she was online and could check her email. She answered her messages and wrote one to Mollie, her niece, who was taking care of her house in New Jersey. It was short because of all the things she didn't want to say, and deliberately lighthearted.

By seven o'clock she had found her way down to the beach.

3

caption:

Uprooted

At first sight, the beach made Lindsey feel more unsettled than ever. It had sand, yes, but the sand was gray, and it was littered with seaweed, rough black rocks, and the hulks of trees that had washed ashore. So different from the smooth white crescents she was used to!

Except for the gulls that flew overhead, it was deserted.

She took a breath of the sea-chilled air and shivered in the mist that hung over the water. Too dispirited to move, she stared across the gray swells that stretched, gray upon gray, for endless drab miles.

A streak of light glowed at the horizon. It grew wider, shimmering over the waves and tinting the layered clouds with pink. The pink turned to gold—gold that flamed across the sky, blazed through the clouds, and set fire to the sea.

She gazed at the far-flung brilliance, letting its warmth fill the cold gray places inside her.

Comfort.

She walked along the water's edge, faster and faster, and then, with a spurt of happiness, took a firm hold on her camera and began to jog, gulping in huge breaths of air.

Beside her, the silken waves rolled in, drew back, rolled in again. Their murmuring filled her ears and soothed her heart.

This was what she needed. Just let go and . . . and . . . what?

Let Vance go, and get on with her work.

She slowed. That was it. She was here to produce the best possible feature for the magazine. Maybe the best thing she'd ever done. Focus on that, and she'd be okay.

She detoured to study a tree that lay among others at the high-tide line. Its roots thrust upward, and its bleached trunk, half-buried in sand, looked desolate in the morning light. She reached for her camera.

She'd brought the Mamiya, her newest film camera because this compact model was ideal for traveling. The Nikon digital was fine for color shots, but for good black-and-whites, there was nothing like the Mamiya.

She took a dozen shots of the tree and slipped her camera back into its case with satisfaction.

As she started down the beach once more, her cell phone rang. She had turned it on in case Remi called, but this was . . . *Vance.* Her fingers holding the phone tightened into a fist.

His voice was confident, upbeat. "Hi, Lin! Whew! My flight just got in. I'm so sorry about the weekend. Tried to phone, but couldn't get you."

Liar. Not even a voice mail.

When she didn't answer, he said, "Lin? Are you there?"

"Yes."

"I'm really sorry, Lin. Something came up, and I missed my plane." He was good at sounding contrite, and he knew it. His voice grew cheerful. "But I'm here now. We can still get together. I can't wait! Where are you, anyway?"

She hardened her heart. "What about your wife?"

Silence.

"Lin, honey, I was going to tell you. And anyway, we haven't done anything wrong—you're such a prude—there's no harm in a couple of kisses."

"I don't date married men, Vance."

"You're upset, Lin, and I really don't blame you." (So charming!) "But take it easy, okay? Just relax for a minute and let's talk. We've had some good talks together, haven't we? Pretend I'm right there beside you and—"

"—No." It came out as a croak, so she tried again. "No! Listen to me. I don't date married men."

"But Lin! She doesn't understand me, not the way you do."

Uh-huh. The tawdry line of unfaithful husbands since the world began.

"Goodbye."

She turned off the phone, shoved it into her pocket, sat down on a fallen tree, and jumped up again. Her shoes made angry slapping sounds as she began to jog, slowly, without joy.

How could she have been so stupid? Why hadn't she seen this coming? He'd always insisted that they lunch in small, obscure cafés. ("More romantic, don't you think?") He rarely came to her office alone. ("You know how Darlene talks.") And he was never in town on weekends.

It wasn't as if she didn't know about men who led double lives. Her own father had been two different people: a smiling, kindly, upright person at church; and a demanding, puritanical tyrant at home.

She ran faster. Don't forget the others: Derek, her first love and the best teacher she'd ever had. Art, the photographer who shot stupendous landscapes and told stupendous lies. And Kent, who had posed as a writer.

Far ahead, she saw someone standing by a rampart of black rocks that tumbled into the ocean, so she turned and jogged the rest of the way back.

Vance was not going to get away with this. Soon as she returned to New York, she and Edric were going to have a talk. She could count on Edric. She and the old man had been friends for years, and their discussions had become important policy-making sessions with a direct link to the magazine's success.

Their first talk had been six years ago, when Edric asked her to help him with his fledgling magazine. In his tiny office he'd plied her with French pastries and good coffee while he described his dream, and finally she'd agreed to partner with him. She had even bought shares in the magazine.

She jogged as far as the uprooted trees and slowed. Something about those useless, ragged, up-flung roots gave her a sense of desolation.

That's how she felt: uprooted. And all because of one blond guy who happened to be good-looking, wealthy, and moderately witty. Ridiculous.

She headed toward the rocky steps that led up to Cameron's Roost. Maybe she should phone Edric right away about Vance. Fire him! Vance's performance as a marketing manager hadn't been exactly stellar—too many people perceived him as arrogant. She could emphasize that.

She ran up the steps and along the path that curved around to the front of the house.

Inside, she stopped to take off her jacket, and Belinda bustled out of the kitchen. "You're doing better, I'm sure. Would you like breakfast?"

She looked so hopeful that Lindsey hesitated before declining. "Not today, thank you. I have to get right to work."

There was that phone call to Remi, and maybe one to Edric, after the interview with Ben Fletcher.

"Yes, you're a busy lady. Here—" Belinda hurried into

the kitchen and came back with a cinnamon roll on a plate. "My sister makes these. They're not too bad. I'll bring you up some more tea."

And stay to talk, no doubt. "Really, I'm much better, thank you," Lindsey said.

"But this tea is Shula's special blend! BrainWhiz. She told me she created it especially for the working woman."

"In that case, thank you."

"You'll like it, I'm sure." Belinda paused, her dark eyes glinting behind her glasses. "You're not happy, are you? Looks to me like you've got a bit of man trouble. You'll get over it." She smiled a tight smile. "We always do."

Lindsey murmured something and went up the stairs as fast as she could without running. She hurried through the room, hanging up towels and clothes, making the bed, and setting out her work folders on the desk.

A photograph from one of her folders slid into view, then two more. Slowly she picked them up: black-and-white studies she'd done of Vance's face.

Go away!

She tore the photos lengthwise into strips, found a box of matches in the kitchen cupboard, and held a flame to each piece. Finally she was done, with only a pile of ashes in the sink.

A knocking sounded at the door. Belinda.

She hurried to open it, just a little.

"I thought I smelled smoke," Belinda said. "Are you all right?"

"Yes, I certainly am. I just got rid of that man you mentioned."

"Good for you! They're scoundrels, all of them."

Lindsey took the teapot from her with thanks. After she'd closed the door, she caught sight of a gray tail whisking under the bed. "As long as you don't say anything," she told it, "you may stay."

24

Now, back to work. She should phone Remi. Where was his number? On the contact list in her cell phone? No. Not in the file either. What about in his last email?

The cat crept out from under the bed and leaped onto the leather chair. While her laptop booted up, she sipped the tea, watching the cat smooth his fur, and then she opened her mailbox.

One from Vance, already.

He was good with words. His poetry could charm the slime off a slug. Don't read it.

She deleted the message and, determined to show herself that she was serious, went through all her old emails and deleted everything he'd ever sent her. Two hundred and forty-six of them. He'd been prolific in the past year, hadn't he?

But she had been too. So blind!

She took another drink of tea. Getting rid of the electronic Vance seemed to give her a giddy sense of disentanglement. Or was it the tea? BrainWhiz?

Here was Remi's most recent email. When she'd last seen it, she'd been in such a hurry that she hadn't read it all the way through.

His cell phone number was there in the first paragraph, and a few sentences later he'd written:

Okay, I've got to tell you about something wonderful that happened to me. It's long, so read it when you have time.

For once she had the time.

Remember Timothy, the old storekeeper in New Jersey? He used to talk to me about God. And he kept telling me bits of verses from the Bible, which kind of drove me crazy. Worse than Colin.

Who was Colin? She'd have to ask.

Guess you don't know that I grew up a Muslim. I never told anybody.

She looked away from the screen. Remi, a Muslim?

25

When he first came to the Pine Barrens, she'd thought there was something different about him, that he might have a French or Spanish background. But—a Muslim?

Anyway, Timothy kept talking to me. One day I kind of blew up and told him that the Quran is the only uncorrupted word of God, and that it was transmitted through the Prophet from God.

She smiled. Timothy wouldn't have argued with him. He'd have quietly pointed him to the Bible.

Remi went on to describe his many discussions with Timothy, his reading of the Gospel of Matthew, and his gradual realization that Christ wasn't just a prophet.

Then Timothy showed me the third chapter of John. Those first twenty verses really got to me. Verse 16 is WOW! I began to understand, just a little, that Jesus Christ lived and died because he loved me—even me!!

Those days I was plenty scared since I had ignored God all my life. But I kept reading the Bible, and Christ became a real person to me. Finally, one night I told God that I was going to quit dodging the truth. I admitted that Jesus Christ is Lord of heaven and earth. I thanked him for paying the death-price for my sins . . . !!!!!!

Lin, I felt like I'd stepped out of a cave into sparkling sunlight.

She leaned back from her computer. True, during those last weeks before he left to come back here, Remi had seemed much happier. She'd known that Timothy was praying for him, but she hadn't paid much attention.

Like walking out of a cave?

She could still remember that feeling. When she was eight years old, she'd gone to church camp for the first time. Her teacher, Miss Sandy, talked about God as if he were someone who lived in her house, which was quite amazing because he was also the one who had made the whole world and had written the Bible.

Finally, on the last day of camp, Lindsey had a serious conversation with God—Miss Sandy's God—thinking it strange but nice that he would send his Son to take the punishment for her sins. For sure, she had plenty of sins.

Miss Sandy's face glowed. "Now you're part of God's family," she said. "Why don't you come to Bible Club at my house? You can get to know him better."

As soon as she got home, Lindsey asked if she could go to Bible Club. Every Tuesday!

Her father had looked up from his plate, and she could still see the way his lip curled. He pursed his mouth, making it look wrinkled as a prune, and he'd said no-of-course-not-that-woman-doesn't-belong-to-our-church.

For the first time in her life, Lindsey rebelled. She cried and screamed, falling dramatically to the floor, but she was no match for her father. He had sent her to her room, shouted Bible verses at her, and worst of all, decreed no desserts for a month. She had never seen Miss Sandy again.

Lindsey sighed. It was long ago and far away; both her parents were dead. Although her transaction with God had been real enough, she hadn't thought about it much until lately, as she'd watched him changing her niece, Mollie.

She sipped her tea, considered taking a close-up of the sleeping cat, and on an impulse, hit REPLY.

She told Remi how happy she was for him and added the little story of how she had also come to believe in Christ. She didn't say that most of the time she felt as if she had somehow slid back into the cave. Let him enjoy the sunlight. He hadn't messed up his life.

While she was typing, she puzzled over the reference he'd mentioned. John 3:16? What did it say? She knew that verse. Of course she knew it.

She sent the email, closed her laptop, and checked the bookshelves behind the leather chair. No Bible here; nothing but a few novels, a history of Washington State, and a dictionary.

What was that verse? She could see herself jumping up in Sunday school and reciting it—beating out the other kids—and gleefully unwrapping her candy bar.

She shook her head in frustration. Why couldn't she remember? Was this what old age felt like?

She'd have to find out. Back in New Jersey, when Remi and Mollie traded quotations from Shakespeare, she couldn't play their game. But one thing she knew was Bible verses—her father had seen to that. If Remi was going to start quoting verses, she'd make sure she could keep up with him.

In the meantime, she'd better give him a call.

Remi answered immediately, brightening her day. "Hi, Lin! I was hoping to hear from you soon."

He seemed to know that she had come to Cameron Bay early, but fortunately, he didn't ask why. On her part, she was careful not to say anything about his recent email in case he mentioned that verse again.

They agreed on four o'clock this afternoon for her visit to Cedar Run Kennels.

"I think everything will be okay," he said. "I sure hope so." He gave her directions to the kennels.

After she'd said goodbye, Lindsey remembered that she had wanted to get a map of the area, if such a thing were available, and went downstairs to ask Belinda.

Before she knew it, she was sitting at the kitchen table, eating a thick roast beef sandwich made with the best rye bread she'd ever tasted.

"From the bakery," Belinda said with a shrug. "My sister married a man who was determined to have his own bakery, and she has to work hard, poor thing. She's not a Cameron, you know. Her father was different than mine."

Belinda paused, as if to reflect on the unfortunate sister, and asked, "What about your family? Is it historical?"

"The Dumonts were French Huguenots," Lindsey said. She could still hear Great-Grandpapa's withered voice telling stories of their early days in New Jersey.

"How nice," Belinda said, and she hurried on with more details of her pioneering great-grandfather Ezekiel and his building exploits in this part of the West coast.

Lindsey gazed outside. Like her room upstairs, the kitchen had sliding glass doors with a wide deck and trees beyond.

As soon as she had a chance, she asked about the map, and Belinda said she should try the bookstore.

"You have a bookstore here?"

"Yes, it's run by the nicest boy, a Native American, believe it or not. I think it's just wonderful to see one of them trying to manage a business venture."

"I'm glad to hear it. I like bookstores."

"I stop by whenever I can. I make it a point to browse the Native American crafts. I don't always understand them, but I feel that they are enriching."

Lindsey got up to put her dishes into the dishwasher, thinking that she could go to the bookstore on her way to meet Ben Fletcher. If she left right away, she'd have time to do some browsing of her own. And perhaps be enriched as well. Was there a touch of superiority in Belinda's remarks? It was hard to tell.

The houses of Cameron Bay clung to the steep hillside, looking precarious enough that a bad rainstorm could send the whole town sliding into the water. Bay Street, logically enough, fronted the water, and as she drove down it, she passed a large white house with a gambrel roof and a red sign: *Brandt's Bread*. Belinda's hardworking sister must live there.

The second street up had a post office on the corner, and nearby, the bookstore.

The store looked like any other boxy white house,

except for the honey-colored post in front. Someone had chiseled the outline of a fish at the top of the post, and below it, block letters that spelled: **BOOKS**.

A carved wooden sign on the door assured her that the store was open, and she stepped quietly inside.

On top of the closest bookshelf, a Siamese cat was sitting—or rather, had arranged himself—as if to survey all who came or went.

Lindsey put a hand on her camera case. A nearby window lit up the cat's face, making an aureole of his creamy fur, and the dark background provided contrast. A natural chiaroscuro. His pose was reminiscent of the Great Sphinx of Egypt, as was his opaque stare.

The scene was perfectly composed, right in front of her. Black-and-white, of course.

She stepped to one side and quietly pulled out her Mamiya. She readied the camera, and the cat watched her without blinking, as if he knew that his role included looking inscrutable. For a moment longer, she studied him—the shadows from his forward-swiveled ears, the light that touched his whiskers—then she began.

She worked quickly because as soon as someone noticed what she was up to, the opportunity would be lost.

Done.

As she was putting away her camera, a voice spoke behind her. "I see that you and my cat are getting to know each other."

This must be the Native American boy. He was tall, with broad shoulders and a lean, intelligent face, probably in his thirties. He looked amused.

"I hope you don't mind," she said. Then, with a candor that surprised herself, she added, "I find it best to shoot first and apologize later."

"Perfectly understandable, and Kumtux considers it no less than his due."

"Kumtux is a beautiful sight," she said. "A most royal personage. What does his name mean?"

"His full title is *Yaka Iskum Kumtux*, which means, 'He knows about things,' but we are permitted to call him Kumtux. I am Fraser Denton, his humble caretaker, known simply as Fraser."

She smiled into the man's luminous brown eyes, saw contentment there, and a suggestion of something else. Grief, perhaps.

She glanced away, down to her camera. "I have a question for the humble caretaker."

A gray-haired man with a reddish face stepped around the end of a bookshelf. He wore the trousers and collared shirt of a businessman, and he carried himself as if he owned the town.

"I apologize for interrupting," he said, "but I couldn't help noticing you with your camera."

She put on her polite smile, and waited.

He cleared his throat. "You look familiar. Have I met you somewhere before? My name is Quincy Corbin. Please remind me—yours is . . . ?"

Such a tired old pickup line.

Fraser must have thought the same thing because she caught the shadow of a grin on his face.

"I'm Lindsey Dumont. How do you do?"

He cleared his throat again and said, "Welcome to Cameron Bay."

"Thank you." This conversation was already limping. Maybe it would die soon.

His cell phone rang. He pulled it out, looked at it, and said, "Unfortunately, I must speak with this person. Please excuse me? Fraser—I'll have to get back to you about that book order."

He strode purposefully out the door.

Fraser's grin had widened. "I suspect you will see Quinn

again. By the way, I had a special order for your book the other day. Now—how may I help you?"

Why would anyone out here order her book?

"I'm looking for a map of the area," she said. "Do you have anything like that?"

Fraser nodded and took her through a wide archway to a second room that extended down the side of the building. They passed shelves of paperbacks, used books, a table heaped with bargain books, and on her left, a potbellied stove. Finally, he stopped to twirl a wire rack that held maps.

She thanked him, and he left her to look through them on her own.

After she found the map she wanted, she browsed through the paperbacks and wandered over to the shelves of used books, where she chose a worn collection of Sherlock Holmes stories and a ragged book about the Olympic Peninsula.

Into the corner was wedged a small Bible, and she pulled it out. It was made with cheap paper and imitation leather, the kind of Bible that churches often gave as prizes. She could get this for only a dollar and look up that verse of Remi's.

She flipped through it. The pages were yellowed and brittle, but none of them were falling out, and the shiny blue cover looked almost new.

Conscious of time passing, she took her books to the front room, where Fraser stood at a wooden counter. Behind him, the wall was hung with carvings and small framed paintings. The Native American crafts, no doubt.

As he rang up her purchases, she thought how nice it was that he didn't hover. Or ask questions. "Thank you," she said. "I'll be back."

"I'm glad to hear that," he said, and he looked as if he meant it.

As she turned away, he picked up a knife from the counter. Next time she was here, she'd ask about those carvings. The cat had disappeared. No doubt his royal business took him elsewhere.

As soon as she reached the car, she opened the Bible and found John 3:16. Of course! She closed her eyes and recited it. At least now she was ready for Remi. He'd said something about the first twenty verses, but she could read them later.

Time to get over to Cedar Run Kennels. She drove down Bay Street and out onto the highway.

She couldn't wait to see Remi again. And get that interview.

Edric had been a little irritable lately, probably worried about circulation, but he would be pleased with this feature. It had the potential for an award. Maybe Vance would take her out to celebrate . . .

No! She swerved to avoid a man on his bike and found herself on the wrong side of the highway with a truck coming at her. She jerked the car back into her lane, giving him an apologetic wave.

She took a quick breath. Forget Vance. Think about all these trees. Wonderful trees, taller than any she'd seen.

Remi had said there'd be two large spruce trees and a sign on her left. Slow down. This was it.

caption:

Dark, Darker

Lindsey followed the gravel driveway to a cluster of buildings with pastures behind them and woods beyond.

To her left was a brown two-story house, and to her right, a barn-shaped building that probably housed the kennels. Built into the barn were individual wire pens that would connect to indoor kennels, one for each dog. This looked like a classy operation.

The dogs in a fenced exercise field caught sight of her and started barking. She smiled at the familiar sound. Were any of them dingo dogs?

She looked for the distinctive honey-gold coat and curled tail. No. Ben Fletcher probably kept them separate.

Remi's dented black truck stood between the house and the barn. He must have driven it all the way here from New Jersey.

As she parked, Remi came out of the barn and hurried towards her. Close beside him trotted a small dark-haired girl with caramel-colored skin.

Lindsey opened her car door, and a black-and-white terrier darted up, barking hysterically.

Remi's face broke into a grin. He ran the last few steps and threw his arms around her in a boyish hug. "Hey, Lin, it's so good to see you!"

She looked up with a quick *I've-missed-you* smile, and he caught it, grinning even more.

He wasn't wearing his baseball cap, and his wavy black hair was a little longer, but he had the same sparkling eyes she remembered.

She stepped back, still smiling, and saw enmity in the eyes of the little girl.

"Who is this, Remi?" She had to raise her voice over the dog's frantic barking.

"Quiet, Spot!" Remi said.

He put a hand on the child's thin shoulder. "This is Ginni, my little sister."

"Hi, Ginni," she said. "I've come to take pictures of your dogs. They're pretty special, I hear."

The child gave her a cold stare and snatched at Spot's collar. The dog quieted, gazing up at them and wagging his stub of a tail.

A small boy, plump and blond, peered at her from around Remi's truck.

Remi called to him, "Where's Dad?" and the boy shook his head.

Remi's face tightened. "Do you mind waiting a minute, Lin? He was inside just now. I'm afraid there might be a problem. I'll go see what I can find out."

He walked off, the child clinging to his hand, and disappeared into the barn.

The boy had gone away too, and she was left with Spot, who eyed her every move, presumably guarding the homestead against this intruder.

She went down on one knee and held out her hand. "You're a nice little guy, aren't you, Spot?" He snuffled at her hand and let her scratch behind his ears, panting in appreciation, his tail going strong.

"Don't you touch my dog!" Ginni's voice.

Remi had come back, Ginni still attached, and she glared at Lindsey as she spoke.

More worrisome was the troubled look on Remi's face, and Lindsey looked past him to the doorway of the barn. A solidly-built Native American stood there: Ben Fletcher. He watched her with a cold stare that was eerily reminiscent of Ginni's.

Thin, sharp wires—equally cold—pulled her shoulders tight.

"Lin, I'm sorry," Remi muttered. "He . . . um . . . can't talk to you right now."

"It's not convenient. I understand," she said. "Perhaps we could arrange for a better time."

The child put her little nose into the air. "You're a *journalist*. My daddy said to get rid of you."

"Ginni!" Remi frowned at her, and she burst into tears, hiding her face against him.

But Lindsey had retreated to the Jeep. She lowered the window and made herself speak calmly. "Not a good day, I see."

Remi leaned in through the window. "I'm really sorry," he said. "I'll phone you."

No doubt Ginni was listening to every word. "Sure, that's fine," Lindsey said.

"I liked your email." Remi took out a small flash drive and handed it to her. "Here's something for you to listen to—when you get a chance to upload it. Hey, take a day off. Explore the area. This is fantastic country."

She smiled into his worried eyes. "It's okay, Remi. Call me when you can."

The blond boy ducked out from behind Remi's truck again, smiling and waving goodbye. Conscious of all the watching eyes, she backed down the driveway with care.

She turned left onto the highway. Yes, instead of going back to Cameron Bay, she'd drive up the coast. After all,

Remi had said to explore.

Think positively. This wasn't the first time she'd had a kennel owner bail out on her, and Remi would be the best possible advocate for a future meeting.

She glanced at the flash drive on the console beside her. How thoughtful of him! She'd listen to it tonight. For now, she would concentrate on this beautiful coastline.

Before long, she was driving with a thick spruce forest on her left, and a rocky strip of beach on her right. The water—the Strait of Juan de Fuca—was deep blue, with a ridge of land rising like a mirage on its far side. According to the map, that was Vancouver Island. Someday she'd get over there too.

She rounded a bend and found herself beside a pebbled beach that was wider and more rugged than the others she'd seen. Photos? Yes!

First she used the Nikon so she could get the colors: reddish drift-logs, black rocks, and curling blue waves. With the Mamiya, she took two shots, one of an especially large boulder patched with sun-lit moss—should be interesting in black-and-white—and the other of an odd little island, round as a ragged biscuit and topped with bushes.

She drove on, but an empty feeling reminded her that it had been a long time since that quick lunch with Belinda. After miles and miles, it seemed, she came upon a scattered group of houses that called themselves the Greater Olympics Resort. Here was a general store where she could buy vinegar for her darkroom, and at the edge of town, a Sandwich Hut.

She ate the bland turkey sandwich in her car, washed it down with coffee that tasted suspiciously like instant, and decided to turn back. She'd shot the last of her black-and-white roll, so now she could develop it. First, set up the darkroom—that would be something she could do tonight.

To keep from thinking about Vance?

She felt her cheeks redden with anger. Well, yes. She spun the wheels as she turned off the shoulder onto the highway. Look at this scenery. Appreciate it! On one side rose cliffs of rough gray stone, hung with ferns and moss, topped by cedars that gathered the dusk into their branches. On the other side, the sea whispered peaceably. She opened her window, and the breeze cooled her face.

He was only a man. So why had she panicked when she found out that he was a two-timing jerk?

She'd always thought of herself as capable and self-reliant: in charge of her life and doing a good job. And she'd never been a got-to-get-married person, either.

Perhaps she had enjoyed, too much, the security she felt when she was with Vance. Perhaps she had let down her guard, for once. Perhaps she had started to hope . . .

No *perhaps* about it; she'd been a fool.

She braked to let a squirrel dart across the road. Enough of this agonizing! Her darkroom. Think about it some more. Did that bathroom have a ventilating fan?

At Cameron's Roost, the windows were dark and Belinda's Subaru was gone.

Good. No delays, no questions, Lindsey told herself. She could get upstairs right away and set to work.

The bathroom had plenty of space, and Belinda, or one of her esteemed relatives, had even installed a fan.

She put the enlarger, the timer, and the print paper at one end of the long counter, with the safelight close by. The developing trays and the water bath tray would have to go in the tub, but she'd done that on trips before and it had worked out fine.

Besides, that's what Boris Spremo did when he went to Africa. And, like him, she would hang a clothesline beneath the shower rod to dry the film. A folded towel under the door would keep out the light.

She backed up to survey the arrangement and almost tripped over the cat. He must have followed her in. "Make sure you stay out of here," she said, and shut the door.

The cat gave her a dignified I-wouldn't-think-of-intruding look and stalked down the room to sit on the windowsill.

After she'd mixed up the chemicals, she revised her plan for developing the film tonight. Too tired. Instead, she slid the bottles under the counter and sat down to read her bookstore find, *Remarkable Olympics*.

The photos of forests and rocky beaches reminded her of this afternoon's incident at the kennels. If Ben Fletcher didn't change his mind, her project was in serious trouble. She had planned it as a two-part series, and this second feature was to be the culminating piece, pulling everything together.

The page in front of her dissolved slowly into fragments, and she felt a warning twinge of pain in one temple. Not again.

She closed the book and stood cautiously to her feet. Maybe she could derail the headache if she drank some PainFree and went right to bed. No pills, please. She had to be able to function tomorrow.

Rain, splattering against the windows, awoke her. She opened her eyes to gray morning light. No headache. That tea of Shula's must have done her some good.

She sat up slowly, with immense gratitude. She'd forgotten to close the draperies, and from here the view was a tapestry of pearl and green touched with silver.

And she was hungry. The mini-refrigerator was empty and she really should go shopping today. Meanwhile, the fragrance of coffee hung in the air, a silent invitation. Belinda had said something about breakfast, hadn't she?

Belinda, wearing a navy wool pantsuit and dark red

lipstick, smiled when she saw her. "Oh, good morning! You've come down for breakfast today. I was hoping you would. I'm sorry to have missed you last night. Sit here. How do you like your eggs? Scrambled? Good. I'll get your coffee first thing. It's Café Vita. And look, blackberry scones that my sister sent over."

This hardworking sister, whoever she might be, made wonderful scones. Lindsey started to ask about her, but Belinda was intent on a history lesson this morning, beginning with a Spanish expedition in 1592 led by Juan de Fuca, followed much later by settlers . . . .

Lindsey helped herself to another scone and buttered it, trying to listen while Belinda spoke of the pretty little park Grandfather Samuel had built for the children of Cameron Bay. Belinda thought it should have his name on it, and maybe even a statue, but no one seemed to . . .

Lindsey ate the last bit of her scone. What about a nice big grocery store? That's what this town really needed.

Belinda had started discussing the area businesses and her words grabbed Lindsey's attention.

"Dogs," Belinda was saying. "He put every penny they had into it, he and Natalie, both. Ben Fletcher is quite enterprising—one of those Makah, you know—and I admire his industry, but I'm afraid he'll never . . . I saw him the other day, and I think he still has problems. All the time he was growing up, if it wasn't alcohol, it was women, and sometimes both. Of course we shouldn't judge one another, I'm sure."

She poured more coffee for them both, smiling her tight little smile. "His dogs are quite unique, I've heard. You might want to go see them. Be sure to take your camera."

Time for her to go back upstairs. Could it be true, what Belinda had said about Ben Fletcher?

Lindsey finished her coffee, remarked on the excellent breakfast, and gently detached herself from the web of

Belinda's concern.

The cat was waiting, curled up in the leather chair, as if ready to further document the activities of this uncommon human being.

"The first thing," Lindsey said, "is to figure out what we have, and where to go from here."

With a start, she realized that she had addressed the cat. She gave an incredulous laugh. She used to chuckle when Mollie talked to her cat—and now she was doing it too.

She frowned at the cat, who twitched his ears, and opened her laptop. Should she phone Edric and tell him what happened? No. Not yet.

But she could look critically at the photos she'd taken for the Carolina dogs feature. Some still needed framing; all of them needed captions. As far as the text was concerned, she didn't want to finalize it until she'd talked to Ben Fletcher. His insights would be priceless. She had to get to that man and the knowledge inside his head.

She began working on the best shots of the Carolina dogs, conscious of stalling for time. A vacuum cleaner hummed in the hall outside her room. Please, Belinda, don't decide to stop in for a chat.

Her cell phone rang. Remi. Maybe good news?

He was speaking low and fast. "Hi. I'm sorry about yesterday, but really, it's not because of you. Oh-oh. This isn't going to work. Wait a minute, I'm going outside."

So no one could overhear?

"This is better," he said. "Hey, I've got to tell you, something bad is going on around here. I don't know what. I'm afraid Ben's changed from . . . what he used to be like."

She dropped onto the rug and leaned her head against the leather chair. "There's no hurry," she said, hoping it was true. "I can stay around for a couple of days." She had budgeted two weeks, allowing time for several interviews.

"Great! I've been talking to him a little. He's worried, and it's got to be connected with the dogs."

"Remi, can I ask you something?"

"Sure."

"I don't want to offend, but has he been drinking lately?"

"Ben? Nope, not since Colin got ahold of him."

Colin again. Must be a friend of the family.

"Don't worry," Remi was saying. "It will work out for good. I'm trying to trust God in this." He paused. "Did you get a chance to listen to that file I gave you?"

"Not yet, but I will."

"Here come the kids. I'll keep you in the loop. Bye."

She closed her phone and let it lie on the rug.

The cat rose, stretched, and peered at her over the edge of the chair. "Not so good, Skookum," she said. "The prospects for this feature are looking worse and worse. I hope Ben Fletcher gets over whatever is bothering him. Soon."

Back to work. Try out some captions.

Someone was knocking at her door. With a sigh, she put down her pencil and went to open it.

Belinda, just stopping by, said that she'd been given some fresh whole-wheat walnut bread and would Lindsey like to have a sandwich?

As she spoke, Belinda glanced around the room. No doubt she noticed the unmade bed, and the clothes on the trunk, and the folders scattered across the desk.

Hurriedly, wanting her to leave, Lindsey said, "Yes, thank you. That would be very nice. Give me a couple of minutes and I'll be right down."

After the door closed, she went back to the desk and began stacking folders into piles.

A clattering sound came from the stairs, then a series of dull thuds and a terrible silence.

5

caption:

Jack in Black

Belinda lay unmoving at the foot of the stairs, her legs tangled in the hose of the vacuum cleaner. She was still breathing—Lindsey checked that first—but her face was white, except for a red patch on one temple, and her eyes were closed.

Where was the phone down here?

Belinda groaned. "My glasses."

"Stay still," Lindsey said. "I'm going to phone 911."

"No!" Belinda raised herself onto an elbow then sank down against the bottom step. "Too far. Port Angeles. Waste of time."

She took a gasping breath. "I'm okay. But my ankle—it hurts. Get my sister. Where's my glasses?"

"Here they are." Lindsey handed her the glasses, still intact. "What's your sister's name? Do you know her number?"

Belinda put on her glasses and closed her eyes. "Alexa. She won't hear the phone, not at lunch time."

While Lindsey was still trying to decide what to do, Belinda opened her eyes again. "You'll have to go down there. The bakery."

Lindsey hesitated, reluctant to leave. What if she had

43

internal bleeding? "Okay," she said at last. "I'll go get her."

"She's a nurse," Belinda said. "Wastes her time baking bread when she's a nurse."

Lindsey ran upstairs for her car keys, pulled the blanket off her bed, and ran back down to cover Belinda with it. "Don't you move," she said.

Brandt's Bread wasn't far, just down the hill and a short distance along Bay Street. When she walked inside, the first thing she noticed was the aroma of freshly baked bread, and the second was the noise.

She couldn't imagine where they'd all come from, but the room was full of customers: weather-beaten men; women with their children; a scattering of tourists; and three old loners. Everyone was talking, the espresso maker was hissing, cups and dishes clattered, and a rack of cinnamon rolls, towed by a dark-haired girl, rattled its way toward the display cases.

Belinda was right. Alexa, wherever she was, couldn't have heard a trumpet in here, much less a phone. She edged through the tables to speak to the girl behind the cash register.

"Is Alexa here?"

The girl nodded, pointing down the counter to where a slender chestnut-haired woman was arranging cookies on a tray. "Alexa?"

The woman slid the tray into the display case and turned toward them with a smile. "May I help you?"

"I've come about your sister," Lindsey said. "She's had a fall."

"Oh, no!" The brown eyes widened. "Is she okay?"

"She's conscious, but her ankle hurts. She's asking for you."

Alexa glanced across the crowded café and back to the girl. "Ruth, ask Rosie to help you out here. Listen for the phone, okay? I'll get back as soon as I can."

She took a small medical bag from under the counter, and a few minutes later, they were parking in front of Cameron's Roost. Alexa hurried through the door and knelt beside her sister.

Belinda gave them both a determined stare. "You can help me up, and I'll be okay. It's just my ankle. I'll walk it off."

"No, you won't." Alexa was taking off her sister's expensive leather shoes. "Look at this."

Belinda's left ankle was already beginning to swell. Alexa took the foot in one hand and gently rotated it.

"Ouch! That hurts."

"I guess it does. But you're fortunate—it doesn't seem to be broken." Alexa gave her a stern look. "When we lift you up, I want you to lean on us and on your good leg. Don't put even the tiniest bit of weight on that ankle. We're going to get you into bed."

Belinda looked as if she would like to object, but Alexa had gone into Belinda's apartment, just off the kitchen. She gave Lindsey a smile as she returned. "This won't be easy. Keep your back straight."

Together they hoisted Belinda to her feet and moved toward the bedroom. "Bed to the left," Alexa said, and a minute later they lowered Belinda onto it.

She lay there, watchful, as Alexa took two satin-covered pillows from a chaise longue and put them under the injured ankle.

"Sorry! I don't think I did my share," Lindsey said. "You must lift weights for a living."

Alexa laughed. "Just about. Those pails of flour aren't light."

"I'm not staying in bed," Belinda said. She looked tiny beneath the bed's ornate headboard, and the room, insistently Victorian with its rose-sprigged wallpaper and glass ornaments, seemed to crowd in around her.

"Should I get her an ice pack?" Lindsey said.

"A plastic bag with ice cubes will do fine," Alexa said.

She turned to her sister. "You really should have someone look at that ankle."

"Call Shula."

Alexa shrugged. "Whatever. What's her number?"

"It's by the phone." Belinda glanced at Lindsey. "I'm sorry—I didn't mean to be rude," she said. "Alexa, this is Lindsey Dumont, the famous photographer."

Lindsey winced.

Alexa paused halfway out the door, and Lindsey knew she'd sensed her embarrassment. "An honor," Alexa said. "Such a pity that we should meet under these regrettable circumstances."

She sent Lindsey a private smile and added, "Please excuse me, ladies. I have to make a phone call, and then I'd better get back to work."

"I'll get the ice," Lindsey said. Maybe she could get back to work too.

But Shula arrived soon after. Instead of the plump, elderly friend Lindsey had expected, she was petite, with bright eyes in a heart-shaped face and spiky black hair.

She hurried into Belinda's room, gave Lindsey a quick nod, and turned her attention to the figure on the bed. "What in the world have you done to yourself?"

She picked up Belinda's hand and held it, gazing into her eyes. "You're going to be fine, do you hear? Now let me take a look."

Lindsey left the room. Shula could deal with her friend.

Should she go back upstairs? It didn't seem right, not so soon. She slipped out through the sliding doors to the deck.

The morning's rain had become a gossamer mist. Water dripped from the fir branches, and unseen waves pounded on the rocks below. She leaned over the railing into the scents of wet wood, sweet resins, and leaf mold.

This was an attractive place, but maybe she should look for something else. Belinda wouldn't be mobile for a while, and she had no intention of nursing her. The project had to come first. If it didn't fizzle.

She clutched at the railing. It almost seemed that Someone was engineering problems for her, one after another. A punishment that she deserved, no doubt.

Where had that come from?

For years, ever since she'd decided that God had given up on her, she'd hardly thought about him. But when Kent died, the whole situation with him and Mollie had pried open the God-door in her mind. Not that she'd done much about it. Not that she wanted to.

She gazed into the trees, willing to be distracted. Look at the colors here—four shades of green in those branches, and the dark trunks, and that misted sky melting into a gray sea. Worth a photo.

She had almost convinced herself to get a camera when the sliding doors opened and Shula stepped out onto the deck.

"Please excuse my negligence," she said in a low, husky voice. "But when our Belinda is hurting, she needs to be center-stage." She smiled with wry affection as she spoke. "I have been looking forward to meeting you. Belinda has told me about your work."

"I'm glad to be here," Lindsey said.

The woman's eyes looked almost golden in her tanned face. "I have to run now, but I want you to know that I checked Belinda thoroughly. She'll be up and about in a few days, so I hope you aren't thinking about leaving us. Her sister will come by to help, and I'll send Jack over."

She gave Lindsey another quick smile and was gone.

Too late, she remembered Shula's remarkable tea. She'd have to thank her the next time she came.

As she stepped back into the kitchen, she wondered

47

how old Shula was. They might be the same age, but the other woman's face was lined, as if she'd had a difficult life, and the blue-black hair was not a natural color.

Belinda's voice drifted from the bedroom. "Could you possibly make me a cup of chamomile tea? Shula's going to bring me something special, but I got thirsty, just thinking about it."

After she gave Belinda the tea, Lindsey perched on the edge of the chaise longue to listen to her for a while. The woman's fluffy blue nightgown, trimmed with ribbons and lace, made her look older, somehow, and defenseless.

Belinda described how her Great-Grandfather Ezekiel earned his fortune logging the forests around Cameron Bay in the early 1900's, and Lindsey began wondering again about a grocery store. At least she could get that much done.

At the first opportunity, she asked, "Can you tell me where to find a grocery store? I didn't see one in town."

"There's a small one across from the post office, in Thorsen's Motel. Liza Thorsen says her great-grandfather settled here years before mine, but I don't believe her."

Lindsey prodded gently. "And apart from that?"

"For a real store, you'll have to go back down the highway, maybe thirty miles, to Joyce. The Joyce General Store has just about everything." She smiled. "Whenever I visited my grandparents, it was my favorite place to go."

Lindsey stood up. "I think I passed it on the way in. Can I pick up anything for you?"

Belinda took off her glasses and rubbed her eyes. "There's plenty of food in the freezer. Maybe you could get me an elastic bandage—that's Alexa's idea. Do you have time to make us a sandwich before you go? I'd hate for that roast beef to spoil. Alexa's going to bring supper, but sometimes she gets tied up, and it might be quite late."

The Joyce General Store was all that Belinda had said and more, its shelves heaped with goods that ranged from the basics to the whimsical.

Lindsey bought what she needed, admired the incredible length of an old chain saw that hung from a ceiling beam, and hurried back. Maybe she could still get something accomplished today.

When she turned off the highway into Cameron Bay, she looked at the sign with new interest, remembering Belinda's story about old Samuel rounding up the whole town to hoist it into place.

Farther down the hill, another sign, hand-painted, said CAMERON PARK. The long, narrow park beyond it must be the one Belinda had mentioned. It seemed to be deserted, which wasn't surprising for a rainy October afternoon.

After she'd put away the groceries, she checked on Belinda, and while she was there, a rapid tattooing sounded at the front door.

"That's Jack," Belinda said, looking annoyed. "I don't know why he can't knock the way ordinary people do."

Possibly because Jack was not an ordinary person, Lindsey thought after she'd opened the door. A skinny figure hunched into a hooded black jacket stood before her, holding two buckets in his large red hands.

"Brought some stuff for Miz Cameron," the young man said in a reedy voice. His face was childish in its contours, but he wore a tuft of brown beard on his chin.

She smiled, visualizing him in a black-and-white shot, and he straightened up, making himself taller.

"Here's the tea." He handed over a plastic bag, glancing at her with sharp, clever eyes.

He banged the buckets together. "And these. Miz Shula said directions are with 'em."

"Thank you," she said. "I'm Lindsey Dumont. You must be Jack."

"Right on," he said, his face drawn in determined lines. "Jack Jincy. I'm a painter."

49

Did he paint houses or canvas? He seemed more like a house painter, but you never knew.

He thrust his hands into his pockets. "Would you please inquire whether Miz Cameron would like me to do anything for her? I'll stay out here. She doesn't like me tracking in on her floors."

When Lindsey asked, Belinda shook her head. "Tell him not today, thank you. What he really wants is a tip. Could you hand me my purse?"

Lindsey brought the leather handbag from Belinda's desk, and the woman chose a five-dollar bill. "Here. Ask him to come back on Friday if it's convenient."

Jack took the money with a dignified nod. "I'll have to check my calendar, but I think Friday will be fine."

He looked more cheerful now, and he gave her a quick grin as he jumped onto his bicycle and sped down the driveway, swerving to avoid a slow-moving yellow Ford.

The old car grumbled its way up the hill toward her, and Lindsey soon recognized Alexa at the wheel.

She left the front door open for Alexa while she took the buckets and tea into Belinda's room. "Here's your tea, Belinda. Looks like it's called Sprain & Pain." She opened the small canister. "Mmm. Smells good."

"She sent me those buckets too?"

"Yes, with instructions."

"I'll take some tea," Belinda said, "but I don't need those buckets. The ice pack will do. "

Alexa came through the doorway, laden with packages and a slow-cooker, and Lindsey went to help her. "So nice to have you here," she said to Alexa, who smiled as if she knew what she meant.

"I brought Italian chicken for supper," Alexa said, "and Peter's latest sunflower-seed bread."

"Don't bother with those buckets," Belinda called. "Just make me a nice cup of tea."

50

Alexa looked at Lindsey. "Buckets?"

"Shula sent them."

"I'm starved," Alexa said, and lowering her voice, added, "But first, I should probably deal with this foolish insurrection."

She took Shula's note into her sister's room. While she waited, Lindsey put on water for tea and set out dishes for supper. Alexa had brought enough food to last them for days.

"Hot water, then cold water," said Alexa's clear voice.

A dissenting mumble from Belinda.

Alexa's voice, sweetly: "So . . . I'll just phone Shula and tell her you're refusing to follow her instructions, and you don't care whether you ever drive a car again."

Belinda's voice, answering very low.

"Okay," Alexa said. "I'll get those buckets ready and be right back."

Alexa helped her sister soak the ankle, served her supper on a tray, and returned to the kitchen. Her freckled face looked weary, but her smile was wide and warm. "Thanks," she said. "Let's eat out on the deck."

The rain had finally stopped, and the trees sheltered them from the wind. As long as they kept their jackets on, it was pleasant at the little table. Neither of them said much while they ate.

Alexa seemed to be a quiet person, restfully so, and when she did talk, it was about the bread, which her husband had made, mentioning such things as crumb and texture.

"Do you make bread too?" Lindsey said.

Alexa laughed. "No, I just picked that up from listening to Pete. I get to do the fun stuff, like muffins and scones and cookies. Cakes too. That reminds me—I've got a cake to finish decorating tonight. Will you excuse me? But please be sure to drop in and see us, anytime."

She was gone then, and after Lindsey cleaned up the kitchen, she went back upstairs.

She sat down, stared at her computer screen, and wondered about the captions she'd been trying to write. Hours ago.

She'd met some interesting people, but as far as her project was concerned, this day was looking like a waste of time. And from what Remi had said, it wasn't going to improve.

Where was the flash drive he'd given her? Wait. Maybe she'd better read that third chapter of John in case he wanted to talk about it.

What had she done with the Bible? Here, on the desk.

She picked it up, and it fell open to the title page.

For Milly Lindstrom
First Place, Swords Contest
December, 1972

A long time ago. She thumbed through the yellowed pages. Had Milly ever read it?

In Lindsey's Sunday school, they'd given out Bibles as the grand prize for memorizing verses. She had never attained the glory of winning a Bible, but she'd won ribbons. Red ones. Seven of them.

What had happened to Milly? She'd be much older by now. Had she taken to heart any of the verses she'd memorized?

Lindsey turned to the book of John and paused. Not ready for this. Not ready to settle down with anything.

Her gaze rested on the flash drive. She could upload it and—she glanced out the window—maybe she'd go see what that little park was like.

It would help to get outside. Get away.

6

caption:

Salmon by Fraser

Instead of using the sidewalk, Lindsey scuffed through the weedy grass on the shoulder of Bay Street, skirting the line of boulders at its edge. The breeze was tinged with salt, wood smoke, and something else. Fish.

A boat launch of rough, stained concrete slanted down into the water, and a few steps farther, she came to the park sign, planted in gravel and rumpled gray sand. Just past it were picnic tables, fire pits, and a small playground.

She followed a straggling line of bushes to a sandy path that ran beside a seawall at the water's edge. This would be a good place to walk. Now for Remi's gift. What kind of music did he like? She put in her ear buds.

A man's voice, somewhat British, began to speak:

"The Letter to the Romans. Chapter Eight.

There is therefore now no condemnation for those who are in Christ Jesus."

She snatched at phrases as they went by.

Some were frightening:

"*the law of sin and death . . . cannot please God.*"

Others made her breath quicken:

"*we cry, 'Abba, Father' . . . children of God . . . helps us in our weakness.*"

She walked more and more slowly until the path finally ended at a high-backed bench. She stood in front of the bench, mesmerized by what she was hearing.

The passage ended with a joyful declaration:

"I am sure that neither death nor life . . . nor anything else in all creation, will be able to separate us from the love of God in Christ Jesus our Lord."

The triumphant words rang out, filling her with awe and hope and longing. But the echoes faded to gray. The gray became emptiness, jagged and cold.

The cold seemed to slash at her heart, and she pulled out her ear buds.

I cannot deal with this.

The bench was there, solid and time-worn. She dropped onto it. Sea birds flew across the bay into the dusk, and waves lapped against the seawall.

"I am sure . . . I am sure . . ." the voice had said.

I'm not sure. Not at all.

She crossed her arms, hugged them to herself, but found no comfort. The headland turned from misted gray to mauve to black. A bleak wind rose from the water.

Enough of this.

She got stiffly to her feet and pulled up the hood of her jacket—the green Columbia jacket she'd bought with such care, picturing walks with Vance on the Seattle waterfront.

What was he doing tonight?

Her hands clenched. No. It was over.

She hurried along the line of bushes, passed the picnic tables and crossed the gravel, pausing only when she reached Bay Street.

A brisk walk was just what she needed. Get her blood moving. Stretch her tense muscles. This wind was cold!

She would heat up some of the soup she'd bought, and she'd dunk some crackers into it. Maybe add a slice of cheese.

And she needed a cup of plain, ordinary tea. With apologies to Shula, she didn't want anything more whizzing in her brain.

The town looked drowsy, as if it was ready to snug its roofs tight and settle down to sleep. Only a few lights were on, and Bay Street was deserted.

She passed the bakery, glancing at its darkened windows, and someone called, "Lin!"

Remi.

He was heading for his truck, parked beside the bakery. "Taking a walk? Isn't this the prettiest little bay you've ever seen?"

"It certainly is." She pulled her jacket close against a sudden gust of wind.

"You're cold! I'm thinking we might get a storm tonight."

He reached into the back of his truck for a box, and she turned to go on down the street. "Come in!" he said. "There's a couple of us here, pestering Alexa and drinking her coffee."

"But isn't it closed?"

"Not to us—you'll see."

Attracted by the prospect of hot coffee, she followed him around the side of the bakery and through a small door.

It was warm inside and reminiscent of bread. Off to her left was the darkened café area, and in front of her was a pair of wide swinging doors. They squeaked as Remi pushed through with the box, and she followed.

This must be the bakery's workroom. It was well-lit, lined with cupboards, and equipped with stainless steel refrigerators, an oversize stove, and a large mixer set into the counter.

Alexa stood at a worktable in the center of the room, patting down a circle of dough. She looked up with her warm smile. "Hi, Lin! Thanks, Remi. You can put it on the counter. Get Lin some coffee. Have you been out walking?"

"I thought I'd check out the park."

With swift strokes, Alexa cut the dough into triangles. "You mean the park that should have a bronze statue of Samuel Cameron? Has Belinda mentioned that serious oversight to you?"

"She has, indeed."

"Hello, there." It was the bookstore owner, walking toward her from a table set against the back wall.

"Oh, good, you two have met," Alexa said. "Fraser Denton, I know exactly how many currants there are in that pile, so don't you lift a single one. In fact, to avoid temptation, you may put them into the bag and close it tightly."

"Caught again!" A boyish smile crossed his face. "Can't put anything over on this gal," he said to Lindsey. "There you are—all stashed, Lexa. Now I'm a free man. Guess I'll get me some more coffee."

Lindsey thanked Remi with a smile as he handed her a steaming cup. "This smells wonderful. Milk? Thanks. What are you making, Alexa?"

"Just scones. I thought I'd try some with orange zest and coriander—and currants. I've already got one tray baking, so they'll be ready in a minute." She slid a second tray into the oven and set the timer.

"Just scones?" Fraser went to the coffee pot on the counter and filled his cup. "I volunteer to judge the results." He glanced at Lindsey. "Until they're ready, tell me why you're in town."

Remi shot her a worried look, but she had no intention of saying anything about Ben Fletcher.

She leaned against the worktable. "I'm researching the aboriginal past of certain dogs—dingo dogs, to be exact—

and I read of a link to some dogs the Makahs had, years ago. What's your tribal background, Fraser?"

"Haida."

"Would that be the Queen Charlottes, up in Canada?"

"I'm American."

"Prince of Wales Island?"

He smiled. "You've done your homework. Just across the Strait, in Ketchikan."

"Is that where you grew up?"

"Mostly."

"And that's where you learned to carve?"

"I had family on Prince of Wales Island."

"You have a carver in your family?"

He was grinning now. "Yes, I learned from my grandfather. And yes, he taught me everything I know, and he made me go to college too. And then I folded up my teepee and did some traveling."

"But the Haida don't use tepees."

"You are correct. Anyway, I traveled around Alaska and a few other places, earning my way as an itinerant carver—did you get that part? People like that line—and ended up here. Taught school. Opened my bookstore. And what's a nice guy like me doing in a place like this? I'm trying to make a contribution to the culturally deprived constituents of the community, especially my white brethren. Besides, Alexa makes great chocolate chip cookies."

Lindsey burst out laughing and had to put down her cup. "Autobiography in ten seconds flat. You're amazing! I wish Belinda could have heard it."

She sobered. "I didn't mean to be so inquisitive. It sounds as if you've been traumatized by the media. But I did wonder about the carving. You're fortunate. Some things can't be learned in school."

"Show her your latest," Remi said.

Fraser spread out his hands in protest. "Hey! I only brought it over because Alexa begged, and she also threatened me with no handouts for the rest of the week."

Alexa looked up from the worktable. "Yeah, I really had him scared."

"You'll let me see it?" Lindsey said.

"Over here."

He went to the table and she followed, with Remi behind her. He took a small flat-bottomed carving out of a box and set it on the table.

It was a salmon, no more than eight inches long, done in the honey-colored wood that she recognized as cedar.

The gills, the fins, the tail, and the mouth were all skillfully incised, and the eye had a hopeful glint.

"He's got a lot of personality, doesn't he?" Lindsey said.

"It's a she," Remi said. He pointed to a crosshatched circle on the fish's belly. "See her eggs?"

"You're right!" Lindsey said. "I love it. And I like the way her tail flips up. She's swimming upstream?"

Fraser nodded.

"What's your favorite thing to carve?" she said.

Fraser sat down at the table and gazed at the ceiling. She and Remi sat across from him.

"Probably the salmon," he said at last. "And Lin, I see that journalistic glint in your eye. Now you're going to ask me why."

She gave him an encouraging smile.

"I guess it's because they're such complex creatures. We spend millions of dollars to invent guidance systems for our missiles—which, by the way, don't always hit the target—and theirs comes with the package, built-in, and perfectly accurate."

He swirled the coffee in his cup. "It makes me turn to God and praise him."

Alexa spoke from where she stood by the oven. "What I like is how tough they are. How determined. A missile doesn't care if it goes astray, but a salmon seems to care."

"Not to be anthropomorphic," Fraser said, "but that speaks to me of courage."

Alexa put a plate of hot scones on the table, along with knives, napkins, and a tub of butter.

Fraser said, "We will now interrupt our discussion for a moment of grateful silence. These are excellent, Lexa."

"You haven't even tasted one!"

"I have the utmost confidence . . ."

She pushed a napkin toward him. "Now you sound like a politician. Eat."

Lindsey took a bite of her scone, savoring its crisp golden crust and flaky center. "Okay, it's my turn, and I speak with the authority of research. The currants are nice and chewy, the orange adds a bit of edge, and they have a sort of toasty flavor. What does coriander taste like, anyway?"

"Buttery and toasty," Alexa said. "So you get an *A* for your report."

Remi reached for another scone. "I have a question. What's anthropomorphic?"

Fraser gave him an affectionate grin. "Hasn't Colin taught you that word yet? When's he coming into town? Tell him it's been too long."

Remi grinned back. "I'm hoping for Friday. He couldn't come last weekend because of one of his kids." He buttered the scone and took a large bite. "But I can't wait until then. The suspense is killing me."

"Anthropomorphic?" Fraser seemed to enjoy rolling the word off his tongue. "It just means giving human feelings to something else."

Alexa said, "You could argue that the salmon is only

59

doing what God designed her to do, but I agree with you, Fraser. It takes something like courage."

Remi nodded, his face serious now. "Sometimes it takes courage for us to do what God designed us to do."

Alexa smiled. "And that is?"

"Love him," Remi said. "Thou shalt love the Lord with all thy heart and with all thy soul and with all thy mind."

He paused. "To think that the Mighty One who designed the universe actually wants me to love *him?* Blows me away."

"Not everyone would agree with you," Fraser said. "In fact, most people don't think God has a personal interest in us at all."

"Or they think he's just a vapor," Lindsey said, remembering a comment from Vance. "They say God is an amorphous sort of cosmic vapor that floats in and out of reality."

Fraser understood her point. "A comfortable idea because a vapor would make no claims on anyone."

Alexa looked up from her scone. "Claims like, 'You're mine because I created you.'"

"Or," Remi said, "'I suffered because of your sin, and I did that because I loved you.'"

"John 3:16," Lindsey said, smiling at him.

"Yes!" he said. "And Romans 8—that's my latest favorite chapter. Did you get to listen to it?"

She nodded, remembering how she'd felt at the park and wishing she could change the subject.

It must be getting late, and it might storm. Was that rain on the back windows? Perhaps she could use it as an excuse to leave.

Remi leaned toward her, his face alight. "What did you think?"

She held tightly to her cup, stared down into the

creamy brown liquid. *I really don't want to think.*

The silence seemed to unroll down the length of the table, and finally she said, "Those verses at the end. They ripped my heart to shreds."

Had she really said that? In front of these people she hardly knew?

But Fraser's eyes shone, and they were all nodding.

Alexa said quietly, "It's one of my lifeline passages."

She folded her arms across her chest, and Lindsey caught a hint of sadness in the brown eyes as she added, "Christ's love is what holds me together inside."

Lindsey bit her lip.

"And the best part," Alexa said, "is knowing that nothing can separate me from his love. Makes me want to get down on my knees."

"Or shout," Fraser said.

"Yeah," Remi said. "You don't see anything like that in the Quran."

He glanced at Lindsey. "Remember old Timothy? He had me reading the second chapter of Philippians, where Christ came to earth in the form of a miserable little human being—all because of his love. That's what really got to me."

Fraser and Alexa must have known his story because they both nodded.

A minute later, Remi pushed his chair back from the table, looking reluctant. "Well, you artistic types can sit here and talk all night, but our puppies wake up early."

He glanced at the rain streaming down the windows. "Lin, why don't I give you a ride back up to the Roost? Looks pretty wet out there."

Alexa stood up. "Take a couple of these scones with you. Was Belinda asleep when you left?"

Lindsey nodded, and Alexa said, "Then I won't bother her tonight. That tea of Shula's probably put her out."

Belinda was still sleeping when Lindsey let herself into the house, so perhaps Alexa was right.

She turned off the downstairs lights and went up the steps as quietly as she could. The cat seemed to have disappeared. No more talk with anyone tonight.

She went first to the sliding door and pushed it open so she could listen to the wind in the trees. Words and ideas hummed through her brain, elbowing each other for room. Must be all that good coffee.

She turned to the desk and saw her camera lying there. How about developing the roll of film she'd finished up yesterday? It would be interesting to see how the tree photos turned out—and the ones of Fraser's cat.

Her partner Edric liked to tease her about it, but developing was one of her favorite things to do.

He couldn't understand how the whole process intrigued her—setting up the trays, pouring out the chemicals, working by the dimness of the safelight. She even liked the pungent smell of the developer.

She pulled on her protective gloves, flipped on the fan, and set to work. When the negatives were ready, she studied the last few shots with her loupe.

This one of the tree might be acceptable, the way the morning light slanted across the sand. The next one, with the root-shadows, was better. Worth printing. She turned on the enlarger.

Finally the moment came when she could immerse the print paper into its tray of developer and watch the image of the tree take shape. Exhilarating. As if she were creating that tree, right here in the darkness.

Into the stop bath, the fixer, and the wash bath; then she could squeegee it and hang it up to dry.

One shot of Fraser's cat turned out well, so she printed it too.

She pinned it up beside the tree photo and paused,

thinking about the experimental shot she'd taken of Vance, trying for a craggy look in bright sunlight.

She examined the negative but couldn't tell how successful her experiment had been.

Why not print it, just to see?

After she'd exposed the negative, she picked up the print paper with her tongs and dipped it into the developing tray. Slowly Vance's face appeared. There he was, with the smile that haunted her dreams. The shot was over-exposed, but for a second his gaze held hers.

She drew a sharp breath. Was she going to soften up now and start mooning over the two-timing skunk?

"No . . . no," she murmured.

She kept the picture in the solution, gripped the tongs, and watched without moving. His face grew darker and darker until it was lost in blackness.

It was almost like playing God, a friend had said, when you let an image destroy itself.

She lifted out the sheet of wet paper and dropped it into the wastebasket.

Was that what God had done with her? Blacked her out of his mind?

She deserved it.

Watch your step, girl. God's keeping his eyes on you and counting up all your sins.

Her father often said that. His speeches about God had haunted her for years.

She let the tongs clatter into the sink and stripped off her gloves.

But that wasn't what the Bible really said about God.

Like those verses in Romans. And those people tonight—the way they'd quoted verses and talked about God's love—as if they knew it was real. As if they counted on it.

She had listened, wanting to be like them, wanting to

have that love hold her together inside too.

So what about it?

She leaned against the wall, staring at the dusky glow of the safelight.

Was she going to believe what the Bible said about God? A real person? A person who created her and loved her and forgave her and made a way for her to love him back?

She reached for the doorknob, ready to escape, but a question snatched at her. More than half of her life was gone. What was she going to do with the rest of it?

I need to either believe the Bible . . . or . . . keep trying to make it on my own.

Time to decide.

She stepped into the bedroom, away from her thoughts, and the first thing she saw was her rumpled bed. Better take care of that.

She stripped it, took the sheets and blankets to the balcony, shook them out over the railing, remade the bed, hung up her clothes, washed the dishes, and scoured the tiny kitchen sink.

The bathroom! She'd left it in a mess. She pulled on another pair of gloves, put away the chemicals, drained and rinsed the trays and the tub, and wiped off the counter.

She went to her desk and closed down her laptop for the night. She organized the scattered folders, rearranging them twice, and wiped off the dust and cat hair.

Milly's Bible lay on the desk. She picked it up, and once again, emptiness shuddered through her.

She curled up in the brown chair with the Bible.

Romans, chapter eight. Those verses at the end. She had to read them for herself.

Neither death, nor life, nor angels,
nor principalities, nor powers,
nor things present, nor things to come,

Nor height, nor depth,
nor any other creature,
shall be able to separate us from the love of God
which is in Christ Jesus, our Lord.

She hunched forward, closing her eyes.

"Father," she whispered, "I have sinned. Please forgive me, not because I deserve your mercy, but . . . because of your Son." She paused. "I love you for loving me. I want to love you better."

Warmth flowed through her, and with it came an unfamiliar tide of . . . joy?

Thank you, Lord.

She sat at ease, listening to the wind and rain and the distant pounding of the surf.

And a scratching sound. Branches on the window? No. She smiled and stood up. Cat at the door.

The cat leaped onto the leather chair and began to wash his face.

She left the draperies open so she could hear the ocean during the night and started getting ready for bed.

If I really love God, I've got to do something about it.

Yes, she would.

Edric had always said she was a get-up-and-do-it person. She would do her very best for God. He'd show her how to remove Vance from the company—kindly, of course—and how to make her project successful.

But she wouldn't think about it tonight.

Tonight was for letting his love hold her together.

caption:

Flotsam

After last night's storm, Lindsey expected to see the beach glittering with sunlight, but it lay half-hidden by fog. She strolled at the water's edge to watch the waves frothing onto the sand and enjoyed the private, enclosed feeling that fog always gave her.

She'd slept well, for once, with no nightmares, no busy circling thoughts. A gift . . . *Thank you, Lord.*

A wavelet broke across the toe of one shoe and she retreated, walking near the high-tide line to poke through the driftwood and broken shells.

A set of footprints wandered in the same direction she was going. Who else would be out this early?

Ahead, only a dim outline in the fog, a man sat among the uprooted trees. She slowed, unwilling to meet a stranger. Should she turn back? But why should she give up her walk? Just smile and march on past.

A minute later, she recognized the black hair of the young bookstore owner, Fraser Denton. He was seated on the smooth trunk of the tree she had photographed, intent on something in his hands.

As she drew near, he looked up with a smile. "Beautiful morning, isn't it?"

"I was just thinking that." She paused in front of him. "What have you got there?"

"Driftwood. I've been scribbling on it. Take a look." He stood up, pocketing his knife, and handed it to her.

It was hardly six inches long, a piece of gray wood with darker knots and whorls, streamlined by the waves.

"A fish!" Remembering last night's talk, she asked, "A salmon?"

He smiled. "Perhaps."

She looked down at it. "Doing what God designed it to do. Clever how you used that knot for an eye." She smoothed it with a finger. "It feels like satin."

He was watching her now. "Keep it if you wish."

"No, I couldn't. It's yours. You found it, and you saw the fish in it."

"Mine to give as I please." He sat down and took out his knife. "I'll make it look a little more like our salmon."

She sat beside him, watching as his knife cut deftly into the wood. He carved a tiny crosshatched circle in the fish's belly and shaped the tail into an upward flip.

He handed it back to her. "How's that?"

She cradled it in her hands. "Wonderful, Fraser."

"Keep it to remind you." He paused. "When you're fighting your way upstream." He gazed at her. "I think that you are a person of courage."

She shook her head. "A person of foolish, blinding enthusiasms, you mean."

Vance, the prime example.

"But," she said, "God has forgiven me."

His face lit up. "Me too, many times."

He stood to his feet. "And now he's telling me that I have a store to open." With a nod, he turned and left.

She watched him disappear into the fog. Just a young man, but he seemed unusually wise and deep-thinking. He couldn't have had it easy, growing up.

The scrap of driftwood lay in her hand, and she closed her fingers over it as she continued on down the beach.

It would remind her of last night and the decision she'd made.

Courage, Fraser said. She had a feeling that she was going to need it. She slipped the driftwood into her pocket and began to jog faster and faster, with the mist blowing around her and the air tasting deliciously of salt.

Something on the sand, something white, came into view through the fog. As she approached, it took the shape of a ragged towel.

No, it was a dog, a small white dog with black splotches. It lay sprawled at the waterline, and the waves were washing over the inert body, lifting its legs.

She knelt to ease it away from the water. A short-haired terrier, mixed breed. Like the Fletchers' dog, the one that had made such a racket. Spot.

She put a hand on the small white chest and felt it rise and fall. He was alive, but his breathing was rough. What could have happened to him?

Hurrying now, she took off her jacket, spread it in the sand, and lifted the small body onto it. "C'mon Spot, I'm taking you home."

Awkwardly, because of her dangling camera, she picked him up and started back down the beach. He wasn't heavy, but it seemed a long time before she reached the Jeep and could lay him on the seat beside her.

While she started the engine and turned up the heater, she phoned Remi. "I've found a dog," she said. "I think it's Spot. I'm bringing him over."

"Where was he?"

"On the beach. I'll be there in a couple of minutes."

Unwelcome as she might be, surely Ben Fletcher wouldn't turn her away. And—yes, this was a self-serving thought—maybe he'd think more kindly of her now.

Remi was waiting out in front of the kennels with Ben Fletcher beside him. Ginni, still in pajamas, clung to Remi's hand, hopping from one foot to the other.

As soon as the Jeep stopped, Remi opened the passenger door and bent over the dog. He lifted it out, and Ben Fletcher said, "Get him inside."

The two men went ahead into the barn, and she and Ginni followed.

The little girl was shivering, and Lindsey wished she had a jacket to lend her. Someone else must have had the same thought because a tall woman, dark pigtails flying above her pink bathrobe, rushed up to them.

"Ginni! You'll freeze! Put this on." She handed the girl a hooded red sweatshirt, gave Lindsey an apologetic smile, and hurried off.

As Lindsey had expected, the barn was filled with dog pens, and everything looked well-maintained. By the time she and Ginni caught up, the men had laid Spot on a counter and were rubbing him with towels. They watched in silence, Ginni still hopping up and down.

Ben Fletcher spoke to the child without inflection. "Ask Mama to get a box and some hot-water bottles ready." Ginni stopped jiggling and ran off.

The dog was breathing more regularly now, and his short fur was dry, but he seemed to be deeply asleep.

Ben wrapped him in another towel and picked him up, a look of despair on his face. "He acts like he's been drugged. Let's take him inside. Maybe he'll sleep it off."

He spoke to Remi, but his dark eyes stabbed at her. "Not a word to anyone, especially Ginni."

Her wet jacket lay on the counter, and as the men walked away, she picked it up to shake out the sand.

Remi had stopped to wait for her. "Come on in."

"You think I should?"

"Yes. I want you to meet Natalie."

They passed through a screened-in porch with firewood stacked by the door, fishing poles on the wall, and boots piled beside a washing machine at the far end. The door led into a large kitchen that smelled of coffee.

Two boys sat at a table eating cereal. One was the blond boy she'd seen before. "That's Bobby," Remi said to her, "and across from him is Jeffrey."

The older boy, maybe twelve, was light-skinned, with dark, intelligent eyes. He gave her a thoughtful glance and kept eating.

Ben was nowhere to be seen.

"Here's our Mama," Remi said, a smile in his voice.

The woman had changed into jeans and a pink sweatshirt, and she was hurrying to greet Lindsey.

"You are so kind!" she said. "You rescued our Spot!"

She had a beautiful face—burnished brown eyes, high cheek bones, perfect skin—and her shining black hair was pulled into a ponytail.

She took Lindsey's arm and drew her farther into the room. "Let me get you some coffee."

Ginni was crouched over a box in the corner behind the kitchen table, but she stood up to listen when Natalie handed Lindsey the coffee and asked how she had found the dog.

Lindsey explained what had happened. Perhaps Ginni would be a little less hostile.

But the child's dark brows were knitting themselves into a frown, and when she finished, Ginni burst out, "Don't you listen to her, Mama! She did it herself! She made it all up because . . . because . . . she wants to take pictures of our dogs and ruin us all."

Little Bobby stared at her, his spoon in mid-air.

Natalie turned pale. "Hush, child! It's not true. You mustn't talk like that."

Jeffrey said, "Ginni, quit! You're telling stories again."

70

Ginni began to sob, and she ran into the next room.

Once again, Natalie put a hand on Lindsey's arm. "Please, don't pay any attention to our little girl. She's upset these days. Would you like to sit down and have breakfast? I made coffee cake."

Lindsey smiled. "Thank you, but not today."

Her jeans were cold and damp, the coffee was bitter, and she'd rather be anywhere else than in this kitchen.

Remi walked with her out to the Jeep. "You know, if I were you, I'd stop by this afternoon, just to ask about the dog, and see what's going on. Ben's in shock right now for some reason I can't figure out."

He paused, frowning. "But Natalie will calm him down, and by then he should be over this. You did us a big favor. He might even let you watch him training the dogs."

"What about Ginni?"

"Poor Ginni." He smiled like a doting father. "I think she's jealous. She wants you to be the Enemy. Don't worry about her." He gazed past Lindsey to the kennels. "But I'd sure like to know what's going on."

"I'd better give you a call before I come," Lindsey said, "to see if it's okay."

"That's a good idea."

Belinda must have heard her key turn in the lock because she called out, "There you are!"

When Lindsey looked in through the bedroom door, Belinda said, "I thought you might be sleeping in."

Lindsey avoided the unspoken question and asked, "How was your night?"

The plump face sagged with longsuffering. "Shula's tea helped, but I finally had to take some pain pills."

Before Lindsey could think what to say next, she went on. "If you wouldn't mind filling those two buckets with water, I'd appreciate it. Alexa made me promise to do that hot-cold treatment. I hate it, but anything's better than being a cripple for the rest of my life. She's bringing supper over tonight. Have you eaten breakfast yet?"

"Let me run upstairs for a few minutes," Lindsey said, "and I'll come back down to help you."

She was so cold and sticky with saltwater that a quick shower was the only solution. Besides, it sounded as if Belinda was going to keep her occupied for a while.

Her jacket would have to be washed since it smelled like wet dog. What about Fraser's salmon—was it ruined? She drew it out of the pocket.

The tip that formed the fish's tail was dark and wet, but she had to laugh at herself. This scrap of driftwood had probably spent months in seawater. It would be fine.

Fifteen minutes later, she was comfortable in dry clothes and downstairs filling the two buckets for Belinda.

Belinda wanted only tea and toast, and after Lindsey had taken in the tray, she toasted herself a thick slice of Alexa's raisin bread, spread it with peanut butter, and carried it and her coffee out onto the deck.

The toast reminded her of the warm breakfast smells in Natalie's kitchen and, less pleasantly, of Ginni's outburst. She could still see the unease on Natalie's face and in Remi's dark eyes. Ginni's peculiar words echoed: "and ruin us all." Not a child's expression. She must have heard it from her parents.

What had happened to that dog? Presumably he'd lived near the ocean all his life, so he couldn't have wandered into the waves out of ignorance.

Drugged? Ben had said that.

Belinda's voice, calling her, came faintly through the sliding doors. Almost eleven o'clock, and she had work to do. The feature on the Carolina dogs wasn't nearly finished, and she definitely had to phone Edric.

She swallowed the last of her coffee and took her

dishes into the kitchen. Belinda had dressed herself and was lying on her bed—neatly made—looking worn out.

"I know you're busy," she said in a plaintive voice, "but if you could just make me a fresh pot of that Pain & Sprain, I won't bother you anymore."

As soon as she'd taken Belinda her tea, she hurried upstairs. First, Edric.

Even though he left the planning and execution of the feature stories to her, he liked to hear the details of any on-going project. Sometimes he had suggestions, with varying degrees of usefulness, and she always tried to incorporate them when she could.

Edric answered her call right away. "Hey Lin! Getting worried about you. What's happening out there? One of those Olympic grizzlies get you?"

He'd started chewing gum to keep from smoking, and she could hear him chomping rapidly. A good sign.

"Hi! I meant to call yesterday, but it got too late." She tried to match his upbeat tone. "I've run into a bit of a problem here. This kennel owner's not so sure anymore he wants to do the feature. Maybe just nerves, maybe something else."

"Okay, well, I'm on another line, but see what you can do about it and give me an update."

"Sure, I'll call back tomorrow if I can."

Good. He didn't sound particularly concerned. She sent a quick email to Mollie, telling about the beach she'd found and asking how she and Nathan were getting along—but those two were so much in love, it was a joke to even ask.

She set to work again on the Carolina dog photos.

Much later, she stopped for a moment to stretch. What was that banging? Front door? Must be Jack. She hurried down the stairs, calling to Belinda, "I'll get it."

He held a wooden crutch upraised, preparing to hit the door again, and made a wry face. "Thought you'd hear me

73

sometime soon."

He thrust the pair of crutches at her. "Where's this all-important night-light the old lady's yammering about?"

She looked him squarely in the eyes. Blue eyes, unremarkable except for a sly gleam. "Good afternoon, Jack."

He shook back his hair. "Good afternoon, Miz Dumont. Sorry. I guess it wasn't you who phoned Miz Shula three times already this morning." His voice was glossed with repentance that might be genuine. "That reminds me. She sent a note for you—here."

"Thank you." She put the envelope into her pocket and took the crutches from him. "Let's find out about this night-light."

There were two lights, it turned out, one in Belinda's bathroom and the other by her bed. Jack must have guessed what might be wrong because he screwed in replacement bulbs, taken from somewhere in the depths of his black jacket, and soon left, bearing with him Belinda's generous donation, as she put it, to his college fund.

Belinda had to try out the crutches right away, and she staggered out to the kitchen, insisting that she would make lunch for them both. Lindsey tried to hurry the process along as much as she could, and, feeling only slightly guilty, took her sandwich upstairs.

The cat must have followed her because he was there, twining around Lindsey's ankles when she sat down to eat. "Don't make me regret this," she said, and dangled a sliver of beef in front of his nose. He took the meat delicately in his teeth and leaped onto the top of the brown chair.

Lindsey read Shula's note while she ate. It was an invitation, handwritten in neat script on thick ivory paper. Shula was asking her to come for tea, "just the two of us," tomorrow afternoon.

That would be nice. She dropped the note onto her desk.

She found herself thinking again about Ginni's dog, hoping he would recover. Terriers were a tough breed. Maybe it wasn't too soon to phone Remi.

His voice was cheerful and reassuring. "Everything seems fine. Spot's beginning to wake up. Come on over."

There was no sign of activity in the exercise area, but the small fenced enclosure behind the barn held almost a dozen dogs. Her breath quickened. Golden-brown coats, upright ears, whiplash curling tails.

From this distance, she couldn't be sure, but their color and body shape were similar to the Carolina dogs. If only Ben Fletcher would talk to her about them!

A couple of dogs were walking back and forth, but others seemed to be napping, and one was nosing a ball in the grass beside the fence.

Remi was there to greet her and so was Ginni, wearing a frown. Together they went into the kitchen, where Natalie was making cookies. She smiled at them, and Lindsey smiled back as she followed Remi to the box in the corner.

Ginni ran ahead to kneel beside it, putting a protective hand on Spot.

Remi bent low and spoke to the sleeping dog. "Hey, Spot, hey there, boy! Time to wake up, don't you think?"

The dog stirred, yawned, and pulled himself up onto his haunches.

Lindsey smiled at the sight. "He's looking much better, isn't he?"

She turned to Ginni, intending to say something about how glad she was, when the dark-haired boy—Jeffrey—burst into the kitchen.

"Mama! There's something wrong with the Makah dogs. Where's Dad?"

"In the barn." Natalie wiped her hands on her apron,

75

asking, "What—?" but the boy had already run outside, yelling.

Remi jumped up and headed for the door with Ginni close behind. Lindsey followed.

Ben Fletcher was already striding into the fenced area. He bent over one of the dogs that Lindsey had thought was napping.

Now she wondered whether it was ill. The dog lay quiet as Ben ran his hands over its body, inspecting its mouth and checking its eyes and ears.

Even as she watched, she catalogued the dog's physical characteristics. Exactly the same as the Carolina dogs.

Remi had darted toward the second dog on the ground. "This one too."

There were four dogs on the ground, and two or three others, still standing, looked dazed.

Lindsey began to wish she hadn't come, and sure enough, as Ben Fletcher glanced up, looking incredulous, he saw her standing there.

His face went blank and cold. "Remi!" He jerked his head toward her in an unmistakable gesture.

Remi got up from the dog he was examining, and she said quickly, "Stay with the dogs. I'll leave."

But Ginni had her own comment to make. "I hate you!" she cried. "Every time you come here, something bad happens!"

Remi spun around. "Ginni! You go into the house." The little girl clenched her fists and ran off.

Lindsey let herself through the gate and glanced back. Remi had pulled out his cell phone and was punching in numbers. He'd be calling the vet.

caption:

Drama

Once again, Lindsey turned left from the Fletcher's driveway and followed the highway up the coast.

The practical side of her remarked that she probably should head back to New York, but all she could do was stare ahead, feeling as dazed as those dogs.

"Lord," she whispered. "What should I do?"

A gravel road branched off the highway to her right and she took it, hoping it would lead to the ocean. The road followed a pebbled creek that flowed rapidly over boulders and fallen trees, and when it ended in a clearing, she got out to walk.

The path beside the creek took her through moss-hung trees, passed a small cabin, and climbed through dense forest.

A picture of Ginni came to mind—Ginni clinging to Remi, sobbing in anguish, glaring at Lindsey. With her light skin and curly hair, she wouldn't be Ben and Natalie's child, so most likely she was adopted. An unhappy little girl. And now this!

The path crested a ridge and revealed a strip of gleaming ocean, but for once it didn't lift her spirits. She stopped to lean against a granite boulder.

Ginni was right. Bad things had happened ever since she'd arrived.

But something strange was going on at the kennels. Something destructive.

Make that *someone*. Did someone want to destroy Ben Fletcher and his family?

So . . . was she going to pack up her cameras and her regrets and . . . let them deal with it?

She traced a dark vein in the surface of the rock, thinking that she'd be smart to give up on the project, but a chill seemed to grow inside her.

And with it, a question rose: did God know about this?

The answer came automatically, drilled into her since childhood: of course he did.

He knew she would come all the way out here for the most important photos of her career and run into disaster.

Why?

She shivered in the pale sunlight. If I really love him, she told herself, I'll trust him to lead me in the right direction, whether it looks smart or not.

"Lord? Show me . . . ?"

Ginni's face came slowly into focus, and behind her, the field of golden-brown dogs.

Lindsey sighed. Should she hang onto her project—even if it meant getting tangled up in Ben's problems?

Do it. Start with those too-sleepy dogs.

She turned back, taking the uneven path at a fast stride. As she rounded the last bend, she discovered that a maroon truck was parked next to her Jeep.

A short distance upstream—in the middle of the creek—stood a man wearing hip boots, holding a pickaxe.

Quincy Corbin.

He looked up and waved as she reached the door of her car, and then he was splashing out of the water, coming toward her with a broad smile.

A lock of gray hair hung down over his forehead, and he was spattered with mud, but somehow it suited him better than his city clothes.

"Miss Dumont, what a pleasant surprise!" he said. "I didn't recognize your car. You caught me working—I'm trying to keep my creek open. Whenever we have a big storm, the rocks shift or trees fall, and I'm quite dependent on this water, so I have to do some clearing."

From his proprietary air, she wondered whether she'd been trespassing. "I didn't realize this was your land," she said. "I happened to find the creek and went for a walk."

"You're welcome to walk here any time. This is Thorsen's Creek, one of the prettiest around."

His smile was heartwarming, especially after what had happened at the kennels.

Was that his cabin she'd passed? "You must live around here," she said.

"I do, but on the other side of the highway. I own part of the old Thorsen homestead. If you'd gone just a little farther down the road, you'd have come to my driveway. You might have seen some of my beauties in the front."

Beauties?

He leaned against his truck. "Cashmeres. You're looking puzzled, and I don't blame you. Here's a little background. All my life I've wanted to raise cashmeres, so after I made my bundle, I sold my company, came over here, and started living my dream."

"Good for you," she said. "A lot of people never get the chance."

She smiled to encourage him. Cashmere meant sweaters, didn't it? What was he talking about?

He smiled back, his face turning red. "You're a very understanding lady."

He cleared his throat. "It hasn't been easy, I can tell you. Goats are resourceful creatures. They can live on

79

weeds or rough browse, but the best care produces the best hair, so it's just good business sense to pamper them a little."

So it was goats.

She nodded, touched by his earnestness, and took out her car keys.

"I'm sorry you have to go," he said. "You're probably very busy. I see you have your camera with you. Fraser, the bookstore owner, said you're a photographer. It must be a fascinating occupation."

"It is." She opened the car door.

He cleared his throat again. "Maybe I'll see you in town sometime. I'd be glad to buy you a cup of coffee. We have a great little bakery. What do you think?"

"Maybe sometime," she said, and slid inside.

He looked forlorn, standing there in his muddy boots, so she smiled at him again as she drove off.

Her smile faded as soon as she reached the highway. Might as well go back to the Roost. There must be plenty for a busy lady like her to do.

But all she did was spend the next few hours doing laundry, listening to Belinda while they ate Alexa's chicken soup, and wishing that Remi would call.

When her phone rang, she was standing on the balcony watching sparrows flit through the maple tree. His voice was solemn. "Lin, I'm bringing a load of wood into town tonight. Have you got time to talk?"

"Yes, of course." She tried to feel hopeful.

"Fraser's store? I should get there around eight."

The bookstore looked closed, but Remi's truck was parked at a side entrance, and he came outside to meet her. The door opened into the far end of the bookstore's second room.

Fraser was stacking wood next to the stove, and he

looked up with a smile. Was he going to be part of this meeting? Apparently not. He brought them hot cocoa and returned to the counter in the front room.

The area to her right seemed to have been designed as a children's nook. What a good idea!

A high-backed, upholstered bench had been built into the corner, just right for reading. A low table stood in front of the bench with a small bookcase beside it that held books, paper, and crayons.

Remi gestured to the bench and sat down on one end. She set her cup on the low table and curled up on the other end of the bench, facing him.

He looked handsome in his chocolate-brown sweater, but his eyes had lost their sparkle. He gazed at her for a minute and began. "I think you deserve an explanation—at least, as much as I know. Especially since you came all this way to get those photos."

This did not sound promising. She curved her cold hands around her cup.

He frowned. "There's something going on, and I don't know what it is. I already told you that Ben has changed. He seems to be worried about something."

He picked up his cup and held onto it. "Anyway, we talked to the vet, and he said it sounds like a virus."

"How long before they're over it?"

"Dr. Bridges said a week or so. He's not sure."

That was going to be too long. She drank some cocoa and found it tasteless.

"Tell me about Ben Fletcher," she said. "Everything you know."

Remi looked thoughtful. "I only know him as this kind, quiet guy who gave me a home and a job when I badly needed one. He loves kids."

"He has a large family, doesn't he? Are some of them adopted?"

"The oldest are Ruth and Rosie—they work at the bakery—they came from Natalie's sister, who died a couple of years ago," Remi said. "You haven't met Stanley. He's thirteen, Ben and Natalie's own child. Then they adopted Patrick. He's Makah, and sort of like a brother. You saw Jeffery, a really smart kid, and a Christian too. He and little Bobby are foster children."

Lindsey smiled. "And you. Ben hired you to help with the dogs?"

Remi nodded. "He's taught me a lot. He's amazing with dogs. It's like he knows what they're thinking and can make them do what he wants."

He took a long drink of his cocoa. "I don't know anything about Ben's past. You'll have to ask Colin. He's the one who set him straight. If Colin talks to him, I'm sure—"

Remi interrupted himself to raise his voice. "Fraser? Did Colin phone yet? Is he coming Friday for sure?"

Fraser turned out the lights in the front part of the store and walked back to join them. "Yes, he's leaving around noon."

"Good." Remi looked brighter. "Sometimes he can't get off—he works at the university library."

He stood up, and Lindsey did too. The meeting must be over.

"I'm sorry," Remi said. "I guess this hasn't been very helpful. But, hey, could we get together again on Friday? Colin will know what to do."

She nodded, and he said, "Fraser, is that okay? After you close?"

Fraser smiled. "Sure. It'll be convenient for Colin since his bedroom is on the other side of that wall. Maybe we can prevail on Alexa to let us have some cookies."

The evening air was invigorating, and she was glad she'd walked down from the Roost. So, what had she learned? A few bits of information about Ben Fletcher that might be helpful. Should she compose a feature on a minority kennel owner who adopts children? Forget it.

And then there was Remi's confidence that Colin, whoever he was, would know what to do. The man sounded like a veritable paragon: kind (look what he did for Ben); educated (a university librarian); intelligent (will unscramble this puzzle); and a good father (takes time with his kids). A friend of Fraser's would also be godly.

She pictured a man with a small paunch, round face, and thinning brown hair. Maybe sporting a ginger-colored moustache too. Particular about details, perhaps, but he'd have a kindly smile.

It might be interesting to meet the Paragon.

In the meantime, what could she do about this situation? If it couldn't be solved, there was no hope for her project.

The next morning, her first thought was the same one that had spiraled through her mind all night. What was she going to tell Edric? Now, as she opened the sliding door and leaned out into the misted air, the answer came in simple clarity.

Tell him the truth: the dogs are sick, nobody knows why, so the project is on hold.

And how would he react? Even after all these years, she couldn't predict with accuracy. Lately, he'd seemed more nervous about everything, so he most likely was going to be upset. And how would he respond when she suggested firing Vance?

Edric didn't really mellow out until after lunch, with its alcoholic boost, so she worked on her laptop and did small chores for Belinda until the time seemed right.

"Hey there," he said, cracking his gum. "What've you got for me?"

"I'm afraid it's not so good." She told him the situation

as concisely as she could and concluded with: "So it looks like we'll have to change the deadline. We could use one of our back-up features—let's see how the bulldog spread will fit."

He groaned. "How can you do this to me, Lin? I really liked your serial idea, and this is a great story, with that Native American as owner."

He added something crude that translated into, "Work on it!" and ended the conversation abruptly. "Gotta run. Call me Monday, okay?"

Slowly she closed her phone. She had wanted to talk to him about Vance—before he returned from the conference—but maybe this wouldn't have been a good time.

Think about the dogs.

The vet hadn't actually seen them. Asking him to come all the way out here would be expensive, but she could try talking to him, couldn't she? Remi had mentioned his name. Was it . . . Bridges?

She spent a few minutes at her laptop and found a phone number for the Bridges Veterinary Clinic, near Port Angeles.

Maybe she should talk to Remi first. Besides, she'd been wondering about a few things herself.

Were only the Makah dogs sick? Did Ben keep them separate from the others? Had they seemed healthy that morning when Jeffrey put them into the exercise area?

Remi's phone rang and rang, and she was trying to decide whether to leave voice mail when he answered.

"Lin!" He sounded out of breath.

"Sorry, is this a bad time?"

He laughed. "I was just chopping some wood."

She asked her questions quickly, and his answers were just as prompt. Only the Makah dogs were sick. Yes, Ben kept them separate. She asked for a list of the symptoms and wrote them down as they talked.

"Do you think anyone will mind if I discuss this with your vet?" she said. Not that Ben Fletcher could think any worse of her than he already did.

"Probably not. If ol' Bridges feels like it, he'll talk your ear off, but he knows his stuff. Wish I had some extra cash and I'd get him to come out here, but Ben can't afford it right now."

"Thanks, Remi. I'll tell you if I learn anything useful."

She phoned Dr. Bridges and he did talk her ear off, but in the process he asked some good questions. He went on to say that he thought the dogs would be okay eventually, and he was going to swing past Ben's way in a week or two, so he'd stop in for a chat.

He added, "Ben's a good man, and he's good to his dogs—I like that." He paused. "Now you've got me curious. Wish I could see a sample of that grass."

"Maybe I can bring you one," she said, and asked for directions to his clinic.

She phoned Remi to see what he thought, and when he volunteered to get her some of the grass, she decided to do it. She had him dig up two samples of turf, one from the center and one from the edge of the pasture, and, as an afterthought, asked him to bring the dogs' ball.

He dropped them off half an hour later and she set off immediately since the clinic closed early on Thursdays. She stopped once, for a drive-thru sandwich, and arrived as the doctor was finishing up.

Dr. Bridges looked much like one of his own patients, a Shih Tzu, perhaps, with his compact body, long white hair falling into his face, and alert black eyes.

Moving deliberately, he took the samples into what he called his lab room, sat down at his desk, and gazed at them. He sniffed at the grass. He pulled it apart, using a pair of steel probes. He picked up the ball with his tongs and examined it under a magnifying glass. "Hmm."

Lindsey leaned back in her chair, trying not to fidget. Let him do it his way, even if it took all night.

He shuffled over to a cabinet and took out a large goose-necked apparatus that combined a fluorescent bulb with a magnifier. He screwed it onto the edge of his desk and put the samples under it. "Hah." Next he slid the ball under it. "Uh huh."

At last he looked up, brushing his hair back. "Not sure. Not sure at all, but there seems to be some sort of residue on the grass—the perimeter grass—and on the ball. It's nothing more than a thin film, but it contains tiny bits of foreign matter."

He took another look, still mumbling to himself. He poked at the grass. "Thought at first we might have run into some poisonous plants."

He glanced at her. "I'm not ruling that out. Could be some growing nearby and the dogs got into it. But, no, Ben keeps his pastures clean, so that's not it."

She waited while he argued with himself.

"But we could have something that was artificially introduced," he said, "something from a plant, mind you, a poisonous one. Let's not be hasty."

He turned off the lamp. "I'm afraid that doesn't add up to a whole lot, but it's the best I can do. Tell you what. Talk to that herb lady in Cameron Bay. She knows the plants in the area better'n anybody. The people too. If someone's trying to do a number on Ben, she might have a guess."

Lindsey asked him every question she could think of, but he was hesitant to say anything definite, so finally she thanked him and left. She'd forgotten to ask about Spot. The two incidents seemed to be linked, but she wasn't sure how.

The herb lady . . . Shula? Should she mention it at their

tea party this afternoon? Better talk to Remi first.

She stopped for a latte—single shot, pumpkin caramel, and it was delicious—then phoned Remi as she drove, summarizing what the vet had told her.

They decided not to say anything to Ben just yet, but Remi wanted to tell Colin when he came. Fine. Let the Paragon figure out this one.

When she asked about questioning Shula, caution crept into Remi's voice. "I don't know, Lin. I don't feel good about that. Maybe don't say anything specific, okay?"

She agreed. This was a small community, and he would want to protect Ben. Even so, it might be an informative tea party if she asked the right questions.

It was almost four o'clock by the time she reached Cameron Bay, so she drove directly to Shula's. It wasn't far out of town, and Jack had told her where to turn off.

The long graveled driveway wound through a spruce forest and ended at a large, two-story house built of cedar. No gingerbread or flower boxes here; just simple, clean lines, glowing wood, and wide windows.

At her knock, Jack opened the door. He wore a black sweatshirt and jeans, and he carried a feather duster.

"Welcome to the castle, Madame," he said, sketching a bow. "M'lady is in the herb room."

He stepped back to let her in and she said, "Hello, Jack. Are you the butler today?"

Was that a twinkle in his eyes? "Yes, Madame, and sadly underpaid, I might add." He flourished the duster toward her right. "This way, please."

She paused in the doorway. Even on this cloudy day, light poured into the room from tall windows hung with draperies of lace filigree. A wide grass mat ran down the stone floor to a grouping of chairs at the far end, and French doors behind them opened onto a garden.

A fragrance that she couldn't identify filled the air.

Incense?

Shula stepped into the room and came to greet her. Today she wore a flowing skirt of pale green and a matching long-sleeved blouse with the sheen of silk.

Lindsey watched her graceful approach, thinking that this felt like a drama. Setting: the elegant, softly-lit room with its mysterious fragrance. Action: enter the lovely hostess, one hand outstretched.

"Lin, I'm glad to see you again," she said, smiling, and took her to a chair that was upholstered in green fabric with geometric raven designs.

Shula seated herself on a facing chair and leaned forward, her spiky black hair catching pinpoints of light. "You've been here for only a few days, but I hope you are enjoying the area."

"It's beautiful," Lindsey said. "I drove up the coast the other day and was just amazed."

She described the beaches she had seen and remarked on the size of the trees, and Shula watched her with an intensity that she hadn't expected.

A woven basket on the floor beside the table caught her eye. It was piled with round glass balls that glistened blue, green, aqua, and amber. "Japanese fishing floats!" she said. "They're beautiful. You've got quite a collection."

Shula looked pleased. She reached into the basket and took out one of the balls, handing it to Lindsey.

It was spherical, almost clear, with a pale aqua tint to the glass. A barnacle shaped like a tiny A-frame house had attached itself to the flattened top of the ball.

"I've never seen one like this," Lindsey said. "The barnacle must have hitched a ride and decided to stay."

"That's an acorn barnacle," Shula said. "Not uncommon, but it adds personality, don't you think?"

"It certainly does." Lindsey replaced the glass ball. "What's the basket made of? It is a nice piece."

"It's Makah," said Shula. "They use cedar fibers to weave their baskets. My sister made this one."

"Is she a Makah?"

"Our father was." Shula gazed at her, and Lindsey had the feeling that the woman could see her thoughts about Ben Fletcher, the dogs, and poisonous herbs, all tangled together inside her mind.

"Lin, you look as if you've had a busy day. Let's get our tea."

Shula rose and went to a long granite-topped counter at the side of the room, and Lindsey followed, curious.

Shula took an earthenware teapot from a cupboard, saying, "I think chamomile, today." She rinsed the teapot with water from a steaming electric kettle, spooned in tiny dried yellow flowers, and refilled it with hot water.

As she worked, Lindsey noticed the ring on her right hand. It was fashioned of three copper wires that circled her finger and twined around themselves to enclose a brilliant tawny stone that might be a topaz.

Shula carried the teapot to the low table between their chairs, returned to the counter, and brought back a tray set with delicate green china mugs, white linen napkins, and a plate of anise cookies.

"I sense that you are troubled," she said in a gentle undertone.

She poured a stream of golden liquid into a cup for Lindsey. "I hope it has nothing to do with us here."

Shula waited, looking kindly and sympathetic, and Lindsey resisted the impulse to confide her fears about Ben Fletcher's dogs. Perhaps another time she'd ask questions, but not now, while her brain seemed to be floating. It couldn't be the tea. Was it the incense?

Shula handed her the plate of cookies, and Lindsey took one with a smile, saying "Licorice is a wonderful flavor, isn't it?"

Shula tilted her head, still inquiring, so she said, "I'm fine, really—it's just jet lag, I suspect. One of these days I'll be able to sleep past five in the morning."

Lindsey took a bite of her cookie. Shula didn't look convinced.

"Oh," Lindsey said, hurrying, "I keep forgetting to thank you for the tea you sent over. It really helped my migraine."

Shula smiled. "I'm glad to hear that. Different people have different reactions to herbal substances, and I was hoping you wouldn't have any adverse side effects from PainFree."

Lindsey examined the black anise seeds in her cookie. "I suppose some herbs can be dangerous, can't they?"

"Absolutely," Shula said. "I have several in my stores that are potentially poisonous. When it's necessary, I know how to use them, but I use only tiny amounts for the shortest possible time. I respect the power of plants—they can change the body and the spirit in dramatic ways."

She told Lindsey about some of her early efforts in making herbal remedies, and the hour passed quickly.

Finally, Lindsey mentioned something about checking on Belinda, and Shula nodded. "I know it's getting late, but please, come with me for a minute."

She led the way into a small kitchen off the herb room. "This is where I make my concoctions, and I just finished a new batch of my skin cream. Would you like a sample?"

"I'd love it."

Shula took out a green jar and spooned a thick white cream into a smaller jar. She handed it to Lindsey. "Try a tiny bit."

The cream was fragrant with lavender and other mingled scents, and she smoothed it onto one hand. "Mmm—this smells fantastic."

Shula looked satisfied. "Good! Massage it in after your shower, and you'll feel like a new woman."

When she left, soon afterwards, Lindsey wondered whether she'd accomplished anything useful.

Perhaps she had learned a little about Shula. It was hard to tell what the real person was like, but she seemed generous and sympathetic.

Sometime later, perhaps, they could talk about the dogs. On the other hand, with the Paragon coming, that might not be necessary.

She let herself into the Roost, and after visiting with Belinda for a few minutes, ran lightly up the stairs. Alexa had asked her to come for supper tonight and meet Peter. That, at least, was something to look forward to.

caption:

The Akitas

The meal with Alexa and Peter was peaceful, all that Lindsey could have hoped for. They ate in the Brandt's comfortable apartment above the bakery, and Alexa served a thick-crusted pizza without apology.

"I like pizza anyway," Lindsey said, "but this is especially good. Plenty of cheese."

"Mott's Pizza," Alexa said. "It's made by a nice old man right here in town. I just love his sauce—it's so sweet and tangy."

Lindsey took note of the man's name, thinking that sometime she'd pick up some for herself.

Alexa's husband, tall and lean, with white-blond hair and a quiet manner, made small talk about the town, the salmon fishermen, and the bread he'd baked that day.

Over their dessert of pumpkin swirl cheesecake, Alexa explained that because he got up at four in the morning to start the bread, Peter went to bed early. Sure enough, while she and Alexa did the dishes, he watched a few minutes of football on TV and disappeared by eight o'clock.

Alexa asked whether she'd like to come along tomorrow afternoon to visit an elderly lady, and Lindsey agreed. Since Alexa looked worn out, she didn't stay late.

Afterward, walking back to the Roost, she thought about the two of them. There was no mistaking the expression on Peter's face when he looked at Alexa, and she often put a hand on his shoulder or his arm as she talked.

They had two college-aged sons, judging from the framed photographs in the living room. They were good-looking boys with Peter's blond hair and Alexa's smile. Alexa hadn't mentioned them, so Lindsey didn't ask, but they were probably off somewhere, working or going to school.

It had been an entirely agreeable evening. So why was she feeling so . . . down? Did she want a life like theirs? Not really.

Children? No, she had decided that a few years ago. Husband? No. She grew more certain of that each day— not worth the pain. The Lord had given her a different life from Alexa's. She should accept it and enjoy what she had.

But when she got back to her room, she couldn't settle down, so she wandered out to the deck. She leaned against the railing and told God how she felt, and finally her tatters of discontent drifted off.

The next morning, heavy fog hid all but the closest trees and muffled the sound of the ocean.

She slept late for once, and when she went out onto the balcony to enjoy the fog's distinctive moist fragrance, she felt the weight of last night's crowding thoughts.

She'd spent too much time speculating about sick dogs, poisonous sprays, and mysterious herbs. All this in spite of Shula's cream, which she'd used as directed. The cream was pleasant, but she didn't feel like a new woman.

Ignore the worries, she told herself. Perhaps, because of tonight's meeting with Remi and Colin, something could be done about Ben's problems, and she could make headway on her project.

Downstairs, the phone rang, and Belinda called up to

her. It was Shula, saying that she'd be distilling some lavender this morning, and she thought Lindsey might want to come and watch.

Why not? She went over right after breakfast.

Shula took her into the herb kitchen and explained how the distiller worked while she packed lavender buds into its onion-shaped dome. The result was a small amount of oil and some floral water that Shula called hydrosol.

"I just do this for fun," Shula said. "The ratio of flowers to oil is about 25 to 1, so I buy most of my essential oils. But they grow excellent lavender down by Sequim."

"Can you use this to make your creams?"

"Yes, after it matures for a couple of months." Shula turned to look outside, where fog still wreathed the trees. "Looks like you're getting an introduction to our fog."

"It's one of my favorite kinds of weather."

"Mine too." Shula half-closed her eyes. "I love the fog. My grandmother used to say she felt closer to the spirits when she walked in the mist. Her best Spirit Guide was the fog spirit, and it is mine as well."

Lindsey pinched a small aromatic bud from a stem of lavender. Shula's voice had a theatrical ring to it.

"Do you really believe that?" she said.

Shula looked surprised. "Not most of the time, I guess. But it's what she taught me, and I loved her. Since she died, I don't know."

She gazed at Lindsey as if she wanted to dissect her. "I know you've got problems—we all do. But you seem sure of yourself. I like that."

Lindsey smiled at her. "Any sureness I have comes from God. He loves me. That keeps me centered. But I'm still not very good at trusting him."

Shula bent over the counter to wipe it off and shook her head. As she finished, she said, "Come, I want to make an introduction."

What now? Lindsey followed her into the herb room.

Shula paused, saying something in a low voice, and from the shadows in the corner, a pair of dogs rose and ambled toward them.

Shula fondled the dark ears of the taller dog. "This is Tyee—his name means *chief*."

"He's gorgeous." Lindsey appraised the dog's powerful shoulders, black-with-brown coat, and deep white chest. Of all the Akitas she'd photographed, this was the most impressive. His intelligent eyes, common to the breed, studied her.

"And this is Pelton, my crazy one." Shula flipped the tail of the smaller dog, a tawny pinto.

She gave another command and both dogs sat, but they remained at attention. "Sometimes they get nervous on foggy days, and I tell myself that they sense the fog spirits. Anyway, I try to keep them with me."

"They're in excellent shape," Lindsey said. "I think Akitas are the most beautiful of the Japanese dogs. I'm wondering how you keep them so fit."

"They run on the beach," Shula said. "You may see us out there sometime. But before I forget, I wanted to ask if you would go out for supper with me, tomorrow night."

"Sounds like fun." She had plenty of time . . . until something positive happened with Ben Fletcher.

"Good! There's a little airport down past Thorsen's Creek. Let's meet there, around five o'clock."

Shula paused. "Why don't you give me your cell phone number so I don't have to bother Belinda? I'll go over to see her, maybe tomorrow."

Shula dismissed the dogs to their corner and paused beside the basket of glass floats.

She picked up the float with a barnacle, saying, "Would you do me a favor?"

Lindsey smiled. "Of course."

"Would you accept this as a small gift from me? I think you're a kindred spirit, Lindsey Dumont. God is so kind to have brought you to me! We're going to have some good times together."

Fog spirits and kindred spirits and God?

Shula handed her the float, and she couldn't refuse it. "I feel like I'm holding a piece of the ocean," she said, looking down at the glistening surface. "Thank you."

Shula's cell phone rang a minute later, and Lindsey took the opportunity to leave, saying that they both had work to do.

The drive back wasn't long enough for her to satisfactorily catalog the impressions swirling through her mind. Shula might think she was a kindred spirit, but something about the woman—even beyond the spirit-talk—was disturbing.

She decided to stop off at her room for lunch; then she'd see if the bookstore had any information on the Makah tribe. She could deepen her research while she waited.

Today Vance would be back in the office. He had already showed a tendency to be highhanded when features weren't ready on time; how was he going to react to the delay on her project?

Fraser had two books about Makah customs, and after lingering in the store for a while, enjoying its bookish atmosphere, she bought them both.

As she paid for them, Fraser said, "Remember your new friend, Quinn? He came in a while ago to ask about you, and I think he's waiting outside. He's a patient man, isn't he?"

She frowned. "I ran into him the other day and we talked a bit. What do you think of him?"

Fraser looked as if he wanted to grin but had decided against it. "Probably not dangerous, if that's what you're asking. A good businessman, but lonely."

"I thought so too." She shrugged as she turned to go.

Quincy was still there, standing beside his truck, studying his cell phone. He looked up. "Miss Dumont! How nice to see you again."

He was wearing city clothes again, and his gray hair looked as if it had been styled expressly to curl over the edge of his collar. He talked about the weather for a few minutes before getting around to asking whether he could buy her a cup of coffee.

Since she wasn't meeting Alexa until four o'clock, she agreed.

At least Quinn wasn't a skinflint. He bought coffee for them both and came back from the register carrying a plate with a generous assortment of cookies. He even made another trip to get her extra cream.

Alexa flitted in and out, replenishing the trays and racks, talking with customers. Apart from a smiling glance, she paid no attention to them.

While she waited, Lindsey looked around the café, admiring the plants in the front windows and the book shelves nearby, well stocked. Paintings hung on the walls with price tags attached, probably done by local artists.

"You like this place?" Quinn asked, sitting back down.

When she nodded, he said, "It's pretty nice for Cameron Bay."

He gazed across the little café with the air of a connoisseur. "It's too bad they don't have doughnuts. My favorite place in Seattle is Top Pot. Great coffee and great doughnuts. They've got books too, but on a grander scale."

His eyes, a pale watery blue, didn't change their flat expression, but he certainly was eloquent.

At first she didn't mind since it saved her the trouble of dredging up something to say, but he talked on and on about his goats, the effect of nutrition on hair growth, and his worries about the expensive new nanny—Ethel—who might not have the best genetic background for breeding.

After a while he asked about her photos, and she described the shots she'd taken on the beaches, avoiding the subject of dogs.

He looked puzzled but didn't ask why she was here. Maybe he thought she was on vacation.

He returned to the subject of himself, telling her about the days when he dreamed of raising goats but had to concentrate on running his company. His two older sisters lived with him and took care of the goats when he had to make a trip out of town.

The details began to blur in her mind, and she was glad when it was four o'clock and the bakery closed.

He escorted her to the Jeep, and when she thanked him for the coffee, said that he hoped they could do this again. Finally he went off, whistling, to his truck.

She sat there until he'd driven away, then went back into the bakery by the side door.

"I'm ready!" Alexa said. "I've got a box of muffins for her. Could you drive us over? There's something wrong with the alternator on our Ford."

"Sure," Lindsey said.

She followed Alexa's directions, and as they drove up the highway, she asked how the day had gone.

"Wild," Alexa said. "But that means a few more dollars, and I'm glad for it. How about you?"

She felt at ease with Alexa. "Wild too, and strange, with a few dull spots."

Alexa smiled. "He seems like a nice enough guy. Doesn't he do something with goats?"

"He does everything with goats. I suspect he eats, sleeps, and dreams goats. Extremely focused, I'll say that for him. Tell me about this lady we're going to visit."

"Her name is Odela Jincy," Alexa said.

"A relative of Jack's?"

"His grandmother. She lives by herself in a little trailer court. Shula owns the trailer court, I think, and Jack does the maintenance for her."

"Anyway, I thought Odela would enjoy meeting you because she loves dogs. I think she was a groomer for one of the big movie studios in California. She'll tell you all about it, if she feels like talking today."

On the way to Sunny Lanes Trailer Court, they passed Shula's driveway and several small houses interspersed with trees. Lindsey turned in at the graveled entrance, and Alexa pointed her to Odela's blue mobile home.

They heard only a muffled answer when Alexa knocked, but Alexa walked right in, carrying the box she'd brought from the bakery. It was warm inside—too warm—and the air was odorous.

Odela didn't seem to feel like talking today. She smiled vaguely when she saw what Alexa carried, nodded as Alexa told her what Lindsey did, and leaned back in her recliner, cradling the box in her small plump hands.

Alexa pointed out the framed photographs and newspaper clippings on the walls. Rin-Tin-Tin and Lassie were the only dogs Lindsey recognized, and she admired them aloud.

While they talked, Alexa opened a window and walked through the small room, picking up towels and clothes. She dropped them into a washing machine and started on the pile of dirty dishes.

Odela smiled as she watched Alexa. "Jack gave me that machine," she said. "He's a good boy." After a pause she held out a string of brilliant pink and burgundy beads. "Do you like my new necklace?"

Lindsey bent over it, saying how pretty it was, and Odela opened a box to show them the black pendant she was making for a customer.

Finally, Alexa said they had to go.

Odela reached for Lindsey's hand. "Please come back? I want to make you a necklace to match your green eyes."

The offer might be just an old woman's effort to earn some money, but Lindsey smiled. "Okay," she said.

"Monday?" Odela said. "How about Monday? Will you be too busy?"

Not the way things were going now.

Lindsey smiled again. "Good. I'll try to stop by Monday morning."

As they drove out of the trailer court, Alexa said, "I'm glad you're going back. That's kind of you."

"I watched her expression while you were working," Lindsey said. "She seems to really appreciate what you do. How does she manage on her own?"

Alexa smiled. "She thinks the world of Jack, and he, surprisingly enough, takes pretty good care of her. She's lonely, though, as you can guess."

Lindsey had just returned to the Roost when Remi phoned, his voice light and high. Colin had arrived. He would eat supper with the Fletchers—Natalie had made her special roast pork—and after he'd talked with Ben, he would come down to Cameron Bay.

"Is eight o'clock at the bookstore okay with you?"

"That's fine," Lindsey said.

And, Mr. Paragon, I hope you have a good talk with Ben. A very good talk.

She put her hope into prayer. "Please, Lord" she said. "You know how important this is."

10

caption:

Blocked

Lindsey kept Belinda company for supper, enjoying a creamy chicken casserole sent by Alexa, and while they ate, she organized her strategy.

Obviously, Ben had a problem with someone, and logically, he wasn't giving interviews. Until his problem was solved or she could get an inside track to Ben, her feature was stalled.

But if Ben changed his mind and would at least talk to her, she could make some progress.

This Colin person seemed to carry a good deal of weight with the Fletchers, so she needed him for an ally. Concentrate on that.

After supper, she dressed as carefully as she would for an important meeting: slim, tailored pants with a green sweater, and the jacket from her dark suit.

When she knocked on the bookstore's side door, Remi let her in, his face glowing.

Behind him, near the woodstove, Fraser stood talking to a square-shouldered man, and they both looked up as she entered.

He was wearing jeans now, and hiking boots, but she recognized the man she'd seen at the coffee shop in Seattle.

He seemed taller than she remembered, and muscular—the kind of man Remi would admire.

"Hi, Lin," Fraser said. "This is Colin McAlister."

She gave him a business-polite smile.

His gaze sharpened, flicked away. His eyes were blue as the central Pacific and just as remote.

"Hello," he said with a nod.

Deep voice. Weathered face. Not the genial librarian she'd expected.

Remi, with touching eagerness, was urging her to sit down, asking whether this was enough milk for her coffee, saying that Alexa would come over later, and why don't we get started.

She smiled at Remi, accepted the cup he handed her, and sat beside him on the bench in the children's nook.

Colin McAlister put his cup on the low table and sat across from them, cross-legged on the floor.

Fraser shook his head, saying, "Please excuse our mountain man. He thinks this is a campfire." He pulled a chair to one end of the table and sat next to her.

Colin gave him an amused glance and bent to drink from his cup. His thick dark hair didn't show any gray, but judging from the lines on his face, he must be in his forties at least.

Lindsey took a sip of coffee and waited for someone else to start.

Remi looked at Colin and said, "Do you think Ben has changed since you saw him last?"

"Yes, I do." The man seemed to be choosing his words with care. "It's been a couple of weeks, but the last time I came over, Ben was full of plans. He talked about more obedience classes, another play area for the dogs, and so forth."

Lindsey watched his eyes: they were intent on Remi and thoughtful.

"And now?" she said.

He glanced at her, then back to Remi. "Ben is worried, as you said. Maybe even frightened, and that's not Ben. Normally, he'd fight back, and when Ben Fletcher fights, he can do a lot of damage."

Remi leaned forward, as if he were hoping for a story. "Ben told me you guys were in the Marines, but he never talks about it."

Colin's hands tightened around his cup. "It's not something you like to talk about," he said in his deep voice. "But that's where I ran into him—Beirut. We worked well together, and we were both from the Northwest. He got into some scrapes, but he was one of the best, and I hated to see him leave."

"He said you kind of adopted him."

"After I left the Corps, I came back here and looked him up. By then he was drifting and needed a place to stay."

Remi grinned. "Like me."

"Yes, but you were different." The blue eyes softened.

Lindsey took note. Did the rough-tough Paragon have a warm spot?

"Ben wrestled with some problems," Colin said. "We worked on them together. He didn't make a decision for Christ, but once he dried out, he seemed receptive. He got started with his dogs, found himself a good wife, and has done very well."

"Yes, he has, until recently," Fraser said. "Lin, it seems you came at an unfortunate time. Tell us about your project."

Remi nodded encouragement, so she gave a brief summary, addressing herself to the man across from her, concluding with the advantages Cedar Run Kennels would gain from being featured in a popular magazine.

While she spoke, Colin studied his cup with a look of frowning abstraction. Was he even listening?

Fraser asked a few questions, and Remi explained how he'd first interested Lindsey in the Makah dogs, but the Paragon didn't say a word.

Somehow she had to reach this man.

She set her cup aside, determined. "I have interviewed kennel owners who were reticent or nervous or just plain dishonest," she said. "I realize that Ben Fletcher has had some setbacks, but he won't even talk to me, and I don't understand why."

Silence.

She lowered her voice. "Colin?"

The dark head came up, the blue eyes wary.

She softened her tone. "Can you help me with that?"

His answer finally came, cool and matter-of-fact. "The reason Ben doesn't want to talk to you is because he sees you as the press, the media. He agreed to an interview when everything was going well, but now he's concerned that his business and his family will suffer if the public finds out what's going on."

So he had been listening.

"Can you tell me what's going on?" she said. "He'll talk to you, won't he? What's he saying?"

Colin shrugged. "He's not talking to me. Not saying anything of substance. He mentioned receiving a note. And that someone might be trying to put him out of business."

Beside her, Remi stiffened. "That fits with what Lin found out from the vet."

"Petty sabotage," Fraser said. "An effective method."

Bad news. But she couldn't let her project fail.

Lindsey's pulse beat light and fast. She rested her arms on the table and leaned forward, focusing all her energy on those blue eyes.

"I'm sorry the dogs are sick. I hate what happened to Spot. But why does it matter for my project? Ben Fletcher is still the only man in the country who knows and breeds Makah dogs."

She had his attention now, but his eyes had gone dark, impenetrable. He must have noticed her watching him and drawing conclusions.

She kept on—she had to—even though her words seemed to be drowning in a night sea. "I won't mention the problems. Just a couple of photos, a few words, that's all I want."

He met her gaze, but she couldn't tell what he was thinking.

I'm not fighting you, she told him silently. I need your help.

"Please, Colin," she said, "I have no right to ask, but could you talk to Ben for me?"

He looked away from her. "I'll do what I can, but I think there's more here than we realize. Unraveling it will take time."

He paused, and regret flickered across his face. "Tonight Ben told me he's closing the kennels. All the boarding dogs will go back tomorrow. And he's not letting anyone near his Makahs."

She dropped her gaze.

She knew the blood was draining from her face, knew it made her pale as death, and she didn't care.

Time? She didn't have time. And this man was no help at all.

"Lin." Fraser's quiet voice.

She turned to him, propping her head on one hand.

His brown eyes steadied her, slowed her pulse. "Remember the other morning on the beach? That scrap of driftwood?"

The salmon. Courage.

"Upstream? That's for sure, Fraser." She gave him a bleak smile. "Thank you." She put on her brisk-and-professional armor and turned back to the other two.

Colin McAlister was studying her as if she were a

105

specimen from another planet, so she looked at Remi.

Remi's voice was indignant. "I'm trying to think why someone would want to do this to Ben."

She thought Colin might answer, but he didn't.

She asked, "What sort of business competition does Ben have?"

"None that I know of," Remi said. "There aren't even any other kennels around here, not until you get down near Sequim."

Alexa came in with a plate of cookies, and Fraser was the one who greeted her, got her some coffee, and insisted that she join them.

She gave Lindsey her warm smile, which was heartening, and, as if she felt tension in the air, told an amusing story about Peter and the time he'd forgotten the yeast in a whole batch of dough and they'd ended up with bricks.

Colin McAlister wore his preoccupied air. He must be still thinking about Ben.

"I remember those bricks," Fraser said with a laugh. "The fascinating part is that Peter made a stack of loaves on the counter, with a sign: *ECO-FRIENDLY BRICKS ONLY 25 cents*. People actually bought them."

Lindsey smiled to show that she wasn't the least bit upset about Ben Fletcher. "What did they use them for?"

"Bookends, I heard, and doorstops, and who knows what else." He grinned at her. "Ol' Quinn even bought a couple for his goat pens."

Remi, having eaten a handful of cookies, got to his feet, smothering a yawn. "Thanks, Lexa, I was starving. Bedtime for me. Tomorrow's going to be a busy day."

He glanced down at her. "Lin?"

"I'm coming." The sooner the better.

"Good night, all," she said.

She took her jacket from the coat-pegs and they went

out the door together.

Remi walked with her to the Jeep. "Let's remember— it's not over yet. We can both hang onto Romans 8."

She looked at him, his young face hopeful in the light from the store window. "Absolutely, Remi. Don't worry about me."

He smiled then. "I've been meaning to ask, what's happening in New Jersey with Timothy and everyone? I miss those guys!"

"Mollie and Nathan are doing fine, of course. I'll ask about Timothy the next time I write."

"Thanks, Lin." He headed for his truck.

Slowly she drove back to the Roost. He was a nice kid. A good friend. So was Alexa, and Fraser too.

Colin McAlister? She probably had offended him tonight by being so intense. But she had to take the chance. It didn't matter what he thought of her, if only he'd talk to Ben.

There was no need for any of them to know that she felt sick with disappointment. She'd counted on this meeting, had done her best, and failed. Colin's news was worse than anything she'd expected, and he himself was worse than contrary.

Slowly she climbed the stairs to her room.

Ben Fletcher's problems seemed out of her reach and the all-important project looked as if it were going to die.

Romans 8, Remi had said. She took her player out to the balcony and stood at the rail, listening to the quiet words as she stared into the darkness.

So Cedar Run Kennels was closed. What next? Colin McAlister had said *time*. Remi had said *it's not over*.

Lord? Help?

That night, she had hoped for sleep, but it came only in bits and pieces, and towards morning she dreamed of Vance and awoke with his voice whispering in her ear. She sat up quickly, ashamed that he was still on her mind.

Get rid of him, as soon as possible.

Six o'clock? Might as well get up. She would read some psalms. They were always a comfort. She sat down with Milly's Bible and opened it to the first Psalm, a page corner crumbling as she turned it.

Blessed is the man who . . .

His delight is in the law of the Lord . . .

It sounded like "Read-your-Bible." Hmm.

He is like a tree . . .

This wasn't her. Not green or fruitful. More like dried up and useless.

Blessed is the man . . .

She found herself praying. "Bless me, Lord? I keep running into walls. And Edric is depending on me for this feature."

Edric had always depended on her, especially now that the magazine was expanding. They'd conferred over each new staff member, the move to bigger offices, and the intricacies of a more complicated budget.

Working at the office for weeks on end made her restless—Edric knew that—and now, with the larger staff, she could travel more often to produce the fresh-voiced, original features that had won the magazine its niche. With Darlene, wireless access, and cell phones, it had worked out well.

Edric had been enthusiastic about her coming out to Washington. "The Makah tribe?" he'd said. "Never heard of them. This could be great stuff."

An idea took shape in the back of her mind. What if she left the Carolina dogs alone for a while and did some in-depth research on the Makah tribe itself? She already had two books about them, and here she was, with their reservation somewhere nearby.

When she finally did get to talk to Ben, (let's be

positive), having a bit of background might be helpful. She could plug the information into place, write the text, and be ready.

Thumping noises came from the kitchen, so she went downstairs for breakfast.

Belinda was full of eager questions about "yesterday," and it took Lindsey a minute to realize that she was referring to her visit with Shula, yesterday morning.

"Quite informative," she told her, and described how Shula had distilled the lavender.

"Huh! She never showed me that."

Lindsey hurried to say that she thought Shula was coming over today, and Belinda looked happier.

"How is your ankle feeling?" Lindsey said.

"It still hurts, and . . ."

They were discussing Belinda's ankle when Lindsey's cell phone rang.

Fraser's voice said, "I hope you don't mind my calling you. Got the number from Remi."

"That's okay. Belinda and I were just sitting here eating breakfast."

"I was wondering, are you still interested in the Makah?"

"Sure."

"We're going to run up to Neah Bay this afternoon. Want to come? You could see part of the reservation."

"I'd like that. What time?"

"Around one, I guess."

"Okay, I'll meet you at the store. Thanks!"

Belinda looked curious, so she explained.

"To Neah Bay?" Belinda's face darkened. "Those Indians! They shoot whales! It makes me squeamish, just to think about it."

She leaned forward, her plump face earnest. "I know it's a right they claim. And we whites have done awful things to them. I'd be the last person to suggest depriving them of their heritage. But couldn't they at least do it in a way that's more consistent with their culture? With harpoons or something, instead of guns?"

Belinda took a sip of her coffee, frowning.

Lindsey waited. Was she going to suggest canoes and medicine men as well?

"And past Neah Bay there's only Cape Flattery—that's all wilderness and eagles," Belinda said. "Are you sure you want to go? It might be dangerous."

"I think I should," Lindsey said. "It's for my project." She had found that mentioning her "project" gave instant credibility to anything she did.

"Do be careful." Belinda smiled her tight, humorless smile. "Alexa goes up there too, but I can't imagine why."

She pulled herself up onto her crutches. "I'd better get things tidied up a bit, if Shula's coming over."

Lindsey glanced over the immaculate kitchen and decided that it was time for her to get to work.

She emailed Mollie again, telling her she was going to visit the Makah reservation, and that Remi was doing fine, and how they both had been blessed by the eighth chapter of Romans. She kept it light and upbeat, asking for news about everyone, especially Timothy.

Shula arrived at mid-morning, and Lindsey stayed upstairs so Belinda could have her to herself. She and Shula could talk tonight at supper.

She booted up her laptop, found a good bit of information about the Makah, and spent the rest of the morning downloading and organizing it.

She ate a quick lunch, took some time with her face and hair, and decided that dark jeans and a sweatshirt—the burgundy one—would do for this trip. More important were her notebook, the voice recorder, and the Nikon.

caption:

Makah

When Lindsey arrived at the bookstore, Fraser was outside, talking to Colin McAlister, and her enthusiasm dimmed. He was coming too?

Fraser explained that this would be a quick trip because he didn't want to leave his store for the entire Saturday afternoon. He was going to pick up some cedar from a friend, and Colin wanted to get some smoked salmon.

Both men insisted that she sit in the front with Fraser, and Colin climbed into the back seat. Wouldn't they have preferred to sit together so they could talk? But Colin was staying with Fraser, so perhaps they could talk at other times.

Not that either of them seemed to be much for conversation. As they started off, Fraser's comfortable old Chevrolet was filled with contemplative silence, a restful change from Belinda's chatter.

Colin didn't say anything about Ben Fletcher, so she assumed that the situation hadn't improved. For Remi's sake, she'd give the man as much credit as she could.

She took out her notebook, glanced at the map, and set up a page for today's trip. She leaned back to enjoy the panorama of white-capped waves and rock-strewn beaches.

111

Fraser broke the silence, pointing out the flock of crows spiraling above them, wondering whether a tribal meeting was taking place.

She laughed and waited for Colin McAlister to say something. A glance at the back seat told her why he'd been so quiet. He had a book in his hand, reading.

Fraser must have noticed because he said, "Such a sad thing, a librarian who doesn't have time to read. What's he got this time, Lin?"

Colin held it up so she could read the title. *Cascade-Olympic Natural History: A Trailside Reference.*

The blue eyes fastened on her. "Ever use one of these?"

"No," she said. "I haven't."

"It's good reading," he said. "I took a couple of my kids on a hike last weekend and saw some unusual mushrooms. Wanted to check on them . . ." His voice trailed off as he bent over the book again.

"I haven't read it either," Fraser said. "But why should I, with him around? If you think of anything to ask, Lin, don't hesitate."

He threw her a comradely smile, and she said, "Now that you mention it, I was wondering about all those rocks piled up on the beaches. The black ones."

"Basalt," Colin said. "I'll show you." He thumbed through his book and leaned forward, opening it to a photograph of the chunky black rock. "It's volcanic—one of the darkest lava mixes."

"And what about those odd little islands? I took a picture of one the other day, but it needs a name."

"Sea stacks. They're made of hard rock, most often a volcanic intrusion. What you're looking at is all that's left after the waves have whittled everything else away."

While she wrote in her notebook, Fraser spoke to Colin over his shoulder. "Really, I should order one of those books so you don't have to keep borrowing it from your library. You could take it along on your next hike. What's another pound or two in your backpack?"

Colin sounded amused. "Thanks, pal. I have the old edition, but I'll take you up on your offer when I have some spare cash." He went back to the book, and silence fell.

Lindsey finished her note about sea stacks. The Paragon didn't seem quite as grim today—perhaps Ben's problems weren't weighing as heavily on his mind. Men were so good at keeping things in compartments.

"This is perfect timing," she said to Fraser. "I've been doing some research about the Makah, but last night I was wishing I could visit the reservation."

She smiled to herself. "Poor Belinda. She's worried about my taking this trip."

"Because of me?"

"No, she admires you. Refers to you as an enterprising young man. But she told me it's dangerous. They shoot whales up here."

Fraser glanced at her and back to the road. "Believe me," he said in a solemn voice, "they'd never mistake you for a whale."

"Thank you."

She felt herself flush and turned to glance out the window. "Look! There's a sea stack. And we're passing through the Greater Olympic Resort."

"Which is neither great nor much of a resort, from what I hear," Fraser said. He was silent for a minute, and he seemed to be smiling to himself. "By the way, Lin, pink becomes you."

Best to ignore this. She made a point of unfolding her map, looking down at it. "Are we there yet?"

Now he was grinning. "Almost, if you can put up with us just a little longer."

Ask him something else. "Do you speak Makah?"

"A bit." He said some words that sounded long and complicated. "Only the elders and a few others speak it fluently these days. Ben Fletcher uses it to train his dogs."

She scribbled a note about this tidbit and looked up as he said, "And here we are. That's the museum off to your left. Worth spending a whole day inside that place."

She folded the map and slipped into her jacket, energized by the rising excitement of on-site research.

In front of the museum stood a pair of enormous totem poles painted in red, black, and green. Between them stretched a sign that made her pick up her voice recorder and start dictating.

"Just entering Neah Bay, 1:30 PM. Here is the Makah museum sign. Says: Welcome to the Makah Cultural Research Center Museum of the Makah Indian Nation. See my photo, following. At first glance this seems an ordinary small fishing community. Compare my notes on the Haida—British Columbia."

She paused the recorder. "Thanks, Fraser. If you'll just drop me off here, I'd like to walk along the waterfront. Pick me up on your way back?"

He looked surprised, and so did Colin, who was putting on his jacket. "Sure," Fraser said. "About half an hour."

He pulled to the side of the road. She collected her shoulder bag and camera, stepped out of the car, and started dictating again. "I'm looking at a red and white sign that says BIG SALMON LAUNCHING. Now I'm going to get a picture of those totem poles."

She walked back to take a photo of the sign, then crossed the road, dictating as she went and taking one photograph after another. It wasn't the best time of day because of the harsh midday shadows, but these would do for a start.

"A wide main street runs along the bay here. A boat

114

launch, fishing boats, and large marina. I'd like to walk out and explore it next time. Sea gulls, lots of them, dipping back and forth over the boats.

"A white building with a rusted door and a black-lettered sign: **Halibut Mortuary**. It must be a walk-in freezer of sorts.

"Dogs everywhere—mongrels, most of them large, all very busy coming and going.

"A small playground with totem pole beside it. Sign: *Place of Rest*.

"Vancouver Island looks quite close, just across the strait. Hills curve around to the north of me, rolling right down to the water."

Much too soon, Fraser drove up beside her. She'd have to come back on her own when she could stay longer.

They drove a few streets over to where Colin had gone to get the salmon. "He's still inside," Fraser said. "He'll be out in a minute."

She admired a red-painted sign on the blue hut: *Salmon HOT from the Smoker.*

Behind the hut stood a mobile home surrounded by children's bikes and parts of old cars, bikes, and toys. A wringer washing machine stood to one side, and under it, a dog watched her puppies.

"Do you think they'd mind if I took some pictures?" she said.

"No, they're used to it," he said. "They'll consider you an off-season tourist."

She stepped out of the car for photos of the amiable mother and scrambling pups. Golden-brown, she noted, but they lacked the other dingo-dog characteristics.

When she returned to the car, she noticed Colin's trail guide lying on the back seat, so she picked it up and leaned against the front fender to page through it.

This write-up about the Olympic Mountains looked

interesting.

"Who's got my book?" Colin stood there, smiling down at her.

So he did know how to smile.

She smiled back. "Please sir, I washed my hands, and I'm not chewing gum."

His smile widened. "What are you looking at?"

She showed him. "Fascinating, how it's a round mountain range."

"Yes, and they've got these areas that form a pattern." He leaned over her, turning pages until he came to a map near the back. "You were asking about basalt. Look at this. They call it the basaltic horseshoe. See the belt of basalt right here, around this major thrust fault?"

Fraser started the engine. "Children, children," he called out his window. "It's time to go."

She handed the book to Colin, and he opened the car door for her. "Do you want to look at it?"

"Thanks, but I'd better work on my notes." Once inside, she asked, "Do you ever take your kids on hikes in the Olympics?"

"Sometimes."

Fraser laughed.

"Understatement?" she said. "Those mountains look as if they'd be fun to try."

"And where do you hike?" Colin said.

"Mostly the Adirondacks in upstate New York. But my favorite so far is a hike outside of Anchorage, at Williwaw Lakes. It's only fourteen miles, but magnificent. I don't have time for much beyond day hikes."

She bent over her notebook.

"You're taking a lot of notes for a photographer," Fraser said. "Plus the audio. You must be a writer too."

"Not by choice," she said, "but when I produce a feature, it needs to include background, sometimes with peripheral information in sidebars, and preferably a story line. It works out best if I write that myself."

"Here's something I've always wondered," Fraser said. "As a photographer, when you first meet a subject, do you sort of catalog his features and then decide how to take the photo?"

"The photographer and me don't stay separate, if that makes sense," she said. "Other photographers might be able to disconnect, but when I first meet a person, whether he's going to be a subject or not, I tend to process him in a certain way."

"And how's that?"

"I see an image of the inner self. Not especially crisp, more like an infrared. Later on, the details may get filled in." She glanced at him. "That sounds kind of mystical, but it's not meant to be. I really haven't thought this through."

"Hmm." He paused. "Out of curiosity, and you don't have to answer this if you don't want to, but when you first saw me . . ."

"That's not easy because by now we've talked quite a bit. But I think, yes . . . this is it . . . your eyes. They were a warm bronze, with the kind of light that comes from inside a person. Happy." She hesitated. "And there was a shadow of something else, like hardship or suffering."

He shook his head. "Stay away from me, lady. When we first met, you just asked for a map. You got all that in one glance?"

"It was a quick impression. I always look at the eyes first."

"Last night . . . ?"

She remembered that Colin was in the back seat. He might or might not be listening, and she lowered her voice.

"Difficult." She gestured out the window. "I felt as if I'd run into one of those rock cliffs. I was thankful for you."

"Okay," he said. "Tell me what you were thinking when you took the picture of Kumtux."

"That's not as hard. His majesty struck me right away. And the way he was posed, the way the light fell on his fur, he was a scene. I visualized him in black-and-white, and that's how I shot him. A great natural chiaroscuro."

"Chiaroscuro," Fraser said. "What a fine word. It has something to do with black-and-white, doesn't it?"

Behind them, the deep voice asked, "How does it apply in photography?"

Lindsey swiveled to look at him. "Much the same as in art. You've got an image with a dark area behind the brighter side of the subject, and a light area of the background behind the shadow side of the subject."

She turned back, picking up the Nikon. "Shadows can be important—and fun sometimes. That reminds me . . . just a minute."

She found the photo she'd just taken of a large dog tearing into an equally large piece of bloody meat.

"See this?" She leaned toward Fraser. "I think it's wonderful."

He glanced at it, then back to the road. "Wonderful? You're an original, Lin. Most women would squirm at the sight of all that blood."

"Wait. Look at it again. Here."

He took the camera. "Okay, now I see it. Pretty cool."

"You like it?"

"Show Colin."

She handed the camera to Colin, and he laughed. "That puppy in the shadows, waiting and hoping? Great shot."

"I like working with shadows," she said. "But I've got a lot to learn. I don't get to do much besides straight shots for the magazine."

As she finished her notes, she asked, "Speaking of

shadows, how is Kumtux doing these days?"

"Just fine," Fraser said. "He rules with peace and dignity."

"Belinda has a cat who visits me—Skookum. Do you know what his name means?"

"Sure," Fraser said. "They're both Chinook jargon words. *Skookum* usually means 'strong or impressive,' which is kind of funny when you think about his personality. He's one of Kumtux's many offspring. Alexa gave him to Belinda a few years ago, thinking she might be lonely."

"Is she a widow?"

"Divorced. She took back her maiden name. Her husband left her for someone else."

Lindsey winced. The other woman. That would explain Belinda's comment about having man trouble.

"Pets are a good thing, aren't they?" Fraser said. "Especially for children. Have you seen how protective Ginni is of Spot? That's probably because she feels so small and vulnerable herself."

"Yes, I sensed that she's a needy little girl. Is she adopted?"

Fraser glanced into the back seat. "Colin?"

"She's with the Fletchers on a foster care basis right now," he said. "Comes from a difficult background."

"How old is she?"

"Nine. Small for her age."

Fraser said, "I'm sure she was thrilled when you brought her dog back, Lin."

"Not at all. Talk about an infrared image—hers was flaming. She hates me, but I don't know why."

"Odd," Fraser said. "She's usually a friendly child. Any ideas, Colin?"

Lindsey turned to look at him as he put a finger in the book to mark his place and leaned forward.

"It's quite understandable, if you're interested in the

119

shocking details," he said, and a smile flickered in his eyes.

"Tell me," she said.

"See, our Ginni thinks the world of Remi, and she's planning to marry him, and then this strange woman shows up, and Remi runs up to her and hugs her. The poor kid can hardly stand it."

"Strange woman?" Fraser said.

"Sorry. Mysterious stranger."

She didn't care what Colin called her. "How did you find out all that?"

His smile grew. "She told me. She crawled onto my lap and whispered it with horror and loathing."

"But she's a resourceful child," Fraser said. "She also gave Colin to understand that she might consider marrying him instead, under certain circumstances."

Colin shrugged, and Fraser went on, "The terms included him giving her another book. About spiders, I believe it was."

"She likes spiders?"

"Loves them, the bigger and uglier, the better," Fraser said. "For a while she had a collection in her room, but Natalie made her move them out to the barn."

"I'd like to give her something as a peace offering," Lindsey said.

"Sure," Fraser said. "How about a nice big hairy spider? You know that beach where we talked?"

"Yes, what's it called, by the way?"

"Thorsen's Beach, named after a Norwegian pioneer. Anyway, at the top edge in all those bushes and trees, you can find some Orb spiders. I like to go and look at their webs. We've had a warm fall, so there should be some still around."

Lindsey thought for a minute. "I know what I'll do. I'll give her a photo she can hang in her room."

"We don't have a place around here to develop it,"

120

Fraser said. "Unless you drive all the way to Port Angeles."

"I'll shoot it in black-and-white and develop it myself."

Colin looked up from his book again. "Where's your darkroom?"

"My room has this huge bathroom, and I've got it set up in there."

"You mix your own chemicals?"

"Yes. I have to use the powdered ones, though, or I'd never get through security at the airports."

Fraser laughed. "Good for you." He slowed to make the turn into Cameron Bay. "Does Belinda know?"

"Not yet," she said. "I guess we'll have to discuss it sometime. Should I worry?"

"No, don't worry." Fraser grinned. "You're the first paying guest she's had at the Roost for a while. She might have a lot to say, but she's not going to evict you."

As Fraser pulled into the parking space beside his store, she started gathering her equipment. She reached for the door, but Colin was already outside, opening it for her.

She'd forgotten how tall he was. As she thanked him, she saw that the blue eyes were alight.

"You are welcome," he said. He even smiled again.

Fraser came around the car to join them.

"Thank you for the trip," she said. "It was a good introduction—I enjoyed it."

"Our pleasure," Fraser said. "I should mention that we're getting together for a small Bible study tonight, if you have time to come."

She paused to think. "I'd like that, but someone's already invited me out for the evening. I'm sure you know her: Shula Murrako."

For some reason, the light went out of Colin's eyes.

"Yes," Fraser said quietly. "We know Shula. Have fun. Unless I'm mistaken, you'll see how the other half lives."

caption:

Starlight

Fraser had told her to have fun tonight, and that's exactly what she meant to do.

She had hurried down to the beach to look for spiders, and among the arching brambles she found two horrible beauties. Using the close-up adapter on her Mamiya, she took enough shots to make sure she had something useful; then she had run back to shower and change for her evening with Shula.

She wouldn't dress up. Her corduroys with a suede jacket and fringed scarf should be good enough.

Not wanting to incite questions, she tiptoed down the stairs feeling like a teenager on an escapade. A night out! Good food, city lights, someplace different.

The airport was the smallest she'd ever seen. The access road simply dead-ended at a long field of green with an orange windsock at the near end and a large gray hangar to one side.

She'd wondered why Shula had said to meet here, and she soon found out. Shula was making a circuit around a green-striped, single-engine plane on floats. She waved and continued with her pre-flight check.

Lindsey walked across the grass to join her, and Shula

greeted her with an enthusiasm that seemed a few notches higher than normal. "Like my plane?"

"It's a beauty," Lindsey said. "I've never ridden in a float plane."

"Love floats!" Shula said.

She took a small stool from the baggage compartment and set it on the ground. "You'll need to get in from this side. Hop on up from here."

Since Lindsey had done some flying herself, the instrument panel looked familiar, and when Shula gave her a headset, she knew how to handle it.

A short, bumpy ride over the grass took them to the end of the runway, and Shula ran through her check list aloud. Finally they were rushing forward. The engine's growl became a roar, the wheels left the ground, and they lifted aloft.

The trees and beaches unrolled below, and Shula made a slow circle to give Lindsey a view of the green Peninsula; then they turned and followed the coastline.

Shula's voice came through the headset. "I thought we could go to Port Townsend," she said. "I'll take you to my favorite little Thai place, and then we can walk around the shops in the historic district."

Fraser was right about "the other half." At Shula's little Thai restaurant they were met by a hostess dressed in formal black, led past costly oriental screens, and seated at a table with silver flatware, carved ivory chopsticks, and fresh roses in a jade vase.

The meal was as good as she'd expected, and over their Ka Bong and Phad See-Eew, Lindsey asked how long Shula had been flying.

Her husband had taught her, Shula explained, and they'd found the plane useful in their real estate business. After he died, she'd taken over the business and kept the plane. It was handy, too, when she wanted to run across to

Seattle for her volunteer work.

Shula asked whether Lindsey had done any more exploring, and she told her about the afternoon's trip to Neah Bay.

Shula looked scornful. "Those guys are just tourists, Lin. If you want to really see that place, let me know. I grew up there. And if you ever want to hear, firsthand, about prejudice, I can tell you about that too."

She changed the subject, asking whether Lindsey ever did freelance photography.

Lindsey told her that she had been freelancing for almost ten years before starting at the magazine, and Shula smiled. "I bought your book," she said. "It's excellent. I was wondering, do you always pose the dogs for your magazine photos?"

"Most of the time we have to. We're usually looking for something in particular, and owners get nervous about candid shots."

Shula seemed satisfied with her answer and asked where she lived in New York. Lindsey told her about her condo in the city and the house in the Pine Barrens she'd inherited, and for the rest of the meal, they talked about land values and real estate.

Afterwards, they strolled through one shop after another, and Lindsey found herself yawning. She'd done this many times with friends, so why did she feel this creeping sense of boredom?

While Shula tried on blouses, she watched faces. Some were proud, some vacant, some cold and disdainful. Did her own face show her restlessness?

Shula chose a blouse with gathered sleeves and cheerfully paid $150.00 for it. Lindsey consulted her personal rule about expensive clothing and decided against another sweater. She reminded herself that she'd spent enough on her cameras to buy a dozen of Shula's blouses.

Was it time to go yet?

On the short flight back, Shula's energy seemed to have faded, and she was silent.

After they reached cruising altitude, Lindsey looked up through the windshield. Stars! She'd forgotten how close they seemed from an airplane's cockpit, and tonight there were millions of them, incredibly brilliant.

"Look at that!" she said.

Shula's head snapped toward her. "Another plane?"

"The stars! As if God has written his name for us. It's amazing."

"What's amazing?" Even through the headset, Shula sounded surprised.

"Him. The way he makes things so beautiful. What if he'd created his stars as plain gray blobs or something? But he knows we need beauty. Or he made us so we'd need beauty and then gave it to us."

"Why would he do that?"

"Because he loves us and wants us to love him."

Shula ran a hand through her black hair. "I don't know, Lin. If it works for you, go for it."

She pointed out the lights below with their respective small towns, and Lindsey had to look away from the stars.

Soon they were circling over the little airport with its cheerful pattern of runway lights, and they landed with only the slightest bump as the wheels touched down.

As they walked toward their cars, Shula said, "I'm glad to hear that you work freelance. Perhaps we can do something together."

Lindsey nodded, wondering what that might involve, and Shula said, "Phone me if you ever want to talk, Lin."

She paused. "Are you enjoying your glass float? My grandmother said that each one has a friendly spirit inside. I like to think she was right."

The ball was still in its box on her desk, so Lindsey

said, "It certainly is beautiful."

Shula put a hand on her shoulder. "You're looking happier tonight. Perhaps it's helping you."

Wrong on both counts.

When Lindsey drove up to the Roost, the living room lights were still on. She opened the car door slowly, reluctant to go inside, and listened to the waves surging against the bluff.

That beach by starlight would be something to see. She could sit and watch the ocean, and maybe she'd feel better.

She walked with care through the tree-shadows and picked her way down the rocky steps to the sand. Still in shadow, she looked first at the ocean, luminous as black satin, then at the long curve of the beach.

Someone else was here.

She recognized him by his height and the set of his shoulders. Colin McAlister. He was walking away from her with his head down, hands in his pockets, kicking something as he went. Like a kid kicking a can along the street.

A minute later he dropped his jacket onto a rock and started jogging along the beach, going faster and faster until he faded into the distance.

She turned and climbed back up the steps. Perhaps he was restless tonight too. Even the Paragon? She'd leave him to it.

In her room, she changed into sweat pants and a loose top; then she took out the glass float and held it up to the light. It shone with a mysterious translucence.

Pretty, yes. But a spirit guide? What made Shula talk like that?

She tilted the ball, thinking she had seen a grain of sand, perhaps, in its shimmering depths, but it was empty.

Empty. That's how she felt. Deflated, even.

The delicious food, the lights, even the plane ride—

126

what did they amount to? If she'd bought that hundred-dollar sweater, would she feel any different than she did now?

She set the ball down beside her voice recorder.

Even the trip to Neah Bay this afternoon—a pleasant diversion—what had it been for?

For the project. Her all-important project.

Why, come to think of it, had she been so upset about Ben last night?

True, if she didn't get the story, it would mean hours of work wasted, but what was that work for? The Magazine. Rich people and their dogs. What good was that?

She couldn't think of a satisfactory answer, but the Mamiya was there on her desk, reminding her that she'd planned to develop the spider photos for tomorrow. She had agreed to go to church with Alexa and Peter, and Remi would be there. She could ask him to take her gift to Ginni.

She set up quickly and soon became absorbed in the developing process. Two of the shots turned out well enough to use. For Ginni, she made a large print that showed the spider's pincers, and for herself, a smaller one with the spider centered on the web. She'd prop it up on her desk to remind her of Ginni.

This, at least, was something real. Maybe even useful.

She had missed that Bible study tonight. Who'd been there? How had it gone?

Tomorrow she would see Alexa.

Once again she awoke early, but she felt as dull as the gray sky. Take a quick run on the beach—that might help.

Off to the east, the sky was turning a pale apricot. Because of the heavy clouds, she wouldn't see a spectacular sunrise, but the light would come, as it always did. Wasn't there a verse somewhere about God's faithfulness being new every morning?

She scrambled down the rock steps and onto the sand, breathing deeply of the salty air.

A few yards ahead, someone walked out of the trees and turned down the beach, moving at a fast trot. It was Alexa, her hair in a high ponytail that caught the light.

Lindsey broke into a run, and Alexa turned to see who was there. "Good morning!" she said with her warm smile. "I thought you might be here."

"I saw you come through the trees. Is there a path?"

"Yes, although only a few of us use it. Belinda likes to think this is an extension of her property, but it's actually open to anyone."

They passed the uprooted trees, and Alexa stopped to take off her shoes. "I like to run on the wet sand," she said, and Lindsey took hers off too.

Cold! Invigorating!

Alexa started off at a fast jog, and Lindsey stayed with her, but by the time they reached the rock pile at the end of the beach, she was glad to slow down.

They paused beside a creek that ran through a channel of sand on its way to the ocean. "Is this Thorsen's Creek?" Lindsey asked, remembering the one she'd followed the other day.

"Yes," Alexa said. "It comes from somewhere back in the hills and winds all around."

They turned back, keeping to a fast walk. "This is so nice," Alexa said. "I just love it out here in the morning, but Sunday's the only chance I get. Oh, I wanted to tell you— we're all going to have lunch at Belinda's after church. I brought a roast to put in the slow-cooker. You'll join us, won't you?"

"Sounds good to me," Lindsey said. "I'm hungry already."

When they reached the uprooted trees, Alexa sat

down to brush the sand off her feet, and Lindsey sat beside her.

"You know what?" Lindsey said. "Sometimes I feel like this tree. Dried up. Good for nothing."

Alexa looked out across the waves. "I know what you mean. When I feel like that I have to head for Psalm 1."

"I just read that psalm. It reminds me to read my Bible. But . . ." She hesitated, unsure whether to be candid.

Alexa waited with a calm listening look on her face, so Lindsey plunged ahead.

"Lexa," she said, "I've just recently come back to the Lord, and I want to know him better. I want . . . I want to be the kind of tree that bears fruit for him. All my life, I've heard, 'Read-your-Bible.' I'll admit I haven't done much Bible reading, but it just doesn't click for me."

Alexa was laughing softly. "You are the realest person I've ever met, and I love you for it. Here's something to think about. If you really liked someone and that person said, 'Hey let's get to know each other,' what would you do?"

"I guess . . . I guess I'd try to do things with him. Spend time together."

Alexa nodded. "These terms we use—they're so worn out they've lost their meaning. *Pray. Read your Bible.* But like you said, the way to get to know the Lord is to do things with him."

"I do talk to him. But this read-your-Bible stuff . . ."

She smiled. "Psalm 1 doesn't say 'Read-your-Bible'. Go back and look at it when you get a minute."

She stood up. "The Lord knows that your heart is turned toward him. He'll show you how to bear fruit, and it will be beautiful, useful fruit. I can tell you that."

Tears prickled behind Lindsey's eyes. She stood up too, and Alexa touched her arm. "Let's talk some more. Tuesday, I'd like to drive to Port Angeles. Want to come?"

Lindsey nodded, and Alexa said, "Good. That's something for me to look forward to. Meanwhile, we'll pick you up in an hour. Whew! I hope Peter's got those potatoes scrubbed."

Church turned out to be a gathering of about fifteen people in a square old house up the highway, near the Greater Olympic Resort. The pastor, white-haired and thin, was a retired missionary with a joyful face. They sat on folding chairs in his living room, with a faint aroma of fried bacon in the air.

Remi was there, and Fraser, as well as two or three people from Cameron Bay, and others she didn't recognize. Some were Native Americans, and several men were deeply tanned—fishermen or loggers, perhaps.

Colin McAlister must have left for Seattle last night. He would have arrived late.

Did his wife wait up for him when he went off on his trips? He seemed to visit the Fletchers fairly often. Did she and the children ever come along?

Peter led the singing, which was a surprise. He had a welcoming manner and a pleasant tenor voice, and after a while, everyone was singing heartily. Remi sat in front of them. His voice rose above the others, and she could see the happiness on his face as he sang.

While the pastor was speaking, Remi leaned forward, absorbed. What would it be like to grow up a Muslim and then be grafted into the church of Christ?

The pastor spoke quietly, conversationally, about his experiences as a missionary, and how he'd learned the truth of God's promise, *I will never leave you nor forsake you.*

He talked about the single word, *never*, saying that in the original language it was a combination of negatives, something like: *I will never, no, never leave you, no, never forsake you.*

Lindsey wasn't used to hearing words dissected like that, and afterwards, she wished she'd written it down.

The pastor asked Fraser to close in prayer, and Fraser, instead of mumbling, spoke in a clear voice to God as if he were standing right there with them. He thanked God that he would never forsake his children and asked for his protection in the coming week.

After church, Lindsey remembered to give Remi the photo for Ginni.

He grinned. "If it's a spider, she'll love it."

He and Fraser had also been invited to lunch at the Roost, and Belinda welcomed them, very much the considerate hostess. The kitchen table had been moved to the living room and covered with a tablecloth. They would eat in style.

The men went out onto the deck to talk, and it was just as well because Belinda hobbled around in the kitchen, getting in Alexa's way, giving Lindsey a better knife for slicing the tomatoes, and wiping up spills from the counter.

When Alexa lifted the steaming pot roast from the slow-cooker, Belinda said, "I never do it that way," but Alexa ignored her, and Lindsey kept on with her salad.

Alexa called Peter in to slice the beef and Remi to mash the potatoes, and she had Fraser put chairs around the table, so the meal was soon ready.

Belinda, sitting at the head of the table, said to Peter, "Would you please ask the blessing?"

She directed a gracious smile at Fraser and said, "It is our custom to do this before meals."

Fraser, with remarkable self-control, nodded gravely as he bowed his head, and Lindsey smiled to herself.

After Peter prayed, no one said anything while the dishes of food were being passed, and then appreciative comments flew back and forth.

Lindsey, still thinking about the message, asked, "How

131

does someone learn all that about one word, like the pastor told us this morning?"

"There's books," Peter said. "Study aids. Fraser, you probably have some in your store, don't you?"

"I have a few, but they're not very popular. I could order some."

Remi said, "Lin, you know what would work really well for you? Some of that free software, online. Just download it and you've got different versions, a Bible dictionary, commentaries, and a concordance."

"I've never used a concordance," she said.

"Easy," Fraser said. "Let's say you know that a verse you're thinking of has the word *horse* in it. You just look up *horse*, and it'll show you all the verses in the Bible with that word. Good idea, Remi."

Belinda gave him a surprised glance before turning to Lindsey. "How was your trip to Neah Bay? I never did hear."

"Most interesting. Very helpful for my project." With an effort, she kept from smiling. "We didn't see any whales, though."

Belinda nodded, looking somber. "That's good. You went out last night too, didn't you? I suppose you young people have to have your fun, but this has been a terrible week for me, I'm sure. I'll be glad when I'm not a cripple anymore."

Alexa smiled. "You're not a cripple, Belinda. You get around pretty well."

Her sister pouted. "I've been stuck here in the house for days! I missed the literacy council meeting and the library volunteers' luncheon, and just yesterday, a nice concert in Seattle."

She poked through her salad. "But it will be better now. I won't miss the FRO on Tuesday because Shula's going to take me with her."

She glanced at Lindsey, as if to make sure she was listening. "She's very active with them. And they are quite appreciative. I can't do much actual work myself, but I do make donations."

Remi, who had just taken another helping of meat, put down his fork. "The FRO," he said. "What does that stand for?"

Belinda looked proud of herself. "It's the Family Relief Outreach, a charitable organization. We help them raise money, doing benefits, and concerts, you know. Have you ever heard of it?"

"Yes." His jaw tightened, and Lindsey wondered what the name meant to him.

He picked up his fork and put it back down again, as if he couldn't remember what to do with it.

Belinda was chattering on. "It's a fine group of people. Muslims, you understand. There are some of us who don't mind working with them—it's such a good cause."

Alexa cocked her head. "And what is that cause?" Had she seen the slow flush rising on Remi's neck?

"We raise funds for Muslim orphans and widows," Belinda said. "All these terrible wars! Those poor people in Palestine would starve if it weren't for us."

"So you raise money," Fraser said quietly. "And it goes to the organization?"

"Yes, of course. For the widows and orphans."

Remi said, "Do they give you any details about those widows and orphans?"

Belinda looked offended. "They might, although I can't say for sure. But they tell us we're doing a fine thing and making a difference in many young lives."

She lifted her chin proudly. "Ask Shula. She works with the local leaders and the women and everything. Now, Alexa, did you bring us something nice for dessert?"

Lindsey helped to clear the table. She couldn't help

thinking it was strange that Shula hadn't mentioned her work with an Islamic charity. Would she have wanted Belinda to talk about it so freely?

Remi drained his water glass, pushed back his chair, and stood to his feet.

"Hate to eat and run," he said in a tight voice, "but I do need to get back to work. Thank you for lunch."

He gave Lindsey a burning glance and headed for the door.

"These young people," Belinda said. "So intense! I just don't understand it."

Alexa sliced and served pieces of her German chocolate cake. Its melt-in-your-mouth frosting was her own special recipe, but Lindsey couldn't eat more than a bite. Fraser, across the table from her, looked troubled too.

"I'm going to save my piece of this wonderful cake for a snack," Lindsey said, trying to sound cheerful.

No one wanted coffee, and the meal was soon over. Belinda, saying she was worn out, went into her bedroom, and Peter and Fraser offered to help with the dishes, but Alexa shooed them away, and they left. She and Lindsey cleaned up together.

"What was the matter with Remi?" Alexa said. "I know he used to be a Muslim."

"Not sure," Lindsey said. "I just don't know."

She finished wiping down the counters without voicing her fears.

It must be something in Remi's past, something connected with Islam. She'd seen that look on his face once or twice, back in the Pine Barrens. He wasn't the kind to get upset over trifles.

Maybe he'd talk to her about it.

caption:

Fighting Upstream

Lindsey's first thought on Monday morning was that she should phone Edric. Her second thought was that she didn't want to.

All day yesterday she'd wondered how to tell her partner that Cedar Run had been closed, and she still didn't know. Perhaps she should wait. It was too early anyway. After his lunch, Edric would be in a better mood, and by then she'd have phoned Remi to see whether there might be a scrap of good news.

Meanwhile, why not pay a visit to Odela, as she'd promised? She could pick up some cookies at the bakery. She started brushing her hair and saw the photo of Kumtux on her desk. She had wanted to take it to Fraser. Do that first.

Fraser was unpacking a shipment of books, but he stopped to talk when she came in, and she handed him the photo of Kumtux.

He looked at it, then at her. "This is beautiful! A lovely chiaroscuro. See, I remembered."

He looked back at it. "I don't know what to say."

Fraser at a loss for words? She didn't remark on that, but when he started to return it, she said, "It's yours, if you want it."

He began to protest, and she said quietly, "Mine to give, right?"

"Thank you. I'll see that it acquires a worthy frame."

He slid the photo into its envelope and set it on the counter. "Where are you off to this morning?"

"To see Odela. It's kind of a stalling maneuver. I have to phone my partner and give him the bad news."

"Still fighting upstream?"

She smiled, wishing she felt more courageous. "Still fighting. We'll see what happens."

The bakery café was crowded this morning, and she was glad for Alexa's sake. While she was buying Odela's cookies, Remi walked in the side door, carrying a box. Good. She could ask him her questions now.

She followed him into the workroom.

Alexa was using a small machine to peel and slice apples, and she smiled at them both. "Remi, you got here just in time. We've run out."

She opened the box so Lindsey could see the cinnamon rolls inside. "Natalie does such a great job with these, I buy as many as she can make."

"They smell wonderful," Lindsey said. She caught Remi's frown. "Something else wrong at the kennels?"

"No. The dogs are getting better. Ben's the same. But I have to give you something." He motioned with his head. "In my truck."

At his truck, he reached into the glove compartment, took out an envelope, and handed it to her.

It was the envelope she'd used for Ginni's spider photo. She looked at him and slowly opened it.

Inside was nothing but torn paper.

Sadness rolled across her. She pulled out a handful of scraps and sifted them through her fingers. She was still the Enemy.

"I'm sorry, Lin."

He looked so miserable that she put a hand on his arm. "Just a piece of paper, Remi. No big deal."

"But I know what you meant by it. Please don't give up on Ginni. I talked to her, and I think she's a little sorry. She needs to be around someone like you. It's only been four years since she came to the Fletchers."

"I wondered. She has some problems, doesn't she?"

"She really does, but she's improving. When the Fletchers got her, she'd been badly beaten, and she still doesn't remember anything from those days."

Lindsey had seen battered children, and the memory still hurt. "I'm not giving up on Ginni," she said. "I'll pray for her, too."

"Thanks, Lin. I'm glad the Lord brought you here." He looked relieved. "I'd better get back home."

He drove off, and she stood there with the envelope in one hand and the bag of Odela's cookies in the other, watching him go. Poor Remi! She hadn't had the heart to ask him about the FRO. He was carrying a lot of burdens these days.

"Miss Dumont!" Quincy Corbin was striding down the sidewalk toward her. "Isn't it a fine day?"

She hadn't thought so, but she said, "You're looking cheerful."

"And I feel it too. Ready to celebrate. How about a cup of coffee?"

She put on a smile. Why not?

He wanted to go to the bakery again, and that was okay with her. It turned out that he was celebrating the birth of a kid to Earlene, his favorite nanny, and expected to make a great deal of money from it. He enlarged on this topic at length, and Lindsey was beginning to plan her phone call to Edric when he mentioned Ben Fletcher's name.

"Ben Fletcher?" she said.

"Yes. Thorsen's Creek, where I was working? He's got a couple acres that the creek runs through. I've offered him top dollar for that parcel, but he won't sell."

"What do you think of him?"

Quinn cleared his throat. "Not a whole lot. He's trying to make a go of it with no capital and less education. Doesn't have much business sense, I'd say. Not especially accommodating, either."

"I've heard he's really good with dogs," she said. "Isn't that more important than a college degree?"

"Certainly, if you say so." He smiled at her and immediately ruined the effect by saying. "I want that parcel, but I can wait. Something will happen one of these days, and he'll decide he needs money or he'll give up on the dog business."

She pushed back her chair. "I have to make a phone call to the East coast, so I'd better go now. Thank you for the coffee."

"I understand, being in business myself," he said. "I have a man in town that I need to see, but I've certainly enjoyed talking to you."

She stood up, and he walked her out to her car and said a cheerful goodbye.

Now for Edric. She'd put it off long enough. Slowly she drove back to the Roost. He'd have finished lunch and maybe a glass of wine, so he might be in one of his jovial moods. If they could have a good talk, she'd feel better.

His greeting, "Hey there, Lin! How's it going?" gave her hope, but he wasn't chewing his gum.

"I'm still having problems getting that interview—"

"—I've got problems too, money problems."

And she was spending money on a dead-end story.

"I have a suggestion," she said. "I won't charge this trip to the magazine. Would that help?"

He muttered to himself and finally said, "I hate for you to do that, Lin, but we've got to cut back somewhere."

"And how about trimming the payroll?" She hurried on. "We could share secretaries, and maybe we could replace Vance with someone less expensive and more efficient. He's worked with us for a year now, and I haven't been very impressed with his performance."

Edric began chewing his gum. "Now that's an idea, Lin."

"He's back from the conference, isn't he?"

"Yes. Friday. In fact . . . Hi, Vance, sit down. Be right with you."

To her he said, "Let me think about that, and I'll get back to you. Bye!"

She made a face and put the phone down. He wouldn't call back. He never did. Maybe he'd be smart enough not to listen to Vance.

A blue jay flew past the balcony railing into the trees. She watched it go and let her eyes rest on the water beyond. It was, as Quinn had said, a fine day. The beach would be cool and bright, just the place for when she felt like this.

But first, Odela.

The old lady was pathetically glad to see her. She took the bag of cookies, peeked inside, and giggled. She had Lindsey sit down, and, after they'd talked for a while, heaved herself to her feet and waddled over to a pile of magazines. She chose one and dropped back into her chair with a sigh.

She showed Lindsey a picture of the necklace she wanted to make for her, talking knowledgeably about faceted drops and rutilated quartz.

"It's going to be pretty," Lindsey said. "Do you design the other necklaces too?"

"I sure do," Odela said. "A shop in San Francisco just

ordered five more copies of my Jungle Gold design, so I'm working on that now. It gives me a little mad money."

She looked sly, much like her grandson. "Then I can get my neighbor to buy me something nice to drink."

She began to talk about Jack.

He was kind and thoughtful, unlike most children these days. He fixed the roof when it leaked. He gave her chocolates. He even brought her jewelry from thrift shops that she could take apart and use.

When Lindsey stood up to go, Odela showed her one of Jack's watercolors, an imaginative seascape with green fronds in the foreground. Lindsey could praise it with genuine enthusiasm since he seemed to have a gift for harmonizing his colors.

Odela begged her to come back on Thursday or Friday, saw her to the door, and stood there waving as she drove off.

Now for the beach, at last.

She took her camera and the copy of Psalm 1 she had written out for herself. Last night, as soon as she'd read it again, she'd seen what Alexa meant.

The psalm didn't say to read God's law; it said to meditate on it. She'd gone online to find the Bible study software Remi had mentioned and learned about the word *meditate*. It meant "to ponder." To talk to yourself about the meaning.

Okay, so she'd ponder.

The waves were rolling in fast, crashing onto the sand with a pleasant tumult, and she matched her pace to their energy. She said the verses aloud, lifting her face to the breeze as she went, and soon her spirits lifted too. This was a promise, right? Blessings and fruitfulness! What more could she ask for?

She'd almost reached the rocks at the end of the beach when she realized that Jack and his easel stood nearby.

He waved her over with one of his flourishing gestures, so she went to see what he wanted. He wore oversize blue-mirrored sunglasses with his usual black outfit, and he was painting.

It was a typical seascape, but he'd added a light green wash that gave the scene a dreamy, unfocused effect.

"Mmm," she said, and he looked gratified.

He took a swig from a bottle half-filled with a murky liquid, stepped back, and added a dab of white to the foreground.

"That's a start," he said. "Now I add the other stuff."

"I saw one of your paintings at your grandmother's," she said. "It's truly original."

A smile twisted his mouth. "Hmm. Not sure how to take that."

She smiled. "I'm not qualified to say whether it's good or not, but I like to see originality. I was wondering how you do it."

"Spoken like a true artist." He took another drink from the bottle. "Nice to have another artist around. We're so often misunderstood. Got to hang together."

Because of the sunglasses, she couldn't tell whether he was mocking himself.

His voice rose a little higher. "Tell you what. I'm coming over to the Roost on Wednesday—gotta clean up for some bigwig. I'll bring a couple of finished paintings for you to see."

He took off his glasses, and gave her an earnest look. "Not to buy. Just for an opinion. Guess I'm getting discouraged."

His eyes gleamed. "Of course, there's always a chance the old lady will want to buy one. She's loaded."

He glanced down the beach and his face hardened.

He slid the dark glasses back on. "Here's our pretty little witch with her doggies. Time for me to dee-camp."

141

He packed up fast. "See you Wednesday," he said over his shoulder, and climbed across the rocks until he reached the edge of the creek.

Lindsey watched him go, keeping an eye on Shula, who was striding down the beach with her dogs frisking ahead of her. Pretty little witch? Why would he say that of his employer?

She did look pretty today in her green jogging outfit, a filmy white scarf streaming in the breeze. She waved as she drew near. "Hi, Lin!"

Lindsey went to meet her, and Shula said, "I love this weather! I just had to get out and thought I might as well bring them too."

While they talked, the two Akitas wandered off to investigate the driftwood at the high-tide line. The older dog began digging rapidly, making the sand fly, and the younger one soon joined him.

Shula whirled at the sound of digging. "Tyee! Pelton!" she shouted. "Stop that!" The older dog lifted his head and gazed at her, looking worried.

The younger dog was still digging, which seemed to make her furious. "No, you don't! Pelton!"

She started toward him, and he froze. He backed away, staring at her.

"That's better." She kicked the sand into the hole, her face distorted with anger, and the dogs watched as she stamped it down.

"Now—" she said, and added something in another language. The dogs turned and ran down the beach.

She linked her arm through Lindsey's, smiling up at her. "Let's go get a cup of tea."

"If you wish," Lindsey said, troubled at what she'd just seen. It had been unusual behavior for both owner and dogs. Especially since Akitas are not easily cowed.

As before, Shula made their tea in the herb room and

they drank it sitting beside the French doors, looking out at her sunlit herb garden.

She put a plate of tiny chocolate éclairs on the low table, and Lindsey remembered seeing them at the bakery. "Help yourself," Shula said. "I could eat these all day."

Lindsey took one and ate it in tiny bites, savoring the creamy custard filling and trying to make it last.

When they'd finished their tea, Shula said, "I have a proposition for you." She gave Lindsey a winning smile. "Let's go look at my map."

She took Lindsey into the kitchen to stand in front of a large topographic map of the Olympic Peninsula.

"I don't know how familiar you are with the area," Shula said, "but it's pretty big and plenty wild. Here's Cameron Bay." She put a pink-tipped finger on the map. "And here's the beach we were on this morning."

"What are the colored pins?"

"My properties." Shula looked proud and eager. "I mean, the properties I'm trying to sell."

She put a finger on a gold pin farther up the coast. "This one's top dog. It comes with beach frontage, nice trees, a fairly modern home, and a couple of cabins in the back. Accessible from the highway too."

She dropped her voice. "It could sell for more than a million."

"Really?" Lindsey said. "Way out there?"

"You'd be surprised what people will spend to get away. And I have a prospective client."

She looked at Lindsey, her eyes turning golden. "Problem is, he wants more than a scenic view; he wants a place for his Labs to play and swim. I know that if I can just get him out here, he'll love it. That's where you come in, my friend."

Shula glanced at her and back to the map. "I'd like to do a presentation for him—a slide show or something—

143

with my dogs running on that beach, and once he sees it, I'm sure he'll want to have his dogs running there too. What do you think?"

Lindsey kept her eyes on the gold pin. Not for free. It would have to be a business arrangement all the way. Especially now since she was paying for this trip.

"It's a good idea," she said. "Why don't you hire a professional and have it done right?"

"But Lin, you are a professional. I want to hire you."

"First," Lindsey said, "let's talk about what you'd get. I would take some photos—maybe a hundred or so—and trim them down to the best twenty-five and put them into a PowerPoint presentation. It won't be a movie. Is that going to be okay?"

"Sure. I know you'll do a good job. And I'll pay your going rate."

She did some quick arithmetic, gave Shula the package price, and Shula said, "Done deal. How about Wednesday, early afternoon?"

Lindsey nodded. Good thing the Nikon was digital or the cost of film would ruin her. "I'll meet you here so Belinda won't worry."

"Right." Shula looked indulgent. "My one-person fan club, that's our Belinda."

As they turned from the map, Lindsey saw a silver-framed photo on Shula's desk. She stopped to look at it. "May I?"

At Shula's nod, she picked it up and studied the girl's face. "Your sister?"

Again Shula nodded.

The girl had a lighter skin than Shula's, dark eyes, and curly dark hair. She eyed the photographer with a saucy smile, one arm around a much younger Shula.

"What's her name?"

Shula sighed, extending a graceful hand for the photo.

144

Lindsey gave it to her. Drama mode coming on?

"Her name was Cheree." Shula's face grew pensive. "She was beautiful and talented. You should have seen her doing the tribal dances!" Shula's voice softened. "My big sister, and all through high school she was my mother, my father, my idol."

Her lips tightened. "I had to watch her anguish while she waited for her man to come back from the army. She'd loved him for years. When he finally returned, he wouldn't have anything to do with her, and she ran off to Seattle."

A ballad of disappointment and lost loves.

Shula smoothed her hand across the glass and replaced the photo on her desk, but she didn't move. She gazed at it, twisting the topaz ring on her finger. "I will never forget my sister," she said, her voice low and hard. "I will see justice done."

She recovered almost immediately, and, as she walked away from the desk, began talking about the big real estate deal she'd closed last weekend.

Lindsey left soon after, but blurred Shula-images drifted through her mind: Shula's face when she glared at the dogs. When she smiled at Lindsey. When she gazed at her sister's picture.

Lindsey felt as if she were looking at the woman through a fogged lens, and nothing fit together. Where was the real Shula?

Another question edged forward. Shula could have hired a photographer to produce a video for less than Lindsey was charging. Why hadn't she?

No answers came to her, but from deep inside rose a warning: *Proceed with caution.*

The next morning, Lindsey awoke late, and she took her time getting dressed.

It was raining, anyway, and she'd stayed up after

midnight, working. Since the Makah project was stalled, she'd decided to finalize the Carolina feature, adding notes to herself of changes to include if she could ever get to Ben Fletcher.

Yawning, she made the bed and hung up her clothes. The Carolina feature still needed polishing, but she'd promised herself that this morning she would drive up to the reservation and learn everything she could. She might never be so close again.

After a quick breakfast with Belinda, who worried aloud when she heard that she was going up to Neah Bay by herself, she set off.

The rain had slowed, and by the time she reached the highway, it had stopped, but a cool wind blew, and she knew she'd be glad for her jacket.

She turned up the coast, soon passing Shula's driveway on her right, then Odela's trailer court, and a little farther, Cedar Run Kennels, on her left.

She crossed the bridge over Thorsen's Creek, and as she approached the access road to the airport, she saw a small blond boy trudging toward her. Bobby Fletcher? Way out here?

She drove up beside him, and he turned to look. He took a purple sucker out of his mouth long enough to say, "Airplanes!" and sat down by the side of the road.

She parked and walked back to him. "Bobby! What are you doing out here by yourself?"

He smiled around the sucker, saying something garbled, and she gently took his arm. "You look tired," she said. "Did you walk a long way? Let's go home."

He climbed into her Jeep with a sigh. Had he just wandered off?

She hoped Remi would be there, but it was Natalie who ran outside, clucking with distress, and a minute later, the three older boys had surrounded them.

146

"Oh!" Natalie cried, her eyes flashing. "Thank you, thank you so much! Bobby, you bad boy! Why did you run away?" She gave Lindsey an agonized glance. "This has been a terrible morning! He was just playing and . . . oh! Please come inside!"

She looked over her shoulder. "Ginni, come get Bobby and clean him up. He's a sticky mess."

A solemn Ginni took Bobby's hand and led him into the house.

The kitchen table was spread with books and papers, but Natalie told the boys to clear it off. "Stanley and Patrick, you may work in your bedroom," she said. "Jeffrey, into the living room. Remember your test."

She put a plate of cookies on the table, sat down, then jumped up and headed for the stove, saying, "Coffee? Would you like some coffee?" She bent her head and began to sob.

Lindsey put an arm around the soft shoulders. "Let me get the coffee. You sit down. Tell me what happened."

She poured coffee for them both, found milk in the fridge, and sat down across from Natalie.

Where were Remi and Ben?

"So Bobby was playing?" she said. "Outside?"

"I let him go out for playtime, every morning," Natalie said. "I can see the swing set from here. I check on him all the time."

Her words spilled out in a flood. "Ginni plays out there too, but not today. She begged to go into town with Ben and Remi and the boys. I was doing laundry and had to hang up the towels on the line in back, and I thought just for a minute it would be okay. He must have run off or something because all of a sudden he was gone, and Ben came home and we couldn't find him anywhere!"

Her eyes filled with more tears.

Lindsey stirred her coffee, which didn't need stirring.

147

More likely, Bobby had been taken by someone.

Ginni came back, holding onto Bobby. "Do you want him to stay here, Mama?"

"You sit right here beside me, Bobby. Tell me what happened."

Bobby sat down next to her and reached for a cookie.

Natalie pushed his hand away. "No cookies until you tell me."

"Old lady." He looked bored. "White hair. Cookie?"

She frowned. "No, tell me some more. Where was the old lady?"

"Truck."

"She was in a truck? And you went with her? Why did you do that, you bad boy? Don't you know it's dangerous? We've told you a hundred times."

He eyed the plate of cookies and said nothing. Ginni sat down beside him, her dark eyes watchful.

"Bobby," Lindsey said, "did she give you candy?"

He nodded. "She had lots of candy. I got to eat a candy bar, and then I picked the sucker."

He frowned at Ginni. "I want my sucker."

"What color was the truck?" Lindsey said.

He shrugged and put his thumb in his mouth.

"Stop that!" Natalie said. "Tell us about the old lady. What did she have on? What did she say?"

Bobby looked at her, his little face set in stubborn lines. "Big things. In her ears."

Natalie sighed. "I'd give him a spanking if I thought it would make any difference."

"Bobby." Ginni spoke in a gentle voice that Lindsey didn't recognize. "Did she have round things in her ears like Miss Lindsey has?"

He shook his head. "Those are little balls. She had rings. Bigger. Shiny."

Ginni held up a cookie in front of him. "This big?"

"Yes." He reached for it, and she pulled it back. "Were they pretty?"

"Little pink rocks."

"Okay," Ginni said. "So the big shiny things had little pink rocks in them?"

"Yeah." He reached for the cookie again, and she glanced at Natalie, who nodded.

"Thank you, Ginni." Lindsey kept her voice soft. "So now we know it's an old lady with white hair wearing hoop earrings with pink stones in them. And she drives a truck."

She looked at Natalie. "The woman must have seen him playing outside and picked him up. Are you going to call the police?"

"No! Ben won't allow it." Natalie frowned. "I think I know who's doing this, but Ben won't let me say."

Lindsey wondered why, but all she said was, "Where are Ben and Remi?"

"In the woods. They thought Bobby might have gone to see the new path they're making."

Natalie glanced at the kitchen clock. "I've been going crazy, waiting for them, and Remi's phone doesn't work right anymore. They should be back soon."

Ben would find her in the middle of another disaster. She had to leave right away.

As she stood up, Natalie did too. "Thank you so much!" She put a hand on Lindsey's arm. "Please forgive Ben for the way he's been acting—he is terribly worried these days. But Remi is right. You love God like he does, and you are a good friend."

"Thank you, Natalie," she said. "I'm glad for that. Be sure to phone if I can ever help you."

She was conscious of Ginni's eyes upon her, but she knew better than to say anything, and she left as quickly as possible. The one person she didn't want to run into was Ben Fletcher.

14

caption:

Cruelty

Lindsey turned back toward Cameron Bay since she wouldn't have time to drive up to the reservation and still meet Alexa for their trip to Port Angeles.

She had tried to be calm in the face of Natalie's despair, but now . . . anxiety clawed at her.

This was more than petty sabotage. Abducting a child like that, from their own front yard? Criminal. Who would want so desperately to harm the Fletchers?

She met Alexa at the bakery, and when Lindsey offered to drive, Alexa agreed, saying something about the price of gas. Soon Alexa confided that she and Peter were beginning to wonder whether the bakery should stay open this winter. The fishing business had been slow this fall, and the best part of the salmon season was coming to a close.

"It's nice when I can take time off, like today," Alexa said, "but not when it comes to paying the bills."

She glanced at Lindsey. "That's enough whining from me. What's on your mind, Lin?"

At least, with Alexa she could be transparent.

"Natalie had a bad scare this morning. Bobby was playing outside, and some woman drove right up and took him away in her truck. The old candy trick. She must have dropped him off at the airport because I found him walking back down the access road."

Alexa's face went pale. "Oh, no! Did he say what the woman looked like?"

"Old, with white hair. And hoop earrings with pink stones in them."

"There's no one like that in Cameron Bay," Alexa said, "or anywhere around here that I know of. Do you think it's connected with the kennel problems?"

"It's bizarre happening number three, or four, if you count the note to Ben. Someone's really out to get them."

"But why take the child away and then leave him?"

"A warning, perhaps. What kind of a person would do that to a child?"

Alexa looked out of the window as if she were trying to think of an answer. Maybe she was praying.

It seemed that an acre of trees went by before she said anything more. "Poor Ben! He's going to flip."

"Poor Ben?" Lindsey exclaimed. "What's the matter with that man, anyway?"

She tried to choke back her indignation, failed, and went on. "Natalie said he wouldn't call the police. She has some suspicions, but he won't let her say anything. She's terrified. He's this big tough Marine, and all he does is clam up? Are his dogs more important to him than his family?"

Alexa sighed. "I don't know. Ben's got this thing about the police—he had a couple of bad experiences when he was growing up. But now . . ."

She shook her head. "I've been praying for that family. And I've been trying to talk to Natalie about the Lord. She's not ready to listen. I think there's a lot going on here that we don't understand."

"Colin McAlister said that the other night."

And he knew a lot more than he was saying, she was sure of it.

Alexa looked out the window again. "So what did you think of Remi's friend?"

"He's not what I expected. Not the friendliest sort. Like talking to one of those rocks on the beach."

Alexa smiled. "What did you expect?"

"Somebody helpful, maybe. Soft body, sharp brain, that type. Bookish, being a librarian. What does he do at the library, anyway? I can't see him standing at a desk, checking out books all day."

"No, he's a research librarian, I think they call it. He gives reference help in his subject area, does consultations, instructs students."

"That sounds interesting, at least," Lindsey said.

To be fair, she had to add, "Of course, there's no reason he should care about my project. I could tell that he was worried about Ben."

"We all are, and Ben's a particular friend of his. He's only human."

Lindsey was tempted to remark, "Oh, is he? I hadn't noticed."

But the man might be a friend of Alexa's too, so she said, "He did thaw a little on that trip to Neah Bay. And it doesn't matter, anyway. I'll get along with him for Remi's sake."

She touched Alexa's arm. "We can't all be warm-hearted like you. Your smile makes my day."

Alexa's eyes glistened. "Thank you, Lin. I hope God keeps you here for a long time."

That wasn't the plan, but she smiled in agreement. "Now tell me where we're going."

They shopped first at a big wholesale store in Port Angeles; then they stopped at a thrift shop on the outskirts of town. "I'd like to dress up the café a little," Alexa said. "Sometimes I find good stuff here."

She picked out a few items, including two glass cake

stands. Lindsey found three strings of turquoise beads that Odela might be able to use, and they strolled past the women's clothes.

They tried on sweaters, narrowed their choices, and Lindsey persuaded Alexa to let her pay for them.

Two sweaters for nine dollars.

Alexa's was an ivory cable-stitched pullover that looked stunning with her bright hair. Hers was mint green with three little buttons at the neck, in cashmere. They'd wear them on Sunday.

While they waited in line, Lindsey fingered the soft green wool of her sweater. Too bad Quinn wasn't going to be at church. He'd like the cashmere, if he noticed it.

What did she think of him, anyway? Not sure. He was a good source of information, if nothing else.

They ate lunch at a sub shop, and Lindsey bought mocha lattes at the Thanks-a-Latte in Joyce.

According to Lindsey's reckoning, they were more than halfway back when Alexa said, "Let's stop at Pillar Point. Do you have time?"

"Sure!"

At Alexa's direction, she turned off the highway onto a road that followed a wide, rushing creek. The Pysht River, Alexa said.

The road ended in a parking lot that faced a narrow beach strewn with pebbles and green seaweed. They stood at its edge for a minute, looking out at ruffled gray water enclosed by headlands.

Another perfect little bay. Same drifting clouds. Same cool, salty breeze.

"I like this place," Lindsey said. "*Pysht*. Sounds like a place to tell secrets."

Alexa laughed. "It's an Indian name. It means 'Wind blows from all directions.' Come over here—I want to show you something."

153

Alexa led the way into the trees at one side of the parking lot and along a faint path that climbed through ferns and moss-covered boulders into a forest of evergreens.

She jumped across a marshy creek, climbed a long, slippery bank, and pulled herself up onto an outcropping of granite.

Lindsey followed. The granite formed a mossy shelf with room for two, and spruce branches hung low, enclosing them. Water gleamed in the distance. She felt as if she were looking out of a porthole.

"My secret place," Alexa said.

"It's lovely," Lindsey said. "Look at these incredible trees." A verse came to mind and she said it aloud, "*He is like a tree planted by streams of water.* Must have been a stream like the Pysht River."

Alexa laughed. "You've been working on Psalm 1."

"Yes, I went back and read it again. You're right. *Meditate.* How do you meditate?"

"I take a piece of Scripture and chew it over, think about it. I do other Bible reading, but the chewing part is what feeds me the most."

Lindsey bent over a clump of moss with tiny mushrooms poking up from it.

She'd been enjoying God's love, taking comfort from it. But was she someone like Natalie, not ready to listen? Was it time to get serious about knowing Him?

"I've been thinking about what we call fun," she said. "Most of it feels empty. Useless. I don't want to be a bunch of withered leaves."

Alexa nodded. "I'm with you. It's my great fear that I'll get all caught up with busyness, trying to survive financially and so forth, and end up with nothing."

She paused, looking off toward the ocean. "That's one reason I visit Odela. I'm obeying the command to help

154

those in need, and I also get a reminder of what I could become."

Her voice grew solemn. "Todd doesn't understand that. He's still after the fun stuff."

"Todd is one of your sons?"

"Yes, he's a student at the University of Washington. Tommy's my other son. He . . . was in the army." Quickly she went on. "But Lin, here's an idea. I'd like to start reading the book of Philippians. Could we study it together?"

Lindsey clasped her arms around her knees. Did she want to commit to something like this?

She hedged. "How would that work out?"

"We'd each do our own study, but we can get together and talk about what we're learning. And even after you leave, we could do it by email."

Lindsey nodded. After she left, she'd better stay in touch with someone like Alexa. And if she really meant it— if she wanted to become that fruitful tree—she should do this.

She smiled. "I'd like that. How does the study part work?"

"First, I read the whole book straight through. This one's really short. Then I take a couple of verses at a time and meditate on them. You heard Remi, about the online Bible study helps?"

"Yes," Lindsey said, "and I've already got some tools downloaded. I like them."

"So do I. We can use them to help us study and get a little to chew on each day. But if I were you, I'd keep reading through the Psalms, and I'll join you. Let's see what God brings to pass."

"That's a kind of frightening thought," Lindsey said. "When I was growing up, it seemed that God was someone to be scared of."

Alexa smiled. "But now you've got Romans 8. Above all else, remember that he's someone who loves you."

She sat up onto her knees. "Peter will be wondering, so we'd better go, but first, let's talk to the Lord."

Her conversational tone didn't change as she bowed her head, saying, "Lord, we want to be strong, growing trees. We want to bear fruit. Thank you for putting this desire into our hearts. Show us how to make it happen."

Her voice broke. "And Father, have mercy on Ben Fletcher. Whatever's wrong, have mercy on him."

They slid down from one rock to the next and walked back to the Jeep in silence, but it was a contented silence.

Lindsey picked up an especially large fir cone for her desk, and thankfulness ran through her like a song.

That evening she read through the whole book of Philippians, then went back to the first chapter and read it in another version.

She paused at verse 6. *And I am sure of this, that he who began a good work in you will bring it to completion . . .*

I am sure. Like Romans 8:38. *I am sure that neither . . . nor . . . nor . . .*

There were plenty of things she wasn't sure about. She had spent all evening finishing the Carolina dogs feature, but she didn't know what to do with it. Send it in? Hang onto it?

And she had to phone Edric tomorrow, no matter what. Should she tell him about Bobby? Should she push him a little harder about Vance?

By the next morning, the clouds they'd seen at Pillar Point had moved in and pulled a rippled coverlet across the sky. Lindsey took her usual jog on the beach and decided that she'd give Edric another call about Vance.

She scuffed her feet through the sand. Get rid of Vance. It would be a wonderful answer to prayer.

She phoned as soon as she returned to her room, and

Edric answered right away. "Hey there! I've got some great news." He paused, cracking his gum.

"What's that? Fresh cinnamon rolls in the break room?"

He laughed, and she waited, staring outside. "Those were the days, weren't they, Lin? No, I've got something even better. Our money problems are solved."

Her neck stiffened with alarm. "Why's that?"

"Vance has invested a couple hundred thousand in the magazine."

She reached blindly for the leather chair and lowered herself into it. "So, how did this come about?"

"I sold him some of my shares."

His shares? Edric must have been desperate. He'd always insisted on keeping his eighty percent intact.

"But you still have a majority?"

Edric stopped chewing his gum. "I forgot to tell you. I sold ten percent to my sister a while back. You were in Alaska, I think."

She rubbed at her neck. Like it was her fault he did something so stupid?

He sounded defiant. "Sure, I've got only thirty percent left, but that's not so terrible. I had to do it." He let loose a string of profanity. "Lin, for the sake of the magazine, I had to do it."

For-the-Sake-of-the-Magazine. How often had she heard that mantra—and chanted it herself—over the past six years?

And now Edric was worried, waiting for her to scold him, but she couldn't. It was too late.

Her thoughts raced, warning her: *Pick up the pieces. Vance is going to be calling the shots. Get yourself some immunity.*

"I guess you do what you have to, Edric." She kept her voice level. "By the way, the project out here has stalled, but I'd like to hang around and see what happens."

Before he could say anything, she went on in the firmest voice she could muster. "I'm going to start taking some of my personal days. Effective yesterday. I won't be available to anyone except you."

"Sure, whatever you want is fine with me." He sounded relieved. "Call me when you've got some news."

She turned off the phone and lurched to her feet. She wandered over to her desk and back to the glass doors. So much for a wonderful answer to prayer.

Prayer? She should pray, but her mind was choked with resentment as thick and gray as the clouds outside.

She swung away from the balcony, remembering Shula's photos. This afternoon, no matter what, she had to shoot those photos.

She tidied up the room. She packed her shoulder bag with granola bars and water, voice recorder, pen, and notebook. She checked her cameras.

Professional and efficient, wasn't she? Yes, except for the churning inside her.

Five minutes later, she was down the steps and out the door, pretending she didn't hear Belinda's question.

It was while she was driving up the slope leading to the highway that she remembered Alexa's words, "Above all else, remember that he's someone who loves you."

She gripped the steering wheel. "I'm sorry, Father," she whispered. "I shouldn't be so upset. But this looks really bad to me."

At least she had finished up the Carolina dogs feature, so it was ready in case they asked for it. She might as well accept reality. Much too soon, Vance would be running the magazine.

Edric must have been terribly worried to sell his shares.

Or Vance had been very persuasive.

She turned onto the highway. But she owned twenty percent of those shares, and with Edric's thirty, they still carried some weight. Would it make a difference?

"Lord, I'm falling apart," she whispered. "I need your love to hold me together. And I really need to do a good job at this photo shoot."

She drove in silence for the next half hour, letting herself think about nothing but the rocky coastline and the requirements of the project ahead of her. It could be a pleasant afternoon—the beach, the beautiful dogs, and her camera.

By the time she reached the turnoff, she had the peace she needed, at least for now.

Shula was already there on the beach, waiting beside her green pickup. The dogs were out, sniffing at the driftwood. Today they both wore black collars. Shock collars.

Why? These were well-trained dogs. Shock collars might be useful in the right situation, but she'd always felt that shocking dogs was perilously close to abuse.

"Isn't this a gorgeous place?" Shula said. "Done anything interesting since I saw you last?"

"One rather strange thing," Lindsey said.

Everyone probably knew about Bobby's escapade, but she was curious about Shula's reaction. "I happened to find one of Ben Fletcher's children, up near the airport. Apparently someone took him—kidnapped him—when he was playing outside."

Shula picked up a gull's feather. "So where was his mother?"

"Right there. She can see the swing set from the kitchen. But you know how it is—she couldn't stand there watching him the whole time. All of a sudden he was gone."

"And then Natalie had hysterics, no doubt." Shula tore the feather apart, rib by rib, letting the shreds float down to the sand. "I heard that the Fletchers have run into trouble with their dogs. They must have enemies."

"Enemies?" Lindsey said. "Like who?"

"There's one person who comes to mind. His property adjoins, and he'd sure like to have a couple of their acres."

"Quincy Corbin? But Bobby said it was a woman."

"Corbin has two sisters who baby him. Maybe one of them helped him out a bit. Not that he really needs the land, mind you. He owns property all over the peninsula. He's smart."

Lindsey frowned. Quinn had told her he wanted Ben's land, but she hadn't made the connection. It did give him a motive. Worth thinking about.

"Let's get started," she said. "First, have the dogs just run, wherever they want to go, but moving fast."

This beach wasn't as long as Thorsen's, but it was fairly wide, and it had an open stretch of sand that ended at a headland with a picturesque little sea stack.

She started shooting, and the dogs performed well. Their colors—black, caramel, and white—would show beautifully against the sand and water.

They ran and splashed and frolicked in response to Shula's commands. She held a transmitter, but for now she was controlling them by voice.

Lindsey ran with them, getting one good shot after another, even catching a cloud of birds that rose as the dogs converged on a jutting rock, midway down the beach.

The younger one, Pelton, was beginning to tire, judging from the way he was panting, but Shula didn't seem to notice. She drove them hard, right up to the sea stack, which was separated from the shore by a rush of swirling water.

Lindsey was still shooting when Shula shouted, "Jump, Tyee! Jump!"

The big dog glanced at the sea stack, gathered his legs,

sailed across, and scrabbled for a foothold on the rough, corrugated side of the rock.

"Great!" Lindsey said. "Got it!"

Shula wasn't finished. "Come on, Pelton. Jump!"

The smaller dog ran back and forth, looking at the water, whining.

Shula held out the transmitter. He gave a screaming snarl and launched himself toward the rock.

Lindsey gasped. He'd never make it.

The dog shrieked again, dropped into the water, floundered in the current for an agonizing second, then paddled back to the beach. He dragged himself up onto the sand and fell into a heap.

Lindsey started toward him, hating what she'd seen, but Shula stopped her with a gesture. "Leave him. He'll behave better next time."

To Lindsey's amazement, the woman laughed. "Men and dogs. They're just like children. Need to take a firm hand, or they'll run right over you. Now get one more of Tyee on the sea stack."

Lindsey closed her camera. "No more. I'll work with what I've got." She slid the camera into its case. "I don't like the way you treat your dogs, Shula."

She turned to walk down the beach, but Shula caught up with her.

"They're my dogs," Shula said. "And I know how to handle them. These two are rebellious. I've got to show them that I'm the boss." Her eyes glittered with anger.

Lindsey looked away from her.

Shula was furious again, and it was about something more than a disobedient dog.

They walked the length of the beach in silence. As they turned to go up the bank to their cars, Shula muttered, "Sorry, Lin. They just make me so mad sometimes."

"I guess we all do things we're sorry for," Lindsey said,

conscious of the outrage that still sizzled inside her. "I'll get this finished and bring it over tomorrow."

Shula smiled, looking satisfied. "Thanks! I really appreciate it." She headed for her truck.

Lindsey waited in her Jeep, fidgeting with her camera and notebook, until Shula had loaded up her dogs and driven off.

She folded her arms across the steering wheel and rested her head against them. Her neck still ached. What was going on with Shula?

The knobby lump of her watch reminded her of the time. She'd promised to arrange flowers for Belinda, who was worried about a guest arriving tonight. The bigwig, as Jack called him.

Stop all this thinking. Hurry. Do something with the flowers. Take a shower. Get dressed. Try to be elegant and entertaining so poor Belinda won't have to deal with him by herself at supper.

Please? Belinda had said.

Sure. But why was this man so important?

Lindsey started the Jeep and eased it back down the rutted gravel road.

Anything would be better than watching a dog in pain. She would never forget the rancher in Montana who'd horsewhipped his dogs until they stood still for the camera. Shula's brand of cruelty seemed even worse.

caption:

Diamonds and Pudge

When Lindsey arrived, she found Jack in the kitchen, as he'd said, polishing a silver filigreed basket. Belinda had driven off to buy a particular wine. The table had been moved into the living room and spread with a white linen cloth, and something delicious seemed to be roasting in the oven.

He put down his rag. "Here—I brought them. Can you take a quick look?"

From a green truck that looked like Shula's, he carried in two paintings and stood them against the sofa.

One showed a red-and-white lighthouse on a ragged gray island surrounded by foaming seas.

"That's pretty," she said. "Where is it?"

"Up past Neah Bay, off of Cape Flattery. It's called Tatoosh Island."

The other was a seascape, but it was done in Jack's distinctive style that made her feel as if she were looking through a curtain of ferns. "This is definitely your strength, Jack. I really like it."

"Do you? My big dream is to go to art school. I've got a lot to learn."

A humble statement, unlike Jack. But perhaps Jack the

artist was different from the Jack she was used to.

"I know what you mean," she said. "I often feel that way. Good for you."

He grinned, satisfied, and took the paintings outside.

By the time he returned, she had taken the flowers from the florist's box and was sorting them on the counter.

"What's so remarkable about this guest?" she said.

His mouth quirked. "Some lawyer, doing a job for one of her old friends. She wants to show him she's not a country bumpkin like the rest of us. Probably one of those slick Seattle types, so watch yourself, m'lady."

"Not to worry. No *slick* for me." She started with the yellow chrysanthemums and added the larkspur, a stem at a time. "I hope it's a good meal. I spent a couple of hours on the beach, and I'm starved."

"Photos of those special doggies? How'd it turn out?"

Jack always seemed to know what was going on. Did he realize how Shula treated her dogs?

"The photos will be fine. The dogs were cooperative."

"Yeah, with her, it's cooperate or die, like Stalin."

Another stem of larkspur. Better not comment on that.

"Did she train them herself?"

"Her?" He held the silver piece under the faucet, rinsing it. "Nah, she had them professionally trained. They're genuine attack dogs in case you didn't know."

"Really?"

"Yeah, I saw them knock over some hiker who was looking for a handout. They would've torn him apart if she hadn't stopped them. Every once in a while she throws them a rabbit to practice on, just for fun."

Now a sprig of pine. "Kind of bloody."

"It's the Indian in her. Most of her commands are Makah, anyway."

A knock sounded on the door, accompanied by

164

Belinda's plaintive voice, and Lindsey went to answer it. Just as well. She'd heard enough.

After she'd carried Belinda's packages into the kitchen, she pointed out the two vases of flowers she'd arranged and escaped up the stairs. Now for a hot shower.

Max Lougherbrey didn't fit the big-city image Jack had projected, but he did fit almost too well into his dark trousers, yellow shirt, and canary-colored sweater vest.

The vest bulged rather markedly in the front, and Mr. Lougherbrey didn't seem aware of that.

He greeted her with urbane confidence and gave her a flattering amount of attention until Belinda put a platter of roast beef and potatoes on the table.

At Belinda's urging, he helped himself liberally, as he had with the minestrone soup, the rolls, the salad, and the wine.

Lindsey took the opportunity to eat heartily herself, being careful to compliment Belinda. She really was a good cook.

While he worked his way through second helpings, the lawyer remarked on the fine flight he'd had over, what fun it was to fly his new Beechcraft King Air, and the superior attributes of a low-wing airplane.

Belinda spoke knowingly of Shula's Cessna 206, and he nodded, saying that he liked the smoothness and reliability of the turboprops; after a pause, he added that Cessnas were good airplanes too.

He planted his elbows on the table, clasping and unclasping his hands.

They were small white plump hands, and he'd decorated his stubby fingers with rings. A diamond-encrusted wedding ring was dwarfed by the others: a wide platinum band set with more diamonds, a silver ring that was heavy with onyx and diamonds, and a ruby-studded signet.

Odd, with such pudgy hands, that he'd want to draw attention to them. Perhaps he didn't know better.

He gestured, emphasizing his point to Belinda, and the diamonds sparkled in the candlelight.

Diamonds and pudge.

As he continued his exposition, he took another roll from the silver bread basket, the one Jack had polished.

Lindsey pictured Jack's hands: oversized, reddened, stained with paint. No rings. Much to be preferred.

Or Fraser's brown hands: slender and skilled. No rings.

Or even Colin McAlister's hands: big, capable-looking hands, the fingers long and tapered, clasped around his coffee cup or leafing through a book. No rings.

She put down her fork. Not that it mattered whether Colin wore a ring. Vance didn't wear a wedding ring either. Some married men didn't.

She took a firm hold on her glass of water, and as she drank, told herself to think about something else. The water—it tasted cool and fresh, didn't it?

"Miss Dumont?" Max Lougherbrey's voice seemed to come from a distance. "Are you feeling unwell?"

She must have been sitting with her eyes closed.

She made an effort to smile at him. "No, I'm fine." She laughed. "Just thinking, I guess."

He smiled back. "Too much of that is dangerous, they say. I was just telling Ms. Cameron how . . . ah . . . exceptionally remote this place is. But I'm happy to work with Mr. Gunning. I'm his Seattle associate, you know, and I certainly am glad to fly out here to do this bit of business on his behalf."

Belinda smiled at Lindsey. "Mr. Gunning is a lawyer too, a friend of our family for years and years. He and his charming wife used to come out here frequently."

Lindsey tried to look attentive. What did Mr. Gunning

have to do with anything?

The lawyer began to enlarge on the political eminence of Mr. Gunning and interrupted himself to say, "I hope you can tell me how to find Ben Fletcher."

"It's not at all difficult," Belinda said. "I'll be happy to show you."

"Excellent." He poured himself more wine and leaned back in his chair. "A fine meal! I'll have to tell Mr. Gunning what a good cook you are."

Belinda looked gratified. "We still have dessert."

She hurried into the kitchen and returned with a small cheesecake, elegantly garnished with whipped cream and pecans. "Here we are!"

Alexa's handiwork.

Belinda disappeared again, returning with coffee.

"Thank you. Thank you indeed," Mr. Lougherbrey said, smiling at the cheesecake.

Belinda sliced and served the cake with the ease of long practice; then she tasted her piece and nodded in approval. "So," she said, smiling, "You've come to see Ben Fletcher? Is he in some sort of trouble?"

"Not at all." The lawyer glanced at Lindsey, as if to make sure she was listening. "A rather nice thing for him. Quite interesting, I must say."

He leaned toward her. "A will. It was lost for a few years, but now it's been located. It concerns his little girl, Virginia."

Belinda corrected him. "You mean his foster child. They call her Ginni."

He furrowed his brows, steepling those hands in front of him, and said with judicial certainty, "His *own* child, the will indicates. Yes, it does, quite clearly."

Aware, too late, of the surprise on Belinda's face, he gave them a stern look. "Now, ladies," he said, turning from one to the other, "I must beg for your discretion. I

167

assumed this detail was common knowledge."

Belinda smiled. "Of course, Mr. Lougherbrey. Now tell me some more about my friends, the Gunnings. Do you think he'll run for governor?"

It seemed the ideal moment to leave, and Lindsey did so, with renewed thanks for the meal, saying that she had work to do. It was true because if she was going to have that project done for Shula tomorrow, she had to make a good start on it tonight.

She closed her door softly behind her and made sure it was locked since Mr. Lougherbrey's room was nearby.

First, change into work clothes. Next, download the photos from the Nikon. Then, take a look and see what we have, and . . . it was no use.

She wasn't going to get anything done until her mind stopped buzzing. Think it through.

Ben Fletcher was Ginni's father? Obviously, Natalie was not her mother. Ginni had lived with them as a foster child for four years.

She felt as if she'd been handed an important bit of information, but she didn't know what to do with it.

Who else knew?

Ben's closest friend, Colin McAlister. He knew; she was sure of it. Perhaps that's why he'd been so close-mouthed the other night. But what did this have to do with the dogs?

Should she ask him? No, she didn't feel like doing that.

What about Fraser? If he knew, there was no point in saying anything, and if he didn't, it was because Colin hadn't told him. She would respect that decision. Same for Alexa and Remi.

For now, she'd have to file away this puzzling information and get to work on something she did understand.

By noon the next day, Max Lougherbrey had left, and Lindsey, who had worked all morning on the presentation for Shula, was glad to have the house to herself.

Belinda might have been eager to discuss the mysterious will, but she had gone to visit Shula and then into Port Angeles to buy a new suit.

The presentation was ready, Lindsey told herself, but she had time for a quick run on the beach, and she'd better take advantage of it.

She let the wind blow across her face and through her hair, hoping it would blow away the fogginess of a too-short night. She'd worked late and had awakened early to the sound of Vance's voice in her dream. Would she ever be rid of that man?

And then there was Edric. Really, she should phone him again—he might need an ally against Vance.

She broke into a sprint, and her pounding feet kept time with her thoughts. Even though she was on personal days, she wasn't going to stay here indefinitely, waiting to see what terrible thing happened next.

What could she do that was proactive? Talk to Shula? Find out what she knew about Ben Fletcher? How would that help? Was she feeling desperate again? Had she forgotten the verses she'd read this morning and last night?

At the far end of the beach, Jack stepped out from the trees, carrying his backpack and easel. He set it up in the usual place and waved her to come over.

By the time she got there, he was putting the last touches on a painting. She studied it with interest: a seascape with long green filaments growing across it. He had a piece of moss hanging off one end of the easel and he was mixing his greens to match it.

He stepped back, cocking his head. "Too surreal?"

"No," she said. "Moss and vines! You've got great ideas, Jack."

He took a swig from the bottle on his easel, gesturing. "Nah. It's this FlowerFire. Sharpens the eye. Better than weed. You might find it useful in your work too."

Not likely. To humor him, she asked, "Where do you get it?"

"Miz Shula. Charges me an exorbitant amount. She whips up some pretty weird concoctions, but this one really works. She takes it herself."

He put the bottle back. "She ever give you a ride in her plane? You'll see what I mean."

Lindsey nodded, remembering Shula's edge of excitement that night.

"I'd think twice before flying with that lady." He stirred his brush into a jar of water, tinting it green. "She tanks up with a big dose beforehand, and it sure does set her on fire."

He tilted his head, looking secretive. "Speaking of fireworks—has she told you her opinion of Ben Fletcher?"

"Not really. What do you know about Ben?"

Jack shrugged. "An okay guy. Works hard. Really cool with dogs." He swished the brush back and forth, pulled it out, and tapped off the droplets of water. "I don't have much use for him, personally. He fired me—didn't even give me a second chance—and it's hard to take that from an Indian."

She let the slur go by. "Why'd he fire you?"

Again Jack shrugged, excusing himself. "Forgot something. Grams says he's overprotective of his dogs. Anyhow, it turned out okay because I got hired by Miz Shula. Some of her jobs are worthy of my talents."

A peculiar thing to say.

He was grinning now, a crooked, sly grin. "I can tell you one thing: no one hates Ben Fletcher as much as she does."

"How come?"

"Dunno." He turned back to his painting, but Lindsey had a feeling that he knew exactly why—if she could

170

believe him at all.

There was no point in hanging around any longer, and since this was Thursday, she'd better make that visit to Odela.

"See you, Jack," she said.

"Uh-huh." He chewed on his lip, staring at the canvas, and didn't look up.

When Lindsey knocked, Odela called out a greeting. It sounded more effusive than usual, but she went inside, threaded her way through the clutter, and handed Odela the piece of cheesecake she'd brought.

Odela looked up with a wavering smile. "It is our dear friend—lookit this! She has come to see Odela. What a treat! Shake her hand."

Without moving, she continued in a hoarse voice, "Hello, my dear. Odela had a bad night, but she is very glad you came. Odela will enjoy this cake. Jack doesn't bring her cake. He doesn't want her to get fat."

She patted the chair beside her, and as Lindsey sat down, the old woman leaned toward her. "Odela is worried."

Her breath reeked of alcohol. So that was it.

"Odela worries a lot about Jack. He is very smart. He is a nice boy, but he gets into trouble. Odela had to move here with him. Odela will tell her dear friend a secret. Wait."

She reached back to tug at something behind her, finally pulling a slender bottle out from under the cushion.

After taking a sip, she smiled. "Odela feels better now. She has her secrets, and Jack has his. He likes to put on his costumes and go out to scare people. Odela thinks that is not very nice, but he never hurts anybody, he says."

Odela began mumbling to herself, and Lindsey got up to wash the dishes in the sink. It was much too hot in here,

171

and the steaming water didn't help at all.

She took off her sweater. What was this about costumes?

Odela watched her, still smiling, and raised her voice, keeping up a steady monologue, partly about Jack and partly about the dogs she had cared for.

Finally she fell silent, and Lindsey decided to leave. She would save the beads she'd brought for another time. Maybe tomorrow.

Odela didn't seem to notice when she said goodbye, and she stepped outside with relief. Cool air!

Now it was off to Shula's. She'd show her the presentation and get away as soon as she could.

They watched the presentation together on Shula's laptop, and Shula praised it lavishly and wrote Lindsey a check for the full amount.

"Before I forget," Shula said, "I'm having a couple of Muslim girls over tomorrow evening. Could you possibly join us for supper? I'm sure you'll find it interesting—you're such a people person."

Was she? But Lindsey said, "I can come if you'd like. What time?"

"Around six. Nothing formal. Just wear what you had on the other night."

Shula gestured at the laptop. "I can't get over how good you are with your camera—and running down the beach at the same time! You could make a lot of money doing promos like this."

Lindsey smiled. "It's not my favorite thing. Maybe once in a while."

"You could do promos that are more challenging." Shula tilted her head. "It would pay tremendously well."

When Lindsey didn't answer, she said, "Of course, you're busy with the magazine, aren't you? How's the current feature shaping up?"

Cautiously, Lindsey said, "I've collected a lot of information so far."

"What about the photos?"

"Photos?"

"Come on, Lin. You need photos of Ben Fletcher's dogs if you're doing a feature on them."

How had she found out? But this was a small town.

"I've having a little trouble getting the photos. Ben's been busy and . . ."

"Not very cooperative, right? You don't have to be evasive with me. I've known Ben Fletcher for years, and I can imagine what you're going through."

Lindsey zipped Shula's check into her shoulder bag. Time to leave.

"Look," Shula said, "I want to help you. You need those photos, right? Let's go talk to Ben."

"I don't think so." Especially since Shula hated Ben, according to Jack. "Really, it's not necessary," Lindsey said. "I can—"

Shula jumped up, took her hand, pulled her out of her chair. "You shy thing! If you don't ask, you're not going to get. And I know how to handle Ben Fletcher."

Was this the break she'd been waiting for? It didn't feel right. But Shula was towing her out of the door.

"C'mon. I'm driving. It'll just take a minute, and it might be fun."

The woman's face was alive with . . . excitement? Mischief? It was hard to tell, but this felt more and more like a mistake.

Shula drove down the highway at break-neck speed, whipped her car up the Fletchers' driveway, and stopped with a flourish behind Ben's truck.

"I'll be right back," she said, and by the time she stepped out of her car, Ben was striding across the gravel.

No one else was in sight. Remi's truck was gone.

Shula moved toward him, a tiny, graceful figure, and he halted beside his truck, as solid and daunting as Lindsey had ever seen him.

"Hello, Ben," Shula said. "Haven't seen you for a while." Her voice was low and husky. Provocative.

"That's right." He looked ill at ease.

How would a man be affected by those dancing eyes?

"I have brought my good friend, Lindsey Dumont."

"I know her." He didn't take his eyes from Shula.

Shula tilted her head and spoke in a sweetly imploring voice. "Ben, I've come to ask a favor. Won't you let her take a couple pictures of your dogs? She'll write good things about them."

"No one comes near my dogs," he growled. "Not until I find out . . . something."

She stepped close, so close that she might be going to embrace him, and put a hand on his sleeve. She looked up at him, speaking abruptly in Makah.

All Lindsey could decipher was a name: Ginni.

Ben shook her hand off and folded his arms in front of him. He said something, clipped and furious, and Shula raised her small pert chin as she answered.

She leaned back from him. "So be it, Ben Fletcher. Take the consequences."

She whirled away, and his angry stare followed.

She marched to the car, swinging her hips, and slid inside. "That's that, Lin. No photos. I'm sorry."

But she didn't look sorry. Malicious, perhaps. The hint of a smile curved her lips, and the golden eyes held a gleam of triumph.

On the short drive back, Shula chattered about a mountain property she was trying to sell, as if the whole encounter had never happened.

But it had, and Lindsey's throat clenched until she

could hardly breathe. The undercurrents had been much too real. And yes, the woman did hate Ben.

Once they returned to Shula's house, she left immediately, and she didn't catch her breath until she turned out onto the highway.

She should never have let Shula take charge like that. What was going on between those two?

And as far as her project was concerned, Shula had made everything worse. What did Ben think of her now? And what about Remi, when he heard?

She had to talk to someone. Fraser.

He stood at the counter, carving, and he glanced up with a smile. "What can I do for you, Lin?"

She was so glad to see his dark, calm face that she could hardly keep her voice from trembling. "Do you have a minute, Fraser? Can I buy you lunch?"

His warm brown eyes rested on her for a minute. "I have a customer coming to pick up a book, so I can't leave," he said. "But I never did eat lunch, now that you mention it. Why don't you get us a couple of sandwiches from the bakery?"

"Good idea. What would you like?"

"Corned beef on rye with extra sauerkraut," he said. "No pickle."

"I'll be right back."

She bought herself a chicken sandwich and added a few chocolate-chip cookies to the order, moving like an robot, wondering if this was another mistake.

They sat in the children's nook because he could see the front door from there, and he asked a blessing on the food. They ate in silence, or at least, he ate heartily and she nibbled at her sandwich. After a few minutes, she pushed it aside.

Should she have come to him like this? He'd think her

a spineless idiot. Right.

She got up to pour their coffee and sat down, but hers was too hot, so she emptied half of it into the drinking fountain, filled her cup with cold water, and stared at it, remembering the expression on Shula's face.

He reached for a cookie and said, "Tell me, Lin."

She took a gulp of water and almost choked. "I did something stupid, and it can't be fixed, but I hope you don't mind my telling you."

She could have wept at the kindness in his eyes.

At his nod, she described the whole incident, beginning with Shula's first questions about the magazine project.

He asked, "What could you have done differently?"

"I could have refused and walked out of her house." She poked at her sandwich. "It makes me mad because that's not my style, letting people push me into things."

"I know." He smiled, as if to himself. "But it's not your style to be rude, and you have hopes for Shula. Did you have any idea she'd handle it the way she did?"

"No. I didn't realize she knew him that well. But now it's going to look like I went running to her with my troubles and forced my way in. I've tried not to pester Ben."

"You haven't been the least bit pushy," he said with quiet assurance. "Don't beat yourself up about this. We all know Shula. And Colin's not going to—"

She shook her head impatiently, and he stopped.

Why did people keep bringing up that man's name? He didn't even live here.

"With all due respect, I don't care what Colin McAlister thinks. I'm worried about Ben. And Remi."

"And your project," he said with a quiet smile.

"My project?" Defeat gnawed at her. "It's virtually dead. And I'm taking personal days off." She sighed. "Ben and Remi will think I put Shula up to it. I'd hate that."

Fraser drank from his cup, slowly. "There's a lot of

history that you don't know." He paused. "What's the Lord been saying to you in his Word?"

"You ask the hardest questions." She thought for a minute. "Okay. Philippians. Something about *He who began a good work in you will* . . . finish it."

His eyes shone. "So, can you accept this from his hand? Part of his working in your life?"

She nodded.

"And if you wish you'd done something differently, tell him that. But don't worry about Ben and Remi. They'll know Shula engineered the whole thing. And Remi would always give you the benefit of any doubt. You know that."

"I guess so."

He put his cup down. "I think God is working out something, and I think he's using you. Can you be patient with what he's doing?"

"I'll try." She gave him the best smile she could find. "Thank you, Fraser."

A customer had come into the store, so he stood to his feet, but he paused, gazing at her. "Any time you want to talk, I'm here, Lin. Remember that."

She left from the side door and walked down the hill to Bay Street, telling herself that they'd had a good talk and now she was encouraged.

Fraser had been more than kind. He was right. Let go of what happened. She added her own advice: Be smarter the next time you're with Shula.

She had hoped Fraser would say something about Ben and Shula, but she'd learned only that there had been a relationship between them, as she suspected. Of course he wouldn't tell her. He was a friend who kept secrets.

16

caption:

Multiple Exposures

Lindsey took her time on the way back to the Roost, and she had just parked in the driveway when her cell phone rang. Remi.

"Hi, Lin—how's it going?" he said.

Her stomach twisted. "Kind of a strange day."

She walked around the side of the house to where the bluff overlooked the water.

"Yeah." He paused. "I just found out that you and Shula came over here."

"We did. I wish we hadn't. It really backfired. I'm sorry."

There, she'd said it.

"I was wondering what happened."

She found a rock to sit on, and she told him.

For a minute, he was quiet. Finally he said, "Ben's been in bad shape ever since that lawyer came over this morning. Natalie had gone into town, and the lawyer talked to Ben for a long time. Then—"

CALL LOST, her phone said.

She phoned him back immediately. *Your call has been forwarded . . .*

A second later, her phone rang.

"Sorry, Lin. My phone's been acting up. Anyway, after talking to that lawyer, the visit from Shula just about sent him over the edge."

So Ben hadn't told Remi about the will.

Lindsey remembered the anger in Ben's eyes. "Shula said something to him right at the end, and I couldn't hear it, but he almost exploded. It's like she was taunting him the whole time."

"Don't feel bad, Lin. She was using you for an excuse. He's already told her not to come around here. That's because one day she dropped in and started sweet-talking Ginni."

"Ginni? How come?"

"I guess Ginni is actually her sister's child."

"Cheree?"

"Yeah, I'm not sure of the details. But wow! I've never seen Ben this upset. He took a can of beer and his knife out to the woods for a couple of hours. Now he's walking around looking sick."

"How's Natalie?"

"Okay, all things considered. Back when they got Ginni, she went along with Ben, so she knows about the connection to Shula. And you probably haven't noticed, but Natalie and Shula . . . um . . . don't get along very well."

He paused. "Colin's coming back out this weekend, so that might help."

Lindsey stared into the darkened bushes. But . . . Ben and Cheree? Even the Paragon couldn't fix this.

"Does he come out every weekend?" she said.

"Almost. Whenever he can get away."

"What about his kids?"

"His kids at the university? He spends a lot of his spare time hiking and stuff with them, but the Fletchers are really his family. And these days, Ben sure needs him."

A babble of children's voices rose in the background

and Remi said, "Guess I'd better go. Thanks, Lin."

"Thanks, Remi," she mumbled.

She couldn't see much of the water, but the waves were there, swishing against the rocks below. Dusk had fallen, and behind the overhanging branches, the sky was deepening to gray. Maybe if she sat still—just watched the sky and listened to the waves—she could think.

No, this was too much to process. All she could do was make a list.

She'd told Remi what happened and he didn't seem to blame her.

She'd learned that something in the will had upset Ben.

And that Ginni was Ben's daughter, Shula's niece.

And that Colin McAlister wasn't safely married, as she'd thought. (Not especially pertinent, but it would keep her from asking about his wife and children.)

A light drizzle began to fall, and after a while she realized that she was stiff and cold. She stood up to stretch, turned, and went into the house.

"My goodness, you're all wet, I'm sure," Belinda said, but Lindsey smiled and kept going.

She hadn't made it halfway up the stairs when the phone rang, and a minute later, Belinda was calling her back.

Quincy Corbin. Would she go to lunch with him tomorrow?

Would she? He was a useful source of information, and besides, if she talked to him a little more, she could decide whether he had any connection with the problems at Cedar Run.

Yes, she would, she told him. When? Where? No, she'd drive her own car, thank you.

That night, she tried to ignore her clamoring thoughts, started reading a Sherlock Holmes story, stopped, and went to the Psalms.

Another page corner broke off. Milly's Bible wasn't holding up well. She'd have to buy a new one.

The next morning after breakfast, she drove a short distance up the coast to explore a different beach.

This one was more rugged than Thorsen's Beach, but the sea stacks offshore were fascinating, and as the light changed, she took one picture after another.

She jogged, pushing herself hard, and finally paused to rest on one of the tall black rocks—basalt, according to Colin McAlister.

While she was looking at the photos she'd taken, her phone rang.

Edric.

He sounded as if he'd had a good lunch. "We've been talking about your problems out there—"

(*WE?* Don't you and I usually discuss these things just between us, Edric?)

"—and Vance doesn't think we can salvage the serial idea, but he'd like us to run the Carolina dogs feature and add a couple photos of those Indian kennels. Sort of a parenthetical comment, how those people are trying to raise the same dogs but have problems."

Not for the world was she going to do such a thing.

"And how would I get these photos?"

"Use your telephoto, girl, like we did last summer on the Arizona ranch. A great feature!"

"I wasn't very proud of that, Edric. Listen, there's someone out to get these people. Their dogs have been poisoned and one of their children has been kidnapped. I can't sneak around taking unauthorized pictures of their business."

"You got a better idea?"

"Yes." The puppy shots she'd taken at the reservation. "I'll send you a sample," she said.

Someone was talking in the background, and Edric said,

"Okay—gotta run. Call me later."

She closed her phone, promising herself that whatever happened, Vance wasn't going to get his way with this. Totally unprofessional. Unscrupulous. Never again would she let herself be pressured into doing it.

After tinkering with three of the best puppy photos, she added the puppy-in-shadows shot that she'd showed to Fraser and sent them off.

As soon as she could, she'd run up to Neah Bay—maybe even get enough shots for a whole feature. Edric would like them, she was sure. What about Vance?

She shrugged. For now she had better things to do than worry about the magazine. These were personal days, right? Enjoy them. For one thing, there was the supper at Shula's with the Muslim girls tonight.

And what about Odela? She would take her the beads she'd found and hope she was feeling better.

First, stop off at the Roost to get Odela another piece of cheesecake from Belinda and change into something cooler.

Odela was sober, and she seemed to be hard at work. She motioned Lindsey close so she could see the necklace of tiny brown beads with silver that she was finishing.

"That's a herringbone-stitched tube," she said. "Those are fun."

"There must be hundreds of beads in that," Lindsey said.

"There sure are," Odela said. "I'm going to mail it today. And I haven't forgotten about yours."

Lindsey sat down beside her, and Odela rummaged in a box.

"I was thinking of raw emeralds for the green stones." Odela held them out in her small palm: polished chunks of deep green with networks of lines running through them.

"Look at those inclusions," Odela said. "I think it makes them look prettier than jeweler emeralds."

"I agree," Lindsey said. "When you're finished, be sure to tell me how much I owe you."

The old woman looked up at her with a shy smile. "Nah. I'm calling this a gift of love. No charge."

"But I could at least pay for your supplies. Those emeralds, and the silver." She touched the silver links.

"Nope. Wear it and think of me, as they say. You going to stay around here for a while?"

"I'm not sure," Lindsey said. "Some things I'd counted on are all messed up."

Odela nodded. "I know about that."

How could she explain to this woman what she was feeling—what it felt like to wait for God to do something? She would try.

"But you know what?" Lindsey said. "I've been reading the Bible. There's promises there from God—"

"—Alexa talks to me about God, and it always makes me sad."

"Why?"

"Because she knows God and I don't. He'd never bother with someone like me."

"I feel sad too, when I think about some of the things I've done," Lindsey said. "If God and I were just people, we wouldn't even be on speaking terms. But God isn't just people. He's made a way so that my bad stuff—my sins—don't separate me from him anymore."

"See, I told you, you're lucky."

"He did it for you too, Odela. He punished his Son for our sins. Mine and yours. It's a gift of love, like the necklace you're making for me. He paid all the costs."

The old eyes filled with tears, but she brushed them away. "I heard about that. Maybe I'll think about it some more, when I get time."

"I hope you do," Lindsey said. "Oh, here are some beads. I found them in a store and thought of you."

She left soon after, thinking that she'd buy a Bible for Odela when she bought herself a new one, and while she was unlocking her car, Jack rode up on his bike.

He jumped off it, his face wind-burned and happy. "Guess where I've been?"

"I never could."

"Remember the painting I did of Tatoosh Island? I went up to the overlook to watch some eagles."

"But that's Cape Flattery! You biked all the way up?"

"Yup. Sometimes I borrow Shula's truck, but this time I didn't take any painting stuff. Just went for fun."

"You amaze me, really!"

He looked pleased and stood a little straighter in his black jacket. "I'll tell you something else. I've got a cabin up there—it's an old heap I found. My eagle eyrie, I call it. A great place to crash when I've been painting all day."

"From the map, it looks like wilderness. Don't you ever get lost?"

"Sure, sometimes. But I'm careful. Like for my cabin, I just have to go to the overlook, and there's some roads going off it, but I know that my road is at seven o'clock. I keep it hidden behind brambles, and if I stay on it—with a couple turns—I'm okay."

"Seven o'clock?"

"It's my own invention. You start with the island at twelve o'clock."

"Ingenious," she said.

"Maybe I'll show you sometime. My cabin's going to be quite cool. I've already got the eagle up."

"An eagle? I hope it's not a real one."

"Brass. I found it in someone's trash. Looks real nice over my front door."

Odela's voice reached them. She stood at the door with

a package. "It's all ready, Jack. Hurry, so you don't miss the mail."

"I have to hurry, too," Lindsey said. "See you around, Jack."

She left, heading toward the restaurant Quinn had described, and when she turned into the parking lot, she saw that his truck was already there.

It wasn't much more than a diner, but it was clean, and this Friday noon, it was crowded with men, some wearing camouflage jackets, who looked as if they worked outdoors.

Quinn escorted her to a booth with a speaker that hung over their heads. Whoever was dropping coins into the juke box must have a fondness for country music, and apparently this meal was going to be accompanied by mournful songs about lost dreams and a faithful dog.

"I'll be right back," Quinn said. He strolled up to the counter and returned with a pitcher of strong black tea and a plate of something that looked like folded tortillas.

These were Indian Tacos, he told her, the best eating on the whole coast.

He helped himself to one, took a large bite, and orange grease oozed from the other end.

It was an unfamiliar sort of taco—thick, soft, and brown-fried. After her first bite, she peeked inside: plenty of greasy fried hamburger, a green chili, shreds of head lettuce, and cheese that had melted into the grease from the meat and ran out onto her hand.

He didn't seem to notice when she stopped eating, and he told her the latest news about his breeding program— thriving; his sisters—they don't have much time for me; and his house—lots of space, you'd like it.

She also learned that he owned the cabin where Jack lived on Thorsen's Creek, that Jack wasn't doing a good job cleaning up the goat pens, and that Jack had tried to sell him a painting and was going to be evicted if he didn't start working harder.

He asked about her work and, without getting any details, told her to fight for her rights and by the way, the next time she was at the Fletcher's, could she remind Ben that he really wanted that property?

Was he the one causing Ben's problems? Not likely.

Quinn gazed at her with hope. Would she want to come and see his spread sometime? He could introduce her to Earlene and Ethel.

Lindsey searched her memory. The sisters? No, the breeder nannies.

She sidestepped the invitation and began making remarks about getting back to work, and finally he took the hint. He walked her to the Jeep, said how marvelous it was to talk to her—and how lonely he was—and waved as she drove off.

The information about Jack might be useful, but apart from that . . . What had she expected, anyway? Chalk it up to experience.

She stopped at the bakery for a quick sandwich, ate it in her car, and drove over to the bookstore. Fraser, standing at the counter, gave her a smiling glance as she walked in. "How are you today, Lin?"

"Better than the last time you saw me. But I must say that I've just had the least memorable lunch of my life."

"I'm waiting with bated breath."

"I found out what Indian Tacos are."

He grinned, and she said, "Tell me—you wouldn't take a girl out to lunch and feed her Indian Tacos, would you?"

"Depends on whether she's an Indian."

"No! No self-respecting girl would eat those things. Unless she had a death wish."

"You don't like ethnic food?"

"I love ethnic food, especially if it's Oriental, but this

186

wasn't ethnic. It was faux-ethnic-greasy-spoon."

He looked at her, still grinning, and she said, "I can tell you're shocked. What I really came for is a couple of Bibles."

She told him what she wanted, asked his advice, and chose two from the ones he showed her. While she was paying for them, he said, "Would you like to read with Ginni for me?"

"Ginni?" She glanced into the back room and saw her at the table, bent over a sheet of paper.

"Yes, I teach her English and reading. Natalie sends her to me on Wednesday and Friday afternoons. It helps Natalie with the homeschooling. Besides, I enjoy it."

He took a book from under the counter. "I've got your book here. It would be good for her to read with someone besides me."

Lindsey hesitated. Her book was a photo essay, black-and-white photographs of disadvantaged children. Across from each photograph was a descriptive paragraph. How would Ginni relate to these children?

"It's designed for discussion," she said, "not for reading practice."

"So, discuss—that's even better."

"You thought I needed a challenge today, didn't you? I'm not one of her favorite people, remember."

He smiled. "I think it'll be fine."

She hung her jacket on a coat-peg in the back room while Fraser was talking to Ginni.

"Looks like you're doing good work there, Ginni," he said. "Here's Miss Lindsey. Why don't you show her your picture?"

The child looked up with a frown, but something in Fraser's face must have made her decide to cooperate. "Okay."

Lindsey sat down beside her, not too close, and Ginni

pushed the piece of paper in her general direction.

It was a page full of black and green trees, heavily crayoned, with a very small child standing in the midst of them.

"I like your trees," Lindsey said. "They look like the ones around here. I've never seen such huge trees."

Ginni didn't look up, but she took the page back and added another tree. A black one.

Fraser put Lindsey's book in front of her. "I'd like you to read this book with Miss Lindsey. She took the pictures in it, so she can answer all your questions."

The child looked surprised, but she shrugged and opened the book.

She leaned over the first picture. A thin black boy sat nose-to-nose with a fuzzy stuffed lion. He held it by the tail, suspended in the air.

Lindsey couldn't forget Sam. She'd taken dozens of shots, coming back each day, before she caught the look of intense concentration that she wanted.

"What's he doing?" Ginni said.

Fraser still stood there. "Read the words."

Ginni inched closer to the book and read the sentences aloud that introduced Samuel and his lion, Alfie, and said that he was teaching Alfie to sing.

Ginni looked at Lindsey. "Why's he doing that?"

"Sam didn't have a mother or father or any brothers and sisters," she said. "All he had was Alfie. So he sang to him every day and every night."

Ginni was nodding.

"After a while, he thought he could hear Alfie singing back to him. Just one song—'Jingle Bells'—his favorite. He decided to try teaching him another song, and that's what he's doing here."

Ginni nodded again. "He's pretending, of course. Sometimes I talk to Spot and pretend that he talks back to me. But I never tried teaching him to sing."

She took another look at the boy and slowly turned the page.

She looked first at the picture of a plump girl with blond hair that fell across her face. The girl sat hunched into a chair, holding a fluffy gray-plush cat against her face. Her eyes were closed.

"That's Ramona and Kit," Lindsey said.

"Is she asleep?"

Fraser had gone, but Ginni knew what to do, and she read the paragraph aloud. It said that Ramona couldn't see Kit, but she liked to touch Kit's soft fur, and her tickly whiskers, and her button nose.

"How come she can't see Kit?" Ginni said.

"Ramona's blind," Lindsey said. "How do you think that would feel?"

Ginni closed her eyes and opened them again quickly. "Awful! I'd hate it." She stared at the picture for a minute and put a gentle finger on the cat's nose. "I'm glad she's got Kit."

Fraser was having a busy afternoon, with customers coming and going, and before long, Lindsey heard a voice she recognized. She sensed that Colin McAlister stood in the front room, watching them.

Ginni started to turn the page, glanced up, and saw him.

"Mister Colin!" She scrambled across the table and ran up the aisle.

He stepped out to meet her, opening his arms wide, and she flew into them. He picked her up as easily as if she were three years old, carried her to the table, and stopped there, smiling past her at Lindsey.

"What are you reading, Ginni?" he said in his deep voice.

"A book. Let's go for a walk."

"I'd like to see this book."

189

She put her arms around his neck and sighed. "Okay. That woman was telling me about it."

He sat down, but his knees didn't fit under the table, so he shifted Ginni onto the bench between them.

"And do you remember what this lady's name is?"

She leaned back, gave him a charming smile, and shook her head.

His voice grew firm. "Yes, you do. Tell me, Ginni."

"Miss Lindsey."

"Right. Now let's read a little more."

Ginni pulled the book closer and turned the page. "Oh, it's Spot!"

The black-and-white dog did resemble Spot, but Colin had seen a difference. "What about his ears?"

"Yeah," Ginni said. "They're bigger."

She studied the photo. The small, Hispanic-looking boy was lying on his back with the toy dog crouched on his belly. His left hand, heavily bandaged, lay beside him. With the other, he held the dog by its neck.

Ginni looked at Lindsey. "What's he doing?"

She smiled. "Read it."

Ginni read far enough to find out that the boy's name was Tomas. She twisted around to look up at Colin. "She knows these kids. She talked to them."

She touched Lindsey's arm. "What happened to his hand?"

"It got cut."

He'd slashed it the week before, deliberately grabbing a teacher's scissors in a fit of anger. One of the aides had done something that offended him.

Ginni was silent. "He looks sad or mad or something. How come?"

Lindsey sighed in spite of herself. "He cut himself on purpose and we don't know why. His dog is the only one Tomas will talk to, and even then, Tomas whispers, so no one else can hear."

Colin looked at her over Ginni's head. "You really know these children?"

"I told you—" Ginni began.

He flipped to the book's front cover. "Photographs by Lindsey Dumont. You're right, Ginni."

But Ginni had lost interest. She lifted her head at the sound of Natalie's voice, edged across Colin, and ran into the front room.

Almost immediately, Fraser called to them. "Miss Lindsey? Mister Colin? Ginni has something she wants to say to you."

"Uh-huh," he said, "I didn't think she'd get away with that."

They joined Fraser and Natalie, who stood by the counter, looking down at Ginni. She ran to Colin and grabbed his hand, saying, "Thank you for reading with me, Mister Colin." She turned, still holding onto him, and gave Lindsey a worried look.

Lindsey went down on one knee, at eye level with the child, and said softly, "Thank you, Ginni, for reading with me."

Ginni's lip quivered. "Thank you, Miss Lindsey."

Colin patted Ginni's shoulder and she ran off, with Natalie hurrying after her.

Lindsey watched them go.

Ginni was a complicated child. Perhaps they could be friends after all. She turned back to where the men stood.

"Thanks for helping out with Ginni," Fraser said. "I think she enjoyed it. She's making progress." He gestured to the end of the counter. "Don't forget your books. The other one you ordered should be in tomorrow."

As she started to pick up the package, he said, "I meant to ask, how was your night out with Shula?"

She shrugged.

"You were supposed to have fun," he said.

"I tried, I really did."

"Not your kind of fun?" Colin said.

"I don't know. I liked the Thai food and the plane ride. I usually enjoy supper and shopping with friends, but after a while it seemed . . . pointless."

She glanced up and saw her photograph of Kumtux, framed and hanging on the wall. "Look what you did with Kumtux! That's a beautiful frame. You carved it, didn't you? May I see?"

Fraser went behind the counter to take it down for her, and she traced the intricate lines with a finger. "I wish I knew more about carving. Do you make a plan?"

"Sort of. Usually in my mind." He put the picture to one side and said, "I have a question, Lin."

Colin was watching her; she knew it without looking, and something about his silent scrutiny made her fidget. Get him talking, that's what she'd do.

She turned. "May I have a word with you about your pal? He seems to have an unfortunate propensity for asking questions. Hard ones."

He smiled down at her. "Unfortunate it is. Also unreasonable and unsettling. We've discussed his problem, and he has tried to reform, but it seems to be unremitting. Especially when there's a full moon."

Very good.

They exchanged a smile, but Fraser said, "Look who's talking! Just the other night in Alexa's kitchen, the first time we had a conversation—and me practically a stranger, somewhat shy, as you know—this lady asked a string of questions that made me dizzy. In less than five minutes."

"That's different," Lindsey said. "I was interviewing you. Didn't you know? In case I do an article on the extraordinary inhabitants of Cameron Bay. I left out a few things. What do you eat for breakfast?"

"You're stalling," Fraser said. "I'm the one with a question now."

"Is he always like this?" she said to Colin. "Is there any hope?"

He looked at her, his blue eyes alight. "Can't escape. Might as well humor him."

"Upstream again," she said. "My life has become a series of fish ladders. Now watch, he's not going to ask me a nice ordinary question about my breakfast or even about f-stops or shutter speeds. It's going to be a hard one. Okay, what's your question?"

"What is an f-stop, anyway?" Fraser said quickly. "I know about short stops, and backstops, and bus stops, but f-stops?"

She laughed. "The man is impossible! The answer is, ask Colin. And it certainly has been an experience, talking with you guys, but I have work to do."

She reached for her package.

"Colin," Fraser said, still behind the counter. "Rope her in and bring her back."

"No, no, I'll come quietly. Do we have to be serious now?"

Fraser nodded.

He did look serious, so she leaned against the counter and waited.

"About Shula," he said. "I was wondering: what's the impression you get of her?"

"That's not fair, especially after yesterday. Let me think." She rested an elbow on the counter and half-closed her eyes. "Fog, maybe."

Fraser gave her an encouraging nod. "Fog?"

"Yes. At least, the impression I get of her is blurred. There's a film technique called deep focus—every element in the picture is clearly visible. I wish I had a deep focus shot of Shula and whatever's around her."

She shook her head. "Fog may not be the best analogy because fog is a happy thing for me. Shula's not a happy person."

"You're right." Colin's voice had chilled.

What did he know about Shula?

"Kind of eerie, Lin," Fraser said.

"Not really. I've done quite a few things with her, and she puzzles me, especially when she plays the drama queen."

"Drama queen?" Fraser said.

"You know—a person who's sort of melodramatic."

He smiled and shook his head. "A serious defect in my education. Go on."

"She can turn it on and off to suit her purpose. And that's another of my questions—her purpose. She wants something from me. I'm not sure what. Maybe it doesn't matter. But I don't want to make any more mistakes like I did yesterday."

She glanced at Colin. He'd been standing beside her, silent, and his eyes had gone dark. She faced him. "You've got that look again."

The ocean at a thousand fathoms. Unreadable. How did he do it?

"You know something," she said. "And you're not going to tell me."

He shrugged, but his deep voice was amiable. "I have only opinions. Not particularly helpful. You'll do better without them, believe me."

She gazed up at him, wanting to see past the inscrutable blue, wanting to understand him, and she sensed the man's strength, his integrity, his kindness. He wasn't being obstructive.

"I do believe you," she said quietly.

He blinked and looked away, as if she'd seen more than he intended.

She turned back to the counter, and oddly enough, Fraser was smiling to himself.

"So," she said, "I'm still running blind. Where did I leave my jacket?"

She went to get it from the back room, and Colin said something to Fraser.

When she returned, Fraser asked, "Do you have plans for supper tonight?"

"Now that's the kind of question I like. But as it happens, I do."

She resisted the impulse to let them wonder. "Shula's having a couple of Muslim girls over for the evening, and she invited me to come. I'll go, but I really don't know why she wants me there."

"Maybe she likes to demonstrate her multicultural spirit," Fraser said. "You'll be Exhibit A: the successful, white, East-coast professional who is also a woman. As well as her friend."

Colin's dark brows had gathered into a frown. Yes, he had opinions about Shula.

"I almost wish I weren't going," she said. "She's got all this anger inside her and she's cruel to her dogs, but I can't just write her off. There's a real person there, somewhere."

She paused, and Fraser gave her a thoughtful nod, so she went on. "When I talk to Shula about God, she asks questions, at least. And now she's got those girls coming. I'm not sure how to respond to them."

Fraser leaned forward. "You're not running blind, Lin. Just be yourself. Remember what we talked about yesterday—the Lord has brought you here for a reason."

"Thanks, Fraser." She smiled at him. "Again."

She picked up her jacket, and Colin took it, stepping close to help her put it on.

She was aware of him, of his height and breadth, but he seemed preoccupied.

She murmured her thanks.

"Remi should know about this supper," he said. "May I tell him?"

She nodded, and Fraser said, "We'll pray for you."

"That's what I need," she said, taking her purse and the package from the counter.

Outside, the afternoon light had started to fade. She'd spent longer in there than she intended. But she might have made some headway with Ginni . . . and what a pair, those two!

She headed toward the Roost. Time for Exhibit A to get dressed.

caption:

Black Eyes

Jack opened the door and ushered her in, wearing a black suit that was only slightly wrinkled. He gave her an elaborate bow.

"Ah," she said, "our faithful butler at work once more. Thank you."

Shula appeared, elegant in gold and white. "Lin! How good to see you again!" Her voice sounded a trifle higher than usual.

She linked her arm with Lindsey's and took her into a stately room with a stone fireplace, tapestries on the walls, and multiple windows that framed a view of forested hills. The sun, as if commanded for the occasion, was setting with crimson streamers.

Three girls stood beside the fireplace, holding goblets. Shula handed a glass of ginger ale to Lindsey and introduced her: "My dear friend, Lindsey Dumont. She's a photographer from New York. You may have seen the book she's published."

Exhibit A. Top score to you, Fraser.

The sisters, students at the university, were attractive in their hijabs. The oldest seemed to be the most talkative, and in the course of the conversation, mentioned their involvement in several MSA events.

Shula glanced at Lindsey. "That's the Muslim Student Association. It has a rather influential presence on campus." She smiled. "Now, shall we eat?"

She led them into a dining alcove at the end of the room, to a table set with silver and china. A uniformed woman served them a lavish catered meal.

Lindsey did her part to keep the conversation flowing as they ate, but the oldest girl seemed to have an agenda, a specifically Islamic one.

"You have no idea," she said, addressing the silver candelabra, "how difficult it is to be Muslim these days. Ever since 9-11, we get treated like we're all terrorists."

"Please," one of her sisters said. "Don't start."

"No, really! People are so quick to stereotype. They think, oh no! Look at her. She's so weird in that head scarf. She must be a terrorist."

The girl paused to cut off a bite of filet mignon. "Why should we be saddled with guilt just because of a few crazies?" She glanced at Lindsey. "What do you think?"

Shula put a restraining hand on the girl's arm, but Lindsey had seen this coming. "You're right," she said. "And it's a shame. People who are unsure of themselves become frightened, and they lash out at the closest vulnerable object. But that's no excuse."

Shula looked gratified. "I'm sure we all agree with you," she said. "Let's talk about the book fair we're working on."

The girls chattered enthusiastically about collecting and selling books, and Lindsey learned that Shula was closely involved with the book fair. Apparently their profits went to an organization they called the FRO.

Hadn't Belinda mentioned the FRO?

The older girl helped herself to more salad. "I was wondering whether we could have a free table too, with leaflets, you know, and maybe some free samples of Arabic calligraphy."

Shula smiled, looking indulgent. "That's an excellent suggestion. I'll discuss it with Kamal."

She looked at Lindsey. "Kamal Hamza. We work together."

She said his name with unconscious tenderness. How deeply was she involved with the FRO?

Shula steered the conversation to the girls' campus activities and, as they ate dessert, to skin care, and the lotions and creams she had made.

When the meal was finished, she showed them around the herb room, and they sat down to try out different fragrances and decide which they liked best.

While the girls discussed their small jars of cream, Shula took Lindsey aside. "I meant to ask you something earlier. Would you mind coming along when I fly the girls back to Seattle? It would be nice to have your company on the return trip."

"You'll just drop them off?"

Shula nodded. "Kamal will pick them up. Please?"

Another one of her schemes? But this seemed harmless.

"Okay," Lindsey said.

The night was clear, and the three girls, sitting in the airplane's back seat, exclaimed over the lights below. Shula pointed out Clallam Bay and Port Angeles, her voice coming through the headset, and the girls chattered among themselves for the rest of the short flight.

Shula didn't say much, and Lindsey thought about the complexities of this woman: her kindness to these girls and to Lindsey herself; her relationship with Ben Fletcher, whatever it was; her questions about God; her curious affinity for Islam.

The display of stars above caught her eye. The last

199

time she'd seen them like this, they'd lit up the ocean and the beach, and the solitary man walking there.

Talk about a complex personality! God had been kind, giving her that glimpse of Colin's character today.

Whether she understood him or not, she'd feel more comfortable with him now. Definitely, he was a private person. And she'd make sure she didn't go down to the beach tonight in case he decided to take another run.

They landed on Lake Union with an impressive splash and taxied over to the dock in front of a restaurant.

Lindsey had planned to stay in the plane, but Shula wanted her to meet Kamal, so she followed Shula, stepping from the float onto the dock, where Kamal waited to greet them.

Kamal Hamza had black hair, light olive skin, and a well-sculpted black goatee. Younger than Shula. He wasn't especially tall, but he radiated an authority that Lindsey could sense.

Shula went to him immediately, putting a possessive hand on his arm. He gave her an intense look and suggested to the girls that they should get themselves some coffee from the restaurant.

He turned to Lindsey. "Miss Dumont," he said in a resonant voice, "I am honored to meet you."

For some reason, the man set her on edge. Behind those glittering black eyes lay something cold.

She smiled without answering.

He fixed his eyes on her and took charge of the conversation, asking about her impressions of Seattle and of Cameron Bay; her favorite park in New York; her opinion of commercial development in the Pine Barrens.

The Pine Barrens? Perhaps Shula had told him about her house in the Pine Barrens.

In the process, he extracted information: her training, her job, and her professional accomplishments.

She soon realized what was happening, and when he began to inquire about her family and her beliefs, she turned the interrogation around with questions of her own.

The girls returned with their coffee, and she welcomed the interruption. Now, at last, they could leave.

They took off with a dramatic surge of power, and after they'd reached cruising altitude, Shula said, "Isn't it a beautiful night? I love to fly! It's my freedom and peace and joy, all wrapped up together."

Lindsey gazed at the stars, pondering how to answer. Flying a small plane was wonderful, yes; but it wasn't her peace and joy.

"Kamal likes to fly too," Shula said. "He just got a new Cessna, a twin-engine, and it's all black leather inside."

She sighed. "Soon as I make some good sales, I'm going to get one like his."

"How did you become interested in Islam?"

"A couple of years ago, I visited the little town of Evry, south of Paris," Shula said. "It's a truly multicultural place. They've got all kinds of colors and faiths and tongues there, and almost a third of them are Muslim."

She glanced at Lindsey, as if to gauge her response. "I loved it. And for once, no one cared about the color of my skin. I got to know some Muslim women and felt a real bond with them. When I came back to Seattle, I met other Muslim women and realized that they get the same kind of harassment I did when I was growing up. I wanted to help them."

Shula's emotion sounded genuine. Lindsey had never experienced prejudice, but she could sympathize.

She asked, "And then you began to work with the FRO?"

"Yes." Shula's voice had a lilt to it. "Because of Kamal. Now we work together on FRO projects, and sometimes we just, you know, go off together. To discuss things, you understand."

Lindsey understood, and she wanted to change the subject, but Shula wasn't finished.

She laughed, deep in her throat. "That man makes me wild, Lin. I'd do just about anything for him."

Shula paused. "As he would for me, I think. He let the girls come tonight. He trusts me with them."

"Are they relatives?"

"His nieces. They had a good time, they said."

That explained Shula's charity, but who could fault her? She was obviously in love with the man.

A minute later, Shula said, "I'm curious. Tell me about the handsome guy who works for the Fletchers. I've seen him in town."

"Remi Lavelle?" A chill gripped the back of Lindsey's neck. Why would Shula connect her with Remi? Did she know he used to be a Muslim?

"That's the one. Gossip has it that you're pretty good friends. You must have known him before you came out here."

Gossip . . . Belinda? Jack?

"Yes. I'm restoring an old house in New Jersey. He worked on it for a while."

"That's nice. I think it's always good to have shared experiences. He looks so intelligent, a perfect match for you. And those gorgeous eyes! I'll bet he knows how to show you a good time."

Her stomach lurched. "He's half my age, Shula. No romance there at all."

"Really?" Shula giggled. "I don't think age should matter, but if you say so . . . I was wondering, where's his family? Has he always lived in New Jersey? Does he ever talk about his beliefs?"

Too many questions about Remi. What was she after?

"He doesn't say much about himself. Tell me how you

met Kamal."

Shula was happy to tell her a great deal about Kamal, some of it too personal, and soon they were circling over the airport. They lined up with the runway lights and landed as smoothly as the last time.

Shula sat in the airplane for a minute. "This was a good evening, Lin. Thank you for coming. We'll have to do it again. Kamal was impressed with you, I could tell."

She giggled again, unlike her usual self. Was it Kamal? Or something else?

"Tell you what," Shula said at last. "If you like tall, dark, and handsome, I can fix you up with a great guy. We could double-date!"

Lindsey tried to laugh. "Thanks, but I'm pretty busy right now."

"What admirable restraint," Shula said. "I think you'll be a good influence on me. I have to go into Seattle over the weekend, but how about getting together for lunch on Tuesday? I might have another photo job for you."

"That might work out," Lindsey said slowly.

Then again, it might not.

As Shula opened the door of the cockpit, the fragrance of wet evergreens blew inside, and Lindsey welcomed it.

They said goodbye, and she drove down the highway with her mind spinning with images from the long day. It was hard to put captions on them, but she tried.

Her musings faded as soon as she walked into her room and saw the file folders beside her laptop. Vance. And his idea of stealing photos. Preposterous. The man had the moral sense of a cockroach.

Enough partying—get to work.

She checked over the Carolina dogs feature to make sure it was ready to go, ignoring her regrets. Tomorrow she'd phone Edric as early as she dared. It was time to get a few things straightened out.

She awoke late the next morning with a vague unease that wasn't heavy enough to call anxiety, as if her mind were filled with the last shreds of a disagreeable dream.

Today she was going to . . . that was it. She was going to phone Edric at home and tell him . . . what?

She sat up in bed and gazed at the silver curtain of rain that veiled the balcony. For one thing, she'd tell him—again—to forget Vance's brilliant suggestion. And she'd enlarge on her idea for a reservation dogs feature.

Her cell phone rang, and she scrambled out of bed to answer it. Alexa's voice was cheerful above the hubbub of bakery sounds. "Lin! Just wanted to ask whether you're doing anything tonight."

"Not really."

"Great! Colin's going to grill. Can you come? Six o'clock, but I sure could use the help if you're early."

"I'd love to, thanks," Lindsey said.

The cat was scratching at the door, so she let him in. He brushed against her ankles, telegraphing a graceful request, and she shared her breakfast with him.

So Colin was going to grill? That meant hot dogs and hamburgers, judging from her past experience with men who cooked. And if he had his nose in a book, the food might end up slightly scorched.

Not that she could talk. Cooking was something she'd never bothered with. Instant oatmeal, grilled cheese, maybe spaghetti and a salad if she felt adventurous; that was all.

She stared at the rain for a few more minutes. Phone Edric and get it over with.

He sounded good-humored today. "Hey there! How's it going? I guess we never did finish our talk. How about Vance's idea?"

"We might want to rethink it." She'd have to say this carefully. "The owner seems to have some personal problems. It might not be wise to take advantage of him or tell the whole world he's in trouble. Besides, other kennel owners on our list would wonder what kind of dirt we'd print about them. We'd jeopardize our good name."

"Okay, you've convinced me. Vance said it might justify the expense of having you out there, all this time."

"Remind him, please, that I am paying my own expenses. And I've been taking personal leave since Wednesday. Did you tell him that?"

"I can't remember—so much going on. But you do whatever you want."

Pain inched up one side of her head. Why did he sound so conciliatory?

She started to tell him about the reservation dogs idea, but he interrupted. "I hope you're coming back soon," he said. "Ever since that Seattle conference, Vance's been really charged up. I'd like to see him as Managing Editor one of these days. He's got good ideas."

She began massaging her temple. "What are some of his good ideas?"

"Oh . . . fewer in-depth features. Maybe get rid of that black-and-white end page. Do more celebrity interviews and spotlight their dogs."

He chewed vigorously. "To start with, he wants to have a meeting of the shareholders—he calls it a board meeting—and get properly organized."

"And what do you think?" Her hands had gone cold.

"It'll be good for the magazine, Lin. Have to be flexible. That's what's important right now. Hey, there's my cell phone. Call me Monday?"

"Sure," she said, but he'd already hung up.

And her mind was going blank. The rain outside was transforming itself into zigzagging lines, a kaleidoscope of shifting silver and green . . .

With a jerk of alarm, she recognized the warning aura of a migraine. "No!"

She put water into the microwave and scrabbled through the tea bags in the kitchen drawer. Shula's tea. Make it double-strength. The last thing she needed was a migraine to put her out of commission until tomorrow.

She swished the tea bags back and forth, watching the water turn to gold. And why was tonight so important? Why did she want to eat hot dogs and hamburgers?

She took a gulp of the tea, burning her tongue, dropped an ice cube into it, and made herself sit down.

Drink it slowly; that's better. Don't think.

She had forgotten the honey, and the liquid was both bitter and pungent, matching her mood. She put a hand over her eyes to shut out the light.

Vance as their Managing Editor? He would manage everything.

She swallowed the last of the tea, stood up carefully so as not to jiggle her head, and closed the draperies. She paused to smooth the cat's silky gray back. "This is Saturday," she told him. "All over these United States, thousands of citizens are having fun. Personally, I am going to start having fun by taking a nap."

She crawled into bed and pulled the blankets up to her chin.

When she awoke, it was early afternoon, her head was clear, and the rain had stopped.

She'd better do some serious thinking about what Edric had said. Go down on the beach. Her mind seemed to work better there, and maybe no one else would be around.

She picked her way over the rain-slick rocks. Vance's "good ideas" sounded ominous.

Trim back the features?—they were her department. Scrap the black-and-white?—they were her specialty.

He must be doing this on purpose.

More interviews with celebrities? It would change the whole tone of the magazine.

Edric had always said that she would take over when he retired. Should she go back and defend her turf?

But she was *here*, and she had a unique opportunity to explore the reservation and study its dogs.

Just a few more days—would it matter?

Foam-speckled waves broke at her feet, coming again and again, like the questions. And she had no answers.

She kept her walk short since she wanted to do some errands before going to help Alexa with supper. First, the bookstore.

Fraser greeted her cheerfully. "Got the book you ordered. It looks pretty good."

"I decided to do some more studying," she said, and paid for it. "Ansel Adams is the best."

"How'd it go last night, Lin?"

She told him as much as she thought appropriate. Some things you didn't discuss with a guy, even Fraser.

It wouldn't hurt to mention Shula's double-date idea, so she finished with that.

He grinned. "You don't want to double-date with tall, dark, and handsome? I thought that was the dream of every American girl."

"Good-looking's okay, but not handsome, not for me. They're usually spoiled rotten. And especially not with eyes like Kamal's."

Fraser was serious now. "What's your impression of him?"

"Hard, cold, maybe dangerous. His eyes suggest it, anyway." Enough talk about men. "So how's your day going?"

He slid the book into a bag. "Just fine, thank you. Never a dull moment, of course. Speaking of dates, one of your admirers was just in here, asking about you."

He grinned. "I must inquire, are you in good health? How's your stamina? That was on the questionnaire."

She stared at him. "Good health? He's checking me out like he does his breeder goats?"

Fraser backed away in mock alarm. "Don't bite my head off, lady. Quinn's the one who asked."

"I hope you told him I'm prone to fainting fits?"

Fraser shook his head. "I had to admit that you jog on the beach."

Without permission, her voice rose. "Well, I am so sorry! He'll just have to find someone else to take care of him in his old age."

"Unfortunately, he seems serious. He commissioned me to find out what you think of him. To suggest a liaison. And he offered me a bundle for that photo of Kumtux."

"The frame is worth plenty."

"He didn't want the frame. Just the photo."

"Why?"

"Because he watched you take it, and anything made by your hands . . . Quite poetic. I'll spare you the details."

"Spare me this whole conversation. Don't encourage him."

Fraser grinned again. "You could do worse. You could work by his side, photographing his goats. Just think—a whole gallery of goats. And he's a rich man."

"I know that, and it's a strike against him. He reeks of money."

She picked up the book, remembering the man's self-absorption, and felt the hot blood rise into her face.

"Good health? Stamina? The more I think about it, what arrogance! After two cups of coffee and a sandwich in a greasy spoon? I hate fried food anyway—he didn't even bother to find out!"

"Guess that means *no?*" Fraser said.

"All capitals: NO. He's so typical! I can tell you—I am through with men. Been there done that. Finished!"

A peculiar expression flitted across his face, but she

didn't pause to wonder about it.

She turned to leave and almost ran full-tilt into Colin McAlister.

"Excuse me," she said, addressing the top button of his shirt.

She stepped around him and marched outside to her Jeep, slamming the door as if Quincy himself were in hot pursuit.

How long had Colin been standing there? She hadn't meant for him to hear that tirade.

"I don't care," she said aloud, and started the engine.

18

caption:

Chopped Walnuts

Alexa greeted her with a relieved smile. "I'm sure glad to see you. I'm way behind! Do you know how to operate one of these things?"

She nudged the apple machine with an elbow and returned to the cake she was decorating.

"I've seen you do it," Lindsey said, "so I probably can."

"Great. Apples are in the fridge. We'll need about three or four. You can use the machine to peel and slice them."

Lindsey had sliced the first two apples when Colin came through the back door, saying, "Hey, Lexa, I hope we've got some more charcoal."

He stopped at the sight of her. "Hello."

"In that corner cupboard," Alexa said.

"Good." He smiled then, and Lindsey gave him a quick smile in return.

"She's got you working too?" He pulled out the bag of charcoal and paused beside her, lifting a curl of red peel from the machine. "Were you saving this for anything?"

"I don't think so," Lindsey said. "Alexa, do you need any peels for that cake of yours? Extra fiber?"

Alexa looked up from a pink rosette and grinned. "All

yours, Lin. Make him beg."

"I'll be nice since he's the cook."

"Thankya kindly, ma'am." Colin snapped off the peel, tilted his head back to drop it into his mouth, and left.

Alexa nodded. "He's such a kid sometimes."

Lindsey fed another apple into the machine. A new side of the Paragon?

When the apples were sliced, Alexa told her how to toss them with sugar and cinnamon, and by the time she'd done that, Alexa had finished the cake. She'd written *Happy Birthday* and decorated it with prancing pink ponies and rosebuds.

"What do you think?" Alexa wiped a smudge of frosting off her arm.

"Pretty!" Lindsey said.

"Good! Into the box it goes. The mother is supposed to pick it up."

Alexa plopped a bag of walnuts onto the counter. "Could you please chop a handful of these? For the tart. I'll make the caramel sauce."

Lindsey looked doubtfully at Alexa's assortment of knives, decided she could best manage a short one, and found a cutting board. She poured out a pile of nuts, chose a walnut half and cut it into quarters, then cut it again into eighths. Small enough.

She chose another walnut half, a nice plump one, and had started working on it when Colin returned.

He glanced over her shoulder and kept walking without any discernible change of expression. But he was amused, she could tell.

"What?" she said.

He stopped, raising an eyebrow.

She persisted. "So how do you chop nuts?"

The corners of his mouth turned up, and the blue eyes studied her for a minute. After her outburst this afternoon, he was probably wondering how best to handle this temperamental female.

"There's really no right way," he said, "but I'll show you how I do it."

She was going to hand him the knife, but he chose another one—long and rather wicked-looking—and leaned over the cutting board. He corralled the nuts with one big hand, sent the knife flashing through them, and they ended up in a pile on the far side of the board.

Ah, yes. Paragon-with-a-knife.

He slanted a look at her from under his dark brows, and she nodded.

"Impressive. And you still have all your fingers?"

"Yes, ma'am. I forgot to mention, it helps if you stand on one foot . . ."

"Colin, that's enough," Alexa said. "I can't afford to lose my good helper. Don't I smell something burning?"

"I hope not." He turned to the stove. "But I've got to get started on the squash."

He was quiet then, moving with confidence from refrigerator to counter to stove.

Alexa had Lindsey arrange the apples over the custard cream-cheese base that was chilling in a pie shell, and then they sprinkled on the walnuts and drizzled it with caramel.

Next on Alexa's list was a salad, and while Lindsey worked on it, she kept an eye on what Colin was doing.

He had sliced two striped squashes, hacking them apart with a knife the size of a small machete, and then he peeled them and cut them into chunks. Now he was chopping something green that looked different from parsley.

She went over to see. "What's that?"

"Here." He picked up a needled green sprig, crushing it as he gave it to her. "Rosemary."

He handed her a small oval leaf. "Sage."

She held them in her palm and sniffed. "Mmm."

"I agree," he said. He melted butter in a small pan and dropped the herbs into it.

She went back to slice a cucumber, and by the time she finished, he had the squash in a second skillet. He added the buttered herbs along with water, apple cider, and vinegar.

Lindsey covered the salad and set it in the refrigerator, then edged back over to see how the squash was doing.

"Here." He handed her the wooden spoon he'd been using. "Mind stirring it for me? Oh, I forgot the salt." He shook some salt into his hand and sprinkled it over the squash while she stirred, gingerly.

"I'm going out to check the charcoal, and I'll be right back," he said. "But first let me show you something."

He used the spoon to scrape the sauce from the bottom of the skillet so it flowed over the squash. "In a couple of minutes the sauce will start getting thicker, and you'll want to lift it gently from the bottom of the pan." He handed the spoon back to her.

"What if it burns?" she said.

"It won't. Just keep stirring."

This was going to taste good. The cubes of squash were golden, and cider-scented steam rose into her face.

When he returned, he glanced at the squash, took a paper bag from the refrigerator, and dumped out some floppy-looking, ragged, splotched shapes.

"Chanterelle mushrooms," he said, brushing them off.

He did something with the mushrooms that involved another skillet—and butter, garlic, and savory bits of green—and went off again.

He came back almost immediately and put a cookie sheet of thinly sliced baguette rounds into the oven.

By now the sauce she'd been stirring had boiled down to a butterscotch glaze that coated each piece of squash. He glanced at it, nodded, and speared a piece for her to taste.

"Perfect," she said. "What kind of squash is this?"

"Delicata. My favorite, but any winter squash would work."

He took the baguette rounds out of the oven, flipped them over with casual dexterity, and put them back in.

Alexa was setting the table by the back wall, and Lindsey was going to ask whether she could help when Colin turned off the burner under the squash and took the toasted breads out of the oven.

He handed her a small spoon. "You've just been promoted," he said. "All you need to do is put a spoonful of the chanterelle mixture on each of these, and I'll go start the salmon. Then we'll be ready to eat."

It wasn't very hard. The mushroom mixture clumped together to make dark little mounds on the bread, and she was almost done when he came back.

"Did you taste it?"

She shook her head.

He grinned. "Trusting soul."

She looked up at him. "On the contrary, I'm waiting for you to taste it first."

His eyes brightened with laughter. He picked up a piece of bread, tore it in half, added a small spoonful to each half, and handed one to her. "I dare you."

"What a way to go." She kept her eyes on his while she took a bite.

He grinned and ate his piece whole.

"Good," she said. It really was, with an unexpected richness.

He chewed, frowning slightly. "Does it need more salt? Wait."

He took the cover off a small glass canister and sprinkled two coarse grains of salt onto the rest of her piece. "Now."

She ate it. "Still good," she said with a laugh. "But you credit me with a more discerning palate than I really have."

He smiled, sprinkled a few grains of salt over the rest of the chanterelle toasts, and went off to tend the salmon.

Fraser and Remi arrived, and Peter came in from his nap, and they stood around looking hungry, so Alexa told them to sit down.

Peter sat at one end and Fraser at the other, with Lindsey next to him and Remi on her left. Alexa brought over the bowl of salad, saying, "I'm keeping the rest warm," and sat beside Peter, leaving a place for Colin next to her.

Lindsey eyed her empty plate, then she joined the others in looking expectantly at the back door.

Fraser had just suggested that they might want to pray in faith for either the meal or the cook, when the door swung open.

Colin came in with a platter that held a plank of singed wood crowned with a filet of grilled salmon. He set the platter in the center of the table, and Alexa hurried to put out the squash and chanterelle toasts.

"Now," Fraser said. "We pray with thankful hearts!" and he asked a blessing on the food.

It was the largest filet of salmon she'd ever seen, and possibly the most attractive, delicately browned on top with the rich pink flesh showing through.

After her first forkful, she was sure she'd never eaten anything more delicious.

She glanced up, saw Colin watching her, and nodded. "Wonderful."

He didn't reply, but the blue eyes gleamed.

Alexa sighed in contentment. "What kind is it, Colin? I get them confused."

"Sockeye," he said. "The King has higher fat content, but I think this tastes better. They use it in sushi bars."

"Your chanterelle toasts are excellent," Peter said. "Mushrooms from the Pike Place Market?"

"Of course." Colin was eating one, slowly, and she

knew he was still thinking about the salt.

He nodded at her. "Better."

"The cedar plank intrigues me," Fraser said. "You scorch them and I carve them. I hope your cedar wasn't as expensive as mine."

"It's just a cedar shingle, no additives," Colin said. "But you're supposed to be able to taste the cedar."

"Now that you mention it, pal . . ." Fraser grinned at him.

"Careful with the criticism," Alexa said, looking mischievous. "We like your experiments, Colin. And I, for one, can taste the cedar." She glanced across at Lindsey. "I'm sure Lin can too."

"Definitely," she said. "Although I don't usually nibble on cedar shingles, so I was a bit confused at first."

Alexa shook her head. "I think Fraser's a bad influence on you."

Remi, who had been eating heartily, helped himself to more squash and salmon. He grinned at Fraser. "We give thanks to Brother Salmon," he said, "for providing us with this meal so we can live."

"Logic slightly flawed," Fraser said. "Brother Salmon didn't intend for us to eat him. He was just trying to do his one big thing. In fact, we probably interfered with his purpose by catching him."

"I've been thinking about that," Alexa said.

"Catching salmon?" Colin said.

"No." She waved her fork at him. "We were talking about salmon the other night, how they do what God designed them for, and then Remi pointed out that God designed us to love him."

"How are you defining 'love God'?" Colin said.

"That's it," Alexa said. "What do we mean when we say we love God? How does that work out in real life?"

Peter spoke quietly from his end of the table. "It's got

216

to be more than an abstraction or even a happy feeling."

Fraser nodded, helping himself to another piece of salmon. "It's a kind of love that goes beyond emotion."

A verse floated into Lindsey's mind, memorized long ago. Something about love and obedience. "But don't you think it will always be just an abstraction," she said, "until we demonstrate it, like . . . like . . . *If you love me, keep my commandments.*"

"You hit it right on," Fraser said. "Genuine love for God implies obedience."

"Like Christ!" Remi said. "Um . . . somewhere in John." He pulled a New Testament out of his pocket.

"Try chapter 14," Colin said.

"Yes, here's your verse, Lin. And then, right at the end: *I do as the Father commanded me, so that the world may know that I love the Father.*"

Alexa nodded. "His obedience meant going to the Cross."

"You're right. Our salvation," Remi said. He was quiet for a minute, and then he added, "When mercy seasons justice."

Colin looked up from his plate. "*The Merchant of Venice.*"

"So you're still reading Shakespeare?" Lindsey asked Remi.

Alexa stood to her feet. "Okay, while you're talking Shakespeare, I'll get dessert."

Lindsey pushed her chair back. "Can I help?"

"I'm just going to slice it up. No ceremony. It won't take a minute."

Peter got to his feet as well. "I'll be right back—need to check my bread."

Lindsey turned to Remi. "Last year it was *Macbeth*. Why are you reading *The Merchant of Venice* now?"

"I just wanted to remember how it goes. I've always

217

liked Shakespeare. Colin had some videos."

Lindsey nodded. He'd said something once about staying with Colin. She took the stack of plates to the sink and helped Alexa serve the plates of apple tart.

Peter came back, and while they ate, Colin said, "I like what you do with this custard, Lexa. I always look forward to it."

Alexa smiled. "Lin was a big help."

"Right," she said. "I cut up the apples." She glanced at Colin. "And two walnut halves."

He gave her an amused look but didn't say anything. Fraser, though, was quick to grasp what had happened. With a straight face, he said, "Lin, you're a wonder. All that topping from one walnut."

They were still laughing when the phone rang.

Alexa answered it, said something, and hung up. "Sounds like I'll have to deliver that cake."

She looked at the clock. "It's six-thirty already. Song Fest! I don't want to start late. Peter, you've got the raisin bread to finish. Fraser, you're going to get the Richardsons, right? And I'll pick up the Thorsen sisters when I deliver the cake."

Lindsey turned from the sink. "Song Fest?"

"Sorry, I didn't tell you about it," Alexa said. "We have a kind of public song service on alternate Saturday nights at the store. Can you stay?"

"Yes. What can I do?"

"Good! The guys have to set up, and you could help them. Take along some cookies for afterwards."

Alexa had started clearing the table, so Lindsey finished it for her, arranged a plateful of cookies, and carried it over to Fraser's store.

Remi showed her where the folding chairs were kept, and she set them up in rows, following his instructions. He and Colin stood in front of the chairs, tuning their guitars.

As she finished, Remi called her over. "Lin, I heard about Shula's party with those Muslim girls. How'd it go?"

"Interesting, and a little unsettling," she said. "They seem like nice girls—loyal Muslims for sure. They're active in the Muslim student organization at the university."

"The MSA is big on campus," Colin said.

"Sounds like it. And they're deeply involved in the FRO. They're working with Shula on a book fair to raise funds. Very enthusiastic."

"Working with Shula?" Colin said. "What's the reason for that connection?"

"At first I wondered too, but then I noticed she's got something going on with Kamal Hamza. He's a leader in the FRO, and those girls are his nieces."

Remi leaned his guitar against a chair. "Lin? Colin?" His eyes had lost their sparkle. "Got a minute?"

Colin must have suspected what he was going to say. He frowned. "Remi, you don't need to tell us anything. Are you sure . . . ?"

"Yeah, you're my best friends."

Colin looked at her. He was assessing her again, and she couldn't blame him. He'd done a lot for Remi, and perhaps, in his estimation, she was too friendly with Shula.

She met the probing blue gaze with assurance. *You can trust me. I love the boy too.*

He must have been satisfied because he said to Remi, "The so-called Family Relief Outreach?"

"It poses as a charitable organization," Remi said, "and—briefly—the money it raises does go to widows and orphans, but they're relatives of the men who gave their lives to jihad. Its mission is to encourage jihad."

Colin nodded. "Hamas connections?"

"Right. They may also buy guns, which is harder to prove. But there's something else."

He looked at his friend. "I'm sorry I didn't tell you."

Colin shook his head dismissively, and Remi went on. "My home wasn't in St. Louis. It was Chicago. I lived there with my uncle's family. He owned an antiques store, and he had an American passport, but he worked as a front man for the FRO. I found that out after they murdered a friend of mine, a non-Muslim. I almost got myself killed too. So I left."

He took a breath, let it out slowly, and looked at Colin again. "I ended up in Seattle, as you know. You took care of me for a while, and then you set me up to work with the Fletchers. Remember when I ran off again?"

Colin nodded, his jaw tight. It must have been hard on him.

"Here's what made me do it," Remi said. "I had come into Seattle that day on the ferry, and I saw one of my uncle's men there, watching. Abu Alam. Somehow, he had caught up with me. I took off again because I was scared he'd follow me back to Cameron Bay and the Fletchers."

His eyes grew somber. "I didn't even dare to phone. That's why I sent all those post cards."

Colin nodded again, and Remi said, "I traveled around and ended up with a job in a little town in the Pine Barrens. I thought it was a good place to disappear. That's where I got to know Lin. She's been like a big sister to me."

He glanced at her with the shadow of a smile. "But when I heard that my uncle and Abu had been killed on a trip to Saudi, I decided to come back here."

He frowned. "I knew there was an Algerian Islamic group in Seattle, but if I'd known the FRO had such an active branch, I probably would have stayed away. I couldn't believe it when Belinda started talking about them like it was some ladies' aid society."

"So you're in danger?" Lindsey said.

He shrugged.

Colin stepped close to him, putting a hand on his

shoulder. "We'll talk again, Remi, but don't let it throw you."

He glanced at her and back to Remi. "Lindsey and I will stand with you on this. Want to pray?"

Remi nodded, and Colin prayed. He thanked God for protecting his child and asked him to give Remi courage and wisdom.

His voice held an affectionate note that she hadn't heard before.

Colin finished, and she had a quick memory of Shula's voice, intense, almost fanatic, when she spoke of Kamal. Without meaning to, she shuddered.

"Hey, don't look like that, big sister," Remi said. He gave her a one-armed hug. "I'll be okay."

She managed to smile at him. "I was thinking about Shula. But I know the Lord will keep you safe. And I'll be praying."

Colin had picked up his guitar and was strumming it, watching them with a smile that mellowed his dark gaze.

Finally he spoke to Remi. "What do you want to sing?"

A car crunched on the gravel outside and stopped. Lindsey took a handful of the stapled song sheets and concentrated on handing them out, one for each chair.

Fraser arrived with the Richardsons, who turned out to be a young Native American couple, and their baby. They were followed by Alexa and the Thorsen sisters, one of whom was the postmistress.

Peter set up coffee and punch on a folding table by the wood stove, and Lindsey put the plate of cookies there.

Colin took charge, easily the leader. He must have taught school. No, he'd been an officer in the Marines.

She sat at the back, and Alexa joined her, with Peter slipping in beside them later on. The group wasn't very large, but it soon became apparent that they liked to sing.

First it was "Your Mercy Flows," then "Speak, O Lord," and "My Savior, My God."

Remi and Colin sang a duet, with Colin doing something fast and rippling in the guitar accompaniment, his deep baritone blending with Remi's tenor.

"In Christ alone my hope is found,
He is my Light, my Strength, my Song."
Could she say that?
"My Comforter, my All in All . . ."
Was he really?
"Here in the love of Christ I stand."

They finished, and Colin began strumming "It is Well with My Soul," leading with his voice.

The music swept into her soul, but it brought only a dull ache.

Alexa's clear soprano rose beside her, joyful in spite of business worries and a wayward son . . .

Fraser sang with his head tilted back, eyes half-closed. He'd probably faced more than his share of hardship, and as a Native American, a Christian, and an artist, he must lead a solitary life . . .

Colin and Remi, dark heads bent over their guitars, exchanged a smile as they sang. Remi had dared to confide in her and Colin tonight, trusting them with information that put him in danger . . .

All was *well?* Yes, for them.

She listened to them sing, and the ache seemed to grow. It scraped at her throat and weighted her bones and deepened into a longing that was tinged with grief.

This small group—their warmth, their kindness, the way they loved God and spoke so often of him—was different from anything she had ever known.

Tonight's meal, for example, with its camaraderie and the talk of Christ. She was hungry for this fellowship, the talks with Alexa and with Fraser.

She took a deep, calming breath.

Yes, she liked these people. They were remarkable—friendly and God-centered. But she had come here to do a job, and she had already stayed too long. If she didn't get back to the magazine soon, Vance would take control.

When the singing ended, she leaned over to Alexa. "Thanks for everything," she said. "There's something I have to do, so I'll go now."

"Okay." Alexa put a hand on hers and smiled. "See you tomorrow for church? Remember, we're wearing our new sweaters. I'll give you a call just before we leave."

Lindsey nodded and snatched up her jacket. Colin turned to watch as she reached the door.

Lindsey and I, he'd said. It was the first time he'd used her name, and something about his tone . . .

The wind was cold, gusting strong into her face, and it gave her something to fight against as she hurried up the street.

This was no time for sentiment, she told herself. The Dumont women are tough.

She should check online for flights to New York. If she took a plane from Port Angeles to Seattle, it would be faster than the ferry.

19

caption:

Moss

The rugged shoreline had never been so appealing, the sea so brilliant, the sky so blue as it was the next morning from the back seat of Peter and Alexa's Ford.

Lindsey gazed at it all with mournful fascination. How many more times would she see this?

Think about something else.

She leaned forward. "Alexa, that's a great-looking sweater."

"Thank you! Peter likes it too. Especially the price tag. And yours looks fantastic."

Lindsey had decided to wear it with her all-purpose black skirt, partly because she knew Alexa would be wearing a skirt, and partly for contrast with the mint green.

"Thanks, Lexa." It felt good to wear something new and know it was attractive.

"I love this drive up to church," Alexa said, and Lindsey agreed.

The hillsides glowed yellow and bronze, set off by a variety of evergreens. What would Jack call those different greens? She'd heard him muttering the names of his colors as he mixed them.

She'd have to ask, if she ever saw him again.

Last night, she had kept herself busy: she caught up on email, sent a cheerful note to Mollie, and checked the airline schedules. She could take a morning flight from Port Angeles and easily connect in Seattle for New York.

At the little house-church, she found that it was more crowded than last week. The Richardsons were sitting with Fraser, and they'd brought a friend.

Colin was there too. She hadn't expected to see him again. He sat beside Remi, just in front of them, and during the opening songs she could hear their voices above the rest.

After the pastor read some Scripture, notably verses from the eighth chapter of Romans, he said that today's service would include a testimony from Remi Lavelle.

She was close enough to notice how Colin's jaw tightened as Remi walked up to the front. Considering what Remi had told them last night, this decision must have taken courage.

Remi spoke well. He mentioned briefly that he'd been raised a Muslim, and then he told how the Word of God and three godly men had pointed him to Christ. He referred to the verses in Romans that spoke of adoption and the certainty of Christ's love.

He kept the emphasis on God's mercy, not naming anyone in particular, but Lindsey knew who the men were—Timothy, Fraser, and Colin—and she marveled at what God had done for Remi.

Afterwards, the pastor said a few words about the life-changing power of Christ and closed in prayer. Two of the Native American teens strolled up to talk to Remi.

She followed Alexa out to the porch, and they talked to the Richardson family for several minutes. Lindsey was making funny faces at their baby when Colin and Remi stopped beside her, but it was Remi who spoke.

"Natalie wanted me to ask you over for supper

tomorrow night. Can you come?" He looked as if he thought it was a good idea.

"Yes! I'd love to. What time?"

"Around six, I guess."

She nodded. "Be sure to thank her for me."

This could be a big step forward.

They walked with Peter and Alexa toward the cars, and Remi said, "Wow, Lin, you're looking—I mean, I don't think I've ever seen you in a skirt before."

She stopped and smiled at him. "Thank you."

Teasing, she added, "I assume you were trying to say something nice. You're looking pretty cool yourself."

Peter stopped too, grinning. "Son, let me give you some advice. It's a risky business to get into particulars. You said something about the skirt, but apparently it did not meet with approval. It's the sweater you should have noticed. They both got new sweaters. I've heard about it for days."

Alexa put a hand to her forehead, but Peter kept on.

"Even commenting on the sweater has its pitfalls. For example, if you say, I like your sweater because it reminds me of peas and all the time she's thinking of it as—what's the color, Lin?"

"Mint green." She smiled at Alexa, and they both shrugged.

"Yes—mint green—you're in trouble already. Much safer to say, 'Lin, you look very nice today.' And she'll apply it any way she wants to. But if you're married, it's simpler because you can say to your wife, 'You look delectable in that sweater, and I can't wait to get you away from all these people so I can kiss you properly.'"

"Peter!" Alexa exclaimed, laughing.

He put his arm around her. "Maybe it's not that simple, Remi. I don't know. But until we figure it out, could you come over here and look at my Ford? I have a question about the belts."

Lindsey laughed, watching them go, then realized that Colin still stood beside her. His dark corduroy jacket looked good on him, and the burgundy shirt with its muted plaid was well-chosen. Unlike some bachelors, he knew how to dress.

"Good morning, Lindsey."

She turned to him with a smile, thinking he would pick up on the sweater discussion, but he didn't.

He must have been waiting for the others to leave, and now he spoke rapidly, without his usual confidence. "I was wondering whether you're free for lunch today. I'd like you to meet someone."

She glanced away, forgetting to smile, hesitating. Was this any different than coffee with Quinn? Maybe. But admit it, she was curious about the man.

She looked up and was taken aback by the intensity of his gaze. This must be an important someone.

"Thank you. I'd like that," she said. "I came with Peter and Alexa, though."

He smiled. "I can give you a ride."

He went striding off to speak to them, and soon he returned to take her over to his battered gray Volvo.

He seemed more at ease now, and she leaned back into the upholstered seat while they talked about the church service, Remi's testimony, and the pastor's long, fruitful ministry.

Finally he said, "For lunch, there's a specialty item they have in this area. Indian Tacos. How about it?"

She let his question hang in the air. He'd been talking to Fraser. Rascals, both of them.

"Perhaps just a salad for me," she said. "All of a sudden, I'm not very hungry."

He laughed. "Maybe we can think of something else."

By now they had driven back into Cameron Bay, which puzzled her, and he parked in front of a small store with a

227

large sign that dwarfed it even further: PIZZA.

This must be where Alexa had bought the pizza they'd eaten. Mr. Mott's famous pizza. Okay, pizza was fine.

He came around to open the car door, and they walked together up onto the porch, past a pair of rocking chairs.

Inside, it looked like any take-out pizza place, with a counter displaying packages of chips, and a drinks cooler in the corner. She couldn't see a place to sit, except for the rocking chairs outside, and that didn't strike her as quite his style.

"Colin!" A wizened old Japanese man appeared from behind the counter.

Colin bowed, said something to him in Japanese, and then he spoke in English. "Mr. Matsukata, I would like to present Miss Lindsey Dumont."

The old man beamed at her, his face breaking into a thousand wrinkles, and instinctively she extended her hand. He clasped it in his own, fine-boned and dry, and bent low. "I am so happy to meet you."

She smiled down at him. "I am honored, sir."

"Ah," he said, "such a lady. I am ready for you, Colin. Please come this way."

He took them through a curtain of beads into a long, narrow room.

Tall windows were set into the outside wall, and below them lay a garden composed of gray boulders, small round stones, and bonsai conifers. Water trickled through it, flowing from a miniature waterfall at the far end.

"Lovely," she said.

"You would prefer this table?" Mr. Matsukata led them to the farthest table of three, with the waterfall just beyond. Colin seated her, and the old man handed them menus and disappeared.

A glance at the menu told her that anything here would suit her: this was authentic Japanese food.

Colin bent his head to study the sheet, and the way the light fell across his face made her wish for her Mamiya. The strong line of the jaw. The planes of cheek and temple. The deep smile creases around the eyes.

What about that tiny jagged scar above his eyebrow? Where did he get it? Men liked to talk about themselves, so he'd probably tell her.

He glanced up, the light shifted, and the moment was gone. "What looks good?"

"Whatever you suggest."

Mr. Matsukata reappeared, and Colin and the old man carried on an animated discussion in Japanese, apparently arranging the meal to their mutual satisfaction.

Mr. Matsukata gave her a twinkling glance and said something that made Colin grin, then scurried off.

When he'd gone, Colin said, "I hope you don't mind. It makes him happy to speak his own language, even with a novice like me."

"How did you learn Japanese?"

"A Japanese friend of mine invited me to visit him for the summer, and that's where I got started."

"Did you happen to go to Kyoto? The gardens there are magnificent."

"They are. Do you photograph gardens too?"

"No, it's difficult to do well. But I admire William Corey's work—he gets incredible depth and tone."

Colin looked intrigued. "He probably does a good job with moss. The chequered moss garden in Kyoto is fascinating. I like Seattle's Japanese garden too. They've got some nice moss specimens—especially the tufted moss."

Mr. Matsukata brought out a white porcelain teapot and two round cups, bowed, and left.

Colin asked a blessing on the meal and poured their tea.

"*Genmai-cha!*" She savored the rich aroma. "Such a

229

fragrance! I haven't had this for years."

He nodded, smiling. "I think it's the roasted rice grains they brew with it."

"I'm curious," she said. "Why is Mr. Matsukata living in this little town, making pizza?"

"It's what he wants to do. He used to have a restaurant in Seattle, and now he's retired. Loves it out here. Makes pizza for the tourists and loggers, and special meals for his friends."

Colin turned to look at the garden, saying, "We worked on this together, and he wants me to help him get some moss started. I'd like to try."

He glanced at her. "Mosses are interesting because they don't have a protective epidermis or even true roots. They have to use the nutrients in the air, and some species have adaptations that fit them to live in the strangest places. God has created them with a reproductive system that's incredibly ordered and beautiful."

She sat back to listen. Moss today, instead of goats. Another unusual lunch date. Was it the air out here that bred such men?

She gazed at a tiny stone lantern beside the waterfall. The moss discourse, though, was different from the goat lecture—it was God-centered. Maybe that's why she could sit here all day listening to this man.

Who was he anyway? Soon he'd start talking about himself, and she'd find out.

He fell silent, and she drank her tea, relishing its delicate, nutty flavor.

She glanced past him again, to the waterfall, and realized that he had been studying her face.

Why the analytical expression?

She gave him a questioning smile.

"I was just . . ." He refilled her cup with tea.

His eyes had that deep-sea look again. Unreadable. He

was reluctant to explain, and she should let it go. But how would he react if she didn't?

"Just?"

"Chinese phoenix," he said.

She was out of her depth already.

"Animal, vegetable, or mineral?" she asked, hoping she could figure out what he was talking about.

"Vegetable, I suppose."

Why that gleam of amusement?

"More precisely," he said, "*Fissidens grandifrons.*"

"What color?" She couldn't bluff him. Give up the game.

"Green," he said. "Deep green."

She glanced from him to the garden and back again. "I think I'm missing a connection here."

"It's a kind of a moss, but never mind," he said. "I was just . . ."

She smiled. "That's where we started, isn't it?"

He looked uncomfortable, but she couldn't resist saying, "Just?"

"Your eyes today."

"Oh." She looked down at her teacup and lifted it to her lips, feeling her cheeks grow warm.

He was still eying her, and she sensed that he'd regained his composure.

Watch out.

He grinned. "Know what? Fraser is right."

She slanted a wary glance at him. "Fraser is right about many things, but I'd hesitate to give him carte blanche."

Teasing, she mimicked his choice of words. "*More precisely,* what?"

"You do look good in pink. Especially with a mint-green sweater."

She put down her cup, shaking her head, laughing because she couldn't help it. "Okay, I shouldn't have . . . I mean, I had no idea . . ."

Her cheeks must be flaming by now.

"Let's call it a tie," he said.

He was enjoying this, way too much.

"Turn the page," she said. "Tell me about your kids."

Mr. Matsukata came in and began to serve. For both of them: a dish of rice and a bowl of miso soup studded with white squares of tofu.

Between them: dishes of cabbage pickle and vegetable tempura and a blue plate with diced, red-glazed pork.

Watching, Lindsey said, "What a feast!"

With a flourish, the old man added a green glass plate that held two small squares of something layered with melted cheese, tied like a gift with strips of chives.

"Colin," she said, "please tell him—because it sounds better in Japanese—tell him I am overwhelmed."

He did so, and the old man smiled broadly. He said something in return and hurried away.

She picked up her bowl of miso and drank from it. "What did he say?"

He looked at her over the rim of his bowl. "Sure you want to know?"

"No, never mind," she said. "Japanese is so effusive. Let's just eat. Tell me, what's this square of cheese?"

He grinned. "It's layered with ume paste and nori."

"Nori—that's sheets of seaweed?"

"Right. I like the pickled plum ume paste he uses. Great flavor. Would you like me to put one on your plate?"

"Please do. I suspect you're better with chopsticks. I'd hate to drop it into the miso." She helped herself to the other dishes, and they ate in silence.

Finally he said, "Where'd you hear about my kids?"

"Remi mentioned them."

He explained how he was working with a small group of students who had drifted into the world of drugs. Many

232

of them had started out as good students from middle-class homes, and some even called themselves Christians.

"They learned rules instead of a personal relationship with Christ," he said. "Sometimes they're the hardest to reach."

He gazed at her. "There's one I'm especially concerned about right now. At heart, he's a nice kid. He grew up with plenty of advantages, but his Christianity was all external, and once he hit college life, he got sucked under."

He chose a mushroom from the plate of tempura. "You saw him that day at the First Hill Bakery."

So he remembered.

"You had your hands full," she said. "I'm surprised you noticed me."

"You were watching us. I've learned to be aware of what's going on around me. In some of the places I go, it's important."

"He fascinated me," she said. "All in black, with that look on his face. He would have made a stunning black-and-white."

"So that's what it was. I wondered."

He didn't seem offended that she'd noticed the boy rather than him.

"It's just the way my mind works."

"Maybe that's why you're so good. I like your book, Lindsey. Where'd you go to get photos like that?"

"An orphanage in New York."

"They let you just walk in and take pictures?"

She shook her head. "In grad school, a couple of us did volunteer work there, and afterwards, I kept on. They gave me permission to take photographs, and in return, I ran a little photo club with the older kids. A company donated crates of stuffed animals to the orphanage, and I made use of them."

"The children posed for you?"

She shook her head. "No posed shots. I took hundreds of photos to get what I wanted. Spending time with those children was quite an experience. Such needs!"

She chose a square of pork and ate it slowly. "When I look at Ginni, I seem to see their faces. Did she grow up in Seattle?"

He nodded. "She's had it rough, but she's got a good home now, and I'm praying that someday the Lord will speak to her tough little heart."

She had mentioned Ginni in hopes of turning the conversation toward Ben Fletcher, but he said, "Here's a question: what do you know about Jack Jincy? Ben fired him a while ago, and I wonder whether he's been carrying some kind of grudge."

"We've had a few talks," she said. "He told me why Ben fired him, complete with excuses, and he didn't seem particularly bitter."

She paused to think. "He's clever enough to pull off the things that have been happening, but I think he lacks motivation."

Colin nodded agreement, and she added, "From what I can tell, Jack's goals in life are to get rich and paint. And to take care of his Grams. He's got a concern for her that is touching."

"So he's probably not our man. Not the instigator, at least."

Mr. Matsukata came to clear their plates, and he placed a small fluted glass dish in front of each of them. It held an orange gel with a layer of white at its base.

He smiled at her. "*Khaki*, persimmon jelly," he said. "And here is jasmine tea, especially for the beautiful lady."

She inclined her head. "Thank you, sir."

After he left, she ate her dessert, saying, "Delight upon delight! He is charming, and his food is excellent."

Colin tilted his head to look at her. "You enjoy people,

don't you, Lindsey?"

He always used her full name, lingering over the syllables as if he liked the sound.

"What do you mean?"

"You seem to see something interesting or good in everyone you meet. There's probably not one person in your life that you truly dislike."

"Hmm." She cradled her teacup in both hands and stared into its pale green depths. Even thinking about Vance made the food in her stomach shift queasily.

Change the subject. Get back to Ben.

"You heard Remi invite me over for supper tomorrow night," she said. "I thought my project was dead, but maybe something good's going to happen. Do you think there's a chance?"

He shrugged. "Ben's gone far away from me. As soon as I walk in, he takes off for the woods."

She heard the regret in his voice. "How do you respond when one of your kids behaves like that?"

"I like the way you think." He narrowed his gaze, considering. "With my kids, I keep an eye on them, but I give them plenty of space. I pray a lot. Sometimes, if they're not too far gone physically, I take them on a tough hike. A couple of days in the wilderness can make a man start thinking and listening. You begin to see who you are."

He told her about some of the students he'd worked with, and Mr. Matsukata came to offer them more tea.

She glanced at her watch. Had they really been here for hours? It was time to go.

When they stepped out onto the porch, they paused to look at the rippled blue bay. A stiff wind blew off the water, ruffling her hair, and she lifted her face to it.

"Thank you, Colin," she said, "I needed to get away. This has been a happy . . . I don't know, what's a good word?"

"Interlude?"

She smiled up at him. "Precisely so. Are you going back to Seattle today?"

He nodded. "Back to my other life. Sometimes, I'm not sure I prefer it."

She had another life too.

A fishing boat slipped past the headland, leaving the horizon empty.

"I wish I knew what to do," she said.

He looked down at her with his grave smile. "The Lord knows, Lindsey. You can count on him to show you. In his time."

Again, that odd little twinge of grief. This was what she'd miss most about these friends. The God-focus.

She squared her shoulders. "Right," she said and started down the steps.

caption:

Tatoosh Overlook

When she returned to her room, it seemed airless and dull, so she changed quickly and spent the next hour running on Thorsen's Beach.

The Japanese meal with Colin had been such a happy time that she wasn't going to dissect it, but looking back, he certainly hadn't told her much about himself.

What was he hiding?

During the evening, she thought several times about Remi. Now that he'd spoken in public about his faith, was he in more danger? She prayed for him.

She prayed, too, about Natalie's supper invitation for tomorrow. In her file were the magazine samples she took to interviews, and she set them out. This might be her big chance to talk to Ben.

By the time she went to bed, she'd convinced herself that something good was going to happen.

The next morning, she phoned Edric right away to tell him about the new development, but he interrupted before she finished the first sentence, promising to call back.

He didn't, of course, so she waited for an hour and tried again.

This time he was terse. "What's up, girl?"

She told him, and he said "Can you send us the Carolina dog feature anyway in case that interview bombs? And I sure did like the puppy shots you sent me."

Lindsey smiled inwardly. "I'd like to get some more, and maybe we could do a feature on the reservation dogs."

"Okay," Edric said. "By the way, Vance said we're going to use Tabitha's feature for the next issue."

Tabitha? The just-out-of-college blond snippet who idolized movie stars?

She kept her voice calm. "I haven't seen it, Edric."

"No, but Vance has. He likes it, and that'll have to be good enough."

"Vance said? He likes it? Since when does Vance decide these things?"

"C'mon, Lin. Lighten up. He's just trying to help."

"He's just trying to run the magazine."

Edric chewed his gum with loud smacking sounds. "Might not be such a bad idea. But we'll settle all that at the Board meeting."

"When's this Board meeting?"

"Next Monday. He's got a couple of proposals."

"I want to see those proposals."

"Sure. I'll have Darlene email them to you right way. You tell me what you think. How's that?"

He had the grace to sound embarrassed, but she didn't feel sorry for him. The doddering old man! She said a brief goodbye and hung up.

She jerked back the sliding door and went outside into the drizzle. Things had really changed, hadn't they? She'd been afraid of this—as soon as those shares changed hands.

Rain blew into her face, and she brushed it away. *Trying to pay me back, are you, Vance? We'll have to see about that.*

The cat appeared in the doorway, sniffing the air. He gave her an eloquent look: *Are you out of your mind?* and stepped back inside.

"You're right, Skookum," she said. "I'm doing way too much thinking. It's time to get on with the day."

Shula called to invite her to lunch the next day, and she agreed with reluctance.

Her phone rang again while she was hanging up the clothes that had mysteriously piled themselves onto a chair.

Alexa explained that she had to run up to the Makah reservation and asked whether Lindsey wanted to come along.

Good timing! She could get some more photos. "Only if you'll let me drive," she said, and Alexa agreed.

It had been a wet morning, but as they drove up the coast to Neah Bay, the clouds began to shred into fragments that skittered across a pale blue sky.

Alexa was taking cookies to a friend who taught Home Economics at the school, so she described her friend and the students she taught.

As she listened, Lindsey felt the tension inside her begin to uncoil.

Alexa asked how her reading was coming along, and they spent the rest of the time discussing the verses they were studying in Philippians.

At the reservation, the small houses were quiet and so was the marina. Was everyone out fishing?

Once again, dogs ran everywhere, and Lindsey remarked on them. She had told Alexa about the new feature, and when she reached for her camera, Alexa slowed the car. "I see that look," she said. "Want to take some photos?"

She parked near a bucket marked FISH. Lindsey thanked her with a smile, and Alexa followed as she strolled along the waterfront taking one shot after another.

"These dogs interest me," Lindsey said. "What a grand mix of colors, shapes, and body styles!"

"Your readers will love them," Alexa said.

Lindsey watched a pair of gray puppies tussling in the weeds and circled them, taking a dozen shots.

Finally she stopped. "That should do me for now."

"You could call it 'Reservation Ruffians,'" Alexa said.

"That's a great title," Lindsey said, laughing. "Okay, where does your friend live?"

Alexa's friend wasn't home, so she left her box on the woman's doorstep and rejoined Lindsey in the car.

"Too bad," she said. "I wanted you to meet her. But now we have some time for ourselves." She flashed a smile at Lindsey. "Have you been out to Cape Flattery yet?"

Lindsey shook her head, and Alexa smiled again. "That settles it."

After they'd driven through a broad valley, the road began to climb, with forest on either side, and it finally ended in a parking lot. A sign pointed into the trees: CAPE TRAIL MOST N.W. POINT.

"What's this about N.W. Point?" Lindsey said.

"You'll see. We're going to end up on a headland that is the most northwestern point of the United States."

As they started down a well-kept trail, Alexa said, "Oh! I meant to remind Peter to turn down the slow-cooker."

"Want to use my phone?"

Alexa looked doubtful. "We could try."

Lindsey soon understood Alexa's remark. Her phone spent a long time searching and finally gave up. "Isn't there any cell reception up here?" she said.

"It's spotty at best. Maybe he'll see my note."

"I hope so. Look at these trees! I've been saying that ever since I got here, but these are the biggest yet."

The trees cast deep shadows, broken only by a rare shaft of sunlight. Ferns, the dark-green vigorous kind, grew everywhere, spurting up to three or four feet high.

Alexa pointed out her favorite plants: the leathery green salal and fine-leafed huckleberry, all flourishing.

She paused to kneel by a clump of delicate whitish-green moss. "Another of my favorites. Colin showed it to me."

Lindsey touched one of the flat, rounded leaves. "It looks like stained glass," she said. "What's it called?"

"Clear moss." Alexa got up, brushing at her knees. "Pretty, isn't it?"

Lindsey smiled in agreement. The moss reminded her of Colin, and his reticence yesterday. What would Alexa think about it? She began framing a question as they started off again. Better make it a hypothetical man.

They soon reached an open, marshy area which they crossed on a boardwalk made of thick cedar slabs. Trying for nonchalance, Lindsey said, "Men are strange creatures, aren't they?"

Alexa laughed. "And some are stranger than others."

"I have a theory," Lindsey said. "Men like to talk about themselves. In fact, most of them think they're a fascinating subject. I can't tell you how many times I've sat through a meal listening to every tribulation in the last ten years of a guy's life, and how he triumphed over them all."

She stepped off the boardwalk onto the sodden leaves of the trail. "But once in a while you run into the kind that doesn't."

"The strong, silent type?"

"No, he'll talk, but it's about his friends or his work or some impersonal thing that interests him, like moss."

So much for the hypothetical man.

"You can learn a lot from what a guy says about his friends or his interests," Alexa said calmly. "I think that when these big men who're good at everything run into something they aren't used to, they get nervous. So they stick to safe subjects."

Lindsey smiled to herself. Alexa's comment might be translated as: "The Paragon isn't quite as sure of himself as he might appear."

By now the coast was in sight. The trees thinned, and they were walking beside steep, rocky banks clothed with salal. Far below, white water churned between piles of rough gray rock and sea stacks. The trail ended at a lookout platform set high above the ocean.

"Here's the Pacific," Alexa said. "Just think: on the other side of this . . . is Japan."

Not far offshore lay an island with a tiny lighthouse and waves curling white around its ragged edges. Lindsey recognized it from Jack's painting. Tatoosh, he'd called it.

It was too cold to stand around, so she took a few photos, and they hurried back along the trail. When they reached the Jeep, Alexa said, "Are you hungry? I'm starving."

"Me too," Lindsey said. After talking to Edric, she hadn't felt like eating.

"Good! I brought some stuff, and we can eat at the Tatoosh Overlook."

They took an unpaved road that led uphill to a small clearing edged with wild blackberry bushes.

The wind blew sharp and cold across the unsheltered space, but the sun was almost warm. Alexa unpacked sandwiches and cookies, and they stood beside each other to eat, looking out at the water.

The shoreline of Vancouver Island was a misted blue, and the ocean was much darker, the color of Colin's eyes.

Lindsey checked herself. Why did she keep thinking about him? It had been only a lunch. A good lunch, but still . . . Colin probably brought other women there. His manners were polished, so he probably wasn't new to the dating scene. Why wasn't he married? Was he one of these men who couldn't settle down?

The wind tore at her hair, and she turned away from the ocean.

"I love it up here," Alexa said. "So did Tommy—my son. We used to come together."

She stood with eyes half-closed, her hair streaming behind her like a bronze banner.

"You two had a lot in common?"

She nodded. "We did all kinds of stuff. He was a daredevil, and he'd laugh at me because I was scared to climb a cliff or whatever, and then—just to hear him say, 'Way to go, Mom!'—I would do it."

The lines on her face deepened, but she lifted her chin. "He joined the army, and the day he shipped out, I came up here by myself to pray that the Lord would keep him safe."

She paused. "You know the story in the book of Daniel about the three men who were going to be burned alive, and they told the king that God could deliver them?"

Lindsey nodded. "The fiery furnace."

"They said something else to the king: *But if not*— Like they were still okay if God didn't do what they were hoping for."

Her voice wavered. "So I added that to my prayer for Tommy. *But if not* . . . And then he died with two of his buddies in an ambush attack."

She swung around to face Lindsey. "You know what I'm learning? God never wastes anything, especially when it concerns his children and their sorrows."

Alexa pushed the hair out of her eyes. "The Lord gives us gifts, Lin, wonderful gifts from his loving heart. *People*. I'm learning to hold those gifts in an open hand."

She spread out her hands, palms upward—sturdy, work-worn hands—and stared at them. "I'm learning not to clutch my dear ones to myself. Christ is all I want. He's all I really need."

When Alexa looked up, tears shone in her eyes. "There's my other son, Todd. He's so messed up, poor kid, and I love him so much. But I'm praying that the Lord will have mercy on him. Maybe one of these days, he and Colin will be here the same weekend. Colin's got a gift for reaching kids like Todd."

She pulled a tissue from her pocket. "Sorry! I'm not sure you wanted to hear all that."

Lindsey put an arm around her. "Anything about you, I want to hear."

She leaned her head against the bright hair, and Alexa closed her eyes. "Thanks, Lin."

After a minute, Alexa turned to look again at the ocean. "That Tatoosh out there seems like a mysterious place. A lot of the Native Americans think it's haunted."

"Jack Jincy did a painting of it," Lindsey said. "Pretty good. I guess he likes to come up here and watch the eagles. He's got a cabin—something he's appropriated for himself, I think—but I'm not sure where. He calls it his eagle eyrie. Are there really eagles' nests around here?"

Alexa nodded. "Bald eagles and a few goldens. I think this whole area belongs to the Makah tribe, but that wouldn't bother Jack. It's so wild, it would be easy for someone like him to burrow in."

Lindsey eyed the tangle of bushes that surrounded the clearing. "Easy to get lost?"

"Not if you stay on the main road. It's all the little roads that'll get you into trouble."

On the way back, Alexa told her about the legends that had grown up around Tatoosh Island, and the time went much too quickly.

Lindsey had wanted to talk to her about Vance and Edric, but the issues were complicated, and each day brought new problems. Why should she pile another burden on her new friend?

At the Roost, she ran up the steps to her room and realized that she was humming. A happy afternoon.

More precisely, a happy interlude; another one.

She unlocked the door and went inside, smiling.

Her smile died as the morning's conversation with Edric blazed into her mind.

The proposals would be waiting in her IN-box. She wouldn't look at them now. Concentrate on tonight's meeting with Ben. Well, a supper, at least, and maybe a meeting.

caption:

Shula's Warning

Lindsey had wanted to take something to the Fletcher children, and books came to mind. This would be a good time to go over and see what Fraser had in stock.

He left her alone to browse, which suited her fine. She didn't have the energy for vigorous repartee today.

Kumtux appeared from nowhere, presumably to check on her. She scratched between his ears and remarked on his elegant tail; then he stalked off to attend to other business.

She took her pile of books to the counter, asked Fraser's opinion, and chose one for each child.

He slid her gifts into a bag, saying, "I hope it goes well for you tonight."

"I'm hopeful too, but I don't know. The project is dead. No, it's alive. They want it. No, they're going to use something else. I should have bought plane tickets, but I didn't. I'm getting the sense I should wait, but I don't know why."

She shrugged. "And how is your day going?"

He smiled. "God is doing some surprising things, isn't He? As you said, one fish ladder after another. But waiting sounds like a good idea. You're on personal days anyway, so why not?"

Sure, why not? Except that Vance was destroying the magazine, and every day that passed made it worse.

By the time she left for the Fletchers', she was still feeling optimistic. And when Remi came bounding out to greet her, followed by all the children plus Spot, her hopes rose.

The children liked their books, even Ginni, who said a quiet "Thank you, Miss Lindsey," and ran off with Spot to read *Spiders Up Close*.

In the kitchen, Natalie greeted her with a hug, and Ben looked up from his newspaper with something like a smile. His face was puffy and his eyes deeply shadowed, as if he were ill.

During the meal, he said very little, and while they were still eating Natalie's chocolate cake, he excused himself from the table, saying he had to feed the dogs.

Lindsey watched him go, telling herself that he might come back after he was finished, but even though she stayed later than she wanted to, he never did.

So that was that. Her big breakthrough.

Remi must have been disappointed too because as they walked down the porch steps, he said, "I'm sorry, Lin. I was hoping he'd talk to you, but I'm not surprised. Ben might look okay, but he's in terrible shape."

She leaned against the fender of the Jeep. "And what about you, Remi? I was proud of you, listening to your testimony. I've been praying for you. Should I be worried?"

"I'm not sure what's going to happen."

He stood there looking thoughtful, his face lit by the floodlights on the barn. People-gifts, Alexa had said. This boy was one of them.

"Do you have brothers and sisters?" she said.

He shook his head. "I told you, you're my big sister, and that's it."

"Your aunt . . . ?"

247

"She still lives in Chicago, I guess, with her little boy. My parents died when I was twelve—that's why I went to live in my uncle's home. There's another uncle, but he's back in Saudi, I think."

He smiled. "Don't be sorry for me. I've got a great family here, and Colin and Fraser." He ran his hand over the black surface of the fender. "I've been asking the Lord what to do with my life."

"Good!" she said. "I know the Lord's got something wonderful ahead for you, Remi, and he's going to show you. In his time."

He grinned. "*In his time.* You sound like Colin. He told me that waiting for God is something he's still trying to learn, and it's a hard lesson for him."

"For me too, Remi."

"Let's keep praying for each other," he said with a quiet smile, and she thought how much he'd grown up since she first met him.

That evening, she didn't bother to check her email. Those proposals from Edric? No. She needed to sleep tonight.

The next morning when she returned from the beach, she couldn't put it off any longer.

There were four proposals, all written in the obscure style that she recognized as Vance's.

Pared down, Proposal #1 stated that from now on, magazine business would be run by the Board, which would consist of the shareholders.

Before this, she and Edric had made all the decisions, but now Vance would have a say, and so would Edric's sister, the wealthy and foolish Adina.

Cumbersome at best.

Proposal #2 made Edric lifetime Editor-in-Chief.

Smooth. Edric would like that title. Would he retain

any real power? That remained to be seen.

Proposal #3 made Vance the Managing Editor.

Of course, if he was going to run things, he needed a title.

Proposal #4 made Tabitha the Associate Editor.

Who did Vance think he was kidding? Tabitha might be cute, but she didn't have the brains or experience to handle an editorial position.

Lindsey clicked out of the file and stared at her computer screen. No glittering title for Lindsey Dumont? Maybe, if she behaved, Vance would let her type the mailing labels.

She left the computer and dragged herself to the leather chair. How could she fight this guy and win?

She should have told Edric right away about Vance. She should have gone back to deal with him herself. She should have left a week ago.

But she would have missed . . . a lot.

She covered her face with her hands and bent over her knees. "Lord, help me! I hate all this. And I hate that man."

Her gaze fell on Fraser's driftwood salmon where it lay halfway under the other chair. Skookum must have knocked it off the desktop again. She picked it up.

Created by God. A masterpiece from his hand. For a single purpose.

She traced the flowing line of the fin. "Lord," she said, "thank you for loving me. In all these things I want to . . . *to conquer* . . . because of your love. Show me what to do about this job. And about my life."

Despite Fraser's generous opinion of her, what she needed was courage.

And maybe some tea. Didn't story heroines sip hot tea while making monumental decisions?

Never mind the decisions. A double-shot mocha latte would be ideal, but she'd settle for a cup of strong tea.

Then she would clean the room.

And soon it would be time for lunch with Shula, which she'd really rather skip.

On the way to Shula's, she tried to analyze her reluctance. Perhaps it was because of Friday evening: Shula's too-personal confidences about Kamal. Her questions about Remi. Her giggle.

From what Jack said, Shula had taken a dose of FlowerFire. Maybe she hadn't noticed Lindsey's distaste.

She turned off the highway. Was Shula trying to destroy Ben? Because of Ginni?

Why didn't that ring true? Perhaps she could find out.

She parked in front of the elegant house. Whatever the reason, Shula had to be stopped before something more serious happened. Perhaps, if they had a quiet heart-to-heart talk, she could convince her to just . . . just leave Ben alone.

Today Shula wore a turquoise outfit, her most gracious manners, and an affectionate smile. She took Lindsey's arm as they went into the herb room.

"I have our lunch all ready," she said. "I'm glad you could come. I've had such a dull weekend."

She had arranged tiny steak sandwiches and grapes on the low table with a pot of green tea, and a minute later she brought out bowls of fragrant, spicy soup.

They ate, and Shula talked about the upcoming book fair, and inevitably, Kamal. She described the children she was tutoring under the literacy program and recounted her speech at the recent library board meeting.

Lindsey made an occasional comment, waiting for the right moment to ask the important questions. She could start with the dogs.

"And where are Tyee and Pelton today?" she said.

"In their pen. We went for a nice run this morning, and I think they need some time to themselves. But we're finished eating, aren't we? Let's surprise them with a treat."

She took Lindsey out the French doors, past the herb garden, and through a dense stand of trees on the left side of the house.

Both dogs began to yip as they entered a large clearing. "They're complaining that they haven't been fed for weeks," Shula said.

Lindsey smiled. "I know what you mean. Dogs always say that."

The dogs lived in a long enclosure with a chain link fence and an elaborate doghouse. They still wore their shock collars.

Shula unlocked the gate and went inside. She spoke to them in Makah—from what Jack said—requiring them to sit, stay, and beg; finally she threw them large rawhide bones that they attacked with ferocity.

After a few minutes, Shula said, "Let's go back. I meant to show you my new toy. Today we can start being the healthiest women in town."

Her new toy was a stainless steel juicer. She took a bag of oranges from the refrigerator. "Have you had your bioflavonoids lately? Here's your chance. I like to add a little ginger to give it zing."

A few minutes later, she poured fresh juice for both of them, and they went back to sit in the herb room.

They sipped their juice, agreeing with each other that it was delicious, and Lindsey prayed for wisdom. Should she say anything about Ben?

"How's the real estate business coming?" she said.

"Very well indeed. That presentation you did for me was effective. My client is coming out this afternoon to see the property again, and he's bringing his dogs."

Shula paused. "Kamal viewed your photos too, and he was impressed."

She gave Lindsey a hopeful smile. "We're wondering

whether you might want to work with us on some freelance jobs from time to time."

We? How did Kamal suddenly fit into the picture?

"What did you have in mind?" Lindsey said.

"You must have noticed that he asked you a lot of questions."

"I wondered about it."

"I think he was also being careful." Shula's voice hardened. "There's a lot of anti-Islamic sentiment these days."

"I am a Christian," Lindsey said carefully. "But I do not hate Muslims."

"That's what I told him." Shula sent her a sideways glance. "One of your best friends used to be a Muslim, didn't he?"

Something cold shivered through her. "How did you know that?"

Shula smiled. "In my line of work, I hear just about everything. Does Remi hate his Muslim brothers now?"

"No, he doesn't, not any more than I do. It's the jihadists that I don't care for."

"Of course. We agree on that. And, Lin, you are a sympathetic person, as well as very talented. I pray that you will have a heart for the widows and children of Palestine."

That was it, the FRO.

"If you were to take pictures of those poor children, your work would help us raise money for the families damaged by the war. You could be famous—another Robert Capa."

"There's only one Robert Capa—"

"—And it would be very profitable."

Profitable for all concerned?

"Unfortunately, I'm making plans to go back to New York," Lindsey said. "The magazine has internal problems

252

that I need to straighten out, and it will take all my time."

"Oh, no!" Shula looked genuinely dismayed. "You never did get those photos you wanted, did you? Are you sure you have to leave?"

How could she say, *I'm waiting for God to show me?*

"It depends."

Shula put her glass down on the table with a thump. "It depends on Ben Fletcher, doesn't it?"

Her eyes flashed. "Listen to me! That fine upstanding Indian brave with his precious Indian dogs and his perfect little partridge of a wife—he's nothing but a bum."

This was the moment.

"You're doing all you can to destroy him, aren't you?"

Shula's face rearranged itself into innocence. "Destroy Ben? Why would I do a thing like that?"

"Is it because of Ginni?"

"Why shouldn't I want Ginni to live with me? She's my dead sister's child." Shula's mouth twisted. "He's not fit to take care of her. Look what a mess he's got himself into, with his kennels closed down."

"Because of what you did?"

"Whoever's doing anything, it serves him right." Her voice took on a sharp edge. "Why those people keep adopting children is beyond me. They can hardly afford to feed and clothe the ones they've got. Maybe if Ben spent less on beer, they might have more to go around. And womanizing isn't cheap, either."

Shula put a hand to her eyes. "Okay, okay. I know he's the father, but Ginni is all I have left of my sister, and I can give her a wonderful life."

Drama mode. She didn't love the child.

"Did Ben tell you he's Ginni's father?"

"Of course not. Such a coward." Shula jerked to her feet and went to stand by the French doors. "I had to find out from Belinda, of all people."

Lindsey turned to look at her. "The will?"

"She tells me everything. She's useful that way. Then Max and I had a conversation."

Max? Max Lougherbrey. The lawyer.

"Max and I took a walk together. I'm named in the will, so of course he had to talk to me." Her lips thinned. "A foolish man. He told me much more than he realized."

Shula clasped her hands under her chin, knotting them together so tightly that her fingertips turned white.

"For years, I've had detectives trying to find that will. Turns out Cheree left it with her druggie boyfriend just before she got murdered. He ran away, and it took all this time to find him."

She leaned against the glass, flicking her fingernails across it. "Silly girl. She always was crazy about Ben, but he never cared. Not for anybody. Why wasn't he man enough to leave her alone in the first place?"

Lindsey went to stand beside her. "Shula." She put a hand on the slim shoulder. "Can't you let this go? It's going to eat you alive. God can—"

She shrugged away. "Don't you talk to me about God. Where was He when my sister died? Murdered!"

There was no answer that Shula would accept.

Shula swung back toward her. "I like being your friend, Lin. Don't spoil it! You've been spending way too much time with Miss Sweetness and Light."

She glanced at her watch. "I have an appointment, so I have to leave." Her voice rose. "But I'd advise you to keep out of this nasty business. A friend of Ben Fletcher's is no friend of mine."

She clutched at Lindsey's arm. "Go back to New York if you have to," she said. "We can still do business. I'll miss you—I really will. But Ben Fletcher is bad trouble. Stay away from him."

Lindsey stepped back, and Shula laughed, a harsh,

grating sound. "And listen to me, for your own sake. Watch yourself with that muscle-bound friend of Ben's. He'll string you along until you give him everything—then he'll break your heart. I know."

Her throat hurt. Her neck hurt. Her head hurt.

Just a tension headache.

She really didn't feel like going back to the Roost, especially since Belinda knew that she'd had tea with Shula.

Rain was coming down in sheets, so walking wasn't an option. She'd already spent too much time at the bakery.

Besides, if she was leaving, she didn't want to . . . Didn't want to spend too much time with Alexa? Miss Sweetness and Light, who was fast becoming a dear friend in Christ?

And what about Colin?

She tried to swallow the prickle in her throat. Colin with Shula? Not the man she knew. They must've had a relationship of some kind, even it wasn't as involved as . . . that.

Slowly she drove down the road into Cameron Bay. What to do next? She was hungry; yes, that was it. Stop analyzing. Do something constructive.

She'd get a take-out pizza from Mr. Mott's. The old man's smile would be cheering.

She stood at the counter until a yawning teenager appeared to take her order. He said, loftily, that his grandfather was in Seattle for a few days and did she want pepperoni on that.

She spent the evening reworking the Carolina dogs feature, checked it one last time, and sent it off.

She looked at the photos she'd taken at Neah Bay. Definite potential here. She set to work planning the content, edited and arranged the photos, and sat back.

Reservation Ruffians! One more trip to Neah Bay and she'd have a great feature. Meanwhile, she would send some more teasers to Edric.

When she finished, she phoned Mollie, described Remi's testimony, and asked her to pray for him.

Mollie told her about a hike she'd taken with (marvelous) Nathan and wondered aloud when Lindsey was coming home.

All Lindsey could say was pray for me too, and before she did anything silly like cry, she said goodbye.

What was the matter with her? Dumont women never cried. That's what Great-Grandpapa always said.

She took a long shower, washed her hair, and put fresh pink polish on her toenails, which usually made her feel invincible. Not this time.

She amused herself, as she drifted off to sleep, with scenarios of Vance—caught stealing, caught lying, caught cheating on his wife. Maybe he'd slip up and do something really stupid, and Edric would see what he'd bought into.

She made satisfying captions for each image, but when she awoke the next morning, she felt exhausted.

Never mind. She'd drink two cups of Belinda's excellent coffee, and then she had to phone Edric. Didn't he see what these so-called proposals meant? A Board meeting? What a joke.

Edric answered the phone right away. He wasn't chewing gum, a bad sign.

After she'd presented her points, he said, "Vance has been telling me that we need him because he has good business sense. He thinks you and I have been running the magazine like it's our hobby."

His voice changed, becoming persuasive. "I'll still be editor-in-chief for the rest of my life. That's better than retiring. And you can still be something like features editor or a contributing editor. Vance says he'll see what your attitude is like when you get back, and he'll decide."

"He'll decide, Edric?"

"He wants to increase our profit margin. I trust him."

"But you and I have a contract, remember?"

"I showed it to Vance, and he says it's rather vague. I can still do what I want."

The satisfaction in his voice stung her into a quick reply. "But our understanding was that when you retired, I was going to make the decisions. Remember?"

"Yes, I do." He coughed, an old man's thin, dry cough. "Yes, I remember that, and I know you've put a lot of hard work into the magazine. I don't know what I'd have done without you."

She didn't answer. Let him think about that.

But a hollow place grew inside her. Edric was old. He was weak. He was greedy.

He cleared his throat. "Tell you what, Lin. Make sure you get here for the Board meeting. That sister of mine is quite taken with Vance, so she'll vote with him. But if you and I talk beforehand, we can cook up something together. If we vote the same, we'll still have fifty percent. Then we can negotiate."

Did he really think he could negotiate with someone like Vance?

He interrupted her thoughts. "Okay? And keep me posted. See you soon. Bye."

A flame of anger spurted through her apprehension. She dropped the phone onto her desk. She could storm into that Board meeting and tear those people up by the roots. Thunder and lightning. But to what purpose?

Her mind went blank on that question. No answer. Not anything that satisfied.

Lunch? No. Make some tea. Go for a walk. Was it still raining? A drizzle. But she had this Bible for Odela, and she'd promised to go see her and it was Wednesday already.

Okay, go see Odela. Maybe pack a sandwich and try the other beach afterwards. Dress warmly, but in layers.

Remember it's hot at Odela's.

She had finished making the sandwich when her phone rang, and she snatched it up.

Remi.

LOST CALL.

He phoned back. "Sorry. My phone's acting up again—needs a new battery. I was just wondering, have you seen Ginni?"

"No, I haven't." She glanced at her watch: 2:30 p.m. "She's not with Fraser?"

"She didn't show up for her lessons, and we can't seem to find her. This isn't the first time she's gone off—last week she ended up at the post office, talking to Mrs. Thorsen. After the punishment she got, I didn't think she'd try it again."

"Is there anything I can do?" Lindsey said.

"Pray for us! Ben's thinking Shula might have—I don't know. Anyway, we're going over to Shula's place now."

"I'm just about to leave for Odela's. Call me as soon as you find out anything."

"I'll try. Let me give you Alexa's number and Fraser's too. Just in case."

She changed into a green short-sleeved tee, then layered on a sweater and a hooded sweatshirt. With her Columbia jacket, she'd be warm enough on the beach, even in the rain.

Her shoulder bag was already packed, so she added the sandwich, picked up the Bible for Odela, threw a regretful look at her cameras, and hurried downstairs.

caption:

Storm

Odela took a long time to answer the door, and when she stepped inside, Lindsey understood why. As the woman moved slowly back to her chair, wine fumes drifted behind her.

Should she give her the Bible now, or wait until she was more coherent?

Too late. Odela had seen the bag.

"Odela is pleased to have you visit," she said. "What is this?"

Lindsey handed the bag to her, and she pulled out the Bible. "Odela knows about this book," she said. "Her granny had one. Alexa reads it to Odela sometimes. Maybe Odela will read it too. She is very busy, but she will try. Look what Jack brought her."

Somewhere, Jack had found a box of beaded necklaces, and Odela was sorting the beads into a large plastic box on her lap.

"Would Miss Lindsey like to help Odela? All the red ones go together. You know red?"

"I'll be glad to help," Lindsey said. "And I'll make us some tea."

She might as well take care of the dishes too.

Before starting to work, she took off her jacket, her hooded sweatshirt, and her sweater. Almost comfortable.

After she'd washed the dishes, she wiped down the counter, and under the newspapers she found a pair of hoop earrings. They were as large as cookies and sparkled with pink rhinestones.

She showed them to Odela. "Are these yours?"

"No. Odela does not like glitz. Those belong to Jack. They go with his old lady costume. That boy always leaves his things around. Odela needs to scold him."

So Jack had taken Bobby. Why? And what should she do with this bit of information? File it away for now.

They drank their tea and sorted beads, and for at least half an hour, Odela delivered a rambling monologue about her life before she married.

Lindsey kept her shoulder bag close by so she wouldn't miss Remi's call, and after a while she began to wonder whether he'd tried to phone but couldn't get through.

"Jack brought these pretties for his Grams." Odela smiled. "Jack takes good care of his Grams."

Her expression shifted. "Odela knows a secret. It is Jack's secret. He told it to Odela today. He says it is good, very good. These blue ones are my favorites."

Lindsey chose a multicolor string of beads. Jack probably had a lot of secrets. The inside of his head would be a frightening place to visit.

Odela put a handful of blue beads into a compartment. "Jack has an eeklit."

Eeklit? Eeklet? Eaglet. What was Jack doing with an eaglet?

"He's taking his eeklit for a ride up to his eyrie."

His cabin on Cape Flattery?

Lindsey kept her eyes on the necklace she held and asked, "Did he say anything else?"

"No." Odela sounded confused. "He took a blanket

and my cookies. My favorite cookies. For his golden eeklit. That's what he told Odela."

Odela reached into the cushions behind her and pulled out a slim bottle. "Odela doesn't like Jack going up to his eagle eyrie. It is too far away."

She took a sip from the bottle, then another. "It is much too far. Odela worries when he takes his bike into those wild places."

Lindsey waited, uneasy now.

Odela pushed the bottle back into the cushions. "One day, Odela told him, your Grams doesn't like you going up to that eyrie. It makes her cry. So he drew her a picture. Miss Lindsey likes Jack's pictures. Odela will show her."

She heaved herself to her feet with a grunt and shuffled over to the kitchen nook. "Dishes are all clean. Odela says thank you very, very much."

She pulled open a drawer. "Odela feels like crying now. She needs to look at Jack's picture."

She took a small piece of cardboard from the drawer, sat down again, and propped it in her lap for Lindsey to see. It was a map done in colored inks, showing a road that curved away from a circle labeled **T-OV**. At intervals, the road was marked with tiny sketches, as if they were landmarks.

"That's beautiful," Lindsey said, still sorting beads. "I can see why it makes you happy."

A suspicion took shape in her mind and grew into something dreadful.

Odela sighed. "Odela tries not to worry about Jack. But he has a truck today." She frowned. "Odela heard something in the truck. Eeklits don't cry, do they? You put the red ones in with the blue ones."

"Sorry." Lindsey fished out the red beads, put them right, and reached for her shoulder bag. Notebook. Pen.

She started on a quick sketch of the map. "When did

Jack leave?"

Odela hesitated. "Odela started watching 'Four-legged Famous,' and Jack came in. Jack was whistling."

Lindsey finished the map and snatched up the TV guide. "Four-legged Famous"?

It came on at 2 p.m. More than two hours ago.

"Odela, can I borrow one of your blankets? Do you have a flashlight?"

Odela smiled. "Miss Lindsey is going to help Jack! Look in the closet. Take anything. The TV man said storm."

The first blanket she found was soft and clean, so she grabbed it, and after rooting around in the clutter at the bottom of the closet, she unearthed a flashlight.

Odela had gone to the stove and was pouring hot water into a thermos. "Jack likes tea." She dropped in a tea bag. "I had some cookies." She looked around the kitchen, blinking. "Where did my cookies go?"

"Thank you." Lindsey spooned sugar into the tea and closed the thermos. "I have to run, Odela."

As soon as the door shut behind her, she sprinted for the Jeep. She threw her supplies into the back seat, spun the Jeep down the road, and turned onto the highway.

Once she had settled down to driving more sanely, she phoned Remi. It rang and rang.

Your call has been forwarded to an automated voice-messaging system.

His phone must be on the blink up again.

She left a message anyway: "I talked to Odela. Sounds like Jack has Ginni, if you can believe her. I'm going to check. Phone me."

She kept an eye on the clouds massing ahead of her and the waves kicking up in the Strait. Odela was right so far. A storm did seem to be moving in.

She ate her sandwich as she drove. She drank some

water. Twice more she called Remi.

Now she was driving through Neah Bay and would soon be out of cell phone range. Better try Alexa.

The bakery's phone rang six times, and then Peter's voice invited her to leave a message. She tried again. It would be heartening to talk to Alexa and ask her to pray.

Okay, leave another message. She'd better make it a good one.

"Hi, Lexa. It's 4:45. I'm in Neah Bay, heading for Cape Flattery. From what Odela says, Jack has taken Ginni up to his cabin there. She's drunk, so I'm not sure I can believe her. Don't worry about me. I've got a copy of Odela's map, and food and water, and I'm not afraid of Jack. But there's a storm coming. Pray for me? I'll get back to you as soon as I can."

Maybe Fraser was in his store. She called him and got another answering machine. He must be out looking for Ginni. She left the same message.

There. Did that sound like a competent woman on a mission? She hadn't mentioned that her hands were stiff from clutching at the steering wheel, and that it was getting dark, and rain was splashing onto the windshield. But Alexa and Fraser would pray; she could count on it.

She found the road they'd taken the other day, the one that led up to the Cape Flattery trail, and she turned onto it. The pavement was awash, and her headlights reflected off a curtain of rain.

At the Cape Flattery parking lot, she checked her cell phone. No messages and no signal. She used a precious minute to study her scrawled map and note the landmarks.

First, take the road to T-OV. That must be the Tatoosh Overlook, where she and Alexa had come the other day. From that roughly circular place, another road. Jack had said the one at seven o'clock.

Please guide me, Lord.

The road to the overlook was already running with streams of water, and drenched saplings hung low, but the Jeep climbed steadily upward.

In the clearing, the wind whistled across the car, rocking it, as she drove at a crawl around the perimeter.

Was that the road? Barely an opening in the bushes? She eased the Jeep through the wall of brambles, and found herself on a muddy track that vanished into darkened trees.

She followed it, feeling the slickness under her tires and trying to remember everything she'd learned about driving in mud.

The landmarks crept past.

Here was the first bridge, sagging toward a fast-running stream. She sent the Jeep across it and churned up a hill on the other side.

Turn left and follow the stream—even though it was spreading wider and wider. Don't stop now.

She passed a pile of boulders, bigger than a house.

Stay on the road—watch out—have to go across the stream again.

This bridge was silted with mud, and she glimpsed the faint outlines of tire tracks. A truck had been here.

The road climbed away from the stream, skirting the base of a cliff that looked as tall as the Empire State Building.

She crept along the next ridge, which was slippery in the cascading rain. The Jeep lost traction and slid sideways.

Slow down. Take it slow and steady.

But impatience drummed inside her.

The road turned again. She drove through evergreens and into a forest of young aspens with slender trunks that glistened in the headlights.

Where was Jack?

The cabin should be somewhere after those aspens. Would Ginni be there? If she wasn't, where was she?

Why had Jack done this?

Would she miss the cabin in the dark? She'd better try the first one she came to.

Who had hired Jack?

The road seemed to wind on for miles before her headlights glanced off the corner of something that looked like an abandoned house.

She saw no light and heard no sound except the wind in the trees. No truck was parked here, but tracks showed in the weeds.

She grabbed the flashlight and ran through the rain to the cement blocks that served for steps. Over the front door, a brass eagle watched, its wings outspread.

The flimsy-looking door was locked, and she pounded on it, hardly expecting a response.

She shone the light through a window. On the far side of the room was something like a bed. On the bed was . . . a bundle.

"Ginni? Ginni?" she called.

The person—yes, it was a person, a live person—rolled back and forth.

Should she break the window? But the flashlight was cheap plastic, and her shoes weren't heavy enough. Get a rock? There'd be glass all over, and Jack would know that his eaglet had flown.

Hurry. She circled around to the back and found another door, its frame badly rotted. She rammed her shoulder against it, and the wood gave way.

She pushed past the boxes behind the door, stepped over a hole, and ran to the bed.

It was Ginni—tied up, gagged, and squirming.

"Okay, Ginni, just wait! We'll get out of here." She made her voice light. "Just a minute, little one. Be brave."

She slipped off the child's crude gag, dug through the dishes in the sink for a knife, and sawed at the cheap rope that tied Ginni to the bed.

Taking too long. Hurry, hurry! Before he comes back.

The last strand broke, and she pulled Ginni upright. The child clutched at her silently and Lindsey held her close, patting the thin back.

"We have to go quickly," she said. "Try to walk."

Ginni took a step and stumbled, but Lindsey caught her and propelled her across the room to the back door. It hung half-open, and Ginni recoiled from the blowing rain.

Lindsey tightened her hold on the child. "It'll be warm in my car. Let's run—now!"

They ran through the rain and the wind and the slippery weeds to the Jeep, and finally Ginni was inside, crouching low, sobbing.

Start the engine. Buckle seatbelts. Turn. Don't get stuck in this muddy road.

She patted Ginni's shoulder again and drove with care, trying to keep out of the water that rushed down each side of the road, trying not to worry about the wind that shrieked around them.

Ginni stopped crying. Was she listening to the wind too?

Lindsey pulled her shoulder bag onto the console between them. "Are you hungry, Ginni?"

"No."

"Okay. I can't talk for a minute—let's get a little farther."

What would she do if she ran into Jack? There was no room for passing, and he'd recognize her car.

Something cracked behind them, loud as a gunshot. In the rearview mirror she saw a huge dark shape falling across the road.

"Just a dead old tree." She said it aloud, as much for her benefit as for Ginni's. "That's the kind that gets knocked down in a storm like this. We don't want to go

266

back there anyway."

She drove faster. Get out of this wind. Get under cover. The aspens were just ahead, tossing in the wind.

A groaning sounded in front of her, a creaking—too close—a snapping, a splintering, and a thud.

She slowed to a crawl. Sure enough. The headlights showed a full-grown aspen blocking their way. Farther along came another crash.

She didn't want to listen to any more trees coming down. Time to talk.

"Okay," she said to Ginni. "This is good news, and this is bad news."

"What?"

"We can't get out. That's the bad news." She put a hand on Ginni's arm. "But here's the good news. Jack's truck can't get in. And here's some more good news. The Lord God knows we're here, so we don't have to be afraid."

Ginni hunched in her seat. "Why doesn't he do something about it?"

"I think he will. I think he's going to send Remi to find us."

Lindsey checked her watch, thinking it must be almost midnight. It was eight o'clock.

The child shivered under her hand. The hooded sweatshirt was soaking wet.

"Here," Lindsey said, "let's take this off you."

But Ginni clutched it to herself. "I'll be cold! I'll be so cold!"

"I'll give you mine. See?" She took off the child's sweatshirt and put it with her wet jacket in the back seat; then she helped Ginni put on her sweater.

"There," she said. "How's that?"

"Cold." Ginni hugged herself. "I'm so cold."

"Okay, here's my hoodie too." Lindsey laughed as she zipped it on over the sweater. "You're going to look like a roly-poly."

"What's that?"

"A very small person who wears a hundred sweaters and looks like a big round ball of clothes," Lindsey said, inventing freely. "They have to watch out for hills."

"Why?"

"Once they start rolling, they go all the way to the bottom."

"Oh. I don't care."

"Are you still cold?"

"I think so."

Lindsey reached for the blanket she'd borrowed from Odela. "Look at this. Pink and soft. I'll wrap you up in it and you'll be the Queen of Roly-Polies."

"Hmmm."

A moment later, Ginni said, "I am an Indian Princess, and this will be my robe. Tell me about Remi. How can he find us? Why don't you phone him?"

"My phone doesn't work up here." Lindsey avoided the question of whether Remi's phone was functional. "But I left a message for Mrs. Alexa and one for Mister Fraser, and they'll tell him."

"He better talk to that man—that Jack—who made me come up here," Ginni said. "I hope Remi catches him and beats him up."

Lindsey didn't want to think what Remi would do to Jack. "Right now," she said, "our job is to sit tight and wait for Remi."

She prayed silently that somehow Remi had heard her message and would dare to come and that he'd have wisdom and plenty of gas in his truck.

The Jeep, still pouring out heat, was like a snug, warm ship adrift on an icy sea. Even in short sleeves, she was comfortable. She glanced at the gas gauge. More than half a tank. It should be enough, if she was careful.

It seemed a good idea to have Ginni move into the back seat so she could sleep, but when she suggested it, the little girl clung to her, shaking her head.

"Here's what we'll do," Lindsey said. "You're the Indian princess and I'm your friend, and we'll curl up together all cozy and tell stories.'

Ginni looked at her. "No, you're my big sister. Like with Remi. He told me that."

"Hooray! That makes me an Indian princess too. I've always wanted to be a princess. Let's do it."

They crawled into the back and she let the engine run a little longer, but when they were comfortable under the blanket, she turned it off.

They told each other stories, and Ginni was in the middle of a variation on "The Three Bears" when she interrupted herself.

"Oh, mmm . . . black," she muttered. "Mister Colin wears blue. Remi wears red and so do I. Mama wears pink. Daddy wears brown. . . . mmm."

Ginni paused. "I don't like black. Mmm . . . scary."

"Did Jack scare you?" Lindsey said. "He wears black."

"It wasn't . . . Jack." The child began to tremble. "Someone . . . mmm . . . all black . . . a black thing on the head . . ." Ginni's voice trailed off.

It must have been Shula.

She would have worn a hijab. And she'd hired Jack.

The cold certainty settled deep into Lindsey's bones, and she made a decision: from now on, her job was to protect Ginni.

She slid both arms around the child to hold her close, and the warmth of Ginni's body fired her determination.

"Where did Jack find you?" she said.

"In a house. Somewhere."

"In Cameron Bay?"

Ginni frowned. "I don't think so. I can't remember. I

can't remember! It's like before . . ."

She turned close to Lindsey. "My head hurts. Mister Colin sings to me. Can you sing too?"

Ginni sounded like a much younger child now. What was this about not remembering?

Lindsey sang, still holding her, as the rain pounded on the Jeep and the wind rocked it, and trees seemed to be falling all around them.

After a while, she said, "Ginni, did you eat anything today?"

"Breakfast," she said sleepily. "And a cookie." She was silent for a minute. "Someone gave me a cookie. It had big raisins in it, but it tasted funny."

"Anything else?"

"Jack gave me cookies too, and some water. He was going to get me something nice if I was good. But I didn't want to be good."

Lindsey turned on the engine for a few minutes. She reached into her shoulder bag for a granola bar. "Here's something to eat."

Ginni started to shake her head, and Lindsey hurried to say, "It'll make you feel better. An Indian princess has to stay strong."

"What does an Indian princess eat?"

"Umm . . . I think she'd probably eat a bar like this. With pemmican in it. I'm going to eat one too."

"What's pemmican?"

If she told Ginni it was dried meat mixed with fat . . .

"Special Indian food that makes them strong and brave."

"Does Mister Fraser eat pemmican?"

"I'd certainly think so. Look how strong and brave he is. Ask him sometime."

She smiled to herself at the thought, but her smile dimmed as she checked her watch. Two o'clock in the morning.

She finished her bar and shared the tea with Ginni. It was just what they needed, hot and sweet. Was the wind dying down? This might be one of those storms that blew past quickly.

What if Remi couldn't get directions?

What if the roads washed out completely?

What if trees fell on his truck?

Maybe Fraser would come with him.

Ginni drifted off to sleep, but she awoke half an hour later, whimpering, and Lindsey sang to her again.

She sang every song she could remember, every verse of everything from "Jesus Loves Me" to "Jingle Bells," and Ginni fell asleep once more.

Lindsey's back and shoulders were stiffening, but she didn't want to disturb the child, so she waited as long as possible before shifting to a more comfortable position. The cold was stealing across them in furtive little drafts.

She moved the child aside and leaned forward to turn on the engine.

Ginni sat up and looked around. "Is Remi here yet?"

She sounded more like herself than she had all night. "I dreamed he was here."

She cocked her head. "It stopped raining. Can we go for a walk?"

Lindsey looked at her watch. At three in the morning?

But Ginni was probably as stiff as she was. They could get out and stretch.

"Okay," she said, reaching for her jacket. "We need to stay close to the car and watch out for puddles."

Ginni was already putting on her sneakers. "I'll take my princess robe," she said, and as soon as she stepped outside, she draped the blanket over her shoulders. "This is how they wear their robes."

The air was cold, and a faint breeze rustled through

271

the trees, but it definitely had stopped raining. Ragged clouds scudded across the sky, lit by an unseen moon.

Ginni stopped twirling in her robe. "Listen."

Lindsey could hear it too, the faint whine of . . . what? A chainsaw?

"Remi came! He came!" Ginni shrieked, jumping up and down. "It's him, isn't it?"

"Maybe," Lindsey said. "There's lots of people it could be, like forest rangers or loggers—"

Or Jack.

Ginni started forward, and Lindsey grabbed her hand. "Wait! There's a fallen tree up here. Let's climb across it and look around."

Once they were past the tree, they stopped to listen.

Now, unmistakably, she could hear a truck's engine. Headlights shone through the trees, somewhere along the road to their right.

Ginni jumped up and down. "Can we go? Please? Let's go see?"

"Okay." She dropped the car keys into her pocket. "We'll probably have more trees to climb over, so be careful."

"Can we run?"

"Okay, but you hold onto my hand. We'll be quiet as Indians until we see who it is."

Ginni took off down the road, holding her robe aloft with one hand like a fleeing princess, and Lindsey ran with her. It felt good to get some air into her lungs, and if you didn't mind crashing through puddles, there was just enough light to see the way.

They reached a bend in the road, scrambled across another fallen tree, and then the road stretched clear for a short distance before it curved again. They rounded the second bend, and Ginni cried, "It's his truck. Remi's truck!"

Yes—Remi's truck, with the lights shining at them.

She let go of Ginni's hand, and the child dashed off. Lindsey followed at a fast walk.

Two men were lifting a fallen tree out of the road.

Definitely Remi, and . . . someone taller.

Colin? What was he doing here?

She wanted to laugh, to cry, to sing. Whatever might happen, those two could handle it.

Thank you, Lord.

Ginni ran squealing toward the men. They pitched the tree into the woods and turned to watch her. Lindsey hung back. It was Ginni, after all, that they had come to find.

Ginni darted into Colin's arms, and the next thing Lindsey knew, Remi had run up and was reaching for her.

He smelled like rain and fresh-cut wood, and his voice was jubilant. "Lin, you'll never know—"

His strong young arms went around her in a bear hug, and she hugged him back.

Ginni came to hug Remi, and Lindsey turned to Colin with a smile.

"Hello, Lindsey." His deep voice sounded calm, but he had a coiled intensity about him that was unmistakable.

She laughed in sheer relief. "How did you guys ever find us?"

Remi was picking up the chainsaw and axe, but he stopped to say, "We had to squeeze it out of Jack, and that's some story, I can tell you."

Colin took the saw from him. "How many trees are down between us and your car, Lindsey?"

"Two. It's not very far back."

"Good," he said. "Looks like another storm is coming, and I'd like to get you off the Cape as soon as we can. There's hot cocoa in the truck. Why don't you and Ginni drink some while we take care of those trees?"

His voice was quietly authoritative, and she was happy to obey.

They returned a short time later, and the wind was rising again, muttering through the trees.

With a ridiculously light heart, she left Ginni in the truck and went out to meet them.

"Finished," Remi said, dropping the chainsaw into the back of his truck. "We left the axe by your Jeep, in case."

Colin came up to her, brushing sawdust off his jacket, and in the glare of the headlights, his face looked stern.

"The road's bad in places, with a couple of washouts already, so if it's all right, Remi can take Ginni in his truck and I'll drive your Jeep."

"Sounds good to me." At least she wouldn't have to drive that road again.

"There's room in his truck if you want to go with them."

"I don't think so," she said. "I've got all my stuff in the Jeep, and besides, someone has to pester you and keep you awake."

"Right," he said, and for the first time, he smiled.

He got his backpack from Remi's truck, spoke briefly to him, and waved them off.

caption:

Sunrise

Lindsey and Colin turned to go back up the road, and a hint of rain pattered through the trees.

"Here it comes," he said. "We'd better hurry, or we're going to get wet."

The rain fell—a cold blinding rush of water—before she could move.

"Think so?" She looked up at him, laughing, shaking the rain out of her eyes, and gave him a push. "Race you!" she said, and started running.

She could barely see where she was going through the downpour, but she heard his shout, and a second later he caught up with her.

He grabbed her arm, laughing too, tucked her against his side, and took her along so fast she could hardly stay on her feet.

The rain kept falling, wave after wave after wave, as if an ocean were storming above them. They neared the Jeep, and he shouted, "Got the keys?"

She tried to reach into her pocket, stumbled, and would have fallen if he hadn't caught her. She ducked her head against his jacket, still laughing, pulled out the keys, and dropped them into his hand.

He picked her up as easily as he had Ginni, ran the last few steps to the Jeep, opened the door, and set her down inside. A minute later, he tossed his pack and the axe into the back and fell into the driver's seat.

She sat there, dripping and breathless, smiling at him in the dim light. "I think maybe you won."

"I think it was a tie." He wiped the rain from his face, and she could hear the laughter still in his voice.

He stripped off his wet jacket and put it on the floor in the back, and after the engine was running, she did the same. Maybe the Jeep would warm up fast.

In the meantime, she crossed her arms over her chest and tried not to shiver. Water dripped off her hair in cold little rivulets that ran down her neck. Somehow, her hood must have blown back.

He was driving slowly down the road, which looked like a muddy stream in the headlights, and he said, "Short sleeves?"

"Not to start with." She had to raise her voice over the pounding rain. "I was going to Odela's, so I wore this under my sweater and hoodie because her trailer's always so hot. Ginni's got them now. She was half-frozen when I found her."

He gestured over his shoulder. "I've got something in my pack if you want it."

She pulled his backpack onto the console between them, and the first thing she found was a blue towel, soft and faded from many washings.

"A towel!" Just the thing. "Do you mind?"

He looked amused. "Help yourself."

She buried her face in the towel, then rubbed her hair dry. It might be standing on end, but at least it wasn't dripping.

After she finished with the towel, she looked into the pack and found survival gear—flashlight, compass, lighter, knife, candle stub, snakebite kit, first-aid kit—plus a thermos and a jacket of hunter-green fleece.

"Look at this! You must have been a Boy Scout."

"No," he said. "I learned the hard way. Keep the thermos out. We'll probably need it."

She put on the fleece and laughed. The sleeves were so long they hung below her hands, and when she pulled the hood over her head, she felt as if she were looking out from a cave.

She rolled the sleeves up to her wrists and folded the edge of the hood back so she could see around it.

"It's kind of big on me too," he said, and she laughed again.

"Are your feet dry?"

"Yes, but now that you mention it, they'd be warmer if I sat on them." She took off her hiking boots and tucked her feet up to sit cross-legged.

"All the comforts of home," she said. "Okay, tell me what happened. Remi phoned you in Seattle?"

"Yes, he'd been having trouble with his phone, so he used the one at Fraser's store. That was around three in the afternoon. He told me they thought Ginni had wandered off somewhere, but I decided to come on over."

A fresh gust of rain blew against the Jeep and ran in cascades down the windshield, immobilizing the wipers. He slowed, looking out the side window to keep from going off the road, but he drove with competent ease.

"The ferry had a breakdown, and somewhere near Joyce, the road flooded. I didn't get there until around eight o'clock. But I brought a battery for Remi's phone, so at least we could communicate."

He edged the Jeep past a fallen branch. "Remi and Ben had searched the woods around their place, and Fraser and Peter checked all through town. They talked to everyone they could find."

She pushed the hood farther back. "Remi said something about going over to Shula's."

"He and Ben went to Shula's, twice. The first time, no one was there. The second time, she and Jack were in the kitchen, arguing. Ben went through the whole house and couldn't find Ginni." He paused. "Shula . . ."

"Shula was outraged and innocent," Lindsey said.

"That's about it."

"Jack fed them some story about seeing an old Indian with a little girl in his truck, heading toward Joyce, so they went off on that wild-goose chase. But they did a smart thing. They left Fraser to watch Shula and Jack."

"I wondered how they caught Jack."

He nodded. "Shula took off in her plane and after she left, Jack drove her truck into town for gas and went back to his cabin on Thorsen's Creek.

"Fraser watched for a while, invited himself inside, and found Jack writing a ransom note that he immediately destroyed. He wouldn't talk, so Fraser tied him up and left him to think about his sins, as he put it."

Colin glanced at her. "I don't think I'd like to be tied up by Fraser when he's . . . upset."

"Serves Jack right," she said, but she winced at the thought.

"In the meantime, Peter got back to the bakery, heard your message, then phoned Alexa—out at the Fletchers'—around seven o'clock."

"Where were you by then?"

"Burning up the road somewhere outside of Joyce. I didn't want Ben talking to Jack because he might have killed him. Alexa kept me posted. She went over to Odela's to ask about the map you mentioned, but the woman was too drunk to make sense."

"I worried about that," Lindsey said.

"By the time I got there," Colin said, "Ben had been

drinking again, so I took Remi with me and we went to see Jack."

A silence fell, broken only by the pelting rain.

Lindsey waited. She didn't want to hear what he'd done to Jack, but she had to know.

Finally he said, "I don't beat guys up, Lindsey. In the Corps, I saw enough of that to last me the rest of my life. But I also learned something about men, and it didn't take long to figure Jack out."

Her anxiety slithered away as he continued.

"Jack thought he was quite clever, and that he was going to outwit these thugs who had come to torture him. I didn't have to touch him, but at the end, he told me where to find Ginni. And you. I didn't waste time asking how and why. I just wanted to find you. So we loosened the ropes a bit and left."

She could picture the stubborn, cowering boy, their worry, and their frantic haste.

"Everything slowed us down. Like a rockslide and an overturned truck. Roads were washed out, so we had to go around. And then we got onto that road off the Tatoosh Overlook. It was a nightmare of mud and fallen trees."

"But you got here." She smiled at the memory.

"Yes, we did, and Ginni came running down that road, and there you were."

He reached across the console and took her hand. "That was a happy moment, I can tell you."

"For us, too," she said. But all she could think about was his hand and the warmth of it, wrapped around hers.

No . . . no.

She was leaving, remember? No more men. No more entanglements. No more pain.

She would stop this before it got started.

Under the pretext of opening her shoulder bag, she slid her hand away, and after that, she kept it in her lap.

He didn't say anything, and she asked how Natalie was doing, hoping he hadn't noticed or that it didn't matter.

He answered, but, looking at his profile in the dim light, she could tell by the set of his jaw that he had noticed, and it did matter.

She fidgeted with the rolled cuff at her wrist. This kind, thoughtful man didn't deserve to be slighted.

The windshield wipers scraped at the silence between them, and finally she leaned toward him, peering around the edge of the hood.

"Colin," she said softly, "I'm sorry. It's nothing about you—it's just . . . me."

Had she read him correctly? Her words didn't make very much sense.

He nodded, his taut jaw easing, and without looking at her, answered in a gentle voice. "Never mind, Lindsey."

Her eyes burned with unshed tears. She must be tired. Of course she was—she'd been up all night. And so had he.

Whether it was the warmth of the car or the long night or something else, weariness fell across her.

She settled into the soft fleece of his jacket. "I've got things to tell you," she said, "but I can't keep my eyes open. I'm going to take a quick nap. Do you mind?"

He glanced at her then. "I don't mind. But you saw this road. We've got the worst stretch ahead of us. You're not worried?"

She yawned, leaned back, and closed her eyes. "Not when you're driving."

As she was falling asleep, she roused once to the sound of thunderous rain and beneath it, his low voice, singing to himself.

Later, she felt the Jeep veer sideways, but he must have pulled it back onto the road because it kept crawling forward, and after that she didn't notice anything.

She awoke to find herself crumpled against the door with the seat belt still clamped in place. Slowly she pulled herself upright and winced.

Pain burned through her neck and one arm. She groaned, flexing her shoulders, trying to stretch the pain away, but it grew worse.

He glanced at her. "I saw you going sideways, but I didn't want to disturb you. It hurts?"

"Yes! My goodness! I've never—I should have known better. I was really out."

She leaned forward, then back again, turning her head from side to side. "Bad as a migraine. Where are we?"

"Getting close to Neah Bay. It was slow going for a while there." He glanced at her again.

She rubbed at her neck. "What did I do to myself?"

"Could be a muscle spasm. I might be able to help with that." He paused. "If you'll let me."

"If I'll let you?" She eased her head back against the head rest. "Please, Colin. This is different."

"Just a minute." He drove until he found a place to pull over. "Slide that hood back, and let's see what can be done."

She did so, and he said, "Bend forward. That's it. Rest your head on your knees."

He unsnapped his seat belt, and as he leaned across the console, her stomach clenched. He was so strong, and she was alone. What if . . .

He put a hand on the nape of her neck, and she quivered at his touch.

"It's okay, Lindsey." The quiet voice steadied her.

His other hand cupped her forehead, firm and warm.

"First, let me find out what we've got," he said.

The hand on her neck brushed up through her hair to the base of her skull. He held pressure there; then he worked down her neck, kneading lightly, and the pain began to ease.

His fingers paused when he reached her shoulders. "What's this? No wonder you cramped up. Get ready— you'll be sensitive here."

Both hands gripped the muscles on her shoulders and she winced, shrinking away from him. This was supposed to help?

"Hang on," he said. "Talk to me, Lindsey. What did you do all night? Did you sit up?"

She could hardly think, but she tried to answer. "I held Ginni in my arms. She was scared, and her head hurt."

"Good for you. Wait . . ." Slowly he eased the pressure of his fingers, and as he did so, the pain seemed to float off, and warmth spread across her shoulders.

"She must have been glad you were there," he said. "And now . . . here's your reward."

He started at the base of her neck and worked along her shoulders, and she could feel the precision of his touch through the thin fabric of her shirt.

Slowly, deeply, he massaged her shoulder muscles, and after a few minutes, the center of her being pulsed with warmth, and she tingled from the crown of her head to the tips of her fingers.

"Still hurting?"

"Ummm. No. It's good," she said. "So good."

"It does feel good, doesn't it? I've been there."

He continued, and she drifted off into warmth, and then he said, "Let's see." His fingers traveled lightly over her neck and shoulders. "Yes, that should do for a while."

He rested a hand on the nape of her neck for another minute, warm and soothing, and she didn't want him to take it away. But he did.

He smoothed her hair into place, pulled the jacket close to her neck, and dropped the hood back over her head.

Slowly she sat up. Did he have any idea how she felt?

Those warm, powerful hands . . .

She made sure her face stayed in the shadow of the overhanging hood.

"Better?" He sounded matter-of-fact, as if he'd just tied her shoelace. "Now put your arms out in front of you and take a good long stretch."

While she stretched, he eased the car back onto the road, and when she could trust her voice, she said, "Where did you learn how to do that?"

"In the Corps. Comes in handy." He smiled. "How about some of that coffee now?"

She opened the thermos and poured the steaming liquid into the thermos top. "How come you put in so much milk?"

"I like it that way."

She smiled, handing it to him. "So do I."

"I know."

"Hmm," she said. "You know, I didn't know you knew but I might have known that you'd know—and I can't believe I just said that."

He grinned. "Have some coffee. It might help." He handed the cup back to her.

"Sure you don't want some more?"

"No thanks. Take as much as you'd like, and we'll save the rest. All the good Boy Scouts do that."

"Go, Scouts!"

She poured herself a half-cup. It seemed natural to share his cup, and she leaned back with it, savoring the smooth balance of cream and good coffee—and this perfect moment that shone a hopeful light on everything else.

They could be friends. Just good friends. So much safer.

They were passing the rain-drenched waterfront of Neah Bay. It was lit only by the lights at the marina, where fishing boats still rocked in the wind.

"I'd better phone Alexa," he said. "Maybe she's still at the Fletchers'."

He pulled out his phone. "Hi, Lexa. Just wanted to tell you we're leaving Neah Bay."

"—Not sure. Might depend on that rockslide. Remi and Ginni went on ahead, so they should be getting there soon."

He smiled. "—Yes, she is. Tired, I think, but still quite herself."

"—Sure."

He handed her the phone. "She wants to talk to you."

Alexa's warm voice. "He sounds pretty chipper. Are you really doing okay, Lin?"

"Yes, I really am."

"I'm going home now, but come see me when you get a chance, okay?"

"Thanks, Lexa. I knew you were praying. I'll call you."

Tomorrow.

Don't think about tomorrow. No, tomorrow was today already.

She handed the phone back to him.

"I'm curious," he said. "How did you figure out that Jack had taken Ginni up there? We didn't even know that place existed."

"From time to time, Jack told me things, and Odela too. Then she talked about Jack's eaglet, and some pieces fell into place. Especially when I saw that map. Maybe a wild guess."

"More like intuition," he said. "Fraser thinks you have a gift of insight."

"I can't tell you how many times I've been wrong about something. Or somebody."

Why did Vance have to intrude here?

She put the top back on his thermos and set it beside

284

her. "Now that I think about it, I'm sure it was God's mercy, all the way."

He shook his head. "That road! I kept wondering if I'd find your Jeep stuck somewhere, or worse."

"I did a lot of wondering too. I had some daylight, which helped, and I was desperate."

They slowed for the rockslide, which still covered half the road, and Colin showed her where the log transport truck had overturned.

After they'd edged past, Lindsey said, "So Shula's gone. I wonder what that means."

"Is she still your good friend?"

"No, she's not pleased with me." She tried to remember when she'd seen her last. "We had lunch together, Tuesday, I think. It may be the last time, and I'm sorry. Things got pretty tense at the end."

"The fog blew away?"

She nodded. "Somewhat. I found out that they want me to work for them—to take photos of starving children so people will give more money."

He turned to look at her. "The FRO?"

"Right. The night the Muslim girls came over, I flew back to Seattle with her, and she introduced me to Kamal. Under the guise of friendly conversation, he interviewed me. I must have passed his test because Shula tried to convince me that it would be a fantastic job. Very profitable. She suggested that I could be another Robert Capa. That was the wrong thing to say."

"Robert Capa. The war photographer?"

"Five wars," she said. "His focus was always people. Not politics or profit. I love his shots of children."

"She probably pulled his name off the Internet, just to impress you."

"I told her no, and she was unhappy about that. She knows about Remi's testimony though, and asked whether he hates Muslims now. Then we got onto the subject of Ben. I'm sure I didn't bring it up. But she was spoiling for a fight. There's something in Cheree's will that upsets her."

"So the two of you talked about the will?"

"Shula wasn't very happy that the lawyers found it. I guess she hadn't known . . ." Lindsey paused. "That Ben is Ginni's father."

"How did you find out?" His voice had the smooth contours of an experienced interrogator, but she didn't mind.

"That lawyer who stayed at the Roost. After he drank a little too much, he talked a lot, trying to impress us. Then Belinda told Shula."

"Did you tell anyone?"

"No. I thought you probably knew, and I decided that you had your reasons for keeping it quiet."

He nodded in approval. "Anything more about the will?"

"Shula is named in it. She said she got a lot of information out of that lawyer. Did you know she had detectives searching for it all this time?"

"No."

"But there's something in the will that's important," Lindsey said. Remembering her determination to protect Ginni, she added, "I want to ask Ben about it. Is he still in bad shape?"

"He was when I left. Almost catatonic."

Lindsey sighed without meaning to. "By the time we finished talking, Shula had lost her cool. I asked if she was out to destroy Ben, and she was all innocence, but I could see how much she hates him."

And she wasn't going to think about what else Shula had said.

She asked, "Do you think she's managed to ruin Ben?"

Colin was quiet for a moment, probably debating how

much to tell her.

"Not quite," he said. "I've had some time to pray about it, and what you suggested at lunch got me thinking. I'm going to take him on a hike for a day or two. Some place nearby."

"And then?"

"It depends on how he responds. Right now he won't talk and he won't listen. I've got to get back to Seattle by Sunday. If he's still holding out, I'll take him with me and see what the Lord does. I think this is now-or-never time for Ben."

He hesitated. "Would you mind praying for us?"

She could do that much. "I will pray," she said.

"Thank you." He slowed the car, gazing out of his window. "Lindsey, look at this."

Beyond the dark sea, a streak of flame burned through the mass of heavy clouds on the horizon. A single pinprick of brilliance shone in the sky.

She leaned over to look, delighted. "Oh, it's going to be . . . and there's the morning star! Please, could we stop and watch, just for a minute?"

"Sure." He turned across the road and parked facing the sea.

The flame was widening, glowing, turning the clouds black and the sky above to a deep royal blue. A bird flew out of the clouds and across the water, taking slow, measured wing strokes.

"We have to have the birds, too." She opened her window to let in the cries of gulls.

He was silent, gazing at the sky with a half-smile on his face.

Vancouver Island was still dark, but the cloud bank was paling to gray, the flame was turning pink, and the waves had become molten gold.

"So beautiful! Look how it's changing," she said. "This

reminds me . . ."

She let her voice trail off, hoping he hadn't heard. He'd think it sentimental, and besides, she'd never shared anything personal with him, and besides . . .

"What's it remind you of?"

She pulled her knees up to her chin and sat with her arms clasped around them.

"My first morning here," she said. "I came down to the beach early, and I was . . . angry about something. Hurting. Then the gray light began to change, and everything turned to shimmering pink and gold, and I had all this splendor in front of me."

She smiled. "I didn't know that the Lord was going to give me a new relationship with him, and new friends, but it was so beautiful . . . a comfort."

Why had she told him all that?

Another gull flew past, a silhouette against the brilliant sky, and he turned his head to watch it.

"I think I know what you mean," he said in a slow, remembering voice. "It's my favorite time of day."

His voice changed, grew ragged. "In Beirut, I would come back from night patrol. Filthy. Wretched. I could still smell the blood." He frowned. "I could still taste the fear, like a rotten thing in my mouth."

He paused, and she waited, not daring to move.

"I always looked for the sunrise," he said. "And I'd think, 'I'm not dead yet. I've got a new day and all this beauty.' Even before I knew or cared about God, he was giving me hope."

He passed a hand over his face, scrubbing at the dark stubble on his chin, and after a minute, he mumbled, "I've never told anyone about that."

He turned his head to look at her, the remnants of horror still lingering in his eyes.

Her throat ached with his pain. What do you say to a

man who has just bled in front of you?

"Sometimes it helps to talk," she said softly. "God has been good to both of us, hasn't he? What's that verse? *His compassions fail not . . ."*

"*They are new every morning,*" he said. "*Great is thy faithfulness.*" His gaze brightened, resting on her for a moment longer, and then he turned back to look at the ocean.

Off to her left, a pair of birds rose and circled, then dipped to land on a small sea stack. The bit of rock seemed to bristle with birds. What would it look like, up close?

He must have followed her gaze because he said, "Want to check it out? I'm ready for a stretch."

She smiled, surprised. "Me too."

"Good. Put on your boots and let's go."

They picked their way down the rocky bank and onto the sand. He kept his hands in his pockets and so did she, taking two steps to each of his long strides

He didn't say anything, and that was fine. All she wanted to do was walk beside him in this delectable air and listen to the waves and watch the birds swooping past.

Finally he said, "I've been wondering, what does Ginni have to say?"

"That's something I wanted to ask you about. She told me a little about Jack—what he'd said at the cabin, how he promised to come back, and so on. But she couldn't remember much before that. Just bits and pieces."

Should she tell him her conclusion that Shula had taken the child? No, first get some proof.

"There's a reason Ginni's memory blanks out," he said. "You probably know that she was five years old when she came to live with the Fletchers."

She nodded.

"At first, she wouldn't talk to anyone, and after a few months, she'd say a word or two, but only to Remi."

He slowed, frowning at the sky, where the sunrise had

faded to apricot.

"Here's what happened. Ben got a frantic phone call from Cheree. By the time he and Natalie got there, Cheree had been killed. They found Ginni curled up in a closet where she'd gone to hide, and they took her home with them. She doesn't remember any of it."

"So she's blocked out this trauma too?"

"Most likely."

She shook her head. "Poor little kid."

He started kicking a rock in front of him and kept at it the rest of the way to the sea stack, and she knew he was thinking about Ginni, her fears and needs.

With an effort, she turned her attention from him to the sea stack. This one was heavily overgrown with grass and bushes, and it seemed to be a favorite roosting place. Its many residents, mostly gulls, strutted and preened and took no notice of anything but each other.

As she watched them, Colin smiled at her. "Wish you had your camera?"

"Always." She yawned. "Remi will be wondering where we are."

He yawned himself. "Don't do that! It's contagious. See?" He yawned again. "Yes, he'll wonder, but I just wanted to have . . . a few more minutes."

"Want to jog back?" she said.

"How about another race?"

She laughed. "There'll never be another race like that one. Just a nice relaxing jog, if you please."

They jogged in silence, and he paced himself with her, and too soon, they were back at the Jeep.

He pulled out the thermos, and they shared the rest of the coffee, leaning on the fender, watching as clouds moved in overhead and the waves turned gray.

She lifted her face to the breeze, one more time.

"I like to watch you do that," he said, "with the wind in

your hair."

She looked up at him, standing there with his grave smile, the wind tousling his own dark hair.

A good friend.

She smiled back, and something flickered across his face, but before she could read it, he turned quickly to the Jeep. A minute later they were inside and he was starting the engine.

"We're almost there," he said, "and I can tell you, as soon as we walk in the door, there'll be a crisis. A new one, I mean."

"Really?"

"Count on it. I'd do anything for Ben and Natalie, but that's one reason I stay with Fraser."

"I don't blame you." She pulled her shoulder bag up onto the seat and took out her travel kit. "If there's going to be a crisis, I'd better be prepared."

She glanced into her compact.

Give thanks for waterproof mascara, but some makeup would help, and her hair looked like one of those bushes on the sea stack.

She had a small travel brush that was better than nothing, and she brushed her hair as well as she could, then leaned forward to fluff it out.

He watched with such interest that she was afraid he'd drive off the road.

After a minute he grinned. "Think I'd better shave?"

She glanced at him, smiling. "I kind of like the wild, scruffy look."

His grin widened. "Thankya kindly, ma'am."

caption:

Mister Colin

They were walking into the Fletchers' small enclosed porch when Remi stepped out from the kitchen to meet them. "I was beginning to wonder what happened to you guys."

"We're fine," Colin said in a voice that invited no questions.

Remi glanced at her, his eyes traveling down the oversized jacket, but all he said was, "Natalie's making pancakes and sausage."

His voice had the rough edge of fatigue. "Natalie's been asking for you, Colin. Better go too, Lin. I can't do anything with her."

Colin was already taking off his jacket. "How's Ben?"

Remi, on his way outside, spoke over his shoulder. "Plastered."

Colin gave her a wry glance and pulled the kitchen door open.

Natalie stood beside the stove with her hands over her face, but she looked up and hurried toward them. "There you are!"

She threw her arms around Lindsey. "You found my Ginni! And kept her safe! I will never forget that. I am

292

thinking—you Christians are something else!"

She turned to Colin. "You brought them back, and I'm so thankful." She smiled up at him. "But please, I need your help."

She twisted her hands together. "I am so afraid! Remi says not to worry, but I am so afraid for my little Ginni. That terrible man next door! I'm scared he will try again, and then we'll find her too late. I beg you to help me!"

He had the preoccupied look that she understood now—he was thinking on two or three levels at the same time—but he said, "I'd like to help you, Natalie—"

"—I am so glad! And also, we have no syrup for the pancakes, so could you make some of your special recipe?"

"Sure," Colin said. "But what was the first thing you were asking me?"

"If you could just take Ginni away." Natalie's lovely eyes brimmed with tears. "Take her with you, and she will be safe until we catch that man and put him in jail."

Lindsey almost laughed aloud at the expression that flashed across Colin's face. What chaos Ginni would create in a bachelor's ordered life!

"Take Ginni?" he said.

"Yes, with you. You have room in your nice little house, and he would never think to look for her there. And if he did, you could fight him."

"Wait. Wait just a minute," Colin said. "You have Remi here with you. He can take good care—"

"—No! Not in this house!" The tears spilled over and ran down her cheeks, and still she looked beautiful. "My Ginni has to go away. You're the only one—"

He held up a hand. "Let's not get in a hurry, Natalie. I doubt that your neighbor would do this. But perhaps we can think of something for Ginni."

While he was speaking, an idea came to Lindsey. Why not take Ginni herself? Not for long since she had to leave, but it was one last thing she could do for the Fletchers.

Colin patted Natalie's shoulder, looking fatherly. "Give me a few minutes, and then I'll make the syrup for you, and we can talk, okay?"

She nodded and turned toward the stove, wiping her tears with her apron.

"Lindsey!" Colin put a hand under her elbow and hurried her back out to the porch, all the way down to the end, where the washing machine stood.

She leaned against it, trying to look serious.

"What am I going to do?" he said. "Are you laughing?"

"Not at you, Colin. It's just kind of funny, the way she says to the all-powerful Mister Colin, please keep my child safe and oh, by the way make us some syrup. Large or small, you do it all, don't you?"

His dark brows drew together, and she put a hand on his sleeve. "Listen, she's distraught. There's no way you're going to take that child for her. It's just not going to happen."

"But you don't know Natalie. Once she's decided we need to do something . . ."

"Fair as the moon, terrible as an army with banners, isn't she? But never mind that. I have an idea."

"I was hoping you would."

"What if Ginni came to stay with me for a while?"

He stared at her. "Do you know what you're in for? She can be a little spitfire at times."

She shrugged. "I get along with most children, and besides, it'll be just for a couple of days until I leave. Whatever's going on should be solved by then, don't you think?"

She had hurried past the subject of her leaving, but he noticed.

He caught her gaze and held it. There was something in his eyes that she hadn't seen before, a warmth that wrapped her close to him, bending her will, melting her resolve until she had to look away.

She put a hand on the washing machine and stared down at its cool surface, trying to steady herself.

He was quick to read her face, and he bent to line up the jumble of muddy boots beside the washer, taking a long time at it.

Calmly he answered her question. "I think Natalie's jumping to conclusions, but most likely, they'll find out something soon."

He was giving her a chance to regroup.

He straightened up. "As far as Ginni is concerned, that should work out fine," he said. "I'm sure they'll appreciate it. I certainly do. Why don't you suggest it to Natalie?"

She tried on a smile. "Coward."

"Precisely." He inclined his head, smiling too. "But I need to make that syrup, don't I?" He ushered her back toward the kitchen. "How can we have pancakes without syrup?"

She took a shaky breath. He had allowed her to see his heart, and things would never again be the same between them, but he was behaving as if nothing had happened. Because he knew she wanted it that way.

She would do the same. Better keep busy.

She went to where Natalie stood at the stove and put an arm around her. "Come talk with me for a minute, okay? And we'll let Colin get on with that syrup."

They went into the small dining room next to the kitchen, and after Lindsey had explained her idea, assuring Natalie, twice, that it wouldn't be any trouble, the plan was made for Ginni to stay with her for a few days.

Natalie wanted to give her a bath and pack her clothes, so Remi would bring her over to Cameron Bay later that afternoon.

Lindsey reclaimed her hoodie and sweater from Ginni's

bedroom and folded up Colin's fleece jacket. She would return it to his backpack, on the porch.

Remi came in, heard the plan, began to smile again, and asked about breakfast.

"Yes, yes!" Natalie said. "Let's all sit down and eat."

It was a happy meal, even though Ben's absence was painfully obvious. Colin sat on one side of her and Remi on the other, and they both ate an astonishing number of pancakes.

Rosie and Ruth had already gone to work at the bakery, but the four boys were there. They talked nonstop to Colin, asking him about the landslide and the storm and the time the Jeep slid off the road, but he didn't seem to mind.

Everyone said how good the blueberry syrup was, and Lindsey agreed. It was different from Mrs. Butterpot's for sure, with a pleasing tang.

She asked Colin what was in it and he said something about balsamic vinegar, and when she laughed, saying she wasn't precisely on speaking terms with this mysterious ingredient, he laughed too.

He got up and brought the bottle to the table so she could taste it. "The next time you do a salad," he said, "mix some with a little olive oil, and drizzle it over. It's good!"

For an instant she wished she could make him a salad sometime—in her condo in New York, or in the big kitchen of her New Jersey house—and then she pushed the thought away.

Everyone was clamoring to taste the vinegar too, so she passed it around the table.

Ginni had seemed happy enough when Natalie talked to her about visiting Miss Lindsey for a few days, but now she said nothing and ate only a little, allowing Natalie to fuss over her without complaint. Was her head aching again?

After the meal, Lindsey helped Natalie clean up the kitchen, and as they finished, she asked, "What's the best thing to do when Ginni has a headache? She had a pretty bad one last night."

"I know what helps," Natalie said, "but I can't really explain it." She smiled. "Colin knows. He'll teach you."

She went out of the kitchen and came back with the two of them. She put a hand on the little girl's shoulder, saying, "I want Mister Colin to show Miss Lindsey how to do the massage that helps your headaches."

She glanced at Lindsey. "He's good at this."

"Yes," Lindsey said, careful not to look at him. "I'm sure he is."

"Sit down, Ginni-belle," he said. "Like we usually do."

Natalie hurried away, and the child sat at the kitchen table, pillowing her head on her folded arms, exposing the back of her neck.

"Does your head ache now?" he said.

"Yes, but not too bad."

He bent over, resting his hands on Ginni's shoulders. "Here's where she carries her tension." He took one of his hands away, saying, "Feel these muscles."

Lindsey put a hand on the little shoulder and was surprised to find that her fingertips rested on something that was hard, more like a bone than a muscle.

"So what we do," he said, "is try to loosen it up."

With his fingertips on each of Ginni's shoulders, he started kneading the muscles, using long, slow, strokes

After a minute, he said, "Lindsey, you take this side."

She turned up the cuffs of her sweater and began, watching him massage Ginni's other shoulder and trying to imitate him.

She could feel the muscles begin to soften as she worked, but when she came closer in, toward Ginni's neck, she found a place where the fibers seemed to resist her fingers.

"There's this one spot," she said. "It just doesn't . . ."

She showed him where, and he nodded. "Here's what you do."

He put his hand over hers, kept it there, and slanted a teasing glance at her. "This is different too, isn't it?"

No, it wasn't—his touch made something glow inside her—but she didn't reply. Ever since they'd arrived at the Fletchers', he had treated her with a resolute tenderness that was unnerving.

Not easily discouraged, was he?

Pay attention, she told herself. You've got to learn this.

"The muscle's tight," he said, his hand guiding hers. "Instead of rubbing, you press down. Like this. And hold it for a couple of seconds. Remember how it almost hurts?"

She nodded, telling herself not to remember.

"Slowly, slowly, you ease up." He showed her, and then he took his hand from hers. "Can you feel how the muscle softened?"

"Yes."

"How's that, Ginni?"

"Nice." She sounded sleepy. "Quite nice. Enchanting."

It was an unusual way to use the word, and Lindsey looked at him for an explanation.

He shrugged, smiling, and went on. "Once you've got the release in her shoulders, you can work your way up her neck. Here, center yourself a bit more."

He moved Lindsey directly behind Ginni, put his hand on one side of Ginni's neck, and began to work upward with rhythmic, circular motions.

"Try doing the other side," he said.

Once again she started by imitating him, and then she began to find her own rhythm. "Good," he said. "You've got it."

He took his hand from Ginni's neck. "Now use both

hands and work your way back down."

She did so, moving with care down to the base of Ginni's neck, where she paused for a minute, as he had with her, to finish up.

She straightened. His hand rested on her shoulder, and he gently turned her—unresisting, she had to admit—until she stood within the circle of his arm.

"Natalie has become quite proficient," he was saying, "and I'm sure you'll do fine."

He moved a trifle closer and rambled on, using an absent-minded voice that didn't deceive her for a minute. "Singing will help her too, as you've already found out. Remember, it is tension that causes this kind of pain, and anything you can do to ease her stress will help."

By now, all she could think about was the warmth of his hand, and his arm, not quite touching her. She kept her eyes on his shirt—flannel, a dark blue plaid. She wanted to put a hand on that soft flannel. She wanted to rest her face against it.

She didn't trust herself to look up at him. "Colin McAlister," she said in a low voice, "you are a rascal."

Ginni stirred. She sat up and turned around. "Why is he a rascal?"

Lindsey stepped away, pulling the cuffs of her sweater back into place. "Ask Mister Colin. I'm sure he can explain. I'll see you later, Ginni."

She walked swiftly to the far end of the kitchen, hesitated, then went out onto the porch to think.

She tried to breathe deeply. Yes, *think*, but not about him. What did she need to do before she could leave? Talk to Ben. About that will. Okay. Go find him.

Remi came loping in from the kennels, and while he was pulling off his boots, she asked where Ben was.

"In the living room," he said, "but you're wasting your time. He has clammed up ever since Ginni disappeared.

Even now, he won't talk. Not even to Colin."

Remi sounded desolate, and, remembering the times he'd encouraged her, she said, "It's going to work out for good, Remi. All of this mess. And we'll be praising God."

She left him there, passed through the kitchen, where Colin was reading something to Ginni, through the empty dining room, around a corner, and into the living room.

Ben wasn't, as she'd expected, on the sofa by the TV. He was slumped in a chair in front of a window, and he looked as if he were ninety years old.

When she drew near, he neither moved nor spoke. Deliberately she walked in front of him, between him and the light, but it made no difference. He seemed to stare through her to the trees outside, and the stench of beer hung about him.

For a moment she studied his face: the wide, bronzed forehead, the dull eyes, the grim mouth. This skilled, intelligent man—how sad!

There were no chairs nearby, but a stool had been left under the window, and she pulled it next to him. He didn't move.

She sat in silence for another minute, watching him and praying for wisdom. His hands lay clenched in his lap.

On impulse, she reached over and picked up his fist. It was heavy, cold as a rock.

She leaned close, warming it between both her hands, and said, "Listen to me, Ben Fletcher. We love you. Colin does. Remi does. Natalie does. Your children love you."

He made no reply, but she stayed there, stroking the back of his fist, its veins dark in the brown skin, and the moments dragged by.

Finally the big rough hand began to open.

She turned it over, smoothing the calluses on his palm, and the strong fingers closed over hers.

She smiled to herself. "God loves you too, Ben. He

knows exactly what's going on, and he's going to help us figure it out." She paused. "But I need you to tell me something."

He turned his head then, with a grunt. "What."

"It's about Cheree's will."

Silence.

She persisted. "If you take care of Ginni, then what happens?"

He closed his eyes. "Then she is mine. She has a lot of money, and it comes to me in a . . ." He paused, as if searching for the word. "In a trust."

"And if you can't take care of Ginni, or something happens to her?"

"The sister gets everything." His voice faded into a gust of beer-stained breath, and rose again, strong and bitter. "I will never let her go to that woman. I will never let them hurt my little girl. They will have to kill me."

So that's what it was.

"What can I do for you, Ben?" she said.

"Pray."

"I will pray for you. And you—remember that we love you. Listen to Colin. Tell him what you're thinking."

She let go of his hand and stood up slowly, watching him. He folded his hands together in his lap and went back to staring at the trees.

An open door led into the hall, so she went out that way and Colin met her there.

"Good for you, Lindsey."

"You saw?"

His face softened. "I saw you take his hand."

"It was a fist." She looked up at him. "Ben's in a terrible state. I wanted to reach him."

He nodded, understanding. "What did you say?"

"I told him that we love him and so does God, and that the Lord knows all about what's going on. He seemed to hear me. He even let me ask about the will."

She saw the question in his eyes. "If Ben can't take care of Ginni, Shula gets it all—Ginni and the money. And if Ginni dies, her money goes to Shula. There's a trust."

Weariness crept across her. "It gives Shula a motive." She rubbed at the back of her neck, where the muscles were beginning to ache.

He lifted a hand, but let it drop to his side. "Take a good hot shower, and your neck will feel better. Get some sleep, okay?"

She nodded.

"You've been wonderful," he said, "but you need some rest. You're so pale it worries me. Would you like me to drive you back to town?"

She shook her head. "Not necessary, thank you."

It was time to return to her other life, and she needed to make that transition alone. *Get here and we'll talk*, Edric had told her. She'd probably go on Sunday, or sooner, if another place could be found for Ginni.

She would take remarkable memories with her. But first, she was grateful to this man for all that he'd spent on her behalf, and she should say something.

He stood at a distance from her, as if he'd imposed this restraint on himself.

She stepped toward him, trying to smile. "I may be gone by the time you return, but I want to say this, Colin. You have given me many gifts, and I thank you."

She swallowed against the misery in her throat. "Especially today—the sunrise."

A warmth flamed in his eyes and she recognized it, but all he did was smile in his grave way. "You have my cell phone number. Will you phone me before you leave for the East?"

"Yes." She tried to match his calm, his control. "Have a good trip with Ben. I think he may be ready to listen."

302

As she drove back to Cameron Bay, she had to blink away tears, and she told herself that she was just tired.

Get some rest, he'd said. Take a hot shower.

With encouragement, he would have said more, but she had made it clear that she didn't want him to.

It would be less painful this way, for both of them. Long-distance relationships didn't work. Like with Art, the photographer in Anchorage.

She and Art had taken a few hikes together and shared a few meals. They had emailed for a while, and he even came out to see her. She showed him around New York, lent him some money, and he disappeared.

After she got over it, she decided that she could have lost a lot more than money. Another difficult lesson about men.

Colin would go back to his other world and forget, and so would she.

To credit him, he'd treated her with respect. The only time he'd pushed her boundaries was in that most public of places, the Fletchers' kitchen.

She shook her head to clear it of the memory.

"Lord, I need you!" she said aloud. "I need you to hold me together. Guard my heart. Lead me in a plain path. And help me with this little girl."

caption:

Natalie's Anguish

Lindsey spoke to Belinda right away about having Ginni stay for a few days—with the appropriate fee for double occupancy—and after a moment of shocked silence and a barrage of questions, Belinda agreed.

That afternoon, when Remi brought Ginni over, the first thing the little girl did was tour Lindsey's room, inquisitive as a cat. She glanced at the kitchenette, listened attentively to Lindsey's cautions about the darkroom, and wandered out onto the balcony.

When she came in, she stopped to examine Lindsey's desk. She gazed at the spider web photo but didn't say anything. Lightly she touched the driftwood fish.

"What's this? Can I hold it?"

"Sure. What do you think it looks like?"

Ginni turned it around several ways. "A fish. It's like something Mister Fraser makes."

"Yes, he gave it to me. We think it's a salmon."

"I like him," Ginni said.

Was she referring to Fraser? No, she was making swimming motions with the fish. "Sam the Salmon," she said. "That could be his name. Is it okay?"

Lindsey smiled at her. Ginni had probably seen salmon spawning, so she'd know about eggs. "It's a girl salmon. See the eggs?"

Ginni halfway smiled too. "She'll be Samantha, then." Carefully she set the fish back on the desk.

Apart from that short conversation, she didn't say much. They went for a walk on the beach, and for an early supper, they ate the food that Natalie sent.

While Ginni was sitting on the rug, taking off her shoes, she leaned under the bed and pulled something out. "What's this?" She held up the glass ball.

"It's called a float. Fishermen in Japan use them to keep their nets from sinking."

Ginni fingered the barnacle on the top side. "It's pretty. How'd it get here?"

"It floated all the way. People like to collect them."

"Why do you keep it under your bed?"

Lindsey smiled. "There's a cat who comes to visit me. Sometimes he knocks things off my desk. He must have been playing with it."

"I hope the cat comes back." Ginni held the float up to the light. "There's nothing inside." She put it down, and crawled onto the bed with a book.

Lindsey put the float back onto her desk. Nothing inside . . . You could make a sermon out of that remark.

She didn't feel like checking her email, and when Ginni began to yawn, she did too. "That's contagious, you know."

Ginni looked up. "What?"

Let go of the memory. But now she had to explain.

"When you yawn," she said, "it makes me feel like yawning too. I'm tired. Do you want to go to bed?"

"Yeah."

She gave Ginni the choice of sleeping on the rug, in the brown chair, or in the big bed with her, and Ginni decided on the chair.

She looked comfortable, tucked in with blankets, pillows, and her stuffed spider, but in the middle of the night, Lindsey felt a small body creep under the covers to huddle next to her. She smiled and went back to sleep.

Ginni was still sleeping when Lindsey awoke the next morning. The child lay curled in a tight ball, facing away from her, the stuffed spider clutched in one hand. Her hair fell in curly disarray over her face. Whose job was it to brush out those tangles?

Lindsey slid out of bed, pulled on a sweater, and, moving with care, made a cup of tea. If she could have a few minutes alone with her Bible, she could face the day with more confidence. It was odd but not unpleasant, this need for comfort and sustenance.

She had to do something about the magazine. What? She still had time to get there for the Board meeting.

She turned to the book of Philippians, wondering where Alexa was reading today. She had reached chapter two, and she paused at verses 12 and 13. What did this mean?

Work out your own salvation . . . for it is God who works in you to will and to work for his good pleasure.

Read it again. Chew on it. She underlined the words carefully, with a squiggle under each *work*.

As she thought about the command, it made more sense. It seemed to say that she had all she needed in Christ, and it was her job to take advantage of it. But best was the linking word, *for*. God was working to change her will and make it possible.

She copied the verses onto a sticky note so she could talk to Alexa about them.

Astonishing. God would change her will to fit with his good pleasure?

She leaned back and closed her eyes to pray silently.

"Lord? My will is all focused on what I want to do. This magazine problem. Edric. And Vance. I think I want to do your good pleasure. Part of me is scared to even ask you about it. In case . . . in case it hurts."

Before her mind could spiral off in that direction, she added, "But I'll do anything you want, if you'll give me the courage."

She heard a rustle of sheets and opened her eyes. Ginni was sitting up, watching her.

"What are you doing?" Ginni said.

"Talking to God."

Ginni nodded. "I've seen Fraser do that. It looks like sleeping, only it's not. He says it's better than sleep."

The brown eyes challenged her. "Is it?"

"Yes," Lindsey said. "It makes me happy."

She'd have to see what Alexa thought about those verses, but they looked like dynamite.

Ginni stood up on the bed, bounced once or twice, and jumped onto the floor. "What's it like outside?"

She pulled the draperies open. "It's sunny!" She tugged at the sliding door and slipped out onto the balcony.

Lindsey stood up, enjoying the tang of wood smoke that drifted into the room.

"Are you hungry?" she said. "Let's get dressed and walk down to the bakery for breakfast."

Ginni turned to her with an incredulous look. "Can we? Sit down like we're real customers?"

"If you wish."

Ginni smiled. "Quite enchanting!" She capered back and forth, getting dressed, while Lindsey tidied the room. Her hair stood out around her face like a dark cloud.

"Do you have a hairbrush?" Lindsey said.

"Yeah, I guess I forgot that. It's such a pain."

"You've got pretty hair. It's worth taking care of. Did you know that brushing your hair makes it shine? That's because you're moving the oil from your scalp out to the tips of your hair."

Ginni gave her a quick glance. "Nobody ever told me that." She began to brush her hair with energetic strokes. "You sound like Mister Colin."

Lindsey bent over the bed, straightening the sheets and blankets. "Not really. I don't know anything about moss."

Still brushing, Ginni said, "He knows about moss and spiders and salmon and cedar trees. He knows everything."

"I've noticed." Lindsey shook out a pillow and dropped it onto the bed.

"But he said you're a wise lady."

"He did?" She picked up another pillow.

"I asked him about being a rascal." Ginni stopped brushing to look at her. "First he made me get a dictionary and look up *rascal*. It means something like playful teasing. That's when he said that sometimes he can't help being a rascal, and that you're a wise lady and you understand."

Lindsey pressed the pillow to herself. She turned away, trying to escape the longing in her bones. He'd known Ginni would say something. And he had sent her this apology.

"Oh! I almost forgot!" Ginni said. "He told me to give you lots of hugs. And I haven't even given you one yet."

The child's thin arms went around her waist, and Lindsey sat down on the bed to hug her tightly. "Thank you, Ginni. I like your hugs."

Don't think about him. Sometime soon, she'd forget, and then she'd be fine.

She took the brush from Ginni, smoothed the dark hair back into a ponytail, and clipped it securely. "That will do for now. Let's go."

At the bakery, Ginni had a hard time choosing the four items they were going to share for breakfast, but finally she made up her mind, and they sat at a corner table.

Quincy Corbin stopped by to say that he had to leave on a business trip. "To New York," he said, his glance meaningful. Lindsey, remembering he was lonely, let him talk. His phone rang, extricating her, and he strode off.

The café was less crowded now, most of the breakfast regulars having left, and Alexa came out to visit.

She told Ginni that Mister Fraser had been hoping she'd come to see him this morning, and when they were finished eating, they went over to the bookstore.

Right away, Ginni said, "I want to read Miss Lindsey's book."

"We'll do that," Fraser said. He took his copy from under the counter, along with a storybook. "First, I'd like you to do some reading by yourself."

He handed her the storybook and looked at Lindsey. "I sold that other copy. I'll have to order some more."

"Who in the world's been buying them?"

"Shula special-ordered the first one before you came." He paused to straighten a piece of paper on the counter. "And Colin bought the other one, last weekend."

Why did he have to bring up that name?

She changed the subject, and of course Fraser noticed, and his brown eyes were puzzled.

Quickly as possible, she thanked him for his part in rescuing her and Ginni, thanked him for taking Ginni for a couple of hours, and, with a sense of having stepped past quicksand, went back to the bakery to see whether she could help Alexa.

Alexa was sitting at the worktable, using an ice cream scoop to fill muffin tins from a bucket of batter. Lindsey looked over her shoulder. "Cranberry muffins? Yum. I can do that."

"Would you?" Alexa said. "I'll go mix up a batch of blueberry."

She set to work at the other end of the table. "I

haven't had a chance to tell you, Lin, but I'm glad you left us the message about Ginni. Fraser missed her right away, but we thought she'd wandered off."

"So then what did you do?"

"Waited for Colin, like he said to. Colin wanted to call the police, but Ben wouldn't have it, and they argued, and finally Colin said that if he hadn't found you by daybreak, he was going to get a helicopter out here from Search and Rescue, no matter what Ben said."

Alexa stirred vigorously for a moment. "I've never heard them talk to each other like that, but Ben was half out of it, and Colin was steaming."

Lindsey concentrated on putting a scoop of batter in the exact center of a muffin cup. "Ginni doesn't remember much at all."

"I'm not surprised, considering her history. How's she doing now?"

"She seems okay. Last night she insisted on sleeping in the chair, but halfway through the night she crawled into bed with me." Lindsey smiled at the memory.

Alexa nodded. "She's not as tough as she acts. I'm glad she's with you for a while."

"For starters, I hope they called the police on Jack," Lindsey said.

"Nope, he's gone. Colin and Remi went over yesterday, and there was no sign of him."

"What?" Lindsey put down the scoop.

Alexa shook her head. "I talked to Odela, and she's quite worried. She thought maybe he went to Kalaloch, on the west coast. He's got friends there."

Lunch customers arrived, all at once, and Lindsey helped as much as she could; then she took sandwiches to Fraser and Ginni and came back.

When most of the customers were gone, Alexa made them both a mocha latte from the espresso machine, and they sat down for a late lunch.

Lindsey pulled out the sticky note she'd written and asked her about the verses.

Alexa smiled over her sandwich. "I think you're right. Isn't it like our wonderful God? When he tells us to do something, he supplies what it takes."

"I've got to memorize those verses." Lindsey slid the note back into her pocket.

"Me too," Alexa said. "Let's check up on each other."

She glanced around the empty café. "I'm going to close up early. Rosie and Ruth wanted the day off tomorrow, so there's a lot to get ready."

While they were clearing off the cookie trays in the workroom, Natalie arrived with a box of cinnamon rolls.

Alexa smiled at her. "For that special order? Good!" she said. "Lindsey, could you help to wrap them up?" She hurried back into the café.

On her next trip through the swinging doors, Alexa juggled a pile of baskets with a small white envelope. "I found this on the counter, Natalie. It has your name on it."

Natalie looked pleased. "Mine?"

She tore it open, pulled out a single sheet of paper, and unfolded it.

"No! How could this be?" She dropped into a chair.

She ripped the note in half and threw it across the table, her eyes blazing. "Where did this come from?"

"I found it under a basket of rolls," Alexa said. "Someone must have left it there during the noon rush."

"The will!" Natalie pounded the table top. "He never let me see it. He lied to me! Wills don't lie. But he lied!"

She put her head down and sobbed.

Alexa rested a hand on Natalie's heaving shoulder and exchanged a puzzled glance with Lindsey.

Finally the storm passed, and Natalie looked up, her eyes fierce. "That man! He did this after we were married! I hate him! He's nothing but trouble. Always trouble. The dogs. My children!"

She stood up, drawing herself to her full height. "Not anymore. When he gets back, tell him that I know everything about him and Cheree. And I have gone home. And I never want to see his face again."

"Wait, Natalie," Alexa said. "Let's talk and see—"

"—No talk! Too much talk." Natalie's voice rose to a wail. "I'm taking the boys with me."

She turned to Lindsey, and her face crumpled. "I will trust you with my Ginni. Because you love God. My precious little girl! It's not her fault!"

She snatched up her purse and rushed out of the room.

Alexa had gone pale. She picked up the note, put the torn pieces together, and motioned Lindsey over to read it.

DID YOU KNOW THAT YOUR HUSBAND IS GINNI'S FATHER? LOOK AT THE WILL.

So it had come to light. Lindsey slumped into a chair, burdened with Natalie's grief.

Alexa leaned against the counter. "Poor Natalie!"

She gazed at Lindsey. "You knew, didn't you?"

Lindsey nodded. "Heard it from that blabbermouth lawyer who stayed at the Roost."

"So Belinda knows. That means Shula knows too. Do you think Colin knows?"

"Yes." She shut out the memory of their conversation about this, their comfortable friendship.

"That's right. Ben would have told him."

"What about Fraser?" Lindsey said.

Alexa put her hands over her face, as if she were trying to think.

"He's probably figured it out," she murmured. "But Natalie shouldn't be left alone right now. I'll get Fraser to go over. They're old friends, and maybe he can talk her out of leaving."

She sighed. "The trouble is, Natalie has a terrible temper, and once she makes up her mind, she never changes it."

"I'll pick up Ginni," Lindsey said. Best to keep the child away from all this. So many tangled lives. Men!

She took Ginni to the small grocery store, where Ginni chose lasagna to microwave for supper, and as they walked back to the Roost, Ginni described all the things she had done with Fraser.

He must have gone out of his way to keep her occupied. So now it was up to her.

The beach? Yes, that would wear her out.

They stopped briefly to chat with Belinda, who was upset with Jack for not showing up as scheduled. Questions sparked in her eyes, but she didn't ask them.

They changed into old clothes, and Ginni wanted to bring Samantha, so Lindsey slipped the little driftwood fish into her jacket pocket as they left.

Ginni found a tide pool for Samantha, and because she didn't feel like jogging, Lindsey took photos of the child and stared across the choppy waves.

She thought about Jack with growing indignation.

And what about Shula? That's who had sent the note. She must have returned.

They were criminals, both of them. Look what they'd done! A business destroyed. A family divided. A marriage splintered.

I've got to find some proof, she reminded herself.

The sunlight was beginning to fade, and she was thinking they should go back, when her cell phone rang.

Caller ID told her it was Edric. Working late, wasn't he? Maybe he had good news.

"Hi, there," he said. "I have someone who wants to talk to you."

"Lin! How are you doing?"

It was Vance, using his most charming voice.

"What is it?"

"Hey, I really like the feature you did on the Carolina dogs. We're going to give it plenty of space."

She waited.

"Lin? You still there?"

"Yes."

"But I want you to forget about the Indian projects. I saw the photos you sent Edric—Indian dogs? Nice, but I want to go in another direction."

"I'm off the clock," she said. "Didn't he tell you? I've been on personal days for more than a week now."

Vance sighed, impatient already. "I want you to start acting like a mature woman. Kill that Indian stuff and get back here, right away."

"What right do you have to tell me that?"

"I'm Managing Editor, as of today. You'll just have to accept it." His voice had grown cold. "Let's keep our personal lives out of this. I think we can work together if you decide to cooperate. The magazine is important to me too."

"I'm sure it is."

"How soon can you get back?"

Who was he to order her around?

"I'll come back when I decide to, Vance. You seem to have forgotten that I'm not your assistant. I'm a partner in the company."

"So am I."

"You're a brand new shareholder. And you don't own the place, so it's a bit early to swashbuckle around, dishing out commands."

"You want me to kiss your fingers? You had your chance. You—"

She didn't have to listen to this.

She held the phone away from her ear.

Finally he stopped talking and started yelling, "Lin? Lin?"

"Let me talk to Edric," she said.

Edric's voice came on. "He's just trying to help."

"I'll call you later. Goodbye."

She was already praying as she hung up the phone, and she prayed as they walked back from the beach and as they ate their supper and as she read to Ginni from a book Fraser had sent along.

It was the same prayer, over and over again: *Lord, have mercy on me. Lead me in a plain path because of my enemies.*

By the time they finished, the moon had risen, and it lit the balcony with a soft brilliance. She had always liked taking moonlit shots. How would Ginni's face look in that light? She had to try it.

Ginni thought it was a fine idea. She let Lindsey brush her hair into curls that framed her face, and she draped the pink blanket around her shoulders.

Lindsey took several shots, framed tight. Then she set the aperture small for deep focus and included the background trees, which showed up clearly.

Ginni's little face, with its pensive dark eyes, was lovely by moonlight.

Sooner than she'd expected, Ginni was yawning and ready to go to bed.

Lindsey glanced at the moonlit balcony. She was tired too. But the phone call wouldn't go away, and she had to think this through. Maybe outside.

Ginni burrowed under the blankets with her stuffed spider, looking content. "When are you coming to bed?"

"Not for a while," Lindsey said. "I'm going for a walk. I'll lock the door."

Ginni closed her eyes. "Okay."

It was dark under the trees, and she had to pick her way around the side of the house. Instead of going down to the beach, she went to sit at the edge of the bluff.

In front of her was a tracery of branches, black against the moonlit sky. Below her, water slapped at the rocks, sounding cold and decisive. Like she was going to be. She had come here to make a cool, rational business decision.

Tonight.

She had to decide tonight because if she booked her flights immediately, she could still get back East for that Board meeting.

She'd leave early tomorrow—Saturday—and arrive in New York around midnight. Worst case, she could leave Sunday morning, but she needed Sunday to talk to Edric and plan their approach.

Maybe she could come back here when things were more settled at the magazine.

Come back? Who was she kidding? Once she was in New York, the job would swallow her up.

What about Ginni?

She shifted on the cold rock. She hadn't actually made a promise to Natalie. She had offered to take Ginni for a couple of days, but that was before Vance phoned.

Maybe Alexa and Fraser could handle Ginni until the Fletchers got themselves straightened out.

But wasn't she in the best position to protect the child?

Protect Ginni? That's what she had told herself to do. Was she overreacting?

Shula had masterminded all of this, but really, would she hurt a little girl, her own niece?

Lindsey pulled her knees up to her chin, clasped her arms around them, and tried to concentrate.

The question: *Do I stay here, or do I go back and fight for my job?*

If she went back, she could win.

Once before, she had talked sense into Edric when that drug-sniffing nephew of his wanted to run things.

Vance didn't have her experience or production skills, and neither did his blond playmate. She could make Edric see that, if she got there in time. She had always been a fighter. How could she walk away from this one?

What would she win?

Financial security. It wasn't her dream job, but it paid the bills. She'd dipped into her savings in order to refurbish the old house, and freelance was a risky way to live. Besides, she wasn't sure she still had the knack for doing candid photos.

What else?

The satisfaction of reclaiming the magazine.

She could handle Vance. She might even work with him, but not until she'd taken him down a peg or two. It was time somebody put him in his place.

No one could blame her for leaving Cameron Bay. Her position and the good of her company were at stake.

But what about Ginni?

Up at Cape Flattery, the child had been in real danger. And Bobby could have been hit by a car. Spot had almost drowned.

Shula hated Ben, and she wanted the money. Hadn't she already proved that she was ruthless?

I will trust you with my Ginni. Natalie had said. *Because you love God.*

Natalie wouldn't understand business contingencies. If Lindsey went off to New York, what would Natalie think about God?

Too many questions, like strobe lights whirling in her mind.

She groaned aloud. "Father, rule my foolish heart! How can I know?"

She lurched to her feet and stumbled through the ferns and bushes to an opening beside the water. High above, the moon hung lopsided and brilliant.

317

"Lord," she said, "You told me that you're working your will in my heart. What is your will? Do you want me to go back and fight? I'll do it, gladly."

She lifted her face to the sky. "But maybe you want me to stay here?"

She waited, gazing at the moon-path across the water. Stay?

The glaring lights in her mind faded to a soft, cool shimmer. What was happening?

Grace to you and peace from God our Father and the Lord Jesus Christ.

Peace. That's what it was—this radiance inside her. God was giving her his peace, so she would know.

"Lord? This means stay?"

The peace was still there, almost tangible.

"Thank You."

What should she do next?

Phone Edric. That was it.

"Lord, please give me the right words," she whispered.

She went back to the rock and flipped open her phone. It was much too late to call, but for once she didn't care. This had to be settled.

After five rings, Edric answered with a grunt.

"Edric, this is Lin. Sorry to wake you up, but I wanted to let you know that I won't be at that meeting on Monday."

He yawned. "Lin? Lin? What'd you say?" He'd be sitting up in bed, reaching for his glasses, putting them on.

She told him again, adding, "I have to take care of some things here." Why did she feel so calm?

He spoke in his business voice. "It's up to you. That meeting's going to happen whether you're here or not. With Vance in charge, I can't guarantee your position. Nothing personal, you understand. The magazine has to prosper, and things are going to change."

"Yes." She rested a hand on the rough surface of the rock.

He said something profane, then he added, "Come back, Lin. You've got a great future here."

She'd heard that line before. Back to the old lies. The old crowd. The old life.

With sudden clarity, she knew what to say next.

She squared her shoulders. "Effective immediately, I'm resigning. Darlene can send my final paycheck to the New Jersey address in her file."

Edric mumbled something about working things out.

She interrupted him. "I'll write you a formal letter as soon as I get time. You can read it at the next Board meeting."

He made a sputtering sound. "What's happened to you? Vance says you've got Indians on the brain."

Ben. Natalie. Ginni.

He wouldn't understand, but she had to say it anyway: "These people are my friends, and they're in trouble."

"What're you going to do about a job?"

"I don't know."

"Then you're not as smart as I thought."

She leaned back against the rock. Enough of this.

"Hang onto things as long as you can," she said. "The magazine is your dream, but it's not mine. Goodbye."

She closed her phone. Goodbye to it all.

She waited for panic to rise, but the sense of peace held, solid as the rock beneath her.

What next? Questions surged up against her peace. The job question: where to start looking? The Shula question: what would the woman try next?

Colin.

She found herself praying for him and Ben. Maybe tonight they were sitting by a campfire, high up in the mountains. Talking.

"Open Ben's heart to your love," she whispered. "Lord, have mercy on that man. And please give Colin the wisdom he needs."

She didn't know what else to say about Colin.

Don't think about him.

caption:

Candids

Lindsey might have slept well that night if it weren't for Ginni's nightmares.

Twice Ginni sat up in bed, crying, and each time Lindsey held her and sang her back to sleep.

Then Ginni awoke, saying that her headache was terrible bad.

This was the time to use the skills Colin had taught her. Working on the bed would be awkward, so she had Ginni sit at the desk. It wasn't hard to remember the technique, but it was almost impossible to keep her attention on Ginni's tense shoulders and fragile little neck. His smile lingered in her memory and so did the warmth of his hand.

This is different too, isn't it? . . . Rascal!

"Lord, what am I going to do about him? It's more complicated now."

She set her mind to praying for Ben and let it go at that.

Afterwards, Ginni crawled back into bed, yawning, and they both slept late into a dark, cool day. The smell of coffee reminded Lindsey that she'd told Belinda they'd be down for breakfast.

Ginni liked the pancakes, and in her curiously grown-up way, she told Belinda that they were most delicious, which got the meal off to a good start.

Belinda asked her the usual questions and seemed amazed to learn that Natalie was homeschooling all five of her children.

"Where did your mother go to school, my dear?"

"I don't know." Ginni poured a cascade of syrup over one more pancake. "Maybe nowhere. But she's a lot smarter than any of us, even Daddy." She glanced at Lindsey. "Except Mister Colin."

"Who's that?"

"A friend of Daddy's. He works in the library and comes to see us."

Belinda looked as if she wanted to ask more questions, but Lindsey hurried to finish the meal. "We're going to the beach," she said.

"Be careful," Belinda said. "It looks like it's going to storm."

They took Samantha along, and every once in a while, Ginni stopped to give the fish a swim.

While she waited, Lindsey gazed down the long gray strip of sand. It was as deserted as the first morning she'd hesitated on the rocky steps, but it no longer seemed harsh and rough.

Here she'd seen that first beautiful sunrise, and God had given her comfort. Here, watching Colin on that starlit night, she'd started to think of him as a person. And here, she'd had memorable talks with Fraser and Alexa. She had connected with Jack, and she'd seen Shula run her dogs.

Shula . . .

Lord, what about Shula?

Ginni came skipping up to her. "Where did you take the spider pictures?"

Lindsey found the place, but there wasn't much to see

except the remnants of a sagging web.

Ginni looked thoughtful. "I have an idea."

"What is it?"

"A present. For Remi and Mister Colin."

Lindsey leaned against a rock to smile at her. "Why would you want to give them a present?"

Ginni flipped her ponytail. "Because they rescued us. They're so brave. And quite enchanting."

She looked at Lindsey. "Don't you think so?"

Lindsey blinked. "Now that you mention it, yes."

"Okay, good. I know you'll want to help me. Let's sit down, and I'll tell you about it. Comfortable?"

Nine years old, going on twenty.

"You like taking photos, don't you, Miss Lindsey?"

"Yes," she said. What was the child plotting?

"You have a very nice camera and the black room too."

"Darkroom."

"Right, darkroom," Ginni said. "How about we take some pictures and you develop them and I'll make two special folders."

"What are we going to take pictures of?"

"Me!" Ginni smiled up at her. "Don't you think they'd like that?"

Lindsey had to smile. "I think so. But I'm in charge of the pictures."

Ginni nodded. "And I'm in charge of the folders."

Lindsey went back to get her Mamiya, and she took beach pictures, rock pictures, and log pictures, all starring Ginni.

She tried taking some of them in deep focus to emphasize the waves and driftwood trees as well as the child.

It was vastly different from photographing dogs for the magazine, and she felt the old excitement returning.

Derek. While she was working in his studio, she'd learned the finer points of taking black-and-white candids. He had taught her about deep focus, and he'd overseen her photos of the orphans, goading her to avoid stereotypes, to keep working until she achieved something original.

He'd been a superb professional and a great friend. They became so close that she began to think about marriage, but then she discovered that his greatest love was an envelope of white powder.

After Derek's overdose-suicide, she thought she'd never take a decent candid again, especially of a child. But some of these felt right.

They ate peanut butter sandwiches for lunch, and Lindsey began the developing process. Yesterday's photos weren't especially good, except for one of the deep-focus moonlight shots. She'd caught the tiny face of a raccoon in the trees, watching them.

Some of today's shots were almost worthwhile. She chose six and, after careful work with the enlarger, printed them as 5 x 7 photos.

The cat had crept into the room, unnoticed, and when he edged out from under the bed, Ginni greeted him with an inviting voice. For a long time, she played on the rug with him. She must be missing Spot, although she never complained.

Alexa phoned to ask them for supper, and Ginni was determined that they should take the photos, even though Mister Colin wouldn't be there.

"Remi will come," Ginni said. "I can't wait for him to see them."

Lindsey was glad she'd hurried to finish developing, because even with the hair-dryer treatment, it took a while for them to dry.

Ginni cut up two of Lindsey's manila folders, stapled them, and, using Lindsey's colored pens, decorated them with spiders, dogs, fallen trees, rain, and zigzags of yellow lightning. On the front of each folder, she printed a name, and below it, a row of large red O's.

"What are the O's?" Lindsey said.

"Hugs. Don't you know about hugs? Mister Colin taught me." She dropped her pen and came to put her arms around Lindsey. "I almost forgot your hug today."

Lindsey hugged her back. "I'm glad you're here, Ginni. You are a delight to me."

The child gazed at her for a minute, but she said nothing and went back to her folders.

When it was time to get dressed, Ginni watched Lindsey brush her hair, and she started on her own without being prompted. "How do you get yours so ruffly and shiny?" she said.

"It might be the way it's cut. And I brush it, too. Yours is long enough for a French braid. Would you like me to do it up?"

Ginni's eyes gleamed. "Sure. What's a French braid?"

After Lindsey finished, the little girl looked at herself in the mirror, then paced majestically back and forth. "This," she said, "is enchanting. I feel *quite* like a princess."

Remi was there for supper, as Ginni had hoped, as well as Fraser, and they heartily admired both Ginni's new hairstyle and her gift.

To Alexa, Lindsey said, "I'm sorry I didn't help with anything, but I had an assignment, as you can see."

Alexa smiled, of course, and Fraser suggested that she could do the dishes as penance. She'd felt his gaze during the meal but wasn't sure what it meant, and she was glad that this evening's conversation was light.

Perhaps it was because Ginni was there. The child sat beside Remi, a little more clingy than usual. She asked about Spot and about each of the Makah dogs by name.

Someone must have explained where Ben and Natalie had gone because she didn't mention them.

Tonight was Bible Study, and Alexa hurried to finish up in time. Fraser went to get the Richards family and the Thorsen sisters. Ginni helped Remi set up chairs.

Alexa and Lindsey cleaned up the kitchen. She wanted to tell Alexa what she'd decided, but the right moment didn't come.

Bible Study was led by Fraser, and in Colin's absence, Remi took over the opening song service. Alexa and Peter sat in the back row, and Lindsey sat there too, with Ginni between her and Alexa.

Fraser was just beginning to speak when Colin stepped through the side door.

Something inside her quivered to attention.

He sat down next to her, and as he did so, his shoulder brushed hers and stayed there.

"Hello," he whispered.

She gave him a quick smile and looked back to the front, but she'd seen enough to know that he wasn't exhausted, as might be expected after two days of strenuous hiking.

That whiff of aftershave meant he'd just shaved. His hair was still damp from a shower, and he was glowing. Things must have gone well with Ben, or he wouldn't have come back so soon.

She had thought it would be a distraction, sitting close to him, but it wasn't, perhaps because they both wanted to hear what Fraser said.

Fraser spoke from a passage in Isaiah, chapter forty: *The Lord is the everlasting God, the Creator of the ends of the earth. He does not faint or grow weary . . . He gives power to the faint, and to him who has no might he increases strength.*

She leaned over to share her Bible with Colin because

326

it was a different translation and he wanted to see how it read. His Bible was well-used, with notes written in a small neat hand, and, like him, she made notes in hers.

Fraser was a good teacher. He didn't lecture. He asked thought-provoking questions and managed to get the small group talking about the passage.

When Fraser had finished praying, Colin ducked his head close to hers. "Let's go for a walk, okay?"

Alexa must have heard because she said, "I'll keep Ginni," and by the time Lindsey reached the door, Colin had taken down her jacket and was holding it for her.

As soon as they were outside, she said, "You came back early! How's Ben?"

He smiled. "Worn out. Contrite. The Lord's done some amazing things, these past two days." He paused to look down at her. "He made a decision last night to follow Christ."

"That's wonderful news." She smiled up at him, enjoying the delight in his face. But he probably didn't know about Natalie.

Colin said, "Ben's got a rough road ahead of himself, but everything will be different now."

They started walking again, and she sighed inwardly. Better get it over with. "His rough road starts now, I'm afraid. Natalie got a note yesterday about Ginni."

"I thought it would catch up with him. How'd she take it?"

"She's gone. Took the children back home."

"Sounds like Natalie. But it's going to be hard for Ben to deal with."

As they reached Bay Street, and she said, "Where to?"

"How about that little park? Tell me how you've been. Is Ginni driving you crazy?"

"Not really. She likes to run around on the beach, and that tires her out. Oh, that reminds me—she has a present

327

for you. Make sure you stop by Alexa's and get it, or she'll be devastated. Do you think I should have left her?"

"She'll be fine," he said. "I just wanted to talk for a couple of minutes. You're still here. Something good has happened with your project?"

She didn't have a simple answer. Surely he didn't want to hear about her problems with the magazine.

They had reached the picnic tables, and he turned down the path to the bench at the far end of the seawall.

After they sat down, he said, "From the look on your face, I'm thinking it's not so good, after all."

What could she say?

"It's kind of complicated. I'm sure you don't want to hear all the details, so let's just say it'll be okay."

"No, let's not. I've only heard a few pieces."

He took her hand, purposefully, as if to encourage her. "Tell me from the beginning."

She left her hand enclosed in warmth and told him about her friendship with Edric and their agreement, years ago, and how the magazine had grown and they'd hired more staff, including Vance as marketing manager.

She didn't mention her relationship with Vance, but she described how things had changed since she'd been away, and she emphasized Vance's corrosive influence.

She paused before telling him about her decision to resign, thinking he would sympathize with her about Vance.

At first he said nothing. He lifted her hand and held it to his cheek.

He understood.

Slowly he lowered her hand, holding it close to himself. "This man has injured you. Perhaps in more ways than you've told me."

His voice was gentle. "But you need to forgive him, don't you?"

She looked away. "Forgive him? Not a chance."

Alarm skittered up her back, and she hurried to defend herself. "I read somewhere that forgiveness is what you do when you can't handle things—a kind of last resort."

He nodded. "The world's thinkers make statements like that, and at the same time they assure us that forgiveness therapy is effective. It is effective, but making yourself feel better isn't what I'm talking about."

"Tell me one good reason why I should forgive that man."

"There's an important verse in Colossians: *As the Lord has forgiven you, so you also must forgive.*"

He had no idea what that would cost her.

She pulled her hand away and crossed her arms over her chest, feeling small and cold. "But isn't Colossians written to Christians?"

"Christ says, *And whenever you stand praying, forgive, if you have anything against anyone.*"

"Listen, this guy is a scoundrel." Her voice began to shake, and she didn't care. "If I say dear-Vance-I-forgive-you, he'll think I want to . . . to . . . be his mistress."

She hunched deep into her jacket. "I tried to get Edric to fire him, but it was too late. I detest that man, and I'm going to make sure he regrets this."

How trite. How juvenile. But there you have it, Colin McAlister, the real me.

He put an arm along the back of the bench and turned toward her, leaning close, as if to shield her. "It takes courage, Lindsey, to forgive."

"Courage?"

"Yes. Because you're letting go of a debt. This guy owes you a lot, doesn't he?"

She could only nod.

"When you, as a child of God, decide to forgive him, you're trusting God to take over the repayment of that debt. It takes courage because you may never know what God does with it. And you're losing the chance to get even."

A fine theory. Maybe someday, but here and now? Impossible.

She shook her head. "You're mistaken about me. That would take more courage than I've got."

"Precisely."

Why did he have to use that word?

His voice reached for her in the dim light, held her, made her listen when all she wanted to do was squirm away.

"You can't do it alone," he said. "It's Christ who enables you. Remember that passage we heard tonight? *He gives power to the faint.* And there's a great promise in Romans. *In all these things we are more than conquerors through him that loved us.* Ben and I talked through that one quite thoroughly last night."

She thought back to Romans 8. Yes, forgiving Vance would certainly be tribulation and distress. *More than conquerors?* What did that really mean? And how did God give power to the faint?

She glanced at him out of the corner of her eye. He sat without moving, staring out at the waves. Repelled by her? Perhaps, but she sensed that he was thinking about something else.

He took his arm from the back of the bench, leaned forward, and sank his face into his hands.

That dark, bowed head suggested despair, and it made her ache.

For a long moment she listened to the murmur of waves at their feet, and then she said, "Colin?"

"Sorry." He straightened. "Thinking about Ben. Then Shula. I realized that here I am preaching to you, and I've got the same problem with Shula."

330

Maybe now she'd find out. "Why Shula?"

He answered with something like a groan. "She's been Ben's nemesis for years. Chased him until she got him, then they had an affair. She dropped him for a better prospect, but she was furious when he married Natalie."

This was preferable to talking about Vance. "What about Shula's sister?"

His voice hardened. "Cheree was part of it. She set her sights on Ben when they were in school, even though he was years older. She thought he'd marry her when he got out of the Corps, but he didn't. That's when Shula stepped in."

"But Ginni?"

"That happened after he married Natalie, as you know. Cheree had run away to Seattle. She married an old man for his money, and after he died, she set herself up in a thriving drug business.

"One day she pleaded with Ben to come see her, for old time's sake. So he did. He told me that he thought they were just going to talk, but she had another plan. And he fell for it."

He leaned back against the bench, closing his eyes, and his words came out in a rush. "All these years, whenever I've wanted to give up on Ben, God has reminded me how he reached out to me. And now he's been merciful to Ben too. Ben has become a new creature in Christ, but I expect the worst of Shula. I'm praying that for once in his life he'll be smart enough to ignore her."

He sat forward and gave his head a shake, as if to rid himself of an annoying insect.

He glanced at his watch. "I have to drive back to Seattle tonight."

She couldn't think of anything to say except: *Don't leave me here. Don't go away again. Don't make me forgive that man.* So she said nothing.

Slowly he got to his feet.

She looked up at him, standing there as big as a mountain, and wished she were a better person, someone a man like this could admire.

She stood up too, and moved away from the bench. She wasn't going to walk up to the bakery with him and see the pity in his eyes.

"I think I'll stay here for a while," she said quietly.

He gazed at her, and in the dim light, she couldn't read his face.

"Are you sure you'll be all right?" he said.

No, she wasn't at all sure.

Pull yourself together, Lindsey. Send the man on his way.

"Of course." She tried for a smile and failed. "This isn't New York."

Her voice was crisp, cooler than she intended. "Please tell Alexa that I'll be up in a couple of minutes."

"Lindsey?" He took a step toward her and stopped.

She didn't answer—couldn't—and after a minute he turned and slowly walked into the shadows.

She waited until she could no longer hear his footsteps, and then she stumbled away from where they'd been sitting, away from the park lights.

She ended up beside the pile of black rocks that buttressed the jetty.

With an effort, she smothered her despair. She removed the image of his face from her mind. The sea was quiet, gleaming faintly. Be quiet too.

Shula's face came into view, the eyes dark with hatred, the face etched with anger. Did she want to end up like that?

She picked up a chunk of the rough black rock and turned it over in her hands.

As the Lord has forgiven you, so you also must forgive.

A command. Was this a question of obedience?

"Lord," she said, "You know what's in my heart. My anger, and my hatred for Vance. My sin."

Hadn't she, yesterday, said, 'I'll do anything you want, if you'll just give me the courage.'?

Yes, she had. So why was she behaving like this?

She tried to swallow the bitter taste in her mouth, and finally, she said, "Father, this is too much. I need you to work forgiveness in me."

She gripped the piece of rock until its jagged edges cut into her skin. "I will say the words, but you are the only one who can make it happen. Lord! Have mercy on me."

She lifted the rock, threw it into the waves, and heard it splash. "There, Vance. I forgive you."

She waited in silence.

Courage, he'd said. Trust God for the debt.

"I trust you for this, Lord."

Light rain began to fall. She pulled up the hood on her jacket and caught the scent of Colin's aftershave. He'd held this hand of hers against his cheek.

She scrubbed at the back of her hand. She'd lost it with him, hadn't she?

Her eyes filled with scalding tears. So now he knew that she had this guy in her past, and he'd read between the lines, correctly. And he knew what kind of a person she really was.

No wonder he'd left.

"Lord, about Colin, I'm scared. I've never felt like this about anyone."

Her face was streaming with hot tears. "If he's the man he seems to be, I don't deserve him. But *what* is he, really? Another fraud?"

A sob caught in her throat. "Is Shula right about him? I can't bear the thought of him being someone like that . . . and then pretending with me."

The breeze shifted, sending an icy drizzle toward her.

She lifted her face, and the rain chilled her tears, washing them away.

Let him go.

The thought fell across her like a cooling cloud. She held out both hands, palms up, as Alexa had done.

"I'm giving Colin to you, Lord," she said quietly. "Take him away. Take him out of my life."

She waited for peace.

Instead, she had a sense of something unfinished, something more that she should say.

Like Alexa's prayer: *But if not . . .*

She bowed her head over the rain-drenched rock. "But if not, please show me what in the world to do about him."

Her hands were cold and wet, puddled with rain, but she didn't care. She thrust them deep into her pockets. At least this was settled.

"Father, I worship you tonight for your great love to me. My Lord and my God."

She took one last breath of the cool air, turned, crossed the small park, and ran up the hill.

She slowed as she approached the bakery. His car was gone. Good.

She blew her nose, thinking she must look like a mess: red eyes, dripping nose, scraggled hair.

Alexa greeted her with an anxious glance that turned into a smile of relief. "Ginni's been fine, but I think she's getting sleepy."

"So am I," Lindsey said. Such a kind person, Alexa was, not asking questions. "See you tomorrow."

Ginni skipped beside her on the short walk home, chattering about how much Mister Colin had liked her present and Remi too. And how tomorrow she wanted to take Samantha back out to the beach and wasn't it fun staying up late?

It felt good to step into the warmth of her room. Ginni undressed and crawled into bed right away.

Lindsey soon followed, but before long, Shula's face returned to her mind.

Even if Ginni was out of her reach for the moment, Shula wouldn't give up. What was she going to do next?

caption:

The Ring

She took Ginni to church with her the next morning, wondering how well she'd behave since she'd probably never been in a meeting like this.

The little girl seemed content to sit quietly between her and Alexa. She joined in the singing, and after watching Lindsey and Alexa taking notes on the sermon, wrote industriously on a piece of paper that Alexa had given her.

Lindsey bent over her notes. It was odd how a person could smile and answer questions and look perfectly normal on the outside and be hurting—a dull, aching hurt—on the inside. Like a computer program that was running in the background.

She had tried to analyze it while they were driving to church, but it was like putting a finger on an invisible bruise. Does it hurt here? Here?

Why?

She'd had a good night's sleep. She'd eaten breakfast. Ginni had given her a hug. She'd read some encouraging psalms. There was nothing wrong between her and the Lord—she'd asked him about that already. Was it the magazine? No, she still had peace about that decision, although she caught herself worrying about a job. Not any of those. She just hurt.

Ignore it, and maybe it would go away. She would forget him.

Back to that, was she? But thinking about forgetting wasn't forgetting.

Listen to this good sermon.

The pastor spoke on "God's gold," and his text in Revelation made her think again of Shula. *You say, I am rich, I have prospered, and I need nothing, not realizing that you are wretched, pitiable, poor, blind, and naked.*

Pitiable. But how Shula would scorn such a suggestion! She had everything she wanted, except Ben Fletcher's head.

After church, Fraser asked how she was doing, a little less casually than usual, but she assured him that everything was fine (thank you) and that she and Ginni were having a good time together.

"Bring her over tomorrow for a while, why don't you?" he said. "Maybe we can talk a bit, too."

"Sure." To herself, she clarified, Yes, she would bring Ginni over; but no, she wasn't going to talk to him.

He was much too clear-seeing, this good friend. And he knew her too well. She wouldn't be having a talk with anyone until she felt more like herself.

Remi seemed more upbeat than usual, and afterwards, with Ginni clinging to his hand, he walked with Lindsey to her Jeep. He probably wanted to tell her something.

Alexa, ever observant, called Ginni over, and Lindsey asked, "How's Ben doing?"

Remi grinned. "It's amazing, the difference. Of course, he's worn out. Colin worked him hard, and he's torn up about Natalie—the house is so empty—but he's doing okay. We prayed together, Lin. It was wonderful!"

He looked over his shoulder to check on Ginni. "I got a phone call this morning from a guy called Shabbir Hassam. He's Muslim. I knew him when I was living with

Colin. Haven't heard from him for a long time. He's got some questions about the Bible and wants me to come over to Seattle to talk. Today!"

A chill crept into her chest. "Are you going?"

"Yes! This is a great opportunity."

"When?"

"This afternoon." His eyes sparkled. "I've got it all figured out. I can catch the three o'clock ferry if I leave right away."

He cocked his head. "What's the matter?"

"Nothing, I guess." She couldn't explain her sense of danger. "Just a bit worried."

"Big Sister Lin!" He smiled. "Don't you worry! I'm tough, and remember, I know Seattle. I'll stay away from the hoodlums, I promise. We'll just sit at Graf's and talk."

She smiled back, determined not to look worried. "You'll be fine. And I'll pray for you and Shabbir."

"Who's Shabbir?" Ginni said from behind them.

Remi turned. "Someone I know in Seattle. I'm going to visit him."

He knelt down and put an arm around her shoulder. "Now listen to me, Ginni-belle. I want you to take good care of our big sister for me, okay?"

She smiled. "That's easy."

He covered her little face with kisses, making big smacking sounds, until she squealed in delight. Finally he let her go and stood up. "I'm off, Lin. I'll tell you what happens."

It was still there, that cold fear, as she watched him stride away, and it tightened its grip while they ate hamburgers for lunch and again while she and Ginni walked on the beach.

She had already prayed for him, so why did she feel like this? Was it a matter of trust? Or was she supposed to do something else?

Phone Colin.

The idea came without warning, and she was immediately suspicious.

She was supposed to forget about him. And he'd think she was chasing him.

But for Remi's sake?

Colin was already in Seattle. He might be able to . . . what? Tell her not to worry and pick up his book again?

She began to jog, half-heartedly, but soon she turned back, unable to get away from the thought. She sighed in resignation, sat down on a rock, and took out her cell phone.

"McAlister." His voice was deeper and more brisk than she remembered, and it shook her.

All she could say was, "Colin?"

His voice warmed. "Lindsey! Where are you? Are you all right?"

She laughed in nervous relief. "I'm fine. I just . . . I just wanted . . . I just wanted to tell you . . . something. About Remi."

What had happened to her brain?

"It's okay, Lindsey," he said. "Slow down a little. What's going on with Remi?"

She took a calming breath. "He got a phone call from a Muslim friend of his in Seattle who says he wants to talk about the Bible, so he's gone to meet with him."

Silence.

"I thought you might want to know," she said, "and it's probably silly of me but . . ."

"What's this guy's name?"

"Shabbir something. Hassam, I think. Have you heard of him?"

"Hassam? He's a leader in the FRO. Not in a million years is he interested in the Bible, except to burn it."

His voice had gone cold. So he was worried too.

"Did he say where they were going to meet?"

"Graf's, I think. Is that near the university?"

"Pretty close. Do you have any idea which ferry?"

"He mentioned three o'clock. What do you think?"

"I think it's a trap. Hope I'm wrong. Maybe I can catch up with him. I'm glad you thought to phone me."

"Colin! Be careful, please!"

Did she have to say that? The age-old cry of a woman left behind while her gallant knight charged off into battle.

"Pray for us," was his quick response. "I'll call you."

She slid the phone back into her pocket and stood up. Too much sitting around and thinking. Better get some blood moving into her foolish brain. She had sounded thirteen years old on that phone call.

"I'll race you, Ginni!" She took off down the beach and ran until she was stumbling.

Ginni caught up with her and demanded another race, so they ran back together. Then Ginni wanted to wade in the water, and for once she joined her, taking off her shoes and socks to splash in the freezing surf, and still she could hear his deep voice, and his promise: "I'll call you."

That night, Ginni had been asleep for only an hour when she sat up, holding her head. "I'm sorry! It hurts so bad!"

"Okay, Ginni-belle," Lindsey said. "Let's see what we can do."

Lindsey began by massaging the thin shoulders, and at the base of Ginni's neck she found tight muscles, so she worked to loosen them.

"Oh, mmm . . ." Ginni said. "Mmm . . . a lady all black with a pretty ring."

She was silent for a minute. "And . . . a note . . . mmm."

Lindsey kept her hands gentle, still moving.

"Mmm . . . she showed me. It said go with the lady, Ginni-belle. Mmm . . . Mmm . . . I kept crying, and then Jack came."

She didn't say any more, and when Lindsey finished, the child was almost asleep, so she helped her back into bed.

The next morning, she asked Ginni about it.

"Did I say that?" Ginni's eyes grew round. "I thought it was a bad dream."

"You said something about a ring. Do you remember what it looked like?"

"It was pretty. It had wires. Three shiny wires and a big goldy-orange stone."

Shula's unique ring. No doubt now.

After breakfast, Ginni curled up on the bed to read, and Lindsey made an effort to work. She wrote her resignation letter and emailed Darlene, asking to have the personal contents of her office sent to her house in New Jersey.

Next, she emailed Mollie to tell her about the boxes coming from the magazine. They'd have a lot to catch up on when she got back, too much to put into email.

There. She'd accomplished quite enough for one morning. She took Ginni to Fraser for her lessons.

He asked how she was doing and how the night had gone for them and where were they going today and what were they going to do. He didn't even smile.

Was he worried about something?

"Fraser," she said at last. "Dear pal! You are much too young to be a grandmother. In fact, you will never get to be a grandmother, so why not give it up?"

She bit her lip, realizing that she'd used Colin's name for him.

He looked at her, his brown eyes telling her nothing, and then he raised an eyebrow as if he hadn't understood.

"The questions," she said.

"Just wondering." His face was unreadable. "So you're on your way over to Odela's, you said?"

"I need to take back her blanket and thermos, and we might talk a little. Would you like me to phone you when I leave?"

He nodded. "I can tell you how Ginni's doing, and—"

"—I will. And I promise not to drive up to Cape Flattery today. Not even once. But you'd best stay by the phone because you never know what wild idea might strike me next."

She left before she could make any more smart remarks. It seemed easier to be sarcastic when she was hurting like this.

And what had happened to Fraser's sense of humor? Was he coming down with something?

The door to Odela's trailer yawned open. The old woman stood inside, surrounded by cardboard boxes. Jack was there too, piling in clothes and magazines.

Lindsey watched in silence, partly because she was amazed to see Jack here, calmly doing whatever it was, and partly because she had so much to say that she didn't know where to begin.

Jack came to the door. "Hi!" He gave her one of his us-artists-together smiles. "We're moving out."

"So I see."

Before someone wrings your neck?

"I happened to be over in Kalaloch, and I sold another painting."

"How nice."

Or did you steal a few dollars from an old lady?

"I'm going to try art school. Grams says it's a good idea."

"How fortunate for you."

"Yeah, Grams thinks our pretty little witch is a bad

342

influence on me, and maybe she's right. You know what I'd like to do?"

"I have no idea."

"I want to paint really good stuff, on my own, without the help of FlowerFire."

"That's certainly admirable."

He stopped talking long enough to look at her. "What's bugging you?"

"Nothing, except you kidnapped someone dear to me and left her in the woods alone in a storm, and two good men risked their lives to come get us, not to mention that her family was in agony. Not to speak of the time you kidnapped little Bobby Fletcher and left him to walk down a public highway."

She paused for a breath. "You belong behind bars, Jack. I hope the police catch up with you, soon."

At least he looked ashamed. "Hey, I was going to go back up to the cabin, except those guys beat me up so bad I could hardly move. Passed out, I think. Must've had . . . um . . . amnesia."

She wanted to slap him. "Serves you right. I wish they'd broken both your legs. Fraser tied you up, that's all."

"Yeah, but he tortured me with those ropes. And the big guy looked like he was going to kill me, so I decided to tell them where to find her. Didn't kidnap anybody. All I did was take her for a ride. Using my cabin was my own little twist—clever, I thought."

She let that go. "What'd you do it for, Jack?"

He grinned. "Money, what else? The golden passport to my future."

"Who paid you?"

A look of cunning crossed his face. "Funnily enough, Ben Fletcher just asked me the same question. I never reveal my sources. A point of honor."

343

"You mean you're scared she's going to find you and drop a little poison in your tea."

He turned pale, and she knew she'd hit on the truth.

But what was this he'd said about Ben?

"How come you went over to the Fletchers'?"

He drew himself up tall. "Just a man-to-man talk with Ben. Grams said to. In case he was thinking about going to the cops. I told him I was sorry and hadn't meant any harm."

Jack shrugged. "At first I thought he was going to hit me, but then he got the strangest look on his face. That's when he asked me, like you—"

"—Did you tell him?"

"Nope. Lucky for me, his phone rang. The subject under discussion herself."

"Did he say anything?"

"After he hung up, he mumbled, kind of stiff-jawed, 'Come see me, she says.'"

Jack grinned. "When I left, he sure seemed on the warpath."

He lowered his voice, still grinning. "Just between you and me, I think he's gone over there to lift her scalp."

"Why didn't you tell me sooner? When did this happen?"

"Couple minutes ago." His grin faded. "You'd better stay out of it. Those two deserve each other. Let them self-destruct."

"But she'll ruin him."

"Not likely. Have you seen him with a knife? He'll have her pinned before she can even think about her cute little pistol."

"You don't understand!" Lindsey whirled and ran for the Jeep.

She drove as fast as she dared, slowing as she reached the highway. There was no sign of Ben's truck heading for

344

Shula's place.

She was too late. He'd got to her already, and whatever happened was out of her hands.

She hunched over the steering wheel. Go back to Cameron Bay. She'd had enough of their private war.

Oh, Ben! How could you be so stupid? . . . Why these silly tears?

She wiped her eyes, reached into her pocket for a tissue, and her fingers closed around a slender piece of wood. Samantha.

She pulled it out. *A single purpose. Obeying him.*

If she tried to interfere, Shula would hate her. Ben would be furious. It wouldn't do any good, anyway.

Her pulse thundered in her ears. She dropped the driftwood fish onto the console, jerked the steering wheel to the left, and turned down the highway.

This wasn't about Shula or loyalty to friends or even about Colin's earnest hope for Ben Fletcher. It was about a single purpose.

God had given her a sure sense of peace the other night, and now, equally sure, was his command to go. Do what she could.

She flipped open her phone and speed-dialed Fraser. As she'd promised.

She said, "Ben's at Shula's—I'm going there." She snapped the phone shut.

Minutes later, she reached the house.

Ben's truck was there, parked crookedly behind Shula's Toyota. The house stood silent in the pale sunlight. Was he inside? Maybe not. In the distance she could hear the Akitas yipping.

She ran lightly along the path that curved around the side of the house, toward the fringe of cedars.

He stood there motionless, almost invisible in the shadows and low branches.

345

Her pulse had settled to a steady, purposeful thudding. Maybe she wasn't too late. Maybe he would let her talk to him. Maybe Shula wouldn't win this time.

After a long moment, she edged forward without making a sound.

He was watching the dog pen, and one hand rested on the knife in his belt.

Have you seen him with a knife? He'll have her pinned.

Without turning, he spoke under his breath. "Go away, Lin. This is my business."

Now she had a clear view of the pen. Shula was inside, talking to the dogs in a scolding sort of voice, holding up something that might be a treat.

She crept closer, stopping only when she was an arm's length from him.

The moments ticked by, and still he watched, his face set in grim lines. There was not a whiff of alcohol about him, only the scent of cedar.

"No, Ben," she whispered. "Not just your business. You belong to God now."

He looked at her, his eyes glittering, then back to the dogs.

The silence between them stretched until she couldn't bear it any longer.

"Let God deal with this, Ben."

He took his knife from its sheath and ran a thumb down the side of the blade. "Can't."

She stepped closer, avoiding the knife. "Yes, you can. Remember the verse—we're more than conquerors in Christ."

A breath of air floated past them toward the pen, and a moment later, the older dog stopped yipping. He stared at them, and the young one joined him, at full alert.

Shula saw them too. She said something to the dogs and moved to the open doorway of the pen, holding the transmitter.

"Hello, Lin," she said. "So you've made your choice?" She didn't wait for an answer.

She was looking at Ben, smiling a crooked little smile of triumph. "I thought you'd come, Ben Fletcher. Better give me that kid. I'm going to get her one way or another. You know it. That's why you're scared."

"Never." His voice was deep and harsh.

He moved forward, out of the trees, and Lindsey grabbed at his elbow. "Don't! That's what she wants. Her dogs will kill you."

He shook off her hand. "No." But he sheathed his knife.

Shula muttered to the dogs.

Both Akitas leaped toward them, two hundred pounds of bone and muscle and tearing jaws.

Ben dropped to one knee. "Tyee! Pelton!"

They slowed, looking confused. Ben called something in Makah and the older dog's head came up, ears pricked.

Shula pointed the transmitter, and Ben shouted, "Lin, get back!"

She moved fast, but the younger dog was screaming, swerving toward her. He leaped high and knocked her to the ground.

A dull pain in her leg . . .

Ben grabbed for the dog, sliced off the collar with his knife, and threw him aside.

Shula cried out. The older dog had turned and attacked, going for the transmitter and dragging her down. He stood over her, growling, his jaws locked on her hand.

Ben ran to them, pulled off the dog, and ripped his knife through the collar.

Lindsey struggled to sit up. Something hurt. Leg.

"Stay there, Lin, I'm coming." Fraser's voice spoke from behind her.

He knelt at her side. "Did he get you?"

"Not too bad." She raised herself on one elbow. "Go see about Shula."

Shula was curled up on the ground with her bleeding hand clenched against her chest.

Ben shut the dogs into the pen and came back.

He glanced down at Shula and at Fraser, impassive. "She's in shock. Can you get Alexa out here?"

After Fraser had phoned Alexa, he returned to Lindsey and helped her sit up.

"There's water in my Jeep," she said, and he went to get it.

Ben stooped over Shula, but she began to scream, a high, primitive wail that prickled the hair on Lindsey's arms. He shrugged and came over to where Lindsey was sitting. "Are you okay?"

"Just a scratch, I think. What about Shula?"

"Can't tell."

Fraser had returned with two bottles of water, and Ben motioned with his head. "Can you do something for her? She won't let me near."

"Help me up, Ben," Lindsey said. "I need to talk to her."

He set her onto her feet but kept a hand on her arm. "You sure?"

"Yes, if I can get my legs moving again. There. One of them hurts, but it's workable. Thanks."

"Are you bleeding?" He seemed dazed, but she felt that way too.

"I don't know." She looked down at her torn jeans. "Probably nothing much. Why don't you go out front to wait for Alexa? You could show her where we are."

Ben disappeared into the trees, and she limped over to see Shula. She was quiet now, still clutching her hand, and the bleeding had stopped.

Fraser was kneeling beside her, his hand on her pulse.

She shot Lindsey a glance that made her spirit wilt.

Fraser reached a hand up. "Sit down, Lin."

She did so, slowly, because her legs had gone stiff again, and he handed her a bottle of water.

As she drank, she noticed with surprise that her hand trembled. She stared at the blood on the ground and at the fallen transmitter, feeling colder by the minute.

Finally Ben returned with Alexa. Shula snarled as soon as she heard Ben's voice, so he detoured around them, going from the dog pen to a small tool shed beside it.

Alexa was gently efficient, and at her direction, Fraser helped Shula into the house. Lindsey stayed where she was, thinking that she really should get up.

Fraser came back right away. "Shall we stand up?"

She nodded. "We shall."

But she had to hang onto him as she stood, and once she was back on her feet, he kept an arm around her, or she would have fallen. "You're shaking, Lin. It's just shock. Stay here for a minute." He draped his jacket across her shoulders, and she shivered into it.

"That was a terrible sight," she said. "It's a good thing you came. I guess I do need a grandmother."

Fraser's voice was gentle. "He said to take care of you for him. He was afraid Shula would go after you."

Colin? He cared.

"Don't . . . don't talk about him."

She bent her head, closing her eyes to keep back the tears. "I don't know . . . I'm not sure at all."

Fraser held onto her. After a minute he said, "You'll know, Lin," and she was thankful for his strong arm and for his words.

Finally she looked up. "I'll be okay now. Thanks, Fraser. I don't deserve either of you." She snatched at a breath, hoping for composure. "We'd better go see how Alexa's doing."

caption:

Trees—Blurred

In the kitchen, Alexa was still cleaning Shula's hand. She remarked that Shula really should see a doctor and get a tetanus booster, but Shula snapped out a reply. "I've had one. No doctor."

Alexa nodded and went on with her work.

Fraser made sure Lindsey had her bottle of water, and then he said to Shula, "What can I get for you?"

He made a pot of tea with the herbs she pointed out.

Lindsey sat in the chair where Fraser had left her, declined the tea, and sipped at her water. Everything seemed to be moving in slow motion.

"Fraser," Alexa said, "I don't like Lin's color. See about her leg."

"It's fine," she said, but Alexa gave her a look, and she pulled up the leg of her jeans to check.

An angry red scratch ran down the side of her calf, and teeth marks showed as red indentations in her skin. Half a dozen bruises were already turning blue.

"Sure, it's fine," Alexa said. "Fraser, clean it for me, okay?"

"I can do that," Lindsey said.

"No, indeed. He's done it dozens of times, and that's

how he earns his big bucks as my assistant. Here's some stuff. It'll sting a little."

He was gentle and fast, and when he finished, Alexa had him make two ice bags to hold on the bruises.

By the time Alexa was done, Shula was sitting upright, and she seemed in command of herself once more.

"Thank you, kind neighbors," she said in a cool voice. "I appreciate your help. I think I'll take a nap, so you may leave now."

They left.

"She's still in shock," Alexa said, once they were outside. "Something in that tea was a narcotic. I hope she can manage by herself."

"Yes," Lindsey said. Except for that first bitter glance, Shula had ignored her.

Fraser shrugged. "She's one determined lady, and it's hard to tell what she's going to do. I'd better get back to town. Kind of left in a hurry."

"Thank you again," Lindsey said to him. She could smile now. "Want me to call when I get home?"

"Of course. And after you've locked your door for the night." His eyes were warm with sympathy, but he didn't say anything more. He smiled and went to his car.

Ben was still there, standing beside his truck. He had put the dogs into travel crates, and they stared out from the barred windows.

"She'll be okay, won't she?" he said.

Alexa nodded. "If she's smart enough to get some rest. Are you going to take care of the dogs?"

"Yes. They should be destroyed, but maybe it won't be necessary if I work with them."

He looked at Lindsey. "Thank you. God has been so good to me. I don't deserve—"

"—None of us do," she said.

His dark face crinkled with distress, and she hurried to

351

ask a question. "Why do you think Pelton went for me?"

"The dog was out of his mind with pain. He knew me, and you were a stranger, standing nearby."

"How come he knew you?"

"They used to be my puppies. I raised them and trained them for her with Makah commands. As a gift. Long ago, when we were friends."

He turned to get into his truck but stopped to give her a tired smile. "Colin was right about you."

Whatever that meant. He still hadn't phoned. What was happening to him and Remi?

"Lin, you're kind of pale," Alexa was saying.

"I'm fine."

Or I will be, as soon as he phones. "Please, Lord, protect them both."

Alexa said, "Let's go pick up Ginni—she's with Peter—and then get you some lunch. Maybe that'll help. Would you like me to take Ginni this afternoon?"

"Thanks, but she's no trouble. We haven't had our walk on the beach today. I think it'll do both of us some good."

It was after they'd returned to the Roost and she was changing shoes for their walk, that her cell phone rang.

Colin.

His voice was buoyant. "We've had a bit of a tussle, but we're both okay—thanks for praying. They might let him out of the hospital in a day or two. Then I'll bring him over."

"Oh . . ."

Ginni had pranced over, so she said, "Here comes Ginni." She handed her the phone. "Do you want to say hello to Mister Colin?"

"Sure!" Ginni gave him a full description of what she'd been doing, said a happy "See-you-soon!" and closed the phone before Lindsey could stop her.

She wanted to talk to him some more, find out what happened and whether he'd been hurt. She wanted to listen to that deep voice, wanted to hear what he was thinking.

Should she phone him back?

No. She bent over to tie her shoes and gave herself a silent lecture.

This is the guy you just handed over to the Lord, remember? You can't expect God to take him away if you keep thinking about him. Toughen up.

"Here's your jacket." Ginni was looking at her curiously. "I'm all ready to go."

Go? That's right, to the beach. A walk might be good for her leg.

Quickly she laced up her shoes, and they set off.

Late afternoon on a sunny fall day. What could be more beautiful than those blue waves foaming onto the gray sand? A seagull rode the swells, eyeing them. "He's watching us, isn't he?" Ginni said. "What's he thinking?"

"Probably that he's glad we've come to share his beach. Isn't it nice out here?"

"Yes, indeed," Ginni said, using her grown-up voice. Before long, she found a small tide pool in the rocks and knelt beside it with a cry of pleasure. She dabbled in the water, talking to Samantha about the tiny shells and the sea weed.

If Colin was taking care of Remi, he probably wasn't injured.

Stop it.

She pulled herself up onto one of rocks and sat down among the clumps of moss, wincing as she banged her leg.

A silent prayer surged from deep inside. "Lord, what am I supposed to do about Colin? I don't want any more turmoil right now. I've got to take care of Ginni. And find a job."

She fingered a tuft of velvet moss. "And Lord, I don't have your peace, like you gave me last time. I've just got this horrible mixture of feelings."

She knew better than to trust her feelings.

When she'd been dating Vance, it had felt so good, so right . . . so wrong!

Now admit it. Even though she was doing her best to forget him, she was attracted to this strong-intelligent-kindly man. He had an intriguing quirky streak, and his godliness seemed real.

But many Christian men lived a lie. God knew what Colin was like inside. Couldn't he give her a push in one direction or the other?

She slid down off the rock. "I'm going to take a little walk, Ginni."

"Wait for me! I'm coming too. Race ya!" Ginni scampered ahead, and Lindsey followed as fast as her leg allowed. The words kept time with her steps.

It . . . is . . . God . . .
Who . . . works . . . in . . . you . . .
It . . . is . . . God . . .
Who . . . works . . . in . . . you . . .
It . . . is . . . God . . .

She slowed. That was a promise. God had promised to work his will in her. So let him work.

Ginni, feet flying, passed her with a shout. "I won! I won!"

Alexa phoned to say that she was bringing supper over, so they ate with Belinda at the kitchen table. Belinda was full of talk about yesterday's visit with Shula.

"All sea creatures," she said, "have guardian spirit power. Shula thinks I should have a sea totem to guide and protect me. She's going to help me find one."

Alexa didn't comment, but she looked sad, as if she'd heard this before.

Belinda darted a sharp glance at her. "You think it's rubbish, don't you? I don't see why God couldn't use a little help protecting us."

"I don't think," Alexa said, "that God needs help with anything."

But Belinda wasn't listening. "Shula showed me one of her totems. It's a pretty little heart-shaped rock with a dip in the middle—that's where the spirit power is the strongest. It'd be nice to have something like that. Maybe I wouldn't worry so much."

Alexa stood up and carried her plate to the sink.

Belinda stood up too. "If you girls don't mind, I'll leave the dishes with you this time. I want to go over and see Shula again tonight."

After Belinda left, Lindsey took Alexa up to her room so they could talk and Ginni could do her homework. They made cocoa in the kitchenette, and Alexa asked about the magazine project.

She gave Alexa a brief version of what had happened and what she'd decided.

Alexa drew a startled breath, smiling. "Lin! Really? So you'll be staying here?"

"I'd like to, for a while anyway. It depends on whether I can find a job. I'll be working freelance, and I'll take what I can get."

Alexa's smile grew. "It's selfish, maybe, but I'm so glad. Oh! I can't tell you what this means to me."

Lindsey smiled. "I've never had a friend like you, Lexa."

"I thought for sure you were leaving." Alexa glanced at Ginni, on the other side of the room. "When you-know-who came back from that talk, he looked so miserable, I was afraid you'd . . ."

"Just a sec," Lindsey said. "Let's go out into that nice fresh air."

This friend, wise in the things of the Lord, might be able to give her some advice. And she might know the truth about Shula and Colin.

Ginni was sprawled across the bed, coloring and didn't glance up as they went by. They dragged kitchen chairs out onto the balcony and sat down with their steaming mugs.

"It's really nice out here." Alexa looked around the balcony, and Lindsey was thankful for her restraint, but she had to ask.

"He was miserable? I wouldn't think so. Someone told me he'd break my heart."

Alexa put her mug down on the balcony, picked up a fir cone, and rolled it back and forth in her hands.

"Sounds like Shula. She made quite a determined play for him at one time."

"The way she spoke, I thought they might have been intimate."

"Colin? No way. She would have liked nothing better. Did her best. As soon as he realized what she was up to, he tried to talk some sense into her—with Fraser there—but she made a scene, hung onto him, weeping buckets of tears. Finally she left, and he hasn't spoken to her since."

Lindsey didn't move, but a weight inside her dissolved and slipped away.

Alexa brushed at the small winged seeds on the cone. "And I will tell you something else—because it's not right for that woman to poison your mind against him."

She glanced at Lindsey and back to the cone. "That night, before he went back to Seattle, Colin came into the kitchen for coffee, and he leaned on the counter with this anguished look on his face. He said, 'I've upset her, Lexa. That astonishing woman—she probably detests me. How can I go off now and leave her?'"

Lindsey looked down into her mug of cocoa. She wasn't going to fall apart, just because . . .

She pulled her thoughts together. "But he did leave. We talked, and he found out what I'm really like."

"Yes, he left," Alexa said. "But not before he told me that you needed to be alone, and it was one of the hardest things he'd ever done. He was quiet for a minute, and then he explained how he'd told you about hating Shula. He said it was only fair for you to know the worst about him."

That was the worst? Lindsey gazed into the trees, trying to quiet the uproar inside her.

Finally she said, "Let me ask you something. When you were dating Peter, how did you know he was right for you?"

"I didn't. Not at first." Alexa threw the fir cone over the railing and picked up her mug. "I was terribly worried about making a mistake."

"Not love at first sight?"

"Not a bit. I tried to be sensible and think things through. He was a little older, solid, a mature Christian. But I was young, a new Christian, just out of nursing school, and kind of wild."

She laughed. "Come to think of it, Pete's the one who should have been concerned."

"So what did you do?"

"Got serious about praying. Asked God to close that door if he wasn't right for me. Peter and I did things together, and I kept praying. I talked it over with my mom, and one day, I knew."

Lindsey studied the design on her mug. "So it's not that easy? I feel like I've got two people living inside me."

Alexa gave her a sympathetic glance. "Here's another thought. The Lord was working in Peter's heart too. You might want to consider what Colin's feeling."

"I didn't try to . . ."

"Not on purpose. That first meeting, and on the trip to Neah Bay, you were cool, focused, and from what Fraser told me, quite impressive. Colin didn't say much—except maybe to Fraser—but he asked questions."

"He seemed so inscrutable. Drove me crazy."

"He used to work for Intelligence—that's where he learned to close up like that. But when you were stranded up at Cape Flattery—the look on his face! I knew then. He organized us like he was still in the Marines. He even went back and listened to your message for himself."

Alexa sipped at her cocoa. "He hasn't lost his wits, though. Believe me, he's a wise man. He'll make up his mind, and you'll know it, but even then, he's going to take his time." She smiled. "I've never seen him like this."

Lindsey shifted in her chair. "Maybe it's just that my eyes remind him of moss."

"From him, that may be quite a compliment." Alexa laughed. "He really said that?"

"After a fashion."

"Come to think of it, he's got a couple of degrees in biology, so it makes sense."

"No wonder I feel like I've been put under a microscope." Lindsey tried to laugh but couldn't. "How come he's not married by now, anyway?"

"He had a girl once. She married someone else when he was overseas."

"Heartbroken forever? Oh, sorry—didn't mean to say it like that."

"There was another one," Alexa said. "A long time ago. I don't think she was good for him, and he finally realized that. He told me that he'd given up on finding anyone, that the Lord wanted him to stay single. He and Fraser have that in common."

"Fraser? But he's so young."

"With Fraser, it's really sad. He was engaged to a wonderful girl, and she died of some rare kind of flu. That's when he left Alaska and came down here."

Lindsey stood up and went to lean on the railing. "I'm sorry, Lexa. Maybe I shouldn't be so cynical. But I've let myself get involved with too many guys who seemed to be just great, and in one way or another, each of them turned out to be no good. Especially the last one."

She brushed a dried leaf off the railing, picked up another, and crumbled it into yellow fragments. "I don't know what to do about Colin. But I think I'd be smart to walk away from this. We'll both forget—I keep telling myself that. I've had enough hurt to last me forever."

Alexa came to stand beside her, and she had the sense that her friend was praying.

Finally Alexa said, "Did you marry any of those men?"

"No. And, for what it's worth, I didn't live with any of them, either. Thanks to my puritanical background."

"Maybe the Lord was protecting you." Alexa's voice softened. "Were any of them Christians?"

She shook her head.

"Were you walking close to the Lord yourself?"

"No, I wasn't. I still think it's a wonder that he brought me back."

"God's incredible love, right?" Alexa smiled. "And he clearly showed you what to do about the magazine?"

"He did. Every time I start worrying, I remember how clear he made it."

"And now you expect him to show you—*zap!*—about Colin."

She could only nod.

"Lin, don't you think that as long as you're walking with him . . . ?"

"I hear you." She braced herself against the railing, and her nails dug into the wood. "So . . . I need to trust that God won't play some dirty trick on me and lead me on the wrong path and let me marry a . . . an imposter."

Alexa's silence agreed with her.

Lindsey glanced into the trees, but they had blurred. She bowed her head. "So maybe . . ." Her voice broke. "Maybe I could love him, just a little?"

Alexa put an arm around her. "You could. Stay close to the Lord. Wait and see what he brings to pass."

Lindsey closed her eyes, and all she could see was Colin's face. Wait and see.

She sighed, glimpsed Alexa's smile, and felt herself begin to smile too. "And what are you so happy about, may I ask? I'm taking a big risk here. It's my life that—" She caught Alexa's raised eyebrow "—that's in God's hands. I've got to remember!"

Alexa brushed at her eyes. "I talked to Colin this afternoon. We made some plans for when they let Remi out. We're going to keep him at our place for a few days. Ben has already left to go plead his case with Natalie. Fraser and Colin get to take care of the dogs. Never a dull moment in this little town."

Tap-tap-tap. Ginni was at the glass door, waving the page she had finished.

Soon after, Alexa said she had to leave, and while they were downstairs gathering up her dishes, Belinda came out of her apartment. "I'm worried about Shula," she said. "I thought we'd have a nice cup of tea, but she's not home."

Alexa opened her mouth and closed it again. She must have decided not to say anything about Shula.

"Maybe she went to Seattle," Lindsey said, wondering how well she could fly with an injured hand.

Belinda nodded, looking happier. "That's right! I forgot—she said something about an important meeting with Kamal. That's where she is."

Which meant she had a date. Lindsey exchanged a glance with Alexa and kept scrubbing the slow cooker, but uneasiness tugged at her. What was Shula up to now?

caption:

Carrot Pennies

That night after Ginni was asleep, Lindsey curled up in the leather chair to read. She went to Psalm 16 because its confident tone reflected the way she wanted to feel.

I shall not be shaken . . .

Well, she hoped not. Too many things could shake her, right about now.

"Lord," she whispered, "I've never felt so vulnerable in my life."

Her phone rang, a startling sound in the quiet room, and she leaped for it.

"Lindsey."

Tears stung her eyes and she had to swallow twice and he was saying, "Lindsey? Lindsey?"

She finally managed a word. "Yes."

"I know it's late, but I wanted to—why are you whispering?"

"Because I don't want to wake up Ginni. Wait just a minute."

She stepped into the bathroom, shut the door, and turned on the light. "Okay, this is better."

"Where are you? Outside?"

"No, I'm sitting on the edge of the tub and trying to be

very careful because if I drop my phone it's going to land in the developing pans, and she'll wake up for sure."

He laughed. "That doesn't sound very comfortable. Aren't you cold?"

She looked down at her bare feet. "Chilly, yes."

"I won't talk for long, but I'm driving back from the hospital, and I was thinking about you. Are you okay? Ben told me what happened. So did Fraser. He got there in time to see you go down, and it scared him half to death. How's your leg?"

"Not bad. I took a walk this afternoon."

"Fraser said you were brave."

"A scratch and a couple of bruises, that's all. But I'm glad he came." She reached for a towel and wrapped it around her feet. "How's Ben doing?"

"Not bad. He's gone to see Natalie. He said something about getting a verse tattooed on his arm."

She laughed. "Probably the one you gave him—more than conquerors."

"He said you were sent by God, and I think he's right."

"That sounds so dramatic, like Joan of Arc. I just obeyed. And I was scared, Colin. Do you know what I mean?"

"Yes, I do. Sometimes it's not easy." He paused. "Ah, Lindsey, I've got so much to tell you. Tomorrow won't come soon enough."

"Tomorrow?"

"Yes. Remi's doing better, charming all the nurses, and he talked them into letting him go. Alexa will take good care of him. So I'm planning to bring him over in the afternoon."

Tomorrow. They were coming tomorrow.

"Lindsey?"

"I'm glad, Colin."

"I am too. Sleep well, okay?"

362

After she'd said goodbye, she wished she had asked whether he was injured, but surely he'd have said something? She put on a pair of socks and went to bed.

It had been kind of him to let her know what was happening. More than kind? Maybe? She'd leave it at that.

They arrived by mid-afternoon the next day.

Lindsey arranged a calm expression on her face and stood off to one side. Her calm stayed intact until she saw Remi.

Colin was helping him out of the car, and Remi seemed to be managing fine until he took a step and crumpled. Colin held onto him, saying, "You can't just take off like that, remember? Put the good arm around my neck. Okay, slow. I've got you."

By the time they eased through the door, Remi's face was the color of parchment. Alexa slid a chair forward, and he sank into it.

Colin's gaze traveled across the room and found her. A quiet smile—just quiet and friendly. That was fine.

She had expected him to look different, but he wore the usual jeans and a flannel shirt—a forest green that suited his dark hair. Perhaps only her perspective had changed.

Alexa helped Remi take off his jacket, which was overly large and looked like one of Colin's. His short-sleeved blue shirt was several sizes too big, and his left arm was bandaged from elbow to wrist.

After a minute, he looked up and gave Lindsey a weak grin. She smiled back, flinching inside.

"Plenty of fluids," Alexa said, "and a couple of days of rest, that's what they told me. So Colin, get him up the stairs, and I'll bring him something to drink."

Colin bent over the boy, and Lindsey followed Alexa into the kitchen. "He looks terrible, doesn't he?"

"He certainly does," she said. "He should have stayed put for another day, but no, he wanted to come. He's

363

young and strong—he'll be okay."

She poured orange juice into a large glass. "Meanwhile, here he is with a twisted knee and a three-inch gash in his arm. If Colin hadn't been there, he could have bled to death."

Her eyes glistened. "It was God's mercy that made you phone."

"I'm thankful," Lindsey said. "What about Colin?"

"Says he's okay, and he doesn't do the macho stuff, so he probably is. I'm glad for that." She hurried out the door.

Lindsey had meant to tell her what Ginni remembered about Shula, but there would be time enough later.

Now that the bakery had closed for the day, Lindsey vacuumed the café, wiped down the glass cases, and carried the baked goods back into storage.

She tried not to limp, even though her leg was still stiff and the bruises were tender.

Colin made several trips to and from his car, up and down the stairs. Her heart quickened whenever she saw him, but she made no effort to get his attention or to speak privately with him.

See what God brings to pass.

Suppertime was coming up. She and Alexa had planned the menu, and she knew that carrots needed to be sliced, so she slipped away into the kitchen.

She would do at least a dozen carrots. Everyone liked Alexa's Copper Pennies. Scrub. Peel. Slice. Cook.

She scrubbed the carrots hard, telling herself how well she was doing—so very busy—and then she peeled them. She was slicing the last few carrots when the kitchen doors opened with their tell-tale squeak.

She recognized his step and didn't move.

Wait.

She kept her eyes on the cutting board and said, "If you're looking for Ginni, she's over at the bookstore."

"I'm not looking for Ginni." He stood behind her "Better put down that knife."

She laid it aside and turned.

He put his fingertips on her shoulders—gently, as if he were afraid of breaking something—and searched her face.

She saw the flame in his eyes, as she'd remembered.

He gathered her into his arms.

Warm. Strong. Home.

He stroked her hair without saying anything, and she lowered her face to his shoulder.

The doors squeaked open and Alexa bustled into the room. "Oops! Sorry, you two."

He didn't move, but he said, "That's okay, Lexa, I'm just making up for lost time. Can I help with supper?"

"You sure can. I was hoping you'd do the vegetables and gravy."

He bent low to whisper. "Later, we'll talk, okay?"

She nodded and turned back to the carrots with reluctance. He and Alexa discussed the chicken, which seemed to involve a lemon and embellishments like thyme, sage, and garlic.

It was hard to concentrate, but she sliced the rest of the carrots without nicking a finger. She put them into the microwave to cook and started chopping the other ingredients. She was going to make this all by herself.

He stood nearby, doing something with potatoes and cauliflower and parsley.

After the carrots were tender, she started on the dressing—not very difficult. She mixed it through the carrots and put the dish into the refrigerator. Copper Pennies done.

Alexa left to check on Remi, and Colin took two golden-brown chickens from the oven, poured off the drippings, over-wrapped them with foil, and returned them to the oven. He mashed the potatoes with the cauliflower and herbs; then he started on something at the stove and stayed there, stirring it.

She went over, feeling a little shy, to see what it was.

"I like to watch you cook," she said.

He looked up with a smile. "I like to watch you watch me cook."

He put a hand on her shoulder, his eyes bright, and all she could do was smile. He moved his hand down to her waist and drew her close.

Her arms went around his neck of their own accord. She nestled against him—smooth flannel, solid muscles— and he smelled like parsley and her heart was bounding out of control.

He nuzzled into her hair and a minute later, lifted his head. "Who lit that blaze?"

Breathless, she said, "I think you did. The quiet librarian."

He grinned. "The cool photographer. Make it a tie." He traced the curve of her cheek with a gentle finger. "You like research and so do I. Maybe we should check it out."

He folded her close. "Ah, Lindsey," he said, and she melted into his whispering, and a door opened.

She hid her face in his shoulder.

"It's okay," he said. "Fraser."

"Well, it's about time, pal," Fraser said. "Just don't burn my supper." He got something from a cupboard and left, rather noisily.

Colin reached over, pulled a pan off the burner, and turned back to her, but she was laughing. "This may not be the most efficient way to produce a meal."

He laughed too. "Efficiency isn't what's on my mind right now." He looked over his shoulder at the stove. "You're right. It's going to be bad enough if I burn Fraser's supper, but when Alexa gets back and the gravy isn't done, we're both in big trouble."

The words were hardly out of his mouth when Alexa came in. She didn't look a bit upset. "We can postpone supper, if you guys prefer, but you're going to get enough ribbing as it is."

"Gravy's coming right up," Colin said, smiling at Lindsey.

"And there's something else," Alexa said. "Ginni is with Peter, so this might be a good time to talk. Fraser said she remembered some things, but she sounded confused. We wanted to ask Lin about it."

Lindsey looked at Colin and he nodded. "Yes, let's talk," she said.

When Fraser came in, Alexa said, "Lin, we're wondering how Ginni's been. Have you said anything to Colin about her?"

"No, not yet."

Fraser grinned. "After all, you two have been busy."

She stiffened, but Colin put his arm across her shoulders and laughed. "We certainly have." He smiled down at her. "What happened with Ginni?"

She told herself to take it easy and organized her thoughts. "Ginni had another of her headaches. I was massaging her neck, and in bits and pieces, she described the person who took her. It sounded like Shula, wearing a hijab. The most important point is that Ginni described her ring."

Fraser nodded. "So that's what she meant."

"Shula wears a rather distinctive ring," Alexa said.

"How accurate was she?" Colin said.

"She did well. She noticed the three copper wires and the stone, which she called goldy-orange. It looks like a topaz."

"That's proof!" Alexa said.

"And here's something else," Lindsey said. "Remember when Bobby got picked up? We pried some details out of him, although we didn't know what it meant at the time. He said it was an old lady with things in her ears, and Ginni and I figured out that it meant hoop earrings with pink stones."

Alexa frowned. "I didn't think of Shula. That doesn't sound like her."

"It wasn't. When I was cleaning up Odela's kitchen, I found a pair of earrings exactly like that. She told me they're Jack's and they go with his old-lady costume."

She looked from Alexa to Fraser. "And I would like to say that I am furious with those two and think they should be turned over to the police and fully prosecuted."

Fraser said, "I don't blame you. I think we all feel the same way. But as far as prosecution is concerned, look at what we've got. Jack's a hostile witness, and he won't admit anything."

"I guess Jack didn't actually harm her," Alexa said slowly. "No ransom note."

"But Ginni remembers!" Lindsey exclaimed.

Beside her, Colin said quietly, "That's the problem. All we have is Ginni's memory and your testimony. If we take this to court and they put you on the stand for cross-examination, you'll do fine."

He paused. "But what about Ginni? Do we want her to go through that? And questions will come up about parentage and relationships and so forth."

"You're right," Lindsey said. "I don't want that for her, and besides, Ben and Natalie would never agree." She sighed. "So they're going to get away with what they've done?"

Colin's hand closed on her shoulder, and his calmness flowed into her.

"I spoke to a friend of mine," he said, "and the police will be asking Jack some questions. He's been in trouble before."

"I don't think," Fraser said, "that either of them will get away with what they've done."

At last, Colin finished making his gravy, Alexa took the chicken and vegetables out of the warming oven, and Lindsey put the Copper Pennies on the table.

She and Colin sat close beside each other at supper. Remi, across from them and looking better after his nap, must have seen something in their faces because he watched them with a grin. He caught Lindsey's eye and gave her a vigorous thumbs-up.

She could feel the warm pink creeping up her neck—in a minute Remi would see it. Couldn't let him get away with this, or they'd have no peace. She gave him a stern look. "Young man!"

He put down his fork in mock surprise. "Me?"

"Yes, indeed. You will keep a civil tongue in your head, please."

"Oh, yes! Yes, ma'am." He bobbed his head, trying to smother his grin while everyone, especially Ginni, looked curious.

"Great meal," Fraser said. "Roast chicken, and the mashed whatever-it-is, quite good with the excellent gravy. And the Copper Pennies! Who made them?"

She tried to keep a straight face. "Now aren't we being a little obvious, Fraser? Besides ever-so-cleverly changing the subject, you know I made them. Copper Pennies is one dish that's almost infallible. Want the recipe? Carrots, onions, peppers, and dressing made with a can of tomato soup."

He laughed. "Guilty as charged. But really, you're too hard on yourself. Was your mother a good cook?"

"One of the best."

"Did she let you help her?"

"Help her? I wasn't allowed to set foot in the kitchen."

Fraser gestured to the table at large. "I rest my case."

Ginni whispered something to Remi, and he said, "That means, 'See, I'm right.'"

"Yes," Ginni said. "Miss Lindsey makes good stuff to eat. We had pemmican when we were Indian princesses, waiting for Remi."

Fraser smiled. "How did it taste?"

"*Quite* delicious. She said you eat it all the time. That's why you're so brave and strong."

Lindsey bent over her plate, avoiding Fraser's eye.

"I'll have to get her recipe," he said. "I'm sure Mister Colin would like it too. Wouldn't you, Mister Colin?"

Ginni gave Colin an appraising look and turned to Lindsey. "Am I still your delight? Even when he's—you know—around?"

Someone smothered a laugh, but she kept her eyes on the little girl's face. "Yes, you are, Ginni."

"Good," Ginni said. "What's for dessert?"

"I was hoping someone would ask," Alexa said. "Peter tried his hand at a yeast-raised chocolate cake with mocha cream filling. I'm thinking of hiring him."

Lindsey could feel Colin laughing beside her, and he found her hand under the table and held it, and Peter remarked on Colin's sudden ability to eat left-handed.

But Lindsey smiled and suggested that this marvelous cake be named after Peter, saying that tourists, no doubt, would come from near and far to ask him questions and take his picture.

Peter didn't look enthusiastic about the idea, and no one could think of the perfect Peter-name for the cake, but they agreed that it should be featured in the café.

They were finishing up when the phone rang.

Peter got up to answer it and a minute later he said, "Belinda, now just a minute, just wait, okay? She's right here."

He handed the phone to Alexa. "Your sister. She's hysterical about something."

Alexa listened for a long time, and then she said, "I'm so sorry. Will you be okay driving? Why don't you fly from Port Angeles? Good. Yes, I'll be here."

Slowly she put down the phone. "It's Shula. Last night she flew over to Lake Union. She had an accident when she landed. Something about a speed boat."

She answered the question no one wanted to ask. "Still alive, but injured."

She looked at Colin and Fraser. "You're both pilots. How could that happen?"

Colin shrugged. "Night time. Lights in your eyes. Something on your mind. It takes only a minute."

"I heard she's a good pilot," Fraser said. "Lin, you've flown with her. What do you think?"

"Careful, I'd say and certainly competent. But she seemed a little giddy, and I didn't understand why until Jack told me she tanks up on one of her herbal brews before she flies."

"And she was already on painkillers," Alexa said. "What a shame. I wonder how bad her injuries are."

"Pretty bad, I'd think," Fraser said.

"Belinda's going to the hospital as soon as she can." Alexa glanced at Remi and back again. "You're not looking so well yourself, young man. Off to bed with you, and please do keep a civil tongue in your head."

Colin stood up. "Okay, let's go."

He put a hand on Lindsey's shoulder. "I'll be right back. Ginni can help Alexa with the dishes."

caption:

Promise

They walked towards the little park. Clouds piled dark at the horizon, instead of being laced with gold, the way a film might be scripted, but Lindsey didn't care. Her hand was warm in his, and they were together.

"You're trying not to limp, aren't you?" he said. "How's your leg today?"

"Just a little stiff."

Not one of those oblivious types, was he?

But she wanted to know about Remi. "Why would someone go to the trouble of trying to kill Remi?"

"We've been asking ourselves the same question," Colin said. "Here's a theory. I think our neighbor friend with Muslim sympathies was trying to get rid of Ben's right-hand man and make some points with her boyfriend at the same time."

"Why would they care?"

"He's a Muslim-turned-Christian, an enemy of Islam. And somewhere in the FRO network files, there's probably a description that matches him with a runaway kid who knows too much."

"Do you think they'll try again?"

"Hard to tell," Colin said. "The three men who

attacked us did not come off well, but they left him for dead. Even if they find out that Remi's still alive, they may decide he's not worth the trouble."

He frowned. "I talked to the police, of course. I know a couple of the officers from working with my kids, and one of them went to see Kamal. He knew nothing about the incident and was regretful that such a thing should happen. You can be sure the police will follow through."

They reached the bench where they'd sat before, and he paused. He put his hands on her shoulders, turning her to face him. "I didn't want to leave you like that."

She spoke to the warmth in those blue eyes. "You were right. I had to be alone. I had to get it straightened out."

"I knew you had, as soon as I saw you this afternoon."

"You did?"

"You're not the only one who reads faces. But it's hard, isn't it? I had to struggle with the Shula thing all the way back to Seattle. If it weren't for the Lord, I'd still be hating that woman."

His face stiffened. "I'm not a very good person, Lindsey. You might as well know it."

Tears misted her eyes. "That makes two of us," she said softly.

He blinked, shaking his head. "Let's sit down."

She sat beside him and he pulled her close, and she marveled at the comfort of that strong, enclosing arm.

He reached for her hand. "Much better than last time," he said. "Now tell me what's happening with your job. We got sidetracked."

"You expect me to think, sitting like this?"

"You may have to get used to thinking under duress. Me too. I had to throw out that gravy and start again. Now, about the job? For what it's worth, I estimate that we have only a few minutes."

"You're leaving?"

"Before we get interrupted."

She laughed. "Okay, in summary, I don't have a job anymore. I'm strictly freelance, and it's rather scary."

"Are you serious?"

"Yes, I am." She leaned her head against his shoulder.

"What happened?"

"I decided on Friday evening." She described the proposals, the Board meeting, and how she'd weighed her options.

"Because of Vance?"

She had to think about that. "Yes and no. What he did forced the issue. I was ready to go back and tear him to pieces, but the situation here was more important. And then, while I was talking to Edric, my focus shifted, and I knew that the whole New York scene wasn't for me anymore."

He rested his face against her hair. "And then you were here on Sunday for Remi and Monday for Ben. What an omniscient God we have!"

"I hadn't thought of that. The Board meeting was Monday too."

"So what's next?"

"As soon as I get a minute, I'll look for a job. Let's not mention that I've been pestering the Lord about it for days."

"Your hair smells good," he said. "What do you want to do?"

"Sit here."

He put both arms around her, and laughter rumbled in his chest. "The job?"

"Hmm. That's harder." She half-closed her eyes and leaned back against him. "First choice? Candids. Black-and-white. Photo-essay stuff. Maybe children. But to pay the rent, I'll do anything. Now that Ben and I are on speaking terms, I wonder if he'd let me muck out the dog pens."

"I doubt it. What are you doing this week?"

"A few things—find a less expensive place to live. Downsize that rental car—a motorcycle might be fun. Phone some old contacts."

"Would you have time to come into Seattle?"

"Yes, why?"

"I'd like to take you to a couple of places, and there's someone who wants to meet you."

She sat up. "Who?"

He unzipped his jacket, pulled out the little folder Ginni had made, and handed it to her.

The folder was empty, but it had a business card clipped to it.

Akira Matsukata
New York   Tokyo   London

"Colin! What's this?"

"Remember Mr. Matsukata?"

She nodded.

"This is his son. Publishes beautiful picture books. He has an office in Seattle, so I showed him your book and the photos of Ginni. I thought you might be interested in a freelance project when you weren't busy with dogs."

He paused, grinning, and she wanted to shake him. Or hug him.

"What did he say?"

"He looked at them for a long time and said he'd like to talk to you."

"Did he? Oh!"

He was smiling. "I hoped you'd like the idea."

"Like it? You can't imagine."

His gaze rested on her, the grave look she was coming to love. "When you're happy, your eyes are like green fire."

"I thought it was moss."

"You weren't happy that day, and your eyes had shadows in them." He paused, as if remembering. "The shadowed green was what reminded me of Chinese phoenix—beautiful stuff. It grows near the water. I'll show you, sometime."

He bent his head, murmuring into her hair. "You're such an amazing person, Lindsey. I thank God for you."

Her heart soared. *What is this you have done, Lord?*

"I feel as if I'm living in a dream," he said. "I can't wrap my mind around it."

He put his cheek against her face. "You."

She turned closer. "You," she said, and his lips found hers.

Tender. Warm with promise.

He straightened up, his voice rueful and amused. "I hear little feet. We're about to have company. Do you want me to send her away?"

She smiled, trying to gather herself. "I don't think so. Ginni's had enough to deal with."

"Stay where you are. She'll have to get used to seeing us together."

"I think she's doing very well."

He laughed. "I have never sat through a meal like that one. You know, don't you, that when Fraser teases, it's a great compliment?"

"He's always been so gentle with me—I was taken aback for a minute."

"Only for a minute," he said, and laughed again. "They probably expected you to blush and retreat, but I thought you did just fine."

Ginni ran up to them, ponytail flipping and eyes sparkling. "I have news. Big news!"

Lindsey felt Colin tense, but he spoke calmly. "Come here and give us a hug, Ginni. What's your big news?"

She climbed up onto the bench beside him, put both arms around his neck, and ducked her head under his chin to smile at Lindsey.

"I just talked to my daddy," she said.

Ben Fletcher.

The man she'd counted on to make her project a success. The man Colin had agonized over. The man whose sin had affected each of their lives, whom God had changed into a new creature.

What had Ben told his little girl?

"They're coming home tomorrow—Mama and Daddy and everybody!"

Ginni's voice trembled. She must have picked up on more than they realized.

"Daddy said that God is going to make us into a family again. Isn't that *enchanting?*"

THE DUMONT CHRONICLES

The Dumont family, French Huguenots, settled in New Jersey during Colonial days. Since then, certain of the Dumont women have led lives of adventure. Although they differed in personalities and circumstances, these women had in common the gifts of artistry, courage, and a growing faith in God.

In the next book, Lindsey Dumont begins to enjoy Seattle—and getting to know Colin—until an urgent message from Mollie brings her back to the Pine Barrens. Surrounded by perplexities, she wonders: What will happen to her friendship with Colin, now that they're 2400 miles apart?

Books by Gloria Repp

For ages 2 and up:
Noodle Soup

For ages 7 and up:
A Question of Yams *(also as eBook)*

Tales of Friendship Bog series
Pibbin the Small *(also as eBook and audiobook)*
The Story Shell *(also as eBook and audiobook)*
Trapped *(also as eBook and audiobook)*
Catch a Robber *(also as eBook)*
The Stranger's Secret *(also as eBook)*
Trouble with Zee *(also as eBook)*
A Day for Courage *(also as eBook)*

For ages 9 and up:
The Secret of the Golden Cowrie *(also as eBook)*
Trouble at Silver Pines Inn *(also as eBook)*
The Mystery of the Indian Carvings *(also as eBook)*

Adventures of an Arctic Missionary series
Mik-shrok *(also as eBook)*
Charlie *(also as eBook)*
77 Zebra *(also as eBook)*

For ages 12 and up:
The Stolen Years *(also as eBook)*
Night Flight *(also as eBook)*

For Adults:
Nothing Daunted: The Story of Isobel Kuhn
(also as eBook)

THE DUMONT CHRONICLES
The Forever Stone *(also as eBook)*
Deep Focus *(also as eBook)*

About the Author

Gloria Repp writes books for children and adults from her home in South Carolina . . . and from the New Jersey Pine Barrens . . . and also from Seattle, WA. She enjoys traveling, is an omnivorous reader, and delights in baking projects, gardening, listening to frog songs, and flying in small airplanes.

Stop by her website to send her note! Or browse through the story resources, frog photographs, and background information she has collected about the beautiful New Jersey Pine Barrens. (http://www.gloriarepp.com)

Gloria values your opinion, and she would like to know what you think of *Deep Focus*. If you enjoyed the story, please consider leaving a few words of review on Amazon.com. Your comments will be helpful to other readers. Thank you!